Jo**

to the wild places of southern Africa and, well, anywhere. She's a wife, a mum to two teenagers and slave to two cats. After a career in local economic development, she now writes full-time. Joss is a member of Romance Writers of America and Romance Writers of South Africa.

Charlene Sands is a *USA TODAY* bestselling author of contemporary romance and stories set in the American West. She's been honoured with the National Readers' Choice Award, the CataRomance Reviewers' Choice Award and is a double recipient of the Booksellers' Best Award. Her 2014 Mills & Boon Desire title was named the Best Desire of the Year.

Charlene knows a little something about romance—she married her high school sweetheart! And her perfect day includes reading, drinking mocha cappuccinos, watching Hallmark movies and riding bikes with her hubby. She has two adult children and four sweet young princesses, who make her smile every day. Visit her at www.charlenesands.com to keep up with her new releases and fun contests. Find her on Facebook, Instagram and Twitter, too: Facebook.com/ charlenesandsbooks and Twitter.com/charlenesands

AT THE RANCHER'S PLEASURE

JOSS WOOD

CRAVING A REAL TEXAN

CHARLENE SANDS

MILLS & BOON

Falkirk Community Trust	
30124 03143129 1	
Askews & Holts	
AF	£6.99
GM	

First ... ...ity 2021

... ...lk & Boon, an imprint of HarperCollins*Publishers* Ltd,
1 London Bridge ... ...ondon, SE1 9GF

www.harpercollins.co.uk

1st Floor, Watermarque Building,
Ringsend Road, Dublin 4, Ireland

At the Rancher's Pleasure © 2021 Harlequin Books S.A.
Craving a Real Texan © 2021 Charlene Swink

Special thanks and acknowledgement are given to Joss Wood
for her contribution to the TEXAS CATTLEMAN'S CLUB: HEIR
APPARENT series.

ISBN: 978-0-263-28283-2

0221

AT THE RANCHER'S PLEASURE

JOSS WOOD

One

The runaway groom returns.

Brett Harston winced as he passed through the gates leading to Heritage Ranch, his hands loose on the steering wheel of a brand-new Ford-150 Limited, which he'd picked up in Dallas on his way back from the Cayman Islands. The best thing about being rich was being able to afford private jets, secluded beachside cabins and treating yourself to a new truck.

Not that he deserved to be rewarded for last month's shitshow.

Brett rubbed the back of his neck before hitting the button to lower the electric window. Sweet Texas air rushed inside the cab and he inhaled deeply, some of his tension easing.

He was finally home, the only place he'd wanted to be for the past fortnight.

His staying away was intended to give Lexi some

space, to allow some of the more salacious gossip over him bailing on their wedding to die down. He didn't give a rat's ass what the Royal Reporters—his name for the three biggest gossips in town—had to say—the Harstons had been a favorite subject of Royal gossip for as long as he could remember. But this was, as far as he knew, Lexi Alderidge's first brush with being the focus of the town's speculation.

Being alone in a secluded, luxurious cabin on a private beach that he'd booked for their honeymoon had given him plenty of time to think about why he'd stumbled so close to becoming hitched and stitched.

It had all happened so fast: he'd been caught off guard when his first love—one of a handful of people who'd looked past him being the son of the town drunk—dropped back into his life looking to reignite their intense teenage love affair.

Knocked off his feet, attraction and memories and lust creating a thought stealing concoction, he'd dived right in, casually ignoring the fact that she was fresh off a divorce and clearly on the rebound. After a few weeks of spectacular sex, Lexi suggested getting married and, half asleep, he'd sorta, kinda suggested that they would, sometime way in the future.

But he'd hadn't considered Lexi's selective hearing or the savvy organizational skills of the Alderidge women, namely Lexi and her mom, Violet. Before he had time to wipe the sleep out of his eyes, the news of their engagement was all over Royal and mother and daughter were determined to prove they could arrange a kick-ass wedding in two months.

Winston Alderidge expressed his reservations about their marriage from the get-go, and Brett reluctantly admitted that his disapproval was enough to make him dig in his heels. Lexi's dad had an overinflated opinion of his own status and worth, and Brett, despite his wealth, wasn't good enough for his baby girl. So if Winston said the sky was blue, Brett's instinct was to thwart him by insisting it was green. Winston still made him feel like the poor kid working any extra hours he could for Tweed Huggins, desperate to prove himself.

Brett was now one of the richest landowners in the district, a respected cattle rancher and horse breeder. But to some people, the Alderidges included, he would always be the kid from the wrong side of the tracks.

Bottom line? The combination of his first love returning, putting a spark back in Lexi's eyes with lots of sex and compliments, and feeling like he'd finally belong when he married into one of the most respected families in Royal, overrode his gut instinct that marrying Lexi was a mistake.

Fortunately, he'd come to his senses before it was too late.

While he didn't regret bailing on the wedding, he did regret hurting and embarrassing Lexi. He'd called her, tried to apologize, but Lexi wasn't taking his calls. In a few days, he'd try again.

Brett wasn't proud of himself and, at thirty-eight, he was ashamed he hadn't ended the engagement sooner. But nothing could be changed now. He'd already contacted his lawyer to refund Lexi and the Alderidges any money they'd lost, and he hoped, in time, that Lexi would forgive him. The Royal Reporters would talk about the aborted wedding until something, or someone, more interesting came along to divert their attention.

He swung his car to the right, following the road to his residence, and out of the corner of his eye he caught a flash of a dark ball cap and a glimpse of blond hair pulled back into a stubby tail.

Brett slowed his vehicle and watched as his foreman's teenage daughter stormed up the road toward the ranch house. Stacy often ran the trails snaking over the ranch and she was a talented athlete, Brett admitted.

When she didn't slow down, he realized Stacy wore earbuds because she had yet to hear the growly rumble of his new truck. He noticed the time on his dash, then lifted his wrist to confirm what he was seeing. Yep, it was eleven forty... What the hell was Stacy doing out of school?

Brett slowly approached her. "Why aren't you in school, Stace?" he demanded, irritated with himself and with her for skipping school.

Brett watched as the runner used her index finger to push up the brim of her ball cap, turned—and instead of brown eyes, a deep blue, amused gaze slammed into his.

And, just like that, all the moisture left his mouth. Awareness, hot and dark, ran up and down his spine as he dragged his gaze off those stunning eyes framed by long, thick lashes, to drift over her high cheekbones then drop onto her wide, lush, sensual mouth.

It had been a long time, but Brett recognized her immediately. Sarabeth Edmond wore an aqua-and-black gym shirt, matching yoga pants, and expensive running shoes adorned her feet. The workout gear skimmed over her still slim, toned body. God, she was hot.

As in *smokin'*.

"Hi there."

It was a standard greeting but her raspy voice, deeper than normal, sent shivers up his spine. He wanted to hear her murmuring his name as she wound those longs legs around his hips, as he slid inside her...

Brett sighed and frowned, annoyed at his reaction to this gorgeous woman. He'd all but left his fiancée at the alter two weeks ago; he had no right to be attracted to anyone, let alone Rusty Edmond's ex-wife.

And why was she on his land, running up his drive?

Brett asked the question, conscious of his less-than-gracious delivery.

And it was obvious that Sarabeth heard the irritation in his voice because she arched a perfectly sculpted eyebrow. "I'm renting your cottage, and the real estate agent told me the owner was away and I was welcome to ride any horse but the stallion. Naturally, I didn't think running would be a problem."

Of course it wasn't. He was just being a moron.

Brett rubbed a hand over his jaw. Holy hell, he'd forgotten that he had a new tenant. He did recall an email from his real estate agent telling him she'd rented his guest cottage for three months. But he honestly couldn't remember whether she'd told him who his tenant was or, with all the drama, he'd forgotten.

Opening his door, he exited his vehicle, immediately noticing that Sarabeth was taller than he thought, maybe five-seven or five-eight. But he still had five or six inches on her and a whole lot of muscle.

"Was she mistaken? If so, I'll apologize."

Yeah, her tone was definitely frosty. Brett sighed and held out his hand. "No, I should be apologizing. Welcome to Heritage Ranch. I'm Brett Harston."

"Sarabeth." She placed her hand in his and electricity sizzled over his skin when their palms connected. Yep, he was definitely attracted to her.

Wonderful. He had the hots for the only other person whose return would be as much discussed by the Royal gossips as he was.

Brilliant.

"And I'm sorry for shouting at you for not being in school. I thought you were Stacy, my foreman's daughter."

Sarabeth's smile hit her eyes, and Brett placed his hand on the hood of his truck to anchor himself. Holy shit, that smile! It was goddamn glorious...and every strand of DNA in his system vibrated with appreciation.

He wanted to know whether it tasted as good as it looked.

"Please don't apologize for mistaking me for a teenager. It's been a long time since that happened. A very, very long time."

He didn't believe that. Oh, he knew that Sarabeth had, maybe, ten years on him but she looked his age, probably even younger. Probably because of her slim build and fantastic smooth, olive-skinned complexion.

She had the type of face, and body, that aged well. Very well indeed.

Sarabeth pulled her hand from his and leaned her hip into his truck. "So, did you have a great honeymoon? Where's your bride?"

Brett winced. And so the explanations started. "Yeah, I'm afraid I bailed. I called it off the evening before the wedding, at the rehearsal dinner. I'm surprised you hadn't heard."

Her eyes widened and she winced. "I only arrived in Royal last night so no, I hadn't heard." She sent him a sympathetic smile. "I'm sure the old gossips are in a flutter and are not sure what to discuss first, your botched wedding or my returning to Royal and what apple carts I intend on kicking over."

Brett jammed his hands into the front pockets of his jeans and cocked his head to the side. "And are you planning on kicking over some carts?"

Those fantastic blue eyes held amusement but beyond that, he thought he saw a hint of fear.

"Nope. I'm only here to try and repair my relationship with my son and, hopefully, to meet my grandbaby."

Right, Sarabeth's son Ross had recently discovered he was a father and was head over heels in love with his baby's mama, Charlotte, the executive chef at Sheen, another of Royal's eateries. Good for him. Love and belonging were things that had always eluded him and even when he was handed it on a platter, he couldn't take it.

Lexi didn't love you, and you don't love her. You were both looking for something that wasn't really there.

"Well, feel free to do something outrageous so that you can take the heat off me," Brett suggested, his tone gruff.

Like her outrageous smile, Sarabeth's laugh made his stomach flip over. "Ah, no. While I'm in Texas, I plan on flying under the radar and keeping my nose clean."

Brett nodded. "I plan on doing the same," he said, shrugging, "but I've always been a favorite topic of discussion."

Sarabeth didn't drop her eyes from his, and he could see the curiosity in her expression. But, to her credit, she didn't walk through the door he'd stupidly opened. He wondered if she remembered the stories about his mom, the stories about him. He doubted it. When she lived in Royal she probably had her hands full dealing with Rusty and two small kids.

Brett heard a familiar, excitable whinny and turned to see Bella, one of his favorite mares, standing at the wooden fence of the paddock, her beautiful eyes excited. Yeah, here was a female who'd missed the hell out of him.

Walking over to the fence, he ran his hand down Bella's nose. "Yeah, yeah, I missed you too." He laughed when she nuzzled his pockets looking for carrots before gently rubbing her cheek against his. His horses knew how to suck up. "You're such a flirt, and you know that carrots are an evening treat."

Brett leaned his forehead into Bella's neck and closed his eyes. Animals were so much easier to deal with than people; they were straightforward and uncomplicated and didn't play games. He didn't like subterfuge or dishonesty and he was, generally, brutally straightforward.

Except that lately, he hadn't been. Not with Lexi. God, he was embarrassed and ashamed and felt a little bit sick for the pain and stress he'd caused. He could, easily, cover the bills of the nonwedding but he couldn't wipe away Lexi and the Alderidges' humiliation by writing a quick check.

He remembered standing to the side at the dinner, apart and alone, thinking that he didn't want to hurt Lexi, that he'd rather cut off his hand than do that. But, surrounded by their guests, he realized that what he felt for Lexi was both complex and disorienting, his feelings influenced by his youthful wish to be accepted, to belong, to be anything other than the boy who always stood on the outside of the cool kids looking in.

Along with owning and operating one of the most successful operations in the area, marrying Lexi and being Winston's son-in-law would cement his place in Royal; he would finally, finally belong.

And that he'd just have to sell his soul to do it.

Biting the bullet, he'd pulled Lexi aside and told her he couldn't marry her, that he didn't love her and that she didn't love him either, not the way two people getting married should. She'd cried and he'd walked away, leaving her alone and confused and shocked and, worst of all, blindsided.

And half of Royal witnessed the train wreck that was supposed to be their rehearsal dinner.

God, he was such a bastard.

He felt the brief touch of a hand on his biceps, heard a soft feminine sigh. "Sucks to be you, right?"

Brett opened his eyes to see Sarabeth standing next to him and managed a small smile at her comment. Her eyes radiated sympathy and, best of all, no judgment. Not that her opinion mattered overmuch; she couldn't think any worse of him than he did of himself.

"Why did you run?" she gently asked.

Even if he was in the habit of explaining his actions to friends or strangers, which he wasn't, he wasn't sure if his explanation would make sense. How did he explain that he'd simply been struck by the unassailable truth that he and Lexi weren't each other's *it*?

And that he didn't think he would be marriage material, now or in the future. He was too closed up, too self-reliant, too screwed up to be anyone's husband, lover, partner...

Any woman's *anything*.

That gentle hand patted his shoulder. "You don't have to answer me."

He knew that and he had no intention of doing so. Exposing his soft emotional underbelly wasn't something he ever did, and especially not to a gorgeous stranger with shadows in her eyes.

"But can I say this? This will pass, trust me. It might pass like a kidney stone, with a bunch of pain, but it *will* pass. Everything always does." Sarabeth's smile was soft and understanding, and Brett felt like he could rest within it.

She turned her back on him and walked toward the road. When she hit the road, she pulled her cap down and lifted two fingers to the brim in a goodbye salute.

Then she broke into a smooth run, her body moving with ease and grace.

Damn, the woman was intriguing.

Sarabeth kept up a wicked pace until she came to the cottage she was renting. Braking abruptly at the steps leading up to the porch, she slapped her hands on her thighs and bent over, sucking in some much-needed air.

She was partly winded from her hard run—she could, at forty-eight, still run a seven-minute mile—but a lot of her breathlessness could be attributed to Brett Harston and his mysterious, deep forest green eyes, sooty lashes, thick stubble and hard jaw. His hair, the little that wasn't covered by a black Stetson, was a rich brown and his nose just a little crooked.

And his body... Lord, that *body*. Long legs, narrow hips, a broad, muscular chest and shoulders wide enough to make angels weep. He was a man in the prime of his life, fit and powerful.

Sarabeth straightened up, feeling a little woozy, off-balance. Had she straightened too fast? She sat down on the third step and stretched out her legs, still thinking about Brett's flat stomach and very nice package under that soft denim.

Whoo-boy! It had been a long, long time since she'd given any thought to a man's masculine package...

She'd met a lot of cowboys but Brett Harston was superfine. And ridiculously sexy. And the expression "save a horse and ride a cowboy" suddenly made a great deal of sense.

Not that she would be riding him, or any other Texas cowboy anytime soon.

Sarabeth leaned back on her elbows and tipped her head to the sun. She couldn't believe she was back in

Royal, Texas, after a nearly twenty-year absence. And, despite laying eyes on her luscious landlord—an unexpected treat!—she wished she could say she felt excited about returning to her home state.

She didn't.

When she'd left this part of Texas with only an alimony check, her car and her clothes, she'd promised herself to never return and she didn't like breaking promises, not even those she'd made to herself. But she'd storm hell itself for her children, and she wanted to build on the bourgeoning relationship between her and her previously estranged son, Ross.

She'd never forgive Rusty for alienating her from her children after she left—trash-talking her by blaming her for their divorce, telling them she was no longer interested in being their mother, making it difficult for her to see them… Constantly fighting for a place in their lives, and frequently losing, had broken her heart over and over again. Oh, there had been times where she'd been desperate to tell Gina and Ross that their father was a serial cheater and had been verbally abusive, but she figured one of their parents had to be the adult in the room.

Thankfully Gina started questioning that narrative in her late teens and, these days, her relationship with her daughter was solid…but Ross was a harder nut to crack.

However, he'd recently opened the lines of communication between them, and Sarabeth wasn't going to waste this opportunity to reestablish a relationship with her older child. And she wanted to spend some time with her beautiful grandbaby, Ben.

Forty-eight years old and she was a grandmother… the thought made her smile.

Her kids, and Ben, were the only reason she was back

in this godforsaken town. She didn't like not having two states and thousands of miles between herself and her ex-husband, and full-time snake, Rusty Edmond.

He can't hurt you anymore: you are older, wiser and have a great deal more resources now than when you did when you walked away from Elegance Ranch long ago.

It was strange, and rather wonderful, that she no longer recognized the woman she'd been when she'd married Rusty Edmond a few months after her eighteenth birthday. That timid, insecure, desperate-for-approval girl didn't resonate with her anymore, but Sarabeth had to give herself credit—she'd fought hard, grown and evolved to become the person she was today.

She liked herself nowadays; she could look in the mirror and smile. Sure, she wasn't perfect, but neither was she the train wreck she'd been when she walked out on her marriage, so anxious and desperate to please.

She'd grown up, thank God, and was smarter about people, about love, about relationships. She now accepted that her belief in happy-ever-afters had been badly misplaced, that her faith in fairy-tale heroes had been nonsensical. After years of disappointing relationships, Sarabeth believed her happiness wasn't dependent on a man, that love was a myth and she was wholly and fully responsible for her own bliss.

It had taken her a damn long time, and too many tears, to get to this point in her life.

But the payoff had been worth it in the end. She was strong, feisty and emotionally and financially independent. And after all she'd been through, she could handle her philandering, manipulative and deceitful ex-husband and the rampant gossip her returning to Royal would generate.

Sarabeth removed her phone from the pouch strapped

to her upper arm and checked her fitness app, taking in her pace and her distance. Running on the ranch was going to be a nice change from her treadmill or pounding the sooty streets of LA.

It was her drug and her only addiction. As a teenager, cross-country running had been her way to get out of the house and away from her pageant obsessed mother, Betty. It had been her favorite way to avoid wardrobe selection prep or practice on her violin for an upcoming competition. Pageants had been her mom's obsession, and it had been a world Sarabeth loathed.

And when Rusty Edmond—older, debonair, rich and slick—gave her a way to leave that life by way of marriage, she'd leaped at the opportunity. Betty had been disappointed not to take her all the way to Miss America—*as if!*—but her only child marrying a rich Texas rancher had been a grand second prize.

Betty had been gutted when her marriage ended and, up until the day she died, blamed Sarabeth for not sticking by her man…

Blergh.

Sarabeth stood up, irritated. It had been a while since she'd thought about her mom, her marriage and her pageant-queen past. She'd spent one night in Royal and she was already being ambushed by painful memories…

It was far more fun to think about her hunky landlord.

Two

The next day, Sarabeth heard the sound of hoofbeats and lifted her forehead off her steering wheel to look in her rearview mirror, softly cursing when she saw two riders trotting down the road in her direction.

Although his face was shadowed by the low brim of his black Stetson, Sarabeth instantly recognized the younger of the two riders. Brett Harston. She watched them approach, admiring the rancher's broad shoulders and powerful thighs as he easily controlled the powerful black stallion with a deft touch on the reins, a squeeze of his thighs.

Yep, he was still sinfully sexy. Dammit.

Attraction raised the hair on her forearms and lust scuttled up her skin, making her breasts tingle and her nipples contract. Hot heat settled between her thighs and she squirmed in her seat. Why was she reacting like this? Sure, it had been a while since she'd had sex—a long, dry spell—but this was ridiculous. In her past relationships, sexual attraction came only after she made an emotional connection so her visceral reaction to this younger man confused her. What was going on here? And why did she keep wondering what he looked like naked? Or how it would be to make love to him in the afternoon, in the sunlight, in that lap pool or in the hot tub she could see from her loft bedroom in the cottage?

She was acting like she was considering having a fling with the man, which was crazy. Sarabeth dropped her forehead back onto the steering wheel and she groaned. Why was she even going there, allowing her thoughts to drift in that direction?

Even if he did find her attractive, which wasn't a given thanks to their age difference, Brett was just coming off a bad relationship. He'd left Lexi Alderidge the day before they were due to marry, practically at the alter—Gina had filled her in on the gossip when she stopped by last night and the last thing on his mind was falling into bed with a stranger.

Guys were different from girls, and they had different ways of coping with loss and change. Maybe a rebound fling or a one-night stand was exactly what Brett needed to do. But *not* with Rusty Edmond's ex-wife, Royal's other hot topic of gossip.

Sarabeth banged her hand on the wheel, annoyed that she couldn't stop thinking about him.

"Hi."

She lifted her head to see Brett's face inches from her own on the other side of the open window, then looked past him to see his companion standing between the two horses off the road, twelve or so feet from them. "Hi back."

"Car problems?" Brett asked, placing his strong arms on the frame of her window. Sarabeth shook her head, idly noticing that he had the longest and thickest lashes she'd ever seen on a man, that his eyes held flecks of gold at the center and that, under his soft stubble, he had a small scar on his bottom lip.

He smelled of horse and soap, deodorant and hay... healthy and outdoorsy. Sarabeth felt the urge to place her lips on the cords of his strong neck, to taste the tang of his skin.

She was losing it, she really was.

"Sarabeth? Everything okay?"

Pull yourself together, woman! She swallowed and nodded. "Yeah, everything is fine."

Brett lifted one arrogant eyebrow. "Really? Because I've been watching you for the past fifteen minutes. You drove through the gates, stopped and haven't moved since. I rode over to check whether I can help."

Ah. That.

Sarabeth winced and wrinkled her nose. How could she explain that she'd got to the intersection, had put on her blinker but she'd been unable to steer her car in the direction of Royal? How could she tell him, tell *anyone*, that despite her hard-gained independence and sense of self-worth, she was suddenly terrified of walking down Main Street. Of being unable to hold her head up high, knowing that people were remembering why she left Royal, thinking that she'd abandoned her kids, condemning her because they'd only heard one side of the story.

She'd so desperately wanted to be a good mom to her kids but living with Rusty became untenable—he categorically refused her demand to keep his dick in his pants—and her leaving allowed him to claim that she'd walked out on their marriage and abandoned her children.

Sarabeth felt the familiar burn at the back of her throat and her stinging eyes so she turned her head away and scrabbled in her bag for her sunglasses. She couldn't find them and softly cursed.

"Dammit! Where the hell are they?"

"Where are what?" Brett asked, his deep, husky voice raising goose bumps on her skin.

"My sunglasses!"

Brett lifted his hand, touched her hair and, seconds later, waved her sunglasses in front of her face. *Great way to show him that you are a ditsy old broad about to lose your marbles, Sarabeth.*

"Thanks," she muttered, taking the glasses from his hand and dropping them onto her lap. She fiddled with them, so conscious of his strong, tanned arm, his broad body blocking out the sun, the fullness of his bottom lip.

"Now tell me the reason you are hanging out in my driveway."

She could lie and make up a story. Over the years she'd become quite good at hiding her feelings behind a layer of cool composure, but, for some reason, she thought that Brett might understand her reluctance to drive into town.

She lifted one shoulder in a jerky shrug. "By now, everyone will know that I'm back in Royal, and my marriage and divorce would've been regurgitated and discussed incessantly. Rusty, I'm pretty sure, would've poisoned the well too. I was just debating whether I'm strong enough to walk down Main Street with my head held high."

"You're strong enough," Brett told her.

She smiled at his instantaneous reply. "You don't know me well enough to say that."

"But I know Rusty, and any woman who managed to remain married to that bastard for as long as you did had to have courage."

"That's sweet of you to say but didn't you hear? I was a shrew, stupid and had affairs with anyone who crossed my path."

Brett's eyes narrowed. "BS."

His instinctive defense of her warmed a small part of her heart that had been cold for a very, very long time.

"I've never had much time for your ex, Sarabeth, and, as a rule, I discount ninety percent of the crap he says. And if it's to do with a woman, that percentage rapidly rises." Brett picked a strand of her hair and rubbed it between his fingers, his expression pensive.

After a short, surprisingly comfortable silence, he spoke again. "Don't go anywhere. I'll be back in a sec."

Sarabeth watched his loose, confident stride as he walked back to his companion. They spoke for a few moments and then his friend—employee?—mounted his horse and started to lead Brett's horse away. Frowning, she watched in her side mirrors as Brett approached the passenger side of her door. He yanked the door open and dropped into the passenger seat beside her.

She placed her forearms on the steering wheel and tossed him a puzzled look. "And now?"

"I've been wanting to go into Royal since I returned home yesterday but I've been putting it off, mostly because I didn't want to contend with the looks, the questions and the speculation."

Right. He was, after all, Royal's Runaway Groom.

"So, let's do this together. And hopefully—" Brett sent her a mischievous grin "—we'll blow up Royal's gossip line."

"Can we blow up the gossips while we're at it?" Sarabeth asked, sounding wistful.

"I wish," he replied before gesturing to the open road. "Lead on, Macduff."

A rancher who knew Shakespeare, Sarabeth thought. How refreshing.

And yep, she decided as she started her small SUV, it did up his sexy factor. And that, considering her earlier thoughts, was definitely something she could do without.

Sarabeth felt Brett's eyes on her profile and resisted the urge to squirm. She was rapidly approaching fifty, and he made her feel like a gauche teenager dealing with her first crush. Her hands tightened on the wheel as she drove the still familiar road into Royal. As she approached the impressive gates to Elegance Ranch, Sarabeth sighed and couldn't help slowing down as she caught a glimpse of her old home through the copse of trees. It was as impressive as it had always been, but now it felt cold. And ostentatious.

She far preferred the clean lines of Brett's ranch house. It was big, everything in Texas tended to be, but it hadn't been designed as a showpiece.

He cleared his throat and out of the corner of her eye, she saw him gesture to the mansion. "Do you miss it?"

Sarabeth quickly shook her head. "Hell, no. I missed my kids but the bricks and stone? Never."

"And Rusty?" Brett casually asked.

Sarabeth slowed down to look him squarely in the eye. "Have you met my ex?"

The corners of his mouth twitched in amusement. "Point taken."

Brett leaned his elbow on the frame of the open window and lifted his Stetson up to run his hand through his hair. "Speaking of, Rusty asked me to sit on the advisory board of Soiree on the Bay. It's a music and food and wine festival that is going to be held on Appaloosa Island."

Now wasn't that a blast from the past? Rusty acquired

the small private island in Trinity Bay early in their marriage. They'd built a holiday home there, and she'd loved spending days on their private beach, swimming and making sandcastles with the kids.

When Sarabeth found out that Rusty had taken one or more of his mistresses to their beach house for dirty weekends, she'd refused to set foot on the island again.

"Why you?" Sarabeth asked, wincing at her rude question. But she needed to know how open she could be with Brett. While she didn't intend to trash her ex while she was in town—he was still, after all, her children's father—she didn't want to have to censure her every word.

Especially since everyone already knew that she and Rusty stood on different sides of a cattle grid.

Brett took his time to answer her question. "Probably because I have a lot of money and they think that asking me to be on the board will encourage me to loosen my wallet." His words were neither a boast nor an exaggeration, just a matter-of-fact statement.

"And will it?"

One shoulder lifted in a negligent shrug but when he spoke, it was to ask a question of his own. "You know that he's painted you as a gold digger, right?"

It shouldn't hurt but it did. "Is that all? I thought that I was a gold-digging slut with no morals who abandoned her kids and who dabbled with drugs. I have one or two friends in town, and I've heard that some stories have me biting the heads off chickens too."

Sarabeth heard the bitterness in her voice and winced. She'd trained herself not to care about what Rusty and the not-so-righteous people of Royal thought, but that was a lot easier when she was in California, many miles away from this gossipy small town in East Texas. She'd been back in Royal for only a couple of days, and she was sliding back into her old insecurities and caring too much about how people viewed her.

Strangely, her biggest worry was how Brett viewed her. This was nonsensical because he was only her landlord and she shouldn't care what a guy a decade younger than her thought. But Royal, as always, had the ability to scramble her brains.

"Are you?" Brett quietly asked.

"Am I what?"

"A gold digger?"

Her initial reaction was annoyance that he had the gall to ask her that, then her common sense kicked in and she appreciated his frankness. She far preferred people to shove a knife in her chest while they looked her in the eye than stab her in the back when her eyes were closed.

"No. Not then and not now," Sarabeth eventually answered him. "Back then, all I wanted was access to my kids. I came back to Royal to repair my relationship with Ross, and I also want to get to know Charlotte and spend time with my grandson, Ben."

"If you don't mind me asking, how do you support yourself?" Brett asked, after a short silence. "I mean, my cottage is one of the most expensive rentals in Royal, and you paid three months rent in advance."

Ah, that. How much to tell him? In California, as the founder of *Sarabeths!*, she'd developed a bit of a name for herself and she was semifamous, but here in rural Texas, no one, including her children, had connected her with the now famous company producing organic cosmetics.

She'd recently sold the company and was many, many millions richer…

"Hopefully you demanded, and were awarded, a hefty, lifelong alimony from Rusty."

She wished. And no, because she never had custody of

their kids, her alimony from Rusty was a paltry figure. But she'd made her own money and a lot of it.

Sarabeth decided to keep it simple. "I worked for a cosmetic house, then started to make soaps and creams, selling them at a market. That led to me forming a company and taking the business online. I recently sold it."

She felt Brett's penetrating stare but didn't look at him. When he eventually replied, it was with a few heartfelt, simple words. "Good for you."

Sarabeth saw they were approaching the outskirts of Royal and slowed her car to below the speed limit. She did not need a ticket on her first week back in town.

At the first red traffic light, one of the few in Royal, she turned to look at Brett, who was relaxing in the passenger seat of her vehicle. Rusty, and many of the men she dated, would have either insisted on driving or criticized her handling of the car.

Points for the younger guy, Sarabeth thought wryly. "I was planning on meeting my old friend Jaynie Prince for coffee. Then I need to visit the pharmacy and buy a couple of things from the store. What are your plans for today?"

"I need to have a quick word with Billy Holmes about the Soiree on the Bay festival…" Brett tipped his head to the side. "Have you met him?"

Sarabeth shook her head. "Nope. First time back in Royal in twenty years, remember?"

"Yeah, sorry. Well, Billy seems to be Rusty's protégé, for want of a better word."

She heard a note of hesitancy in his voice that had her curiosity spiking. "You don't like him?"

"He's fine," Brett shrugged. "I didn't click with him but that means nothing—" a brief flash of amusement hit his eyes "—since I'm not the most sociable of guys at the best of times. You might find him charming."

Sarabeth shrugged. "Honestly? I'll take taciturn and grumpy over slick and charming any day of the week."

Brett's smile, natural and full, revealed straight white teeth and made his eyes sparkle. Warmth curled through her, and she felt her breasts tingle in response. That smile should come with a warning...preferably in flashing purple neon.

"I also need to pick up some documents from my lawyer," Brett continued, "so I'll be about an hour. Does that suit you?"

"Perfect," Sarabeth replied, happy that the light turned green so she had an excuse to wrench her eyes off his gorgeous green eyes. Really, it was so unfair that she spent a ton of money on mascara and his eyelashes were longer and thicker than hers.

"I also need a couple of items from the store. Shall I meet you there?"

Sarabeth nodded and, seeing a vacant parking space outside the diner, whipped into it, idly noticing three women standing on the sidewalk. They were around her age, perhaps a little older, had attended her wedding and were dinner guests in what used to be her home. None of them bothered to contact her when she left Royal and they were, as per Jaynie's information, a source of some of the wilder rumors about her.

They hadn't liked her back then—too blond, slim and pretty—and, judging by their narrowed eyes and the slight curl to their bright lips, nothing much had changed.

Sarabeth, knowing a devil was sitting on her shoulder, climbed out of the driver's seat and walked to the hood of her car, placing her booted foot on the bumper behind her. She pushed her sunglasses up into her hair and made eye contact with her once, so-called friends. "Dale, Flora, Hattie…"

She received two frigid nods and an ice-cool "Sarabeth."

An awkward silence dropped between them as their eyes, bright with malicious curiosity, darted between her and Brett, who strolled over to join her. He shoved his phone into the back pocket of his well-fitting jeans and pushed two fingers into the brim of his Stetson, lifting it a fraction. "Ladies, good morning."

"We didn't expect you to show your face in town, Brett Harston," Flora told him with a righteous sniff.

Sarabeth didn't try to hold back her eye roll.

"I live, work and shop in Royal, ladies, so why shouldn't I be here?" he asked, his tone genial but Sarabeth noticed the sparks of annoyance flickering in his eyes. Like her, she suspected that he'd far prefer the town gossips to acknowledge his nonwedding—the glittery elephant on the sidewalk—than keep making vague allusions to it.

"I think they are trying to say that you should be keeping a low profile because you left Lexi Alderidge almost at the altar, Brett," Sarabeth said, deliberately sounding super cheerful and helpful.

Brett's eyes met hers and she caught the quick lift of his eyebrow, the flash of amusement causing his lips to twitch. "Thank you, honey."

Their eyes widened at his casual use of the endearment, and she could mentally imagine the three witches of Royal, Texas, adding two plus two and reaching sixty-billion. Oh, yeah, marvelous, juicy gossip would be flying later.

"You two look to be on very good terms," Dale commented with a trill of laughter that was as fake as her smile.

Three sets of malicious eyes bored into hers, and Sarabeth fought the urge to explain that she and Brett had only recently met, and that *nothing* had happened between them. Then the devil on her shoulder prodded her with the pointy end of its pitchfork, reminding her that she no longer owed anyone any explanations, and that these women had no power over her.

Sarabeth ran her hand down Brett's arm, enjoying the feel of hard muscles under the cool cotton of his shirt, rolled back to his elbows. "Oh, we are," she cooed. "As I'm sure you've heard, we are living together."

Brett's eyes met hers and she saw the tiny shake of his head. Too much? Yep, apparently so. Damn. But, because she was an adult, Sarabeth lifted her chin. "I'm renting his cottage, ladies, that's all," she told them, keeping her voice flat.

"We didn't, for one minute, think anything else," Flora huffed, her eyes bright with dislike. "You are, after all, far too old for him, my dear. He's a man in his prime and you are, well…*not*."

Wow, okay then. They'd definitely honed their bitch skills.

Sarabeth raked her hands through her hair, thinking that she should never have engaged them in conversation. Sometimes it was better not to poke the hornet's nest with a short stick. "Have a good day, ladies." She turned to Brett. "I'll see you in about an hour?"

"Yeah. Enjoy your chat with your friend," Brett replied.

"Thanks." Sarabeth dropped her foot off the bumper, and as she was about to turn away, she felt his hand on her arm. She turned and he lifted his palm to hold the back of her head, tipping her face up. Before she could make sense of what he was doing, his surprisingly soft, delectable lips were on hers. Sarabeth held on to his forearms, her mouth dropping open in shock.

What. The. Holy. Hell?

Brett took advantage of her open mouth and slid his tongue past her teeth and Sarabeth, right there on Main Street, in front of three of its biggest gossips, released what she was sure was an audible moan.

Then her surroundings faded away and all she could think of was getting closer, seeing how her body fit into his. As she was about to draw nearer, Brett took a step back, his hand on the side of her face, his thumb drifting over her cheekbone.

"I will see you later, gorgeous."

He released her and tipped his hat again to the astounded ladies in front of them. "Have a good day, ladies."

Then four sets of female eyes, including Sarabeth's, watched his unbelievably delicious backside, covered by formfitting jeans, walk away.

Three

Brett could feel eyes on his back and on his butt, and forced himself not to scurry away, to keep his gait as normal as possible. He was finding that a bit difficult since the hair on the back of his neck and on his arms was waving in the wind, his mouth was dry and his jeans felt snug across the crotch area.

And that was the only reason why he'd stopped himself from bending Sarabeth over the hood of her vehicle; another few seconds and he would've popped the buttons on his jeans.

Holy hell.

He'd kissed Sarabeth because he'd been pissed at the Royal Reporters' insinuation that this drop-dead gorgeous woman was too old for him—and because he'd seen the hurt in her eyes at their bitchiness. Brett loathed bullies and was ultrasensitive to verbal harassment, and hearing that coven of witches aim their fire at Sarabeth raised his protective instincts and took him straight back to his childhood.

They, or women just like them, verbally stabbed his mom every time she came into town to do their meager shopping, whispering behind hands and closed fists...

Is she sober?

Disgraceful! Why can't she just leave town?

She's hurrying through her shopping so that she can go home to that vodka bottle.

No one bothered to find out the cause of her addiction. She'd been T-boned by a drunk driver—irony was such a bitch!—and broke her back. The doctors said it was a miracle she was able to walk again. But mobility came with a hell of a price, constant and debilitating pain, and after trying a regimen of painkillers—and wiping out all their financial resources—she discovered that vodka and opioids somewhat dulled the pain.

Although he'd just turned twelve, he wasn't surprised when she quickly became addicted to both. But, after a year or two, she lost her job, started drinking in the morning and popping more pills. She spiraled and, a few weeks after his eighteenth birthday, he'd walked into the house in the early hours of the morning after a blissful night spent with Lexi and found her unresponsive on the living room floor, various empty bottles of pills on the worn carpet.

He'd called for an ambulance and started CPR, pumping her heart and blowing air into her lungs. She passed away as the ambulance turned into their drive and Brett blamed himself for not coming home earlier, for not being able to save her.

For not listening, for dismissing her words and brushing her off. If he'd just taken a little time she'd still be here.

Sorry, Mom.

Brett swallowed the lump in his throat as he walked the familiar route to his lawyer's office where he'd arranged to meet Billy, still lost in thought. Seeing his mom in such pain—a shell of the fun, happy, vivacious person she'd been prior to the life-altering car accident—had kick-started his rescue gene.

As a result, he was a sucker for women in trouble, instinctively drawn to gals who needed rescuing, desperate to make things better, to rebalance the scales he'd let tip.

In his early twenties, he'd lent a girlfriend money to fix her car, bought another a plane ticket to New York City to see her sick brother only to realize that there had been no sick brother. He now suspected there wasn't a broken car either. In his midtwenties, he started to wise up, not to fall for every pretty face's sob story and, by his thirties, had developed a pretty good bullshit meter.

But his white knight personality trait had played a part in his hooking up with Lexi again, that and gratitude. Along with Tweed Huggins and Jules, his childhood friend, Lexi attended his mom's funeral, had held his hand as they lowered her cheap coffin into the ground. So when she dropped back into his life, sad after her divorce, he'd confused wanting to help her with true attraction.

They'd made love and it had been nice, fun…safe. They'd both worked hard to make it as good as it could possibly be…

But there had been more heat in one kiss with Sarabeth than he and Lexi had ever generated in bed. Honestly, Brett felt like he'd been attacked by a blowtorch. It had been wild and feral, a crazy connection of want and lust and the need to rip her clothes off…

Brett sighed. He was rapidly approaching forty and he'd had a lot of sex, but that kiss was unlike any he'd experienced before. Her soft lips tasted of coffee and berries, her scent was light, fresh and fragrant, and her body, the little he got to feel, was firm, toned and delightfully feminine.

He wanted her.

Brett, turning the corner, lifted his hand to the back of his neck. He shouldn't be thinking of another woman, not so soon after a broken engagement. Hell, a few weeks ago he'd been convinced he'd marry Lexi, that he'd live with her for the rest of his life.

Yet here he was, after a quick, hard, lush kiss, balls deep in lust with Sarabeth...

He'd had two conversations with her...*two*!

How could he go from legally engaged to sexually enraged in the blink of an eye?

It made absolutely no sense and, because it was taking too much mental energy, he dismissed it as a one-off, a step out of time. Nothing was going to happen with Sarabeth Edmond, not now or ever. He needed to keep his distance from women, concentrate on his business and the ranch, fulfill his obligations to the Soiree on the Bay festival. In other words, he needed to keep his head down and his nose clean.

Brett sighed. He'd caused enough gossip lately, and having lived under the town's collective microscope as a kid, he wasn't keen to relive that experience as an adult.

He'd apologize to Sarabeth, tell her he got a bit carried away, that their kiss was an anomaly. That it wouldn't happen again...

Approaching the squat, red brick building housing his lawyer's offices, he felt his racing heart slow down, his lungs now fully able to take a big breath. He had a ranch to operate; he would not tolerate another distraction of the feminine kind. He could resist those big blue eyes, that beautiful, triangular face with its high cheekbones, her wide, sensuous mouth. A body that wouldn't quit...

Brett felt a heavy hand on his shoulder and he spun around, frowning. He didn't realize his fist was clenched or that his lip was lifted in a snarl.

Billy Holmes took a sharp step back and lifted his own hands. "Whoa, Harston, I come in peace."

Brett forced his shoulders to drop and flexed his hands before holding out his right hand for Billy to shake. "Billy, hi. Sorry, I was miles away."

"I could tell."

Billy fell into step with him. "I'm glad I bumped into you. You've been away so you might not have seen the email I sent out convening a meeting of the festival's committee."

Billy went on to detail the time and date of the meeting and gave Brett a basic rundown of the agenda.

Instead of feeling excited or enthusiastic to get stuck in, Brett felt hesitant. Why was he feeling a little uneasy about getting involved with this festival? A small, bleak voice in his gut was telling him to stay away, but Brett knew that he wouldn't...

Being invited to sit on the advisory committee, along with the other movers and shakers in town, was not something to be taking for granted. It told him—and the greater community, his employees and their families—that he held a certain amount of power and influence in Royal.

And for a man who was once derided and dismissed as the son of the town's most embarrassing drunk, that wasn't a small thing.

The moment she stepped into the Royal Diner, Sarabeth found herself wrapped up in Jaynie Prince's arms and pressed up against her ample bosom. And being hugged like this reminded her of those dark days when she'd first found out about Rusty's affairs, and the dawning knowledge that he'd never love her enough to quit seeing other women. Jaynie, whom Sarabeth met at a wine-tasting gala, had been her shelter in the storm, the only person she'd felt comfortable enough with to share her troubles.

They'd kept in contact over the years, but theirs was the type of friendship that could be picked up after two days or twenty years...

Sarabeth slid into a red leather booth and looked around the diner, smiling. "This place doesn't change, does it?"

Jaynie's smile was wide. "You certainly haven't. God woman, how can you possibly be as skinny as you were in your midtwenties? Don't they have food in California?"

"I have a fast metabolism, you know that," she replied, laughing.

"Prove that you are normal and order one of Amanda's special milkshakes." Jaynie pointed to a board detailing the diner's gourmet drinks. "If you have one and tell me that we're celebrating our reunion, then I will feel morally obliged to ditch my diet and join you."

"We're celebrating our reunion, and I'm having a salted caramel milkshake."

Jaynie grinned, placed their order with a waitress and leaned across the table, her mischievous green eyes dancing with glee. Jaynie's eyes were clear and light, whereas Brett's were a deep, mysterious evergreen. Remembering his mouth on hers, how shaky she felt in the knees and the liquid heat that rushed to that space between her legs, made Sarabeth blush.

"Are you having a hot flash or something?" Jaynie demanded, on a whisper as loud as a foghorn.

Sarabeth slapped her hand. "Back off, sister! I have a couple of years to go before I have to deal with that, as you well know."

Jaynie cocked her head to one side, looking like an inquisitive bird. "Then why are you all flushed and goofy-eyed? I'd love to take credit for your excitement, but I know you don't roll that way."

"How is Laura?" Sarabeth asked, thinking of Jaynie's long-term partner, who worked as a doctor in Joplin, the next town over.

"Fine. She says you must come over for a meal soon. But don't try to distract me. I want to know who or what put that glint in your eyes."

Once Jaynie homed in on a subject, one needed a high-powered missile strike to direct her off course. Besides, if Sarabeth didn't tell her now, she'd soon hear—thanks, gossips!—that Brett kissed her. Jaynie would be hurt she didn't confide in her, and she had too few friends in town to hurt one of the few standing on her side of the fence.

Sarabeth leaned forward and softly told her what happened.

"OMG! You kissed Royal's Runaway Groom?"

Sarabeth winced at her friend's shrill response and felt more than a few eyes swivel in their direction. "Why don't you say that louder, Jaynie? I'm sure the people in the back didn't hear you."

The waitress placed their milkshakes in front of them, sending Sarabeth an approving look. "You kissed Brett? Good for you! Is he a good kisser? I always thought he would be…"

Caught off guard, Sarabeth exchanged a look with Jaynie. The waitress looked about sixteen, and any response seemed inappropriate. Then Amanda Battle, the owner of the Royal Diner, sauntered over to their booth and shepherded the outspoken waitress away.

"She's older than she looks." Jaynie sipped her milkshake, closing her eyes in pure ecstasy, and when she opened them again, pinned Sarabeth to her seat. "Well, *is* he a good kisser? Judging by your floaty face, I'd say yes."

"I do not have a floaty face!"

"Honey, you glided in here on a six-foot cloud," Jaynie replied. "You arrived in Royal two days ago. How the hell did you end up kissing Brett on Main Street in front of the three witches?"

Sarabeth lifted a shoulder. "They said something about him being too young for me. And, duh, that's obvious."

"It's not like you are eighty and he's forty," Jaynie said, sounding a little exasperated.

Sarabeth waved her words away. "Look, they were being bitchy and Brett didn't like that."

"And I know exactly why," the other woman muttered before pushing her fingers into her mop of curls. "Back in the day, his mom was the subject of a lot of mean and horrible gossip."

Sarabeth lifted her eyebrows at this news. "Really? Why?"

"She had a drinking problem," Jaynie quietly replied, and Sarabeth appreciated the lack of judgment in her voice. "He found her passed out on the floor of their home and tried to revive her, but she died in his arms."

Sarabeth lifted her fingers to her lips, distressed. "Oh, that's horrible. When did this happen?"

Jaynie's brow furrowed in thought. "Twenty years ago? You were still here, in Royal, I think."

She winced. "I must've heard about it but, to be honest, I was fighting so many Rusty battles that nothing from the outside world penetrated."

Sarabeth stared out of the window, pulling her bottom lip between her teeth. Now that she knew about his mom and the gossip she'd been subject to, it was clear to her that Brett kissed her because he'd felt sorry for her. It would be natural for him to defend her, to defend *any* woman.

Okay, maybe a kiss was a slightly unorthodox way of doing it, but men were strange creatures...

"I'm sure it was just a pity kiss," Sarabeth told Jaynie and waited for her to agree with her.

"A *pity* kiss?" Jaynie spluttered. She sent her a "honey, you're nuts" look. "Sarabeth, you're a gorgeous woman, and you're so much more than a pity kiss."

Sarabeth reached across the table to squeeze her hand. She had a few friends in LA but none with whom she had such a strong connection, like she was sliding her feet into a welcoming pair of slippers on a freezing day.

But, as much as she loved Jaynie, she'd needed to get her off the topic of Brett Harston. Her girlfriend was an incurable romantic, and if she had her way, she'd have them on the first plane to Vegas before she left the diner. Which meant she had to put the kibosh on any of those thoughts!

"How are your kids?" Sarabeth asked, deftly changing the subject before taking a long sip of her milkshake. *Heaven.*

"All good." Jaynie relayed their latest news before leaning back and tapping a red nail against the side of her glass. "Now, tell me how it's going with Ross."

Sarabeth pushed her hand into her hair and rubbed her scalp. "Well, you know he's always blamed me for not fighting harder for them when Rusty and I split up. I haven't wanted to get caught in the blame game, but I've told him some of what went down but not everything. I still don't think he realizes how hard it was fighting Rusty with minimal resources and no power."

"I'm still angry that that judge gave Rusty custody of the kids and not you. That was a prime example of how wealth and influence and old boys clubs work." Jaynie huffed, looking annoyed. "But Ross is an adult now, Sarabeth, with a child of his own. He's old enough to understand the truth, *your* truth and I'm glad you told him. And, seeing that he and Rusty are not talking—"

"Yeah, I heard that Rusty disowned him because of his relationship with Charlotte. Ugh... I could just...stab him."

Jaynie looked around, worried. "Jeez, hon, don't make statements in here like that! If something happens to Rusty, you'll be the number one suspect."

"I'd be the number one suspect anyway," she muttered. "They always look at wives and ex-wives first. And we watch too many crime shows, Jaynie, we really do."

Sarabeth grinned. She and Jaynie were both huge devotees of true crime documentaries and were convinced they could pull off the perfect murder.

Not that they would...

"So, how are you going to mend fences with Ross?"

"I'm still tiptoeing my way around that," Sarabeth admitted. "Do you have any ideas?"

"Just keep reinforcing the truth. Keep telling him that Rusty started cheating on you a few months after your wedding, that he couldn't keep his pants zipped. Tell him that the gossip he spread around about you made living in Royal untenable so you moved to Dallas, purely to stay close to them. That every time you made arrangements for them to visit you, or for you to visit them, Rusty had an excuse to cancel those visits, telling you they had plans, or weren't interested or were sick. That he put so many barriers between you that, eventually, the wall became too high for you to climb."

Sarabeth felt tears well, angry and annoyed at her younger self. She'd been raised by a pushy mother who believed that her face was her currency—if she couldn't win pageants then marrying a rich man was just as good—and putting up with a man's infidelity was the price one paid for having access to his money and enjoying financial security. Sarabeth violently disagreed, and her relationship with her mother deteriorated rapidly to the point of barely interacting. And for far too many years, she'd had little interaction with Ross and Gina.

She counted her blessings every day that she and Gina were now in a good place, but she'd failed Ross. And she felt so ashamed. "I should've done something different, something else."

"Maybe." Jaynie shrugged. "But you were so damn young when you married Rusty, no more than a kid yourself. Give yourself a break, Sarabeth. You're trying to make amends and that's all you can do."

"But what if Ross refuses to let me be a part of his life?" Sarabeth voiced her biggest worry, the one that kept her awake at night. She wanted to get to know Charlotte and to love, cuddle and spoil her beautiful grandson.

"Have faith that it will all turn out okay, girlfriend, and it will," Jaynie told her, pulling her half-empty glass toward her. "Changing the subject…"

Sarabeth cocked her head, frowning at the naughty glint in the other woman's eyes. What in tarnation was the troublemaker going to say next?

"So, I think you should have an affair with Brett Harston."

Sarabeth nearly spluttered her salted caramel milkshake all over the table. "What! *Why?*"

"Because he's hot, he's single—"

Sarabeth threw her hands up in the air. "He broke up with his fiancée the day before his wedding a couple of weeks ago."

"*Pfft*, he and Lexi Alderidge never made sense to me." Jaynie waved her objection away. "The best cure for heartbreak, not that I think either of them is heartbroken—"

"Lexi must be." Sarabeth crossed her arms over her chest, frowning at her friend. How could she not be? She'd been expecting to get married, for God's sake!

"Brett was Lexi's rebound guy after her divorce. I bet she's more embarrassed than heartbroken," Jaynie stated empathetically. "She needed someone to prop her up after her divorce, and she and Brett drifted toward each other and somehow, God knows how, they started thinking marriage was a good idea. Good thing that Brett saw the light because they are *so* not right for each other."

Darling Jaynie, so decisive. But, despite her friend's ability to read people and situations, she hadn't walked in their shoes, slept in their bed, so she couldn't know for sure what had happened between them. It had to be more complicated than that...

Not that Brett's love life was any of her business. Now or in the future, as she informed her friend.

Jaynie laughed. "We'll just see about that."

No. They wouldn't.

Because there was nothing to see. It was just a kiss, dammit.

An earth shuddering, toe-curling kiss but still...just a kiss.

Four

Well, this was awkward.

Sarabeth and Brett hadn't spoken one word since meeting in the parking lot of the general store. Brett helped her load her sacks of groceries into her vehicle, then opened the driver's side door before walking around to the passenger side. He spent the entire journey back to Heritage Ranch staring out of the window, his expression remote.

Was he upset, angry, regretful?

What was going through his head? And *why* was she obsessing about this?

Sarabeth saw the gates to his ranch in the distance and slapped her hand on the steering wheel, sick of the heavy quiet. "Will you please say something?"

Brett turned his head to look at her. "What do you want me to say?"

Sarabeth rolled her eyes heavenward. Okay, she might have to stop and draw him a picture. "We *kissed*, Brett."

"I remember. I was there."

Having a conversation with him was like pulling teeth. Why was she always attracted to the strong, silent type? Rusty, admittedly, hadn't been—he'd been slick and charming and so damn smooth he could slide *up* walls. But, after him and probably because of him, every man she had a serious or not-so-serious relationship with was reticent and economical with words.

"Shouldn't we discuss it? We did give the gossips grist for their overworked mill."

"Is that a problem for you?" Brett asked.

"No. But it might be a problem for *you*. I'm leaving in three months but you live and work here. You are a member of the Texas Cattleman's Club, and you're a wealthy and respected rancher and businessman." Sarabeth released a breath as she turned the car to pass through the gates leading up to his ranch.

"I'm single. I wasn't cheating on my wife, girlfriend or partner when I kissed you. And, trust me on this, this might be a conservative Texas town but if we had to stop doing business with people who have committed adultery, there wouldn't be many people left to trade with," Brett said.

So, in that regard, not much had changed in Royal.

"So you're not regretting kissing me?" Oh man, could she sound any more insecure? What a stupid question. *Change the subject, Sarabeth, and change it now.*

She pointed to a group of horses in the paddock. "God, they are magnificent. You have beautiful animals, Brett."

As they passed, Sarabeth noticed a russet-colored horse with a distinctive coat of curls. "Did you give that horse a perm?" she quipped, trying to cut through the tension hovering between them.

"That's Percy, he's a Bashkir Curly horse. The breed

is one of the rarest of American descent. I'm thinking about breeding them," he replied. "And no, I very much *don't* regret kissing you."

Well, then. Good.

"And I'd like to do it again as soon as possible."

Sarabeth turned her head to stare at him and forgot to look back at the road. What? *Really?* Where was he going with this?

Brett leaned to the side and placed his hand on the steering wheel, pulling the wheel toward him. Sarabeth's eyes darted to the road and winced when she saw that she'd been heading for a ditch. "I'm not sure where you are going with this…" Braking gently, she stopped the vehicle so that she could give him her full attention and avoid crashing. Brett Harston fried her ability to multitask.

"Just stating a fact," Brett replied, sounding completely unfazed.

Okay. Well. Did that mean he was going to kiss her or not? Brett gestured to the road and Sarabeth accelerated away, both hands gripping the wheel. If that kiss was off the charts hot when they were in public, how would it be when they were alone? How far would he take it? How far would she *let* him go? She didn't know but she wouldn't mind finding out…

Just drive, Edmond. You're playing with fire…

But, after covering just a few yards, she slammed on the brakes again, put the car in park and turned back to him.

Don't do it, Sarabeth, don't step into the flames. But the fire was seductive and she wanted to play…

Hitting the catch on her seat belt, she felt it slide away and she turned to half kneel on the seat. She caught the flash of surprise in Brett's verdant green eyes as she lowered her mouth to his, one hand coming up to touch his jaw, rough with stubble. He was such a man, every inch of him oozing testosterone. Sarabeth nibbled at his mouth with her lips, tracing the seam of his mouth with her tongue. She felt his hand on her hip, heard that masculine growl of approval deep in his throat. Then his hand came up to grip the back of her head, his mouth opened and she lost control of this encounter, of their kiss. His tongue slipped past her teeth to tangle with hers and it was her turn to moan, a primal request for more.

Brett placed both hands on her waist, and without breaking their kiss, lifted her so that she straddled his muscular thighs. There wasn't enough room for her to make an intimate connection, and she wiggled her hips in disappointment. But her dismay turned to elation when he fumbled for the door handle and the door opened, allowing her the room to get closer. Seizing the moment, she instinctively dragged her mound over his erection and they both stilled at the contact.

Sarabeth pulled back to look into his face and she clocked his heavy breathing, the desire raging in his eyes. She wasn't alone in this madness, and that was good to know.

"Come back here," Brett growled.

Sarabeth, feeling like she was sixteen again, dived back in, stroking his shoulder with her palms, testing the texture of his hair, *silky*, and relishing the warm skin beneath the collar of his plain black button-down. Their kiss deepened, and she whimpered when his hand came up to cover her breast, his thumb drifting across her nipple. Ribbons of pleasure skittered across her body and she pressed down on Brett's hard shaft, needing the pleasure only he could give.

The thought that she was too old to be making out in the front seat of a car in broad daylight flitted through her mind, but she impatiently swatted it away. She was long done with living her life according to other people's standards—when it came to her life, hers was the only opinion that mattered!—and figured that as long as she wasn't hurting anyone, she could do whatever the hell she wanted.

And, judging by Brett's very ardent response—he'd pushed his hand down the back of her jeans—he was enjoying this crazy interlude as much as she was...

Sarabeth sighed when he wrenched his mouth off hers to drop kisses along her jawline, across her cheekbone. She arched her neck when he tugged her earlobe into his mouth, gently nibbling her flesh with his teeth. How could such a prosaic, tiny part of her body be so erogenous? If she was this turned on by a hot, demanding kiss and some mild petting, God help her if he got her into bed. She might just spontaneously combust...

A hard rap on the window next to her head made Sarabeth shoot up and she banged her elbow against the side panel of her SUV, causing her to release a couple of low, rude curses. She whipped her head around to look straight into a brown khaki shirt. Her eyes traveled up and she saw the purple-and-white badge of a Texas Game Warden and, from there, up into brown eyes in a swarthy, handsome face.

Oh, God, were they facing a public indecency charge?

Sarabeth hit the button to activate the electric window and pushed back her sure-to-be-messy hair from her forehead. "Yeah, sorry, Officer, we'll get moving."

She caught a flash of white teeth in the officer's smile and heard a snort from Brett. She turned to look at him to see him scowling at the Texas Game Warden. He was going to get them into more trouble if he didn't can his attitude.

Sarabeth lifted her hands. "I'm going to get off him and retake my seat."

"Thank you, ma'am."

"I just don't want you thinking that I'm reaching for a weapon or anything," Sarabeth said, keeping a fixed smile on her face.

"I appreciate that, ma'am."

Brett lifted his hand to his forehead and dug his fingers into his eye sockets. "Holy crap." He groaned when Sarabeth dug her knee into his thigh and cupped his package with his hands. "I don't want kids, honey, but neither do I need to be emasculated."

Sarabeth blushed as she plopped down into her seat. Right, she could've accomplished that maneuver with more dignity. Pulling her shirt down, she glanced in her side mirror to see a black truck parked behind them, blue lights flashing.

How long had the officer been there? Why hadn't they noticed and what had he seen? What was happening here?

Sarabeth watched as the tall, muscular lawman walked around the hood of her vehicle, hands on the belt holding a huge weapon, handcuffs and various doodads she couldn't identify. He looked mean and tough and like he meant business.

"May I see your license and registration, ma'am?" Sarabeth reached for her bag to get her documentation, but Brett's hand on her arm stopped her from pulling it onto her lap. He leaned across her to glare at the officer. "Stop being a dick, dude."

Sarabeth's mouth fell open, and she pinched Brett's arm, rather hard. "Stop antagonizing him, Brett! Just do what he says and he'll let us be on our way."

"Yeah, *Brett*."

"Cut it out, Shaw," Brett growled. He dragged his hand

through his hair before rubbing it over his face. "Jules is a friend, Sarabeth. He's just busting my chops. We're on private land, and we weren't doing anything wrong."

It took Sarabeth a moment for his words to make sense, and when they did, she glared at the officer. "That really wasn't funny!"

"It really was," he replied, leaning his hip against her car. "You seem to be very wary of law enforcement. Anything I should know about?"

Sarabeth stared at him before shaking her head. "No, of course not." The curiosity in his eyes remained, and underneath it, she saw kindness. She lifted her shoulders and let them drop. It couldn't hurt to give him a small explanation. "I dated an African American man back in California. We were stopped once by the police and it… well, it wasn't a pleasant experience. Seeing you so suddenly rattled me."

Jules's lips twitched. "I think Brett had you rattled already."

She blushed, but before she could respond Jules spoke again, his expression radiating sympathy. "I'm really sorry that happened to you, Ms. Edmond."

Sarabeth's eyebrows lifted. "You know who I am?"

"This is Royal, and the gossip is that you and lover boy here—" he jerked his chin in Brett's direction "—locked lips on Main Street."

"That was barely two hours ago," Brett snapped. "How the hell did you hear about that already?"

"Dude—" Jules rolled his eyes "—at the risk of repeating myself, this is *Royal, Texas.* Gossip is carried on the wind. But if you really want to know, Flora told Jenna, her daughter who told her cousin Beth who works at the Saint Tropez Salon. You know that once gossip hits that place it spreads like wildfire. Somehow our dispatcher heard about it, and she told me…"

"Probably because you were hanging over her desk and flirting again," Brett muttered.

Jules lifted his hands in a "what can you do" gesture. "It's what I do best," he admitted and Sarabeth had to smile at his confidence.

"Only matched by your ability to bug the hell out of me," Brett told him. "What are you doing here anyway?"

"I came to see you, idiot."

Brett narrowed his eyes, suspicious. "Why?"

"I've got a barn owl with a hurt wing. I need you to look after it for a spell," Jules replied.

Brett sighed and exited the vehicle. He followed the officer to his truck and Sarabeth admired his longs legs, his excellent butt and his graceful stride. God, he was gorgeous. Panty-melting, bone-shaking hot.

She couldn't wait to kiss him again…and not only his mouth. Nibbling those cords on his neck, sliding her tongue over those muscled shoulders, taking a bite out of those huge biceps…

"I spoke to Brielle but she can't look after him. She's slammed," Jules told Brett after shaking his hand. "And I thought since you are back, and bride free, you could help me out."

"Has Brielle looked at the bird?" Brett asked.

"Mmm. The X-rays show that the wing isn't broken. She thinks its soft tissue damage. It just needs a safe space to rest and recover. It also looks a little under-nourished."

Brett nodded. "Let's take a look."

Sarabeth opened her door, hopped out and followed the men to the back of Jules's big black truck. "Who's Brielle?" she asked as Jules dropped the tailgate.

"She's the local vet," Brett explained as he reached for the pet carrier and pulled it forward. Sarabeth caught a glimpse of big yellow eyes and speckled feathers and noticed a wing tucked very close to the bird's body.

Brett bent down to look inside the carrier. "It's a female, not a male and she's pretty young, maybe a year. She's definitely underweight. She's also got an eye infection."

Jules bent down to look into the carrier, and two sets of massive male shoulders blocked Sarabeth's view of the bird. "I didn't notice that," Jules said.

"Brielle would've. Did she give her any antibiotics?"

The officer stood up and shrugged. "I was rushing between calls so it was a bit of a hurried conversation."

"I'll call her," Brett told him, not taking his eyes off the bird. He placed both hands on the tailgate, his eyes on the owl. "Hey, honey, you're sick and scared, aren't you? I'm going to take such good care of you," he crooned. "You don't know it yet, but you've checked into a great hotel. Let's get you settled, okay, gorgeous girl?"

His entire focus was on the owl, and Sarabeth smiled as he easily lifted the carrier off the tailgate and walked it toward her SUV.

Sarabeth caught Jules's smile. "He's such a sap," he stated, affection in his voice.

"Is this something he does often?" Sarabeth asked as Brett opened the back door of her vehicle and gently lifted the carrier inside.

"All the time," Jules replied. "He emptied out his rehab barn because he was taking a honeymoon, but there's normally a menagerie in the old stable block."

Interesting. Yesterday, she would not have thought that of Brett—he seemed too tough and macho to have such a strong reaction to the weak and wounded. But, after hearing about his mom, his "save everything" streak made sense.

As long as he didn't think she needed rescuing, they'd get along just fine. Sarabeth didn't expect or want a white knight rushing to save her; in fact, she couldn't think of anything that would annoy her more. She'd walked through hell and back to become the strong, self-assured woman she was today, and she'd never let any man take away her hard-won independence.

Jules glanced at Brett and folded his big arms across his chest, looking hard and remote and very, very tough. They both looked at Brett, who was watching the bird, their conversation too low to reach him.

"He's a good guy, Ms. Edmond, and if you want to screw his brains out, I've got no problem with that."

Wow, where the hell had that come from? Oh, maybe because he'd caught them with their mouths fused and Brett's hand down the back of her pants.

"Good of you," Sarabeth sarcastically replied. "But I'm trying to work out what, exactly, anything we do has to do with you."

"I've known Brett since we were kids, and he's my oldest friend," Jules snapped. "I'm *family* and we're close. So if you start to play mind games with him, asking for money, for presents, for a new car, a break on your rent, I will find out."

Ah, he'd heard about and believed the gold digger rumors. Sarabeth stared at him, debating how to respond. It was on the tip of her tongue to tell him that she could, probably, penny for penny, match Brett's wealth. But pride and stubbornness kept the words behind her teeth. It was no one's business but her own how well her business did, how much she'd sold it for and how much she was worth.

And that was a lot...

Brett turned to look at her. "Hey, Sarabeth? I need to get the bird home so can we get moving?"

"Absolutely." That sounded like an awesome idea.

"It was nice meeting you," Sarabeth told Jules, the good manners her mama drilled into her forcing her to speak the lie.

Jules grinned. "No, it wasn't."

"You're right, it wasn't." She was annoyed with him for making assumptions, but she also admired his loyalty to his friend. Not wanting to make an enemy of him— she already had a few in Royal—she briefly touched his arm. "I'm not here to cause trouble, Jules."

He stared at her for a minute before his mouth softened into a small smile. "Glad to hear it, Ms. Edmond."

She'd used Rusty's surname for the best part of thirty years, but here, in Royal, it felt wrong. And weird. She wrinkled her nose. "Just call me Sarabeth."

"Can we please get going?" Brett demanded, sounding impatient. Sarabeth frowned when she saw him climbing into the trunk of her SUV, contorting his big legs around the carrier. Was that really necessary?

Jules shook his head, and when he looked at her again, humor had returned to his eyes. "You've got competition for his attention."

She shut her trunk door on both Brett and the bird and rolled her eyes at Jules. "It was a moment of madness. I doubt it will happen again."

Jules walked her to the driver's door and yanked it open. He gestured her inside. "Yeah, it sure will."

Sarabeth couldn't argue with his emphatic statement because God, she really hoped it would.

Jules, the bastard, didn't know when he wasn't wanted and, despite Brett glaring at him through the back window of Sarabeth's SUV, followed them back to the ranch. After Sarabeth dropped him off at the stable block, she continued on to her cottage, which stood on the other side of his lap pool and hot tub.

When her car disappeared from sight, Brett glared at Jules. "Why are you still here?" he demanded.

Jules picked up the carrier and followed Brett down the path that skirted the stables to the custom-built, small rehabilitation center he'd constructed. Having great facilities was another perk of being stupidly wealthy.

"I wanted to check in with you since we haven't spoken since you denied me the opportunity to be your best man," Jules told him. He waggled his eyebrows and shoved his tongue into his cheek. "But it seems like you are handling the situation just fine."

Brett led him to a small, wire enclosure, big enough for the owl to move around freely but not flap her injured wing. After retrieving a set of thick gloves from his supply closet, he pulled them on and dropped to his haunches to take the owl out of the carrier. The bird attempted to bite him, but Brett ignored her anger and gently placed her in the wire cage. After securing the cage, he stood up and pulled off the gloves. "I need to rehydrate her. Are you going to help me or are you going to bust my ass?"

"Both."

Fair enough. Brett entered the small building that served as a kitchen to prepare food for his injured animals, a storage space and an incubator room. Against the far wall was a series of cages to hold critters that couldn't be placed outside or that needed specialized care. He'd spent many hours in the room, sitting on the floor and nursing an injured animal back to life.

Animals were much less complicated than people. And

damn, while he could do with Jules's help to feed the owl, he'd really wanted to be alone so he could make sense of what had happened with Sarabeth.

One minute they'd been talking about kissing, the next he had his arms full of a fragrant sexy woman.

Brett wanted to believe that he would've eventually come to his senses, but also reluctantly admitted that if Jules arrived ten or fifteen minutes later, he might've found them naked.

It was official: Sarabeth could shut down his synapses.

"Water, glucose."

Brett blinked before frowning at Jules. "What?"

"You need glucose and water to rehydrate the owl and I don't have all day," Jules told him, leaning against a counter, smirking.

He nodded. "Right."

Brett knew Jules would not let the Lexi-Sarabeth matter drop. He gave him ten seconds, maybe twenty, before he raised the subject again.

"Are you going to give me an explanation?"

Five seconds. Wow. Jules was getting impatient with age. And had anyone else demanded an explanation, he would've told them to go to hell but Jules was his oldest friend. Also, the asshole wouldn't budge until he got an answer that satisfied him.

He was stubborn that way…

"You should never have asked Lexi to marry you," Jules stated.

Brett sent him a "well, duh" look. "I know."

"And you should've come to your senses a lot earlier than the day before the wedding."

"Wow, really? Thanks for pointing that out." He mixed the correct amounts of glucose and water and when his friend didn't react to his sarcasm, he sent him a ferocious scowl. "If you're going to make asinine observations then you can just piss off."

"Touchy too." Jules grinned. "Okay, well at least you got out of there before you said 'I do.' But that raises another question…"

And here it came…

"What the hell are you doing kissing the hell out of Sarabeth Edmond two weeks after you ditched Lexi Alderidge?"

"Good question," Brett muttered.

"I mean she's superhot for an old chick…"

Brett's glare was hot enough to melt Jules at fifty paces. "She's hot. Period. With no reference to her age."

The other man lifted his hand and had the grace to look sheepish. "Point taken. My mama and sisters would skin me alive for making such a remark."

Damn straight. Sarabeth was a decade older than him, but who the hell cared? Lust and need and desire and his goddamn body didn't stop to count the years; they wanted what they wanted, and what they wanted was her.

"So, what's happening between you?" Jules asked.

"I met her yesterday, Shaw. Nothing is happening between us." Brett spat the words out.

"I'd believe you but you've kissed her in front of three of the biggest gossips in town, and I just caught you with your tongue down her throat. If I arrived any later, I might have had to bleach my eyeballs. And arrested you for public indecency."

Point. Taken.

Again.

Brett rooted in the cupboard for a plastic syringe and a thin, supple plastic tube. "Nothing is going to happen between us."

"Really? You going with that?"

He banged his forehead against the cupboard door. After a minute, he lifted his head to skewer Jules with a hot glare. "If we sleep together, if it gets that far—"

"It'll get that far. Chemistry like that can't be ignored."

If Jules interrupted him one more time, he was going to thump him. "If it gets that far," he repeated, "it will only be a fling, a couple of hot nights spent with a sexy woman. I'll make damn sure she knows that she can't expect anything more from me. The last thing I need right now is a relationship."

His friend stared at him for a long minute before nodding. Then he stepped forward, slapped his back and Brett stumbled forward. "Can we get on with feeding the owl? Not all of us are wealthy ranchers who run their own schedules. I still have calls to make, work to do."

"And I have your grave to dig," Brett told him.

"You've been threatening to kill me for years. Just hold on until next week, I finally got a date with Mary-Jo on Friday."

"God help her," he muttered, handing Jules the syringe and the feeding tube. "How did you bribe her into going on a date with you?"

Jules turned away and lifted the gloves off the fence post. "Some women recognize class when they see it."

"Obviously Mary-Jo is lacking in that particular skill if she's agreed to be seen in public with you," Brett retorted, happy to have the spotlight moved off him. But he was under no illusions that if Jules could turn the tables back to his love life, such as it was, he would.

Their friendship was rock solid and based on loyalty, kinship and a lifetime of insults.

Five

Sarabeth wiped her damp hands on her tight-fitting jeans and fiddled with the cuff of her men's style, button-down shirt. She glanced at her watch and tapped her index finger on its oversize face. Hours and hours had passed since she'd last seen Brett. It was past six and she'd give him until seven to get over here, but if he didn't show, then she'd track him down and they would have a discussion about how to address their insane sexual attraction.

Or she'd just jump him.

Either way, she'd put an end to her acting like a cat on a hot tin roof.

Sarabeth sat down on the edge of the pretty two-seater couch in the cottage's small sitting room and dug her bare toes into the shaggy woolen rug covering the stone floor. Sighing, she looked toward the wood burner in the corner and wished it was cold enough for a fire. She could easily imagine stretching out on the rug, the heat from the stove warming her naked skin as she watched Brett pull his Henley over his head, push his jeans down his slim hips revealing his...

She released a heartfelt groan, wishing she could kick her own butt. She was being utterly ridiculous, and her inability to stop thinking about her landlord naked was driving her insane...

Sarabeth flung herself backward against the thick cushion and closed her eyes. Since leaving Brett at the stables to tend to the owl, she'd been hyped and utterly unable to concentrate. She veered between being desperate to see him and equally desperate to avoid him because of how out of control he made her feel.

Despite never attending college, Sarabeth considered herself an educated adult, and had graduated summa cum laude from the school of hard knocks. She wasn't a dewy-eyed teenager and knew that sexual attraction was a result of pheromones. Something about Brett made her hot and vice versa. Humans were, as a species, hard-wired to mate, and she wasn't stupid enough to read more into this heady, dizzying situation.

She wanted him, he wanted her. It was simple biology.

Which meant she would not put herself in the position of wanting more from Brett than he could give. Too often in the past, she'd confused sexual attraction with the beginnings of a relationship and she'd had her fingers burned and, in some cases, her heart set on fire... and not in a good way.

No, this time she would be clear thinking about this.

If something happened, and she and Brett had sex, it would be just a fling, a way to sate this terrible yearning. After so many years of looking for love, she was finally comfortable being single and she enjoyed her own company. She was self-sufficient and liked to control her own schedule. And now, not having the responsibility of *Sarabeths!* anymore, she was a free agent and could do what she wanted and go where she pleased. No relationship was worth sacrificing her freedom.

So, if Brett was looking for a relationship—and he couldn't be, not so soon after his botched wedding—he should look elsewhere.

She'd make that clear, if and when, they got to that point—

Sarabeth heard the sharp rap on the door and bolted up, instinctively running a hand over her hair. She launched herself to her feet and started to rush to the door before stopping abruptly. *Slow down, take a breath, don't let him think you were waiting for him...*

Be cool, for God's sake.

But why should she and why was she playing games? She wanted him, and intended to make that clear, so why was she pandering to social conventions? She prized honesty and so, she suspected, did Brett.

Just open the damn door, Edmond.

Sarabeth crossed the small space to the door and pulled it open, promising herself that she would at least say hi before she flung herself into his arms...

Manners, after all, were important.

She fumbled with the doorknob, cursing when her damp hand slid off the knob. Taking a deep, calming breath, she tried again, and there he was, looking rough and tough and so sexy it hurt. Brett had showered; his dark hair was damp and looked like he'd only brushed it out with his fingers. He'd pulled on a soft cashmere V-neck sweater and a pair of soft, black jeans. When she met his eyes, he held up a bottle of wine. "It's a merlot I won at a TCC fundraiser. Apparently, it's really good and freaking expensive."

"Sounds good," Sarabeth replied, her heart rate accelerating. "Did you come over here to drink wine with me?"

"I don't drink so I was going to ply you with it while persuading you to let me take you to bed."

Her mouth curved at his blunt reply. She'd been right about him preferring honesty. So did she. "Excellent, let's start with that and I'll hit the wine later."

Linking her arms around his neck, she stood on her tiptoes to slide her mouth against his. She felt Brett tense, then he groaned and took control of the kiss. One strong arm banded around her back and he hauled her to his body, her aching breasts pushing into his chest. Ah, yes, *this*…

Sarabeth heard him fumbling and pulled back to see Brett trying to place the bottle of wine on the small, decorative table next to the door. She saw him release the bottle but before she could utter a warning, the bottle skimmed the side of the table and shattered on the flagstone floor.

Brett cursed but reacted quickly, lifting her up and off her feet. She felt a couple of droplets of wine hit her bare feet but Brett walked her inside, away from the mess outside her door. She expected him to put her down, but he just turned her and backed her up against the closest wall.

Placing his hands under her thighs, he easily lifted her up and it felt natural to wind her legs around his hips, relying on him to keep her pinned against the wall.

Brett nipped at her mouth, slid his tongue against her bottom lip. "You taste so good…"

"The wine—"

"Can wait," Brett rasped. "I, on the other hand, cannot."

When his mouth covered hers again, Sarabeth tasted the passion in the leisurely exploration of her mouth, in the way he touched her face with calloused fingertips. His hand skimmed the side of her breast and she lifted her chest in that silent, feminine demand for more and groaned when his big hand covered her full breast, learning her form. She sucked his tongue, trying to convey how much she liked what he was doing, that she craved more.

He was so hard, muscular, overwhelmingly male. He smelled like expensive soap and fresh air and a unique scent that was all his own and which she loved.

If she could bottle and package him, she'd make a freaking fortune. Sarabeth buried her nose in his neck and when she'd inhaled her fill, she licked the taut cord of his neck before gently biting down on his skin.

"You are so damn sexy," Brett growled, slanting his head to the side to give her better access.

Being called sexy was so much better than being called beautiful; sexy was about the way she made him feel, not the way she looked. "Kiss me, Brett. Hard and deep, like you mean it."

He didn't hesitate, and when his lips connected with hers, Sarabeth felt like she'd been plugged into an electrical thunderstorm. Brett didn't hold back and poured passion and demand and want into her mouth, silently telling her that they were rapidly hitting the point of no return...

Sarabeth had barely completed the thought when he yanked his head back, looking at her with blazing eyes. "Do you want this? Do you want *me*? Because, if we go any further, this is only going to end one way..."

"With a fabulous orgasm, I hope," Sarabeth cheekily replied.

"I guarantee it," Brett retorted before his eyes turned serious. "I want to make love with you, Sarabeth. Yes or no?"

So straightforward, with no frills or embellishments. God, she loved his say-what-you-mean style of speaking. "Hell, yes."

The corners of his mouth tipped up in a sexy-as-sin smirk. "Good answer."

Sarabeth ran her fingertips down his cheek, stroking her thumb over his full bottom lip. "Couch or bed? Or, quicker still, the rug?"

"Right here," Brett told her as he nibbled his way up her jaw, "will be just fine."

Okay, then. Well, they said that new experiences were a good learning curve...

As she opened her mouth to his raiding tongue, Brett's hand snuck under her shirt, found her covered-with-lace nipple and thumbed it. Sarabeth felt the corresponding flash of lust scuttle through her as she angled her head to allow him deeper access to her mouth. This was different from the kisses they'd shared earlier; there was no restraint and she loved the hint of something wild she could taste on his tongue.

Moving her hands over him, she ran her fingers across his taut stomach, and let them drift lower before settling them low on his narrow hips. Her breasts begged for more, and hearing her silent plea, Brett lowered his head and tongued her through her shirt. She heard his growl of frustration and laughed when he gripped the ends of her shirt and ripped it apart, sending buttons flying.

Well, that was a little barbaric, and too damn hot!

Brett inhaled sharply as he moved the cup of her bra aside to reveal her hard, aroused nipple. She saw his frustration as he took her aching nipple into his mouth. Not hesitating, his tongue slid over her, hot and wet and achingly perfect.

Sarabeth lifted her hand and pushed her fingers into

his hair, arching her back to encourage him to head south and eventually, long minutes later, his hand slipped between her legs and he cupped her mound.

Sarabeth slid her hand over his hip and stretched her hand to brush his erection. It was a faint touch, but she felt the electricity power through him. And when she increased the pressure of her touch, she had Brett moaning aloud.

"I need to be inside you," he muttered. Flipping open the buttons to her jeans, he hurriedly pushed the fabric down her legs, stepping back to look at the transparent panties covering her thin strip of hair. "Oh, yeah. Man, you are smokin'."

His obvious appreciation gave Sarabeth confidence so she pushed his sweater up his chest and pulled it over his head. In between exchanging hot kisses, they removed jeans and his shoes, her shirt and underwear until they were both naked.

And dreams did, Sarabeth decided, come true. Because Brett exceeded every expectation. Wide chest, muscled arms, a ridged stomach and what she'd initially decided was a very nice package was actually hard, long and lovely.

Sarabeth wrapped her hands around his cock and rested her forehead on his chest, looking down. She was so ready for him, needed to know what he felt like deep inside her. So she told him...

In Brett's eyes flames of passion, hunger and want burned brightly, and under her probing touch, he hardened even more. He opened his hand and Sarabeth saw the foil package in his palm and watched as he ripped it open and withdrew the latex, handing it to her with a soft command to cover him. She slid the rubber down his shaft and yelped when Brett's fingers penetrated her folds, spreading her wet juices over her flesh.

And then, somehow, she was back up against the wall, her legs wound tightly around his waist, and he was pushing himself inside her, his face a mask of concentration.

"Man, you're tight. Gorgeous, lovely..." Brett muttered.

"You feel amazing." Sarabeth just managed to form the words before he hit a spot deep inside her and a wave of intense pleasure, crashed over her.

She chanted his name, lifting his hips to get closer, wanting more, needing to ride that bright light again.

"Yeah, baby, again..."

She felt the wave build, swell and then she was flying. Short moments later, from a place far, far away, she heard Brett's satisfied shout. Yep, a multiple orgasm was exactly what she'd wanted, and this one was bigger and brighter than the few she'd had before.

Nice.

Nice, as in too freaking fantastic for words.

Brett fought off another yawn and felt his eyes closing. If he intended to sleep in his own bed tonight, he needed to get going. But it was exceptionally hard to pull his hand off Sarabeth's truly excellent butt, to stop dropping kisses into her hair.

After a second round christening the rug next to her couch, they'd stumbled upstairs to her loft bedroom to clean up in her en suite shower, and that had turned into a heavy petting session. When they finally made it to her bed, they picked up where they left off in the shower...

He was fit and had stamina but, hot damn, he was exhausted. She'd worn him out. Brett really wanted to close his eyes and drift off, but there was the broken bottle on her porch and they still had to have a chat...

They needed to have a conversation so that they could reach a solid understanding...

Sarabeth lifted her head off his chest, and he turned his head to look into her deep, blue eyes. She was, in every way, truly beautiful and he felt honored to have explored her body, to be the one to make her squirm and scream with pleasure. But pleasure was all he could give her...

"Can we have a quick word?" Sarabeth asked.

Brett frowned as she rolled away, not giving him time to answer. She reached for a silk bathrobe and pulled it over her slender body, efficiently tying the belt into a floppy bow. The color was a brilliant blue, close to the shade of her eyes, and he felt himself twitch, once again interested in sliding it off her body...

Three times, dude. You're good but not Superman!

Brett watched as Sarabeth fiddled with her hair, raking her fingers through the thick, shiny strands to create some order. He thought about telling her not to bother, that he'd just muss it up again before reminding himself that he was on his way home. As much as he wanted her underneath him again, he was battling to keep his eyes open. And sleeping over wasn't an option as it tended to give women the wrong idea.

Sarabeth gestured to the bed. "This was fun."

Fun? What a weak word for what they'd done to, and *for* each other. Hot, explosive, set-the-sheets-on-fire were far better descriptors for the sexual heat they'd generated.

"I'd like to do it again but—"

Here it came, the I-need-more-and-I'm-not-the-type-who-does-this-without-a-commitment spiel. He'd heard it all before. Brett swallowed his sigh of irritation. It was just sex—the best sex of his life—why did women always have to complicate a good thing?

While he waited for Sarabeth to continue, Brett constructed a few responses of his own... *"I've just broken up with my fiancée," "I'm not ready for a relationship"* and *"I'm a long way off committing to anybody and I might never again."*

He'd be as kind as he could be, but he'd make his position clear. He refused to give her false hope.

"I hope you're not offended, but that was great sex and I'd like a repeat performance but—"

Another *but*. Brett lifted one eyebrow, waiting for the shoe to drop.

"But I'm not looking for a relationship." Sarabeth rushed the words out, so fast he wasn't sure if he'd heard her correctly. Maybe he'd imagined her "not."

"I'm terribly independent and I like being on my own," she continued. "I've been on my own for a long, long time and I don't see myself being in a relationship. It's too confining, too restricting, so if you're looking for that—and you shouldn't be, you know—then maybe you should look somewhere else."

She didn't want a relationship? Why the hell not? And, excuse me, he wasn't the type of guy who restricted, controlled, or crowded his partners. Relationships were a partnership, not a dictatorship.

Brett opened his mouth to argue and then remembered that she was giving him what he wanted, on a silver platter. So why was he feeling irritated instead of jubilant, annoyed rather than relieved?

Honestly, he was losing his shit...

Sarabeth pulled her bottom lip between her teeth and released it with a little plop. "And, if you don't mind, I'd prefer it if you didn't stay over."

Ah, and because he was a stubborn, contrary man, that was exactly what he now most wanted to do. Snuggled down under her down duvet and crisp sheets, his head supported by this truly exceptional pillow, he felt warm and comfortable. And he didn't…

Want.

To.

Go.

"And I'm sorry about your wine," Sarabeth added.

"Yeah, I just tossed five thousand dollars all over your porch floor."

She winced. "Sorry. Um…"

Brett flipped the covers back and stood up, utterly at ease in his nakedness. He saw Sarabeth's eyes drop to his crotch, saw the interest in those pretty blue depths and smiled grimly. Yeah, she wanted his body but wasn't particularly interested in his mind. He felt, to be honest, a little used.

You're being a hypocrite, Harston, and you damn well know it. Ten minutes ago, you were prepared to give her the same speech but, because she beat you to it, your nose is out of joint. You don't want a relationship, a "just-sex fling" would be amazing, and you're going to mess it all up by being a juvenile dick.

Pull yourself together. Pronto!

Brett walked over to Sarabeth and dropped a kiss on her temple. "Thanks for being honest." He admired candor in a woman. "I appreciate that…and I'm glad we're on the same page."

Sarabeth placed her hand on his bare chest and tipped her head back to look at him. "We are?"

He nodded. "Yep. And yeah, of course I'd like to sleep with you again, for as long as it works for both of us." He wrapped his arms around her and rested his chin in her hair. "Come over tomorrow night and eat with me."

Sarabeth stepped back and pulled a face. "OMG. I never offered you anything to eat. You must be starving!" She placed a hand on her belly and wrinkled her nose. "*I'm* starving."

He laughed, his irritation vanishing. "I'll take great sex over food any day, sweetheart. But tomorrow night we'll eat first and allow ourselves to be distracted afterward."

"Good plan," Sarabeth agreed. "Go on down and find your clothes, and I'll find you a broom and pan to sweep up the broken bottle."

He liked the fact that she didn't offer to do it for him, that she didn't buy into the stereotype that she was the woman therefore she must clean.

Sarabeth was full of surprises, and he couldn't wait to see what else she had up her sleeve.

Six

In Brett's gourmet, barely used kitchen, Sarabeth whisked eggs with buttermilk and eyed the number of dry ingredients for corn bread in the glass bowl in front of her. After ten days of eating many of her meals with Brett—they'd ditched the "no sleeping over" rule after one night, deciding that waking up together was far more fun—she'd realized that the man ate. *A lot.*

So, not being a fan of the microwave meals he kept in his freezer, Sarabeth cooked.

But only because she *wanted* to, not because he expected her to. As a rancher—as a good ole Texan—Sarabeth expected him to assume that she would do the cooking and cleaning. But Brett, she'd come to realize, was more evolved than she'd given him credit for. He employed a housekeeper a couple of days a week to keep his home spotlessly clean and to do his laundry, but he loaded and unloaded his own dishwasher, made coffee and his bed.

Got her wine, rubbed her feet, gave her outstanding orgasms…

"C'mon, get it into the oven, sweetheart."

Sarabeth smiled at Brett, who was standing on the other side of the massive, marble-topped island in the center of his kitchen. "Hungry?"

"I'm always hungry but doubly so today. I rode up to the high meadow to check on a herd. I spent the whole day sitting in the saddle."

They'd taken a couple of rides together and Sarabeth was slowly regaining her youthful confidence. Though being on a horse reminded her that she had muscles in places she'd forgotten about. Actually, sex with Brett did the same.

"I took Bella out for a ride today," she told him, adding the wet ingredients to the dry. "She's a lovely horse and I adore riding her. She's definitely my favorite."

"She was one of my first foals, and I couldn't bear to part with her," Brett told her, picking up the bottle of wine and topping off her glass. He sent her a curious look. "You looked a bit pensive earlier. Anything on your mind?"

"Ah, no. I was just thinking that I like that you don't follow convention."

He used his fingers to transfer some grated cheese from the pile on the counter to his mouth. Sarabeth glared at him and pushed the cheese and the grater toward him. "Replenish the stock, Harston."

"Yes, ma'am. I didn't have a conventional upbringing so I think convention is overrated. But why do you think that?"

She chose her words carefully. "Well, I started cooking for us because I hate microwave meals and I like cooking, but you never asked and best of all, you don't expect me to cook. Or clean."

"Should I?" Brett asked, picking up the grater and cheese.

"No, of course not. I like that you don't, but so many men would."

"You've been hanging out with the wrong type of guys," he said, his big hands making short work of the cheese.

"Tell me about it," she muttered, gently stirring her corn bread mixture. "You're the most normal guy I've been with for years. Hell, you're the *only* guy I've been with for years."

"Really?" Brett asked, obviously surprised. "But you are drop-dead gorgeous."

Sarabeth put the cheese, onion and chilies into the mixture and stirred it through the batter. She laughed as she tipped the mixture into a greased skillet. "You are so good for my ego, Brett."

"Tell me about your marriage to Rusty," Brett asked and because it was a quietly posed question, not a demand, she decided to answer him.

"I was very young, eighteen, he was a lot older. I was naive, he was not. I was there to look good and produce kids and to keep my mouth shut. And I listened and obeyed and I thought we had a good marriage. Then I caught him in our bed with a so-called friend and, with a little digging, I found out he'd had a series of mistresses since we were first married. Apparently, everyone in town knew but me."

And knowing that she was the last person to know really hurt. And she still felt like a fool.

Sarabeth made herself meet Brett's eyes, and she was grateful to see sympathy within those mesmerizing green depths, not pity. "But if I thought he was a bastard during our marriage, it was nothing compared to his fury when I walked out on him. Rusty decides when a relationship is over, no one else. He vowed to punish me and he did. He managed to get custody of the kids, the judge was a friend of his father's, and then he did everything possible to drive a wedge between the kids and me." She cursed the tears in her eyes. "And he succeeded. Damn, I still feel guilty for that."

Brett didn't say anything but instead picked up her wineglass and pushed it into her hand. Sarabeth took a sip, a deep breath and raked her hair back from her face. "So, according to the Royal Reporters, via Jaynie, he's not happy I'm back in town. Apparently, he's telling everyone that I'm looking for money, that I'm broke and that he's waiting for me to come crawling back."

"What a prick," Brett muttered.

Yeah, he was soooo good for her ego.

"Does he know about us?" he asked.

She shrugged. "According to Jaynie, everybody knows about us so I supposed he's heard. Is that a problem for you?"

"Hell, no. I don't give a crap."

Yeah, so blunt and so decisive.

"But he can't be happy about it, and he's going to be really pissed when he finds out I'm ridiculously rich," Sarabeth said. Damn. She hadn't meant to tell him that. Hell, she'd had no intention of telling anybody about the sale of *Sarabeths!*. But Brett was so easy to talk to, and around him, she felt her emotional barriers dropping. She had to be careful, however, because she couldn't start letting multicolored feelings into their monochromatic fling.

They were friends having sex. Period.

But she'd have to tell her kids about *Sarabeths!* at some point, but for now, she was just enjoying knowing that she was financially secure and free.

"I haven't told anyone about my financial situation," she informed Brett, who sat on one of the stools opposite her.

"Why not?"

She looked at him and immediately noticed the blatant curiosity in his eyes. He covered her hand with his and squeezed. "I'd love to hear more but if you don't want to tell me, that's fine too. And it goes without saying that whatever you say on the ranch stays on the ranch."

Sarabeth smiled at his turn of phrase. She walked around the island before coming to stand between his legs. His arms immediately wrapped around her and she leaned into his chest, feeling secure and safe. She was strong, feisty and independent but sometimes it was nice to lean on someone, to confide her worst fears.

He was proving to be her friend as well as her lover...

"Rusty never believed I could do anything, and my mom raised me to capitalize on my looks. Beauty pageants or a good marriage to a very rich man... Those were my two choices. Rusty often told our friends and his business associates I was so lucky to be born beautiful because I was brainless."

Brett released a low, annoyed growl. "A lot of people underestimated me because my mom was a drunk and we were poor," he quietly said. "People are morons."

Weren't they just? "How did you come to own all this?" Sarabeth asked, curious.

"I had a mentor who trusted me enough to be a guarantor on a loan to buy this property. I then worked my ass off. That's the short version of my story. But carry on with yours. I'm fascinated."

Sarabeth took a sip from his wineglass before continuing. "I was living in Dallas and was struggling to get access to my kids. And as they grew older, I had to beg them to visit and when they did, we were all miserable. Rusty basically poisoned them against me. When it became too much, I went to LA and found work in an upmarket cosmetic store. One day I was bored, and I decided to find out how they made the products and was horrified to learn that a lot of the manufacturers use palm oil and experiment on animals—"

She nodded at the distaste on his face. They both loved animals, and with Sarabeth helping with the injured owl and frequently accompanying him when he did his nightly tour of the stables to check on his horses and other farm animals, most of which were rescues, the bond between them deepened every day.

"I started researching other ways to make soaps and lotions, using sustainable products, and I made a few batches. I rather liked them so I made more and started selling them at a market store on the weekends. Quite quickly, I realized I couldn't keep up with demand, and I kinda, sorta went into production and began selling the cosmetics online."

"I feel like a lot more happened than 'kinda, sorta...'" Brett commented.

A million decisions, meetings, the hiring and firing of staff. Sleepless nights and pure terror. Feeling like a god when everything went right, crying in the bathroom when it didn't. It had been the hardest and most rewarding thing she'd ever done in her life. Apart from her kids, of course.

"You started your own business, you know what it takes to become one of the wealthiest guys in the area.

A hell of a lot of hard work, a little luck, some tears and a lot of stress."

"Yep, that."

Sarabeth dropped a kiss onto his mouth and pulled back before they took it further and got distracted. She wanted to tell him the rest, suddenly excited to be confiding in him about her business and her successes. She was at the stage in her life where she no longer required the world's approval but for some inexplicable reason she wanted his.

As casually as she could, she asked him whether he'd heard of *Sarabeths!* "It's a cosmetic line, gold and pink packaging?"

Brett slowly nodded. "A girlfriend a couple of years back wanted a set for Christmas."

Sarabeth's mouth twitched with amusement. "Did you buy it for her?"

"God, no! Far too expensive," Brett replied on an easy grin. She didn't say anything, she just waited for him to connect the dots, which he quickly did. "Wait, are you telling me that the Sarabeth in *Sarabeths!* is you?"

She grinned, delighted, and lifted one shoulder in what she hoped was a casual shrug. "Yep."

"Wow." Brett ran a hand over his chin, surprise flickering in his eyes. "Holy shit, I'm seriously impressed."

"Thanks." Sarabeth tucked her face into his neck and she felt his big hand sliding over her butt. Mmm, nice.

"And you're right, Rusty will be super pissed when he finds out."

Sarabeth knew her smile was just this side of evil. "I know, right?"

Brett patted her butt in a "pay attention" gesture, and she pulled back to look at him. "How much time do we have until the corn bread is ready?" he asked.

Disconcerted by the rapid change of subject, she glanced at her watch. "Uh, fifteen minutes? Twenty?"

"Excellent. Just enough time to take my hot, sexy, *smart* lover to bed."

Brett gave the best compliments, Sarabeth thought. Thanks to her looks being the currency she was taught to trade in, being called beautiful was overrated and meant nothing. But hot was lovely, sexy better and being called smart was the absolute best.

And yeah, when he said things like that she'd follow him anywhere.

By Sunday, after Brett spent three days in Austin visiting a ranch he was considering purchasing, Sarabeth was desperately missing him and actively loathing the fact that she did. He'd invited her to accompany him, but because they'd spent so much time together over the past two weeks, she thought it prudent for them to spend some time apart. Now, on Sunday, she was regretting that decision.

Every pore on her body missed him with an intensity she didn't believe possible. Her bed in the cottage—she didn't feel comfortable sleeping in Brett's bed when he wasn't there—no longer felt welcoming and her once cozy abode now felt cold and empty.

Sarabeth stood on the porch of her cottage and looked anxiously toward the drive, praying she'd soon see the big lights of Brett's truck. On Friday he'd said that he'd be home by lunch on Sunday; it was now dusk and she hadn't heard anything from him.

What was wrong with the man? Had he forgotten how to use his phone? Or to text? Had his battery run down, or, God, had he been in a car accident? How would she know? How could she find out?

Take a breath Sarabeth and calm the hell down. Do try to remember that you are not his girlfriend, wife, partner or significant other. You are the woman he's currently sleeping with, no more and no less. He's under no obligation to tell you where he is and what he is doing. Or when he'd be home.

Anyone on the outside watching her would think that what they had meant something, and it didn't. She was acting like they were a romantic couple instead of treating him like a friend she was having sex with.

And it had to stop.

She had to be clever about this, seriously smart. If she didn't keep an eye on what they were doing and why they were doing it, the lines would blur and confusion would settle in. They were sleeping together because the sex was amazing and their chemistry off the charts.

The fact that they enjoyed each other's company was an additional bonus.

But they should tone it down, keep it cool, keep those lines crisp and sharp. It wasn't wise to spend so much of their out-of-bed time together; hell, maybe they should stop having sex every night.

Though, to be honest, she didn't want to. She loved exploring the depths of her desire with Brett and, because of him, she'd regained or, to be more accurate, *found* her sexual confidence. With this smoking hot, generous and virile man, she was gloriously uninhibited and felt safe to tell him what she did or didn't like. And he listened, learned and made her body sing.

But sex was sex but her longing for connection, for his company, was dangerous, worrying. And it needed to stop. *They* needed to stop...

Not today, tomorrow or the next day but soonish.

Because this couldn't last forever. Nothing this good ever did.

But for now, she'd settle for shoring up her defenses and stop acting like a lovesick teenager waiting for her boyfriend to pick her up for the prom.

Because waiting around, wringing her hands was not something a strong, feisty and independent woman did.

Determined to make a point, to herself and to Brett, Sarabeth picked up her phone and dialed Jaynie. When her friend answered, she forced herself to sound jaunty. "I'm craving pizza. Can I bring a few pies over and a bottle or two of wine?"

"If you're going to drink then you are not driving back," Jaynie told her, "so pack your pj's and your toothbrush."

Perfect, she thought. If she wasn't on the ranch when Brett finally returned, there was no way he'd suspect that she'd been hanging around waiting for him to appear.

Because he'd hate it if he thought she was becoming territorial and, worse, clingy.

From this moment on, she would do her best to get a better handle on this friends-with-benefits thing…

By the time Brett saw Sarabeth's SUV moving up his driveway, he'd built up a fine head of steam. Instead of her being at the cottage when he arrived home the previous night, he'd found her place locked up tight and her car not in its usual parking spot in his six-car garage. He'd tried to call her a few times, both last night and this morning, but his calls went straight to voice mail. And he started to, stupidly he realized, consider calling local hospitals or to get Jules to check whether there had been any accidents in and around Royal.

His overreaction annoyed him.

As did the fact that he was so disappointed that she wasn't home and waiting for him. He didn't buy into that whole, woman-belonged-at-home stereotype but was frustrated that she hadn't sent him a text message to give him a heads-up on her whereabouts...

And he'd lost a half morning's work because he kept finding excuses to hang around the house to be around when she finally made an appearance. Where had she gone? Who had she been with?

Brett ran his hands over his face, irritated with himself and pissed off in general. He hadn't slept well for the past few nights. The hotel bed had been big and lonely, and he'd missed her warmth. Her scent. The way her hair kept catching on his stubble.

And yeah, he missed the sex...

He felt like a lifelong addict who'd suddenly gone cold turkey. Shaky and weird and feeling like he was about to jump out of his skin. He'd never felt like this before...he was generally laid back and easygoing. So it freaked him out that he was annoyed with Sarabeth for going AWOL.

Brett blew out a frustrated breath. He had to get this craving for her under control. What he thought would be a quick fling had turned out to be a lot more intense than he ever imagined, and he needed to corral those emotions. They were having a fling, were bed-buddies, and he could not, *would* not allow his feelings to deepen. Because if he did, Sarabeth would put his heart through the wringer. She was wealthy, independent—emotionally and mentally—and she had no intention of being one-half of a whole ever again.

And with his recent track record, having just made such an unnecessary mess with Lexi, he'd be a fool to jump into that alligator-infested swamp again. He wanted,

no, *needed* a physical relationship devoid of expectations.
And that was what Sarabeth was giving him...

So what, dumbass, was the problem?

He hoped God knew because he sure as hell didn't.

Brett leaned his shoulder against the doorjamb to his
kitchen and watched as Sarabeth pulled into her space,
parking her SUV neatly between his Jet Ski and KTM
450 SX-F dirt bike. It had been a while since he'd ridden the bike but a year, maybe two, since he'd used the
Jet Ski. He had a lot of toys but didn't take the time to
enjoy them.

He ambled over to the garage and by the time he
reached Sarabeth, she was out of the SUV, a small overnight bag hanging off her shoulder. Dressed in jeans and
a simple white, thigh-length sweater, knee-high leather
boots and a colorful, oversize cotton scarf wrapped
around her neck, she looked fresh and lovely.

And damn, he really wanted to take her to bed.

"Hi."

Brett noticed the wariness in eyes the color of liquid
ink as he returned her greeting.

"Good trip?" she asked as he pulled her bag off her
shoulder to carry it for her.

"Good enough," he replied, resisting the temptation
to tell her that he wished she'd come with him, that he'd
missed her company. In bed and out.

"What time did you get back?" Sarabeth casually
asked, but he heard the note of tension in her voice. Had
the same where-is-he, what-is-he-doing thoughts tumbled through her mind? He followed her to her cottage,
making a mental note to replace the warped plank on the
stairs leading up to the front door.

"Eightish," Brett answered. He lifted her bag and allowed it to drop again. "Where did you spend the night?"

Okay, that question wasn't casual at all. It was demanding, rude and very out of order. He closed his eyes after Sarabeth sent him a withering stare, turning her back on him to open the door to the cottage. "You don't have any right to ask me that question in that particular voice, Brett."

She was right, he didn't. But that didn't stop him from dropping her bag to the floor with a thump and slapping his hands on his hips. "No, I don't, but I'm asking it anyway."

"And then do I have the right to interrogate you about your weekend?" Sarabeth coolly asked, placing her handbag on the hall table and her car keys in the pottery bowl.

Since he spent his nights going over balance sheets and profit and loss statements and his days either on horseback or in a pickup inspecting the land, he didn't have anything to hide, as he told her.

"Neither do I," Sarabeth informed him, her back straight and her eyes frosty. "I spent the night with Jaynie and Laura, if you must know."

Relief, as hot and sweet as melted taffy, flowed through him, and he released the pent-up breath he hadn't known he was holding. "Oh. Okay."

"Okay? It's not like I needed your permission, Harston."

Stop digging, boy, you're going to give yourself a hernia. "Of course you don't," Brett told her in an attempt to douse the light of battle in her eyes. "It was just a figure of speech."

They locked eyes and in those gorgeous blue depths, beneath the simmering attraction, he noticed determination and a distance that hadn't been there when he left.

Oh, crap.

He knew that look—he was thirty-eight years old and he'd seen it in the countless women before her. It screamed that she *wantedtotalk*. A phrase to freeze a man's blood.

"I think we should talk…"

Was he a genius or what? He really should've just gone to work this morning instead of hanging around like a crazy, besotted fool.

"Shall we sit down?" Sarabeth gestured to the couch, sitting on the rug where they'd made love that first night they hooked up.

Images of taking her up against the wall blasted his brain and he shook his head. "I'll stand. You obviously have something on your mind so just spit it out."

Sarabeth placed her hands into the back pockets of her jeans and the action raised her chest. Damn, he wished she hadn't brought attention to her perky breasts. He wanted his mouth on her coral-colored nipple, her smooth legs around his hips, her mouth and body under his…

"I think us being apart was a really good thing, and it gave me time to think. I'm sure you enjoyed having some time away from me too."

Sarabeth looked like she was waiting for him to agree with her, but he couldn't do that. He'd had two emotions the past seventy-two hours, horny and frustrated. And lonely. Okay, that was three emotions…

"And I think we should slow this down, take a breath," Sarabeth said.

"Why?"

She shrugged and looked past him. He needed her eyes on him so he lifted his foot and kicked the door closed. Her now irritated eyes returned to his.

"You might be retired, but I need to get to work sometime soon," Brett told her, wincing at the harsh note in his voice, "so can we move this conversation along?"

Her mouth fell open and her irritation morphed into anger. "Is that a crack about my age?"

What? No! He hadn't meant it like that. And she knew her age wasn't an issue. Didn't she? "I'm sleeping with you because you are a sexy, fascinating woman. I don't give a crap about your age. Or mine. So stop putting words in my mouth."

Sarabeth tipped her head back to look at the ceiling, and when she met his eyes again, he saw her rueful expression. "Sorry."

"Accepted. Now tell me what's really going on."

Sarabeth leaned her butt against the back of the couch and looked pensive. He waited while she gathered her thoughts. "I've never done this bed-buddy thing before, but I'm sure it doesn't involve us practically living together two days after our first meeting. We've been spending so much time together that I, well…missed you this weekend."

She sounded desolate, like she was trying to tell him she'd run over his dog or written off his truck. He tried not to let her see his amusement. "I missed you too. Is that such a bad thing?"

Sarabeth threw up her hands, obviously agitated. "As FWBs—"

"As *what*?" Then the acronym clicked and he nodded. "Sorry, got it, carry on."

"We shouldn't be missing each other, it shouldn't be this intense. We're supposed to play it cool, have fun and do our own thing…*apart*. I'm sure we're doing it all wrong!"

Brett rubbed his hand over his mouth, trying to hide his smile. "Says who?"

Sarabeth stared at her feet. "*Cosmopolitan*. Jaynie, who had a couple of these types of relationships before she met Laura. And Google."

He couldn't contain his amusement anymore and grinned. "You're consulting the internet about our love life?"

Sarabeth blushed. "I was doing research. And everything I read says that we are doing this wrong…"

"Bullshit," Brett said, stepping up to her and placing his hands on her slim upper arms. "There is no one right way when it comes to people and attraction, sweetheart, and I refuse to live my life in accordance to a few stupid rules someone posted online."

He brushed a kiss across her mouth and felt her shudder. "Does that feel good?"

"You know it does," Sarabeth whispered.

Brett placed his hand on her breast and felt her nipple pucker. He knew the answer to the question he was about to pose but needed to hear her breathy voice again. "And this? Do you like me touching you here?"

"I like you touching me everywhere."

So honest, so straightforward. He loved it. "And I know how much you love my fingers, and my tongue, between your legs. So, let's agree that, as long as it feels good, let's do it."

"But what if—?"

She broke off her sentence but Brett knew what she was about to ask. What if they started to feel more, what if this thing between them started to deepen? He shook his head. "We won't let this go deeper, Sarabeth, we can't afford to let that happen. Because it would ruin what we have, and what we have, right now, is damn awesome. We're friends who enjoy each other, in and out of bed. Let's not ruin that by embarking on a rules-based relationship."

He felt her sigh, physically saw the tension drain from her body. Then his lover, fierce and fantastic, lifted her head and pushed back her shoulders, lifting her chin and fine jaw. "I won't fall in love with you, Brett. And I know you won't fall in love with me."

He pushed a strand of hair off her forehead, a little disconcerted by her determination. "Why are you so convinced of that?"

"Because, as much fun as we have together, in and out of bed, I don't need you to save me. I'm emotionally independent and I don't need rescuing. And if I did, I would do it myself."

"Yeah, yeah, I get it," Brett huffed, exasperated that she'd pointed out what he considered to be his weakest fault.

"And you need to be needed," Sarabeth added.

He used to need to be needed. But not anymore. He was done with that...

She dealt in honesty but could she take it when it was directed at her? It was time to find out. "And, because you were put down and told you would never be anything but beautiful, and because you were once stripped of power, you need to feel, or be, in control. You think that if you need someone, it's a sign of weakness."

Sarabeth winced before releasing a shaky laugh. "God, if we did end up in a relationship, it would be ludicrously dysfunctional."

Brett winced. "So, let's not do that then?"

"Deal." She nodded and managed a smile. "I'm glad we're both on the same page, Brett. Another question..."

He held his breath, hoping it would be a lot simpler than the ones that had come before. Like most men, he preferred to avoid these conversational, paintball bullets.

"Why aren't we naked yet?" Sarabeth asked, her hands sneaking under his flannel shirt and her fingers dipping beneath the band of his jeans.

That was a damn good question. So, instead of answering, Brett got to work.

Seven

"Sweetheart, you always smell so good," Brett murmured, pushing his nose into the space between her neck and chin, inhaling deeply. "And you are so incredibly hot. I can't wait to get inside you..."

"I haven't thought of much else since I left on Friday and if I don't have you, I'll lose my mind," he added, his voice rough with need.

Sarabeth heard his words, sighed at the rasp in his voice, enjoying the heat building in her stomach and her womb. She still didn't know how to handle his compliments, the sweet mutterings against her skin, in her ear. While they were nice to hear, she had to be careful about believing any of it. Words were easy, especially in the heat of the moment. It wasn't that she thought Brett was being insincere—she believed he meant everything he said—but bedroom words faded and were easily forgotten.

She couldn't allow herself to believe them or get swept away by them. But, man, it was difficult.

It was late on a Monday morning, but there in the living room, he efficiently stripped her of her clothes, his face flushed as he looked down at her bare torso. She placed her hand on his erection and sighed at the proof of his desire. Yeah, he wanted her.

Brett hooked his thumbs into the band of her flesh-colored panties and pulled down the fabric. He stared at her thinner than normal landing strip, and she gasped when he ran his finger over the soft hair. "So pretty."

"I had an appointment at the salon in Royal this morning," she said, impressed that she could form words when he was touching her so intimately.

"Nice."

His appreciation made her smile and Sarabeth, impatient now, widened her legs to encourage him to touch her, deeply and intimately, and ignored his muffled laugh at her impatience. Without warning, Brett dropped to his knees and kissed her hip bone, then the top of her thigh, the inside of her leg, his soft stubble brushing ever so gently over her skin.

She needed his mouth on her sex, on that sweet, demanding bundle of nerves.

Sarabeth gripped the back of the sofa for support. "Brett, I need you. Now. Please, please touch me, or kiss me. Just do something!"

"I like it when you beg," Brett growled, before finally slipping his finger between her folds and touching her... *right there*. Sarabeth shook as electricity shot through her body, sensitizing every inch of her skin. She could barely think, or breathe, and then his hot, thick, talented finger slipped inside her, quickly followed by another. His thumb swept over her clit, and Sarabeth felt the pressure building, fascinated by the rainbow swirling through her.

"Brett, I'm going to come," she whimpered, all her energy focused on the exhilarating tempest she'd been sucked into.

"No, you're not," he told her, sitting back on his haunches, watching her with an intense expression on his face, his fingers still deeply embedded in her.

"Please," Sarabeth sobbed, lifting her hands to finger her own nipples to keep feeding the colors, the rainbow storm. "Brett—you're killing me here."

"Then come for me, baby. Now." His voice, rough and sexy, skittered across her skin. In a fluid movement, he placed his mouth on her mound, swirling his tongue around her clitoris. He sucked her, once and then again and, deep inside her, his fingers widened and curled and Sarabeth became the rainbow storm. Her hips jerked as she pushed herself against his fingers, hardly aware that he'd lifted his head and that he was watching her fly.

After the colors faded and her shaking stopped, after he pulled his hand from her and held her thighs in a loose grip, her eyes slowly started to refocus on his masculine, so very sexy face. Her heart lurched at his tender, penetrating expression. She pushed a hand through her hair and, because the muscles in her legs felt like noodles and her knees like jelly, resumed her grip on the couch.

"You're just looking at me?" she softly asked, a little part of her scared at what he would say.

"I am."

"Why?"

"I know how much you hate being complimented on your looks but you *are* truly beautiful, possibly more so when you come." Brett stood up in a graceful fluid movement and held out his hand. "Come to bed with me?"

Sarabeth quickly nodded. *Of course she would.* His

hand, strong and warm, encircled hers and she followed him, naked, up the stairs to his bedroom.

On Wednesday evening, Brett surprised Sarabeth by telling her that he had made reservations for them to dine at Sheen, Royal's newest, and hippest, restaurant. Because her future daughter-in-law, Charlotte, worked as the executive chef at the popular, built entirely from glass restaurant, Sarabeth knew they were booked out weeks in advance. Brett had to have some serious connections to have secured a table at such short notice, but she'd recently realized her easygoing lover was a formidable businessman—fair but tough—and wielded quite a bit of power in this small town.

And had she known that he wanted to eat at Sheen—it never crossed her mind—she would've asked Charlotte to secure them a booking because Sarabeth knew Charlotte was grateful to her for encouraging Ross to give their relationship another chance. But her son's fiancée had enough on her plate at the moment—a new relationship, an energetic toddler and a blossoming career—and Sarabeth didn't want to cause her any additional stress.

"Hi, Faith." Sarabeth smiled at Sheen's gorgeous manager, whom she knew to be a good friend of Charlotte's. "I'm Sarabeth, Ross's mother."

Faith greeted her with a wide smile and introduced herself to Brett. As they exchanged small talk, Sarabeth looked over the restaurant and caught a glimpse of her reflection in the wall-to-ceiling glass. She was happy she'd chosen the black, silk jumpsuit. The wide legs and fitted bodice suited her lanky frame, the outfit was classy and wouldn't, hopefully, draw attention.

Because being with Brett Harston, his hand in hers, was already garnering curious looks, and she could easily imagine the comments of the snooty patrons seated at the restaurant's tables.

"They are having a torrid affair."

"She's at least a decade older than him."

"Shameless. He was about to marry a month ago and here he is, already with another woman."

She fought the urge to run from the room.

"This way, folks," Faith said, leading them into the lion's den.

Brett placed a hand on her back and practically pushed her toward their table, which was, Sarabeth noticed, one of the best, and most prominent, in the room. "Relax, sweetheart. We're having dinner, not being executed," he whispered in her ear.

She took the seat he pulled out for her and forced a smile onto her face. "I feel like everyone is looking at us."

"They are," Brett casually replied, dropping his big frame into the seat opposite her. Looking at Faith, he ordered Sarabeth's favorite red wine and a club soda for himself. He leaned back in his seat, looking urbane and debonair in a black button-down shirt worn under a very nice, possibly designer, charcoal suit.

Sarabeth frowned at him. "I was hoping you were going to tell me that I was overreacting."

"Nope, everyone in the room is talking about us." Brett shrugged. "They can gossip about me until they turn blue in the face, I don't care. The only person I don't want to be hurt by the gossip is Lexi. And you, obviously."

She liked that he was worried about his ex-fiancée. "Have you spoken to her recently?"

Sarabeth wasn't jealous or feeling insecure...okay, maybe she was a smidgeon jealous and insecure. But she had no right to be—bed-buddies, remember?—and the stupid feelings that occasionally floated to the surface were her problem, not Brett's.

He nodded. "I spoke to her yesterday. She's still super pissed I called the wedding off so late, and she has a right to be. But she did admit it was the right thing to do." Brett tapped his finger against the stem of his empty wineglass. "She asked whether the rumors about us were true."

"What did you tell her?"

Brett shrugged. "The truth. I owed her that much. I told her you are renting a cottage from me and that we're seeing one another. Without being crude, I stressed we are keeping it surface-based, and that it only started a couple of weeks ago and that it isn't serious."

Yet, here they were, eating at Sheen, dressed up nice and smelling good, acting like this was a date. Sarabeth rubbed her forehead with her fingertips, feeling confused. This wasn't what bed-buddies did.

But friends could eat together, and she and Brett were friends. But nothing more.

However, when they got home, they'd end up having seriously hot sex.

Arrgh...

Needing a distraction, Sarabeth looked over to the open kitchen area of Sheen, visible to the guests, smiling when she saw Charlotte in her chef whites. As if feeling her eyes on her, the young woman lifted her head and scanned the restaurant, her smile broadening when she locked eyes with Sarabeth. She turned to another chef, said something, and then she left the kitchen area to make her way across the restaurant.

Sarabeth stood up and held out her hands for Charlotte to take, which she did. They exchanged kisses, and Charlotte surprised Sarabeth when she pulled her in for a tight hug.

When she released her, Sarabeth noticed Charlotte's beautiful brown eyes were moist with emotion. "Since Ross isn't here and I don't know when next I'll get you on your own, I just wanted to say a hundred thank-yous for the part you played in getting Ross to see some sense."

Sarabeth smiled. "Anytime, honey. You look so happy, and so is he, and that's all that matters. How's my baby boy?"

Charlotte grinned. "I presume you are talking about Ben?"

Ross might be fully grown, a gorgeous man, but he'd always be her baby. Sarabeth winked. "This time."

She introduced Brett, and Charlotte stood by their table for the next few minutes exchanging Ben stories. Stepping behind Sarabeth's chair, she watched as the waitress poured her wine, before telling them their meal was on the house. "You don't need to do that, honey!" Sarabeth protested.

Charlotte dropped a kiss on the top of her head. "I really do, I'm so grateful." She straightened and her eyes, never still, drifted across the restaurant, constantly gauging the happiness and satisfaction levels of the customers. Sarabeth saw her spine stiffen, her expression close down and followed the direction of her gaze. She silently cursed when she saw Rusty and Billy Holmes standing at the entrance, talking to Faith.

Damn, the man still had the ability to spoil a nice night out.

Charlotte flashed her a strained smile. "I've got to get back to my station. I've got work to do."

"And you want to avoid Rusty," Sarabeth said, "and I can't blame you."

Charlotte grinned at her caustic tone and walked off,

studiously ignoring her future father-in-law. Sarabeth looked at her ex and wondered what she'd ever seen in him. And why did she never noticed that his eyes were ice cold and his I'm-here-worship-me smile was as smarmy as hell?

Brett clinked his glass of soda against her crystal wine glass and his action pulled her back to her hot date. She hadn't seen her ex-husband for a very long time. Was it wrong to be thrilled that she was looking good and was on a date with a great looking, *younger* guy?

Wrong, no. Egotistical? Maybe. But also very human.

"I take it that Charlotte has no time for Rusty?" Brett asked, his voice low enough not to carry to the neighboring tables.

"Something happened between Rusty and Charlotte when she worked as his chef at Elegance Ranch. Knowing Rusty, I have an idea of what might've happened but, out of respect for Charlotte, I won't verbalize my suspicions." Sarabeth took a sip of her wine, which was full-bodied and rich. "But I do know that Rusty recently used some strong-arm tactics on Ross to get him to stop seeing Charlotte."

Sarabeth caught the flash of distaste in Brett's eyes. "Are he and Rusty talking now?"

Sarabeth rocked her hand from side to side. "I'm not actually sure. I don't think so but I could be wrong."

Brett aimed a glance at the duo, who'd stopped at a table to converse with a distinguished couple Sarabeth vaguely recognized but couldn't place. Billy Holmes rested his hand on Rusty's shoulder, looking very much at home. "He seems fond of Billy," Brett noted.

Sarabeth nodded her agreement. In fact, Rusty and Billy exuded a father and son vibe that was hard to ignore. "From what I've heard from Gina, Billy's been a part of the family for a while. He's a college friend of Ross's. I think Ross, and his brother, Asher, like have Billy around as he seems to be the only one able to manage Rusty. He has a knack of dealing with him in a way that gets results."

"Is it true that Billy adopted Asher?" Brett asked.

Sarabeth nodded. "Asher was fifteen when Rusty married Asher's mother, Stephanie. Ross, Asher and Gina are close in age and they bonded as teenagers. In Ross's and Gina's eyes, Asher is their brother."

Sarabeth wiggled in her seat, conscious Rusty and Billy were on the move again and heading in their direction. She knew Rusty was surreptitiously watching her so she put her hand on Brett's partly, she admitted, to wind Rusty up. But she also touched Brett because she couldn't bear not to. His eyes glinted with amusement, and he lifted her hand to place a lingering kiss in the center of her palm. Sarabeth, as she always did when he touched her, shivered.

"I think that your taste in men has vastly improved, sweetheart," Brett told her, his expression amused. "Your latest lover is your best choice yet."

Sarabeth's lips twitched at his flirting, turned on by his confidence. And he wasn't wrong. "I happen to agree."

"Heads up, they are coming our way. I think they have the table two down from us." Brett turned to her, looking concerned. "Are you okay?"

He was consistently perceptive, always seeming to realize when she was feeling off balance. "He just annoys me, that's all," she said, sounding rueful.

"We can leave if you like," Brett offered.

And have Rusty think that he still intimidated her? Oh, hell no. She was no longer that fragile girl he'd married a lifetime ago. "Absolutely not! My days of being intimidated by that man are long over." She sent him a wicked grin. "Watch and learn."

Sarabeth knew the way Rusty's mind worked and knew he'd be expecting her to cower in her seat, hoping he'd just ignore her. Sarabeth looked around the room, saw that most of the diners were still looking in their direction to see how the first meeting between the ex-spouses played out, and she had no intention of disappointing her audience.

"I'm thinking about giving the gossips something new to talk about in the morning. I'm about to be a little rude and completely fake... Is that okay with you, Brett?" Not that she needed his permission, but it was polite to ask.

He grinned. "Absolutely. Not that the Royal Reporters deserve to be rewarded—Flora is sitting at the back table by the way—but go for it."

Sarabeth stood up, bent down to drop an open mouth kiss on his mouth before turning to face Rusty with open arms. "Rusty! Darling, you're looking well, *for your age*." Knowing how vain he was, she decided to poke him a little more. "*Oh*, how I wish I could be like you and not care about wrinkles, a soft belly, a receding hairline and a complete disregard for fashion."

Rusty, obviously caught off guard by her effusive greeting and backhanded compliments, did a fine imitation of a fish out of water. He opened his mouth to say something, but Billy's hand on his back propelled him past her. So he plopped down in his chair, his face red and his light silver eyes pulsing with rage.

Knowing that more was less and that she'd won the opening battle of their Royal based war, Sarabeth, pretending ignorance and attempting to look innocent, shrugged and took her seat. She flashed Brett a naughty grin.

Well, that was fun.

* * *

Thank God, the meeting was done. Brett pushed his chair back from the boardroom table and shoved the agenda and notes into his leather folder, thinking that some members of the Texas Cattleman's Club really liked the sound of their own voices. The meeting could've been concluded an hour earlier if the good ole boys stuck to the damn point.

Brett, one of the few members not dressed in a suit and tie—they'd have to hog-tie him to put a noose around his neck anytime soon—reached for his favorite black Stetson and jammed it on his head. Rolling his shoulders, he tried to surreptitiously work the knots out of his neck. He needed to get home and go for a long ride or do a brutal gym session. Then he remembered that Ty was out of action with an injured fetlock so it looked like he'd be pulling on his trainers and hitting his home gym.

"Coming for a drink, Brett?"

He turned to see Clint Rockwell standing behind him, dressed, as he was, in jeans, boots and a button-down shirt. Clint was one of the younger TCC members, and unlike some of the older members who'd been around since God was a boy, he didn't think the sun shone out of his own ass.

Brett nodded his agreement. "I'll have a soda."

Clint didn't react to the fact that he, unlike pretty much everyone within these hallowed halls, didn't consume alcohol. Neither had he inquired why. Brett liked people who minded their own business.

As they moved to the bar area of the famous club, Clint asked whether he would visit his ranch to look over a mare he'd recently acquired with a view of breeding her with one of Brett's stallions. The conversation flowed easily and he started to relax, knowing that the other man either didn't know or, more likely, didn't care that he'd walked out on his wedding and was now having an affair with Rusty Edmond's ex-wife.

Brett felt the back of his neck prickle and he slowly turned around, his eyes slamming into Rusty's, who was at his usual spot, which was the far corner at the other end of the bar, a coveted position he'd claimed years ago. Rusty jerked his head in an unmistakable "come here" gesture, and Brett lifted his eyebrows at the impertinence.

Last he checked, he wasn't one of his sons, employees or sycophants.

"You're being summoned," Clint told him.

"Yeah, got that."

Clint drained his glass of whiskey and nodded at Brett's half-empty glass of soda. "Can I get you another?"

Brett shook his head. "I'm good, thanks." His eyes drifted back to Rusty and saw the irritation on the old man's face at his lack of response. Rusty lifted a hand to beckon him over, and it gave Brett pleasure to turn his back and ignore his demand.

If Rusty Edmond wanted to talk to him, he could make the effort to cross the room. He wasn't anyone's damn lapdog.

"He's coming over," Clint told him. "Do you want me to leave?"

"Don't shove off on his account," Brett told him, deliberately ignoring Rusty's approach. He felt the change of energy in the room and slowly, one by one, the conversations died down as the rest of the members noticed something was about to go down.

Wonderful, Brett thought. An altercation with Edmond would be the perfect way to end what had already been a crap day.

"Harston!" Rusty barked at his back.

Brett took his time turning around. Edmond looked down at the drink in his hand and his top lip curled. "Still a wimp about liquor, boy?"

Rusty had been around long enough to know Brett never touched liquor because his mom struggled with alcoholism, but he was pretty sure many of the newer TCC members didn't. But if the jerk was trying to shame him into kowtowing, he didn't know whom he was dealing with.

"My mom was an alcoholic and as a result, I don't drink," Brett said, managing—just—to keep his voice even.

"You can't put lipstick on a pig, Harston. Your mom was a drunk and a slut."

Clint's hand shot out to grab his arm and prevented his fist from connecting with Rusty's jaw. The tension in the room ratcheted up a level, and Brett looked past Rusty to see the disgust on several faces. Yeah, Edmond wasn't doing himself any favors by insulting his mom. Maybe, instead of hitting him, he should just let the dude dig a deeper hole for himself.

"Did you really cross the room just to insult my dead mama, Rusty?" Brett asked, placing his elbow on the bar and crossing his foot over his ankle. He knew that he looked relaxed but, judging by Clint's folded arms and scowling face, he wasn't fooling his ex-Special Forces friend.

"Actually no, but that's always a pleasure," Rusty snarled.

Bastard.

"I actually came over here to inform you that you are no longer welcome to be on the advisory board for the Soiree on the Bay."

What a surprise. *Not.* Brett had been expecting this

to happen since Rusty saw him and Sarabeth dining at Sheen last week.

"And you couldn't do that in private, or on the phone or in an email?" Brett laconically asked.

"You're here, I'm here."

"And so are most of the members of the TCC, Edmond," Brett pointed out. "If your aim is to embarrass me then you are shit out of luck. I don't embarrass easily."

Brett saw a flash of discomfort in Rusty's eyes and decided to push him further. "And I find it very interesting that you all but begged me to sit on the board and now you are kicking me off it. I have to wonder why."

"Do stop. You might hurt yourself taxing that undereducated brain," Rusty retorted, pleased by his cleverness. He looked around for support and frowned when he seemed to receive none. Yep, that's what happened when you acted like a dick.

It was time to stop beating around the bush. "This wouldn't have anything to do with the fact that I am in a relationship with your ex-wife?"

Relationship? No, that was wrong. He was having a fling with Sarabeth and it wasn't going anywhere, but he couldn't announce that to the world. But this fling was nothing like he'd ever experienced before. They ate together, slept together, explored his ranch on horseback together, gone on a romantic date to Sheen…

He wanted to believe that this was only about sex, but he was honestly having trouble convincing himself of that.

The anger flaring in Rusty's eyes and the cords tightening in his neck pulled his attention back to his present problem. "I don't give a damn what that bitch does," Edmond snapped.

Do not wipe the floor with him, Harston. As much as

you want to rearrange his face, justifying an assault to a judge would be tricky. But Rusty calling Sarabeth a bitch had Brett wanting to break his jaw. Or his nose. Or both.

"Be very careful, Edmond."

"She's a gold digger, a useless mother and as thick as a plank," Rusty said, enmity oozing from every pore. "I don't care what she does."

"Really? Strange then because that's the only reason I can think of as to why you no longer want me on the festival's board." Brett downed the rest of his soda and banged his glass on the counter of the bar.

"And you are only sleeping with her because you have mommy issues," Rusty drawled. "I don't like you, Harston, but despite my antipathy, I feel honor-bound to warn you that Sarabeth is a liar, a drain on a man's bank account and she was a crap wife. And she was terrible in the—"

Okay, he was done.

Before Rusty could finish his sentence, Brett's fist flew through the space separating them and he connected with Rusty's jaw, the power of the punch ricocheting up his arm. The old man stumbled backward, turned ashen, but didn't crumple to the floor.

Pity.

Rusty held his jaw and his eyes glinted with embarrassment and fury. "You're going to pay for that, *boy.* You'd better watch your back."

Brett rolled his eyes. "I'm so scared." He turned to Clint. "Can I hit him again? You know, just for fun?"

"I think the sheriff would understand one punch, since he provoked you but a second could be considered assault. So...*no.*"

Brett frowned at Clint. "Damn."

His friend placed his big hand in the middle of Brett's back and urged him to walk away. "Walk, dude. Because I'm sure as hell not bailing you out of jail."

Spending a night, or three or four in the pen would be worth it to see Rusty bloodied and blue.

Eight

By the time Brett got back to Heritage Ranch, about an hour later, the knuckles on his hand had swollen and he was in a sour mood. After parking his truck in his six-car garage, he exited the vehicle and tried to flex his hand, wincing when dots of blood appeared on his bruised knuckles.

Yeah, it stung like a bitch but decking Rusty had been worth it.

He didn't care about being kicked off the advisory board; they'd begged him to join and he had enough work of his own to do without looking for more. But he did care about what Rusty said about his mother and Sarabeth.

You're only sleeping with her because you have mommy issues.

How the hell did a ten-year age difference suddenly equate to Sarabeth being his mommy? He found it hard to believe that in the twenty-first century people could still be so ignorant and intolerant. And, really, Sarabeth and his mom couldn't be more different. Yeah, okay, they'd both been raised to believe that the only worth they had was in their ability to be a wife, to raise kids and in Sarabeth's case, to look good while she put up with Rusty's crap.

And when she realized their marriage wasn't working, Rusty's response wasn't to help or support her, but to take revenge and create a chasm between her and her kids. Fortunately, Sarabeth had risen above her circumstances and made a hell of a success of her life. He desperately wanted to tell Rusty about her business and her wealth, to rub her success in his face, but that wasn't his story to tell.

His mom and Sarabeth were nothing alike. Sarabeth had refused to be a victim and had taken responsibility for her life and choices—she moved away and had forged a new beginning. Yes, she'd left her kids, which he knew had not been an easy decision. But even so, Rusty still tried to control her movements and her life and, from what he understood, took great delight in thwarting her plans. On leaving Texas, she'd established a successful business in California, which she'd grown and operated for fifteen years before cashing it in.

She was interesting, independent and, frankly, incredible.

On the other hand, his mom had stayed in her doublewide, the only place she felt safe. She'd sued the driver who injured her and won a modest settlement, enough, if she was very careful and if she found some employment, to last the rest of her life. But working caused her back to ache and later on, a job interrupted her drinking time. As the money ran out and times got harder, she sank deeper into the bottle, drink and oblivion being all she craved. From the age of fifteen and up, until he found steady work with Tweed Huggins, he'd worked every job he could on every ranch in a ten-mile radius to pay the utilities, to keep his old truck running and to put food on the table, not that she ate much at all.

And to buy her booze…

Brett hated the fact that his most vivid memories were of him taking a half-full vodka bottle from her hand after she'd passed out and dumping it down the sink. He quickly learned to lie, telling her she'd finished it all, knowing she wouldn't remember in the morning.

For most of his childhood, he'd had two mothers, a drunk one and a sober one. When she was sober, she asked about school, his job, made him cookies, promised to be better. When she drank, she cursed him for judging her and blamed him for making her life more difficult than it already was.

And she often told him that she loved booze more than him and that she couldn't be saved.

But he'd tried anyway.

God, how he tried.

Walking without direction, Brett found himself on the path that snaked past his lap pool and led to Sarabeth's cottage. He needed her wide smile, to bury his face in her sweet-smelling neck…he needed to step out of the past and into the present and being with this beautiful, amazing woman was the best way to do that.

Brett approached the porch and hurried up the two steps to her bright red door and lifted his hand to knock. He cursed when his knuckles reminded him that they'd made a forceful connection with Rusty's face. Brett hoped that Rusty's jaw was throbbing like a bitch.

"Brett…"

He turned to see Sarabeth tucked up into the corner of the bench swing hanging from the rafters of the porch roof. Instead of the plain cream-colored covering, she'd placed a colorful throw over the bench and cushions in different colors and textures ran along the back of the wooden slats.

Her hair was pulled up into a messy bun, and her face was makeup free. A long cream jersey reached her midthigh, and her yoga pants were brightly patterned. Fluffy socks covered her feet. A tablet rested in her lap and cute, wire-framed glasses on her nose.

"Hey," he said.

"Hey," Sarabeth replied. "I thought you were at the TCC meeting tonight."

"I was," Brett said, walking over to her. He picked up her legs, sat down next to her and draped her calves over his thighs. Spreading his arms wide along the back of the bench, his fingers brushed her shoulder and he played with the ends of her soft, blond hair.

Sarabeth gasped and lifted his hand to inspect his bloody knuckles. "That needs to be cleaned up."

"I know." He waggled his eyebrows. "Want to play nurse?"

Sarabeth snorted. "You're big enough and ugly enough to disinfect your own wounds, Harston."

He loved the fact that she didn't fuss. Brett smiled. Mommy issues, his ass.

"Who did you hit?" Sarabeth asked, placing her tablet and glasses on the small table next to her. She picked up her glass of red wine and offered it to him, before wincing and pulling it back. "Sorry. Because you keep ordering me wine or bringing me wine, I forget that you don't drink."

Brett, feeling out of sorts and a little irritated, took the wineglass from her hand and took a healthy sip. Her pretty eyebrows rose higher. "Was that a smart move?" she quietly asked.

"Jesus, I'm not an alcoholic!" Brett snapped. "My mother was but I'm not."

Sarabeth folded her arms across her chest, thankfully ignoring his harsh retort. "So she's the reason you don't drink?"

Brett stared off into the distance, not wanting to relive the past and wondering how he could change the subject without hurting Sarabeth's feelings. He never discussed his mother with anyone—there'd never been someone he trusted enough to explain that he both loved and hated her in equal measure. That he wished she'd been stronger, tougher and that she'd loved him more than she loved booze.

Sarabeth rested her head against his arm that lay behind her head, turning her face to kiss his wrist. "Okay, I can tell that's a touchy subject so let's go back to my original question... Who did you punch?"

"Rusty," Brett reluctantly admitted.

She stared at him and he forced himself not to wriggle under the power of her hard stare. He knew she loathed Rusty, but women were strange creatures and she might not appreciate him punching her one-time husband, the father of her children.

"Sorry, I thought you said that you punched Rusty," Sarabeth said, her tone extremely polite.

He had and she damn well knew it. "He was being an asshole."

She kept her face blank for another twenty seconds until she dissolved, her eyes watering with mirth and a low, rumbling, sexy laugh making her shoulders shake.

Right, well, she wasn't pissed. Good.

Tears rolled down her face and the last of Brett's irritation disappeared. There was nothing better than making his woman laugh and if split knuckles were the price to pay for it, he'd gladly sacrifice his hands to the cause.

He folded his arms and watched her, trying not to smile. "Are you done?" he asked when Sarabeth started to hiccup.

"Nearly," she replied, wiping her eyes with the bottom of her shirt, giving him a quick glimpse of her rich, creamy skin. She sniffed, placed her hands on her stomach as if to check her body's response. "Yep, I think so."

Brett waited for the barrage of questions that were about to fall from her lips. She didn't disappoint. "What did he say? Why did you hit him? Did he hit you back? Did his eyes bug out? Did you draw blood? Oh, please, please tell me you broke his nose!"

Brett smiled. "Bloodthirsty creature, aren't you?"

Sarabeth punched his arm and her fist held all the power of a crippled mosquito. "Tell me, dammit!"

"Well, if you'd shut up and let me get a word in, I would," Brett retorted, leaning sideways to drop a quick kiss on her pursed lips. Quickly, and without embellishment, he recounted the evening's events.

Sarabeth placed her hand on her heart. "So you were defending me?"

He rolled his shoulders, feeling uncomfortable with the affection in her eyes. "Sort of, I mean, yes, I suppose so. Rusty is a jerk, and somebody needed to teach him a lesson in respect." Honesty had Brett adding another sentence. "He also made some disparaging comments about my mother."

"Ah." Sarabeth looked down and he saw her shoulders slump. Oh, no, he wasn't going to let her think that she wasn't worth defending.

"He started on my mom and moved on to you and then I lost it and punched him."

"Thank you for defending me," she said softly, looking ridiculously young. "It wasn't necessary, but I appreciate it and I'm sure your mom would too."

Not wanting her to think he was prone to violence, Brett had to clear the air. "I learned to control my temper in my teens because if I punched everyone who made a comment about my mom, I would've spent most of my time in jail," he admitted, feeling weary. "As the town drunk, she was a soft target and easy to disparage. Hell, most of the time I agreed with what they said about her."

"But you still defended her."

"Somebody had to." Brett slid his tired body down the seat to rest his head on the backrest, his legs extended. Then he placed his free hand on Sarabeth's knee. "When she was sober, she tried to be a good mom but when she drank, she became a monster. Life with her was...volatile."

So much for not talking about his mom. But recounting his past to Sarabeth felt like he was lancing a wound, allowing the poison to drain.

"Did family services never get involved?" Sarabeth asked him.

"Back then Royal was a lot more rural than it is now and I think I only remember a lady visiting, twice... maybe three times? Incredibly and coincidentally, my mom was sober every single time she arrived and because there was food in the fridge and the place was clean, and I was attending school, they left me where I was."

"Did you want to leave her?"

It was such a direct, honest question and Brett knew that, no matter his answer, Sarabeth wouldn't judge him. She'd been judged too often—as a wife and a mother—to do that to anyone else. There were, as they both knew, a hundred shades between black and white.

There had been so many times he'd wanted to run away, to leave, but he knew he couldn't. It was his job to look after his mom, to try to save her, and he couldn't do that if he was in foster care or tangled up in the system. And, by the time she got to the point where she was more drunk than sober, he was eighteen and juggling his job with Tweed, his relationship with Lexi and graduating high school.

Shortly after he graduated high school, she got sick. And then a lot sicker. And her mental health rapidly deteriorated.

"No, I wouldn't have gone," he finally answered.

"I didn't think so…"

Brett, enjoying her head resting on his arm, handed over her wineglass and gripped her slim thighs. "I've been thinking about her a lot lately, and how she influenced my life," he said, his voice low. She was the only person he'd ever spoken to about his past and, inexplicably, he wasn't ready to stop, not just yet.

"How so?"

He drew patterns on her thighs with his fingers. "I've been looking at my relationships, starting and ending with Lexi twenty years later. I've noticed a pattern that I seemed to have missed."

"That you are a rescuer and you like to save people?"

He narrowed his eyes at her. "Have you been talking to Jules?"

"You're not that difficult to figure out, Brett," she said, giving him a soft smile. "But carry on, please."

He sighed. "As I was trying to explain, I have a habit of falling for waifs and strays, for women who needed something from me. Then, after I patch them up and make them stronger, I lose interest in them."

Brett felt heat move up his face, uncomfortable with

the way he was running his mouth. But he couldn't seem to stop.

"So, you're saying that you are attracted to vulnerability?"

"Seems like it," he reluctantly admitted. "And, before you point it out, I know it's damn condescending to treat people like my pet project."

"So why do you do it?" Sarabeth quietly asked. "Because we don't do something unless we get something out of it."

He thought for a minute, knowing the answer but unwilling to admit the truth. When she didn't speak, he felt the urge to fill the silence. "I think I did it because it lessened the guilt, at least for a while."

She didn't push him to explain his guilt, instead she just patiently waited for him to continue, in his own time and at his own pace. She seemed to know that if she demanded an answer, he would shut down the conversation. Yeah, he was stubborn that way.

"The guilt was my constant companion." Brett placed his forearm over his eyes and tipped his head back, images of his mom lying on that ragged rug, white and still, bombarding him. "I remember that night so clearly, Sarabeth. I was dating Lexi and my mom asked me to come home early, mumbling something about having 'bad' thoughts, that she was thinking about ending it."

Brett released a harsh sigh. "But Lexi was waiting, I was about to get lucky and she'd had a million 'bad' thoughts before. She'd cried wolf about suicide so often, always when she was very drunk, so I assumed she was rambling, that she didn't mean it. She was, I told myself, looking for attention." He felt his breathing turn shallow and his arm felt heavy across his eyes. "She was still warm when I came home and I tried, I swear

I tried, Sarabeth. I did CPR, mouth-to-mouth, I really tried to save her."

"I know you did, honey."

He told her this much, he might as well get the rest out. "I saw the lights of the ambulance coming up the drive and I gathered the empty bottles of pills and hid them, and stashed the empty vodka bottle in my gym bag.

"The official cause of death was a deadly but accidental combination of pills and booze, but I can't help thinking that it was suicide, that she meant to take her life."

Brett never talked about the night his mom died, not even discussing it with Jules, and he shuddered to think what the Royal Reporters would say if they heard that delicious tidbit. But Sarabeth would never betray his confidence; he knew that like he knew every inch of this ranch.

"Ah, Brett." He dropped his arm from his face when he felt her straddle his thighs. Then she brushed small, comforting kisses on his chin, his jaw, the tip of his nose. "I'm so sorry."

"It is what it is."

"And what it is *is* horrible," Sarabeth insisted, leaning back. She tipped her head to the side, her forehead furrowed. "I don't mean to gloss over your mom's death—and thank you for telling me—but can we go back to your habit of hooking up with waifs and strays?"

"If we must," Brett grumbled. Actually, he was done talking. Talking was exhausting.

"So, what I'm thinking is that I can be your transition girl, woman…whatever."

What the hell was she talking about?

"Sorry?"

Sarabeth flicked her thumbnail against her front teeth. "Well, it sounds like I'm the exact opposite of the women you normally get involved with," she said, looking very at ease perched on his thighs.

Again, what the hell was she going on about?

"I'm not a waif or a stray, Brett. I'm financially independent, emotionally stable—mostly—and I don't want or need you to fix me or my life."

Brett pushed his hand through his hair, not sure where she was going with this. "I know that. I don't *want* to fix you. You're pretty perfect as you are."

Sarabeth grinned. "Now, that's a big, fat lie. I'm stubborn, ridiculously independent and far too proud." She scratched her cheek, looking pensive. "But I'm okay with my flaws…they are a part of me."

She hesitated, as if deciding how to convey her thoughts. "You know, for years I was lost, and had no idea who I was or what I stood for. I turned myself inside out trying to make myself into whatever the man in my life wanted me to be. Once I stopped trying to please the man in my life and started being my authentic self, I was so much happier. I became me. I'm flawed, sure, but I'm strong and I don't need anyone to fix me."

What the hell was he supposed to say to that? "Okay."

"And that's why I think that I could be your transition girl, a bridge for you. Maybe the next time a woman takes your fancy, she'll be more like me, independent and self-sufficient. Because you need someone strong, Brett, you really do."

Taken aback by her words, Brett silently cursed. He didn't want someone *like* her, he wanted her. Clearly he'd had a harder day than he'd imagined because that notion was, as Tweed used to say, hole-in-the-screen-door crazy.

Sarabeth swiped her mouth across his. Before he could gather her closer, she edged away to stand up. After lifting her wineglass to her lips, she held it against her chest and sent him a small smile.

"I know that I shouldn't be saying this, and I'd only ever say this to you, but thank you for decking Rusty. He totally had that coming to him."

"My pleasure." And it had been. But he was still pissed that he hadn't hit him hard enough for his ass to connect with the floor.

Sarabeth planted another hot kiss on his lips before speaking again. "Let's go disinfect your hand, slugger. Who knows what awful germs you picked up smacking that ugly face?"

Brett laughed and followed her inside.

Nine

The next evening, Sarabeth sat in her SUV on Main Street, her fingers gripping the steering wheel as she stared into space, thinking about her conversation with Brett the previous evening.

His revelations about his mother startled her. She'd not expected him to share something so incredibly personal and his frankness, and those hints of vulnerability that he'd allowed her to see, touched her deeply. Too deeply.

It also, despite her blithe talk about just being his "transition girl," made her acknowledge that she didn't want to let him go. That she might, foolishly, want *more*...

She wanted the next woman he fell for to be *her*.

Oh, Lord, she was in a world of trouble. And it was all of her own making...

How could so much have changed in just a few weeks? For years and years, Sarabeth considered herself to be so damn savvy about relationships, thinking she had it all figured out. She'd convinced herself that princes didn't exist, that there were only frogs to be kissed and fairy tales were a lie all little, and big, girls were fed. And after over a decade of treating dating like she was on the pageant stage, giving the judges what they seemed to want with scant regard as to whether she was happy or not, she'd given up men altogether to focus all her energy on *Sarabeths!*

She had plans to travel, to see the world, and she was prepared for those cities, their people and their culture, to mold and change her, to help her grow. But of all the places in the world she intended to visit, she never expected her views about life, and love, to be challenged in Royal, Texas.

She'd thought herself so smart, so cool to be having an affair with a younger, sexy guy, convinced she had this all under control. But she'd never, not for a second, planned on feeling this much for Brett, of teetering on the sharp edge of falling in love.

Sarabeth rested her forehead on her hands and told herself she was getting swept up in the moment, that she was giving a deep and intense conversation more power than it deserved.

They were friends and friends confided in each other...

Sarabeth felt a spurt of annoyance at her rationalization, acknowledging that she was looking for an excuse to justify the way she was feeling. She'd studied enough psychology to know that people tended to lead with their emotions first and make up reasons for why they were acting the way they did afterward.

So what *was* she feeling? Way down deep where only truth resided?

Sarabeth placed her hand on her sternum and forced

herself to get real. She was, she reluctantly admitted, scared of what she was already beginning to feel for Brett.

And, because of her fears, she'd sprouted that nonsense about being his "transition girl," the woman who could bridge the gap between his waifs and strays and someone who didn't require rescuing.

The problem was that a part of her, the hopeless romantic she thought she'd buried years ago, didn't want to be his transition girl but rather his forever girl.

Sarabeth allowed herself a moment to imagine a life spent with Brett, living and loving and shaping the future with him. And it was pretty, and sunshiny and glorious and...

And it was a dream that would never come true.

Because the risks far outweighed the rewards...

For far too long, she'd given her power away, desperate for validation. She'd been the charming beauty queen, then the perfect trophy wife. Eventually she'd left Rusty, thinking it was a new start, but fighting for a place in her kids' lives mentally and emotionally drained her. She'd felt so useless, an abject failure as a wife and a mother, and she'd been desperate for kindness, attention and validation. For anybody to make her feel a little less alone.

And every time she gave people, and men, what they wanted from her, she gave them permission to rip away a part of her soul.

Her business saved her, and as she grew confident in what she was doing, she felt her self-worth growing, her soul regenerating.

And when she finally felt strong enough to be her true authentic self, she promised herself that she would never give away her power again. She categorically refused to allow herself to be hurt again, and if she allowed this relationship with Brett to continue, she had no doubt that would happen.

Bottom line? She'd worked too hard for too long to lose herself again.

Which meant there was only one course of action, a single road to take. She needed to create some distance between them, to start easing away. To allow this relationship to slowly evaporate…

But, right now, she needed to put a smile on her face, as she was meeting Ross, Charlotte and Gina for dinner at the RCW Steakhouse. Her kids weren't fools. If she walked into the restaurant looking even a little sad, they would push and pry and demand explanations.

She had none she wanted to share…

A knock on her window had her jumping, and on seeing Gina's beautiful face, she left the vehicle and embraced her daughter.

"You looked a million miles away, Mom. What on earth were you thinking about?"

"Nothing much," she replied, lying through her teeth.

Gina kissed her cheek and tucked her hand into her elbow, leading her to the entrance of the restaurant. "I don't believe you for one second. I think you were thinking about your sexy landlord."

Yep, her daughter wasn't an idiot.

"I can't believe how Royal has changed since I lived here." Sarabeth swiftly changed the subject before Gina could interrogate her further. She was thoroughly enjoying her new, adult relationship with her grown-up daughter, but she wasn't about to discuss her sex life. Sarabeth, stepping into the steakhouse, shuddered at the thought. "This place is new."

"Mmm," Gina said, nodding. "I've never eaten here before but I've heard the food is fabulous."

The interior wasn't too bad either, with dark wood furniture and heavy drapes. It reminded her of the original clubhouse of the Texas Cattleman's Club back in the day. The hostess approached them and led them to a table in the back where Ross and Charlotte were already seated. They stood up and Sarabeth looked at Charlotte, thinking her sunshine yellow dress looked marvelous against her dark skin. Charlotte dropped a kiss on her cheek and gave Sarabeth a quick hug before taking her seat again.

"Hi, Mom."

Sarabeth smiled at Ross who'd pulled out her chair. She wished they were close enough to hug, but she reminded herself to take baby steps. At least he was calling her mom again and not Sarabeth. Although Sarabeth was a vast improvement from the "Satan's Bride" he'd called her in his teens and early twenties.

Yep, she could live with baby steps. "Thank you, darling."

After they placed their orders for drinks, Sarabeth looked across the table to Charlotte. "How's my boy?"

"Ben's lovely but exhausting. He's with my folks tonight, and I'm sure they'll collapse before he does." Charlotte placed her hand on Ross's arm as she looked around the room, their connection undeniable. Sarabeth smiled; she was so happy Ross had found such an amazing woman to share his life with. "It's so nice to be out, eating someone else's food. I feel like a grown-up!"

Sarabeth laughed. "Anytime you want a date night, I'm happy to take Ben."

Ross started to answer—no doubt about to offer an excuse for her not to have Ben overnight since her son was a very overprotective daddy—but Charlotte spoke before he could. "That would be awesome! Thank you, Sarabeth."

Ross frowned at her. "Honey, I don't think—"

Charlotte's expression turned impatient. "Ross, you told me that Sarabeth was a great mom. You said that she was super responsible but a ton of fun. So please stop being an idiot, darling."

Ross sent Sarabeth a rueful smile. "I did say that and… sorry, Mom. I'm a little overprotective of Ben."

And he was still finding his way back to her. "I was just as protective of the two of you so I get it," she softly said. Deciding to take the risk and address the issue, she placed her hand on Ross's arm. "I made a lot of mistakes, Ross, and I'm so sorry those mistakes hurt you and your sister. But please believe that I did the best I could, with the resources I had."

Ross nodded, looking uncomfortable.

"Are you madly, utterly besotted with Ben, Ross?" Sarabeth asked him, her elbow on the table and her chin resting in her hand.

"Utterly," he immediately responded, love blazing from his eyes.

"And that's how I felt about you and Gina, how I *still* feel. Don't doubt that, sweetheart."

Sarabeth held his emotional gaze, mentally begging him to believe her. When his wariness faded and she caught the hint of emotion, a combination of remorse and hope, Sarabeth felt her tears well and immediately dropped her gaze. She would not embarrass anyone by blubbing like a sentimental fool.

Emotion swirled around them until Charlotte cleared her throat, drawing their attention to the bottle of white wine they'd decided to share. She picked it up and inspected the label. "Ooh, lovely! I tried to order this vintage to put on the wine list at Sheen, but it's hard to come by. Well done, Rafe."

Grateful for the distraction, Sarabeth asked who Rafe was.

"Rafe Cortez-Williams is the owner of the steakhouse, Mom. His family own ranches but he's a restauranteur," Gina explained, her voice holding an uncertain note Sarabeth had never heard before. She tipped her head, wondering why talking about this Rafe character would make Gina sound a little off balance.

"And a good one," Charlotte added, perusing the menu. "His menu is fantastic and the food, so I've heard, is brilliant."

"You're being very complimentary of your competition, baby," Ross said, squeezing her hand.

Charlotte shrugged. "There's enough business in this town for all of us and Sheen, as you know, is doing damn well."

"And I'm so proud of you," Ross told Charlotte.

Gina made a gagging sound, and when Sarabeth looked her way, she rolled her eyes. "Get used to them billing and cooing, Mom, because they never stop."

Charlotte grinned. "And we never will. Now, tell me, Gina, where did you find those shoes? They are to die for!"

Sarabeth leaned to the side and eyed the patent leather in a black-to-red color swirl. They had pointed toes and curved openings and were sky-high. Sarabeth couldn't believe she hadn't noticed them on her daughter earlier; she'd obviously been living on the ranch for too long. "Louboutins?"

Gina lifted her foot so that Sarabeth could see the

distinctive red underside of the shoe. "Yep. A present from me to me."

"Please tell me we are going to talk about something other than shoes and fashions," Ross groaned.

Gina placed her chin in her hand and her smile turned wicked. "We can. Maybe mom could explain why Brett Harston decked our father in the TCC bar yesterday."

Ross's eyes narrowed. "I heard from someone who was there why he punched Rusty and, had I been there, I would've decked him too," he stated, his voice as cold and hard as concrete. "Goddammit, but our father can be an utter prick occasionally."

Gina raised her eyebrows. "Only occasionally?"

Ross acknowledged her quip with a small grin before shaking his head. "Let's not spoil our dinner by talking about him," he suggested.

"But I want to know—"

Sarabeth caught the infinitesimal shake of Ross's head and Gina's equally small nod in return. Message sent and received, she thought, relieved.

"Okay," Gina continued, her eyes full of mischief, "Then let's talk about mom's relationship with Brett instead."

"Let's not," Sarabeth retorted.

Ross groaned and rubbed his hands over his face. "*Ugh.* Mom, you have to know that the whole town is gossiping about you and Brett. He recently dumped his fianceé, you returned and within a few hours fell into his arms—"

Okay, hold on a second, she wasn't liking Ross's judgmental tone. She opened her mouth to defend her relationship with Brett, but Charlotte beat her to it. "Hold on there, sunshine, you're way out of line."

When Ross started to interrupt, she scowled at him

and lifted her index finger. "Your mom is an adult and single, and she has a right to do what she wants with whoever she wants to."

Oh, she really did like Charlotte. In fact, she was starting to love her future daughter-in-law.

"But—" Ross spluttered.

"No, darling, your mom's relationship has nothing to do with any of us." Charlotte picked up her wine glass and winked at Sarabeth. "Though I have to say, I admire your taste. Brett Harston is hot."

"Here, here!" Gina raised her glass as well.

"I'm sitting right here!" Ross protested.

"I'm engaged, not dead, darling," Charlotte informed him, her dark eyes laughing. "But, just to make sure that Ross's head doesn't explode, let's change the subject. I love Gina's shoes but I adore your perfume, Sarabeth. What is it?"

"Men, clothes, shoes and perfume," Ross muttered. "I'm in hell."

Sarabeth couldn't help it; she reached out to clasp his hand. She gently squeezed his fingers and was relieved to feel him squeezing hers back. Yeah, they were getting there.

Sarabeth released his hand and wondered if this was the perfect segue into telling them about the sale of the company. She had to tell them some time, so she might as well use the opportunity that had been presented to her.

"It's a scent I developed called Bold," she answered and waited for one of her daughters, one old and one new, to make the connection.

"Bold, like the one *Sarabeths!* sells?" Gina asked.

"Not *like*, it is the one *Sarabeths!* sells."

She waited for the penny to drop and it didn't, not for a little while. Surprisingly, Ross was the first one to get it and he leaned forward. "What's your connection to the online cosmetic retailer, Mom?"

"You know the company?"

"Charlotte orders their products," he explained. "Did you work for them when you lived in California?"

"Sorta, kinda." Sarabeth blushed and allowed the words to rush out. "It's my company, *was* my company."

Sarabeth gave them a brief rundown of how she started her company and how she built it into the influential company it was today.

Gina held up her hand. "Mom, are you saying that *Sarabeths!* is yours?"

"No, it *was* mine. I signed the sale agreement six months ago and ownership was transferred six weeks ago."

Gina's mouth fell open, and when Sarabeth glanced over at Ross, he looked equally astounded. Charlotte just giggled.

"I still can't believe you're Sarabeth of *Sarabeths!*"

She winced at Gina's rather loud statement. "Shhh, honey! I'm telling you this in confidence. It's not something I want to become public knowledge, not just yet."

"Why not?" Ross demanded. "It's amazing, Mom, *you're* amazing."

Aw, how sweet was he? "Thanks, sweetheart."

"Does anyone else know?" Gina asked, surprise and shock still dancing in her eyes.

She felt her cheeks heat. "Uh, Brett does."

Sarabeth couldn't miss the look Gina and Charlotte shared, nor their raised eyebrows. She didn't want to answer the questions in their eyes— why did you tell him your secret and not us? When did you tell him? Do you trust him with this knowledge?— so she quickly changed the subject.

Hopefully, her next announcement would distract them. "So, I've set up trust funds for both of you, Gina and Ross." She looked at Ross and smiled at his shocked expression. "When the time comes, I'll pay for Ben's, and his siblings', college expenses." She looked at Gina. "I'll do the same for your kids when you have them, honey."

Ross stared at her before lifting her hand and dropping a kiss on her knuckles. "That's very generous of you, Mom," he said gruffly. "Thank you."

Gina half stood to kiss her cheek. "That's such a lovely gesture, Mom, and I so appreciate it. But are you sure you have enough for yourself, to live and so on?"

Sarabeth thought of the many, many millions still in her bank account and nodded. "I have more than enough."

"Thank you, Sarabeth, it's very much appreciated." Charlotte smiled at her and lifted her wineglass in her direction. "I'm really happy for you but, to be honest, I'm glad your wealth is a secret. I'm rather enjoying the notoriety of being the soon-to-be daughter-in-law of Royal's most famous gold digger."

Sarabeth laughed.

"Charlotte's comment raises an interesting question, Mom. Why aren't you broadcasting this from the rooftops?" Gina asked, looking intrigued. "You've been so maligned by the Royal gossips, and this would be a fine way to shut them up."

Sarabeth shrugged. "I no longer need to prove a damn thing to anybody, anymore, and I sure as hell don't owe anyone an explanation."

But she'd told Brett about her marriage and also about the sale of *Sarabeths!*, long before she was ready to tell her kids. What did that mean? Did she even want to go down that rabbit hole? Not really, especially since she'd decided to step back…to ease herself out of his bed, his house and his life.

Brett, not wanting a long-term relationship himself, would probably be incredibly grateful for her dignified retreat and wouldn't, she was convinced, demand an explanation. Reticent and contained, the rugged rancher wasn't one to cause a scene, to make demands or try to cage a bird wanting to fly.

"But, be honest now, there's a part of you that wants to tell Rusty, to rub it in his face," Ross pointed out, pulling her back to the topic at hand.

Maybe. Possibly.

Absolutely.

Sarabeth searched her son's face and eyes, looking for condemnation and she found none. He understood her need to show Rusty that she'd succeeded, on her own terms and without his input and help.

"Well, yeah," she admitted.

Charlotte released a muted whoop! and clicked her glass against Sarabeth's.

"Is it wrong for me to want to be there when you tell him?" Gina asked, her stunning eyes dancing with mirth. "Oh, don't frown at me, Mom! I'm not a kid anymore who needs to be reminded that I should respect my father. He's been an utter bastard to you and Ross and, while I believe he loves us, he's not always a nice man. I'm old enough to know that. So…can we be there when you tell him?"

"Yeah, can we?" Ross demanded.

Sarabeth stared at her children—who were these monsters?—before erupting into peals of laughter. Oh, she should reprimand them but after hearing how Rusty had bad-mouthed her at the Texas Cattleman's Club, she wasn't that much of a saint. Besides, as Gina pointed out, her kids were adults and it was time Rusty learned his actions had consequences.

Brett hated paperwork; he far preferred to be outside in the sun, wind and rain than reading spreadsheets and income and expenditure statements but, like with any other business, they were a necessary evil.

He'd built a small complex behind his garage, composed of three offices, a storage room and a small boardroom. He used the biggest office, the ranch's bookkeeper occupied the other and his ranch foreman used the third. Sitting in his light-filled office, with a view of the pond, he leaned back in his chair and idly watched Percy, his Bashkir Curly stallion and Penny, the caramel Bashkir Curly mare he'd bought last week, ignore each other as they idly munched their way across the paddock. He was well known for his excellent Arabians and pintos, with their exceptional bloodlines and wickedly expensive price tags, but the Curlies were a fun, see-where-it-went project.

Brett heard the ding of an email arriving and turned back to his desk, forcing himself to get through the paperwork. Although he employed both a business manager and an accountant, there were decisions only he, as the owner, could make and that meant reviewing these damn figures.

When he was done, he'd track Sarabeth down and see if she wanted to accompany him to the east boundary of the property to check on a sick cow. It was, according to reports, on the mend but Brett wanted to look in on the animal himself, since it was one of his best breeders.

Well, that was the plan, if he could find Sarabeth. She

frequently lost track of her phone and could be just about anywhere on his vast property. Brett frowned, trying to pinpoint why he felt uneasy. The feeling had been growing stronger over the past few days, and he couldn't nail down what had changed and why.

His uneasiness had something to do with Sarabeth, that much he knew for sure. He wanted to say that she was acting differently but couldn't pinpoint a specific action that justified that conclusion. She was still the happy, nondemanding, easygoing soul he'd come to know but something about her seemed different lately...

Maybe her smile wasn't as bright, maybe it was the smallest hint of hesitancy he sensed in her every time he initiated lovemaking. But, after ten seconds of kissing her, tasting her mounting, undeniable desire for him, he always tossed that thought away. But soon after they were done, he went back to wondering if she was a little more guarded, a touch more distant.

And if so, why?

Brett heard the rap on his office door and, grateful for the distraction, yelled a "come in." Seeing Sarabeth, he immediately stood up, pleased that he wouldn't have to track her down to invite her for a ride. Although, judging by her outfit, a denim jacket worn over a white T-shirt, a black skirt that hit her midcalf and tan sneakers the same color as her bag, she looked like she was planning on heading out.

Damn. He wondered if he could change her mind. A hard ride to the east, a small picnic and after they'd eaten, he'd strip her down and make love to her in the sunlight...

"I don't want to disturb you but I'm heading into town. Do you need anything?"

Her tone was a fraction too cheerful, just a little too

Polly Perfect. Was he reading too much into this? He wasn't, Brett admitted, a master at interpreting women and there was a good chance that he was reading all her wrong.

Brett sat down on the edge of his desk and folded his arms across his chest. "I'm good. You picked up some things for me yesterday, remember?"

She nodded and he caught the flash of unease in her eyes. He wasn't overreacting, dammit. Something was definitely worrying her. "What's going on, Sarabeth?"

Those enormous blue eyes widened, but he didn't buy her innocent look. "What do you mean?"

"Something is going on with you, you're—"

"I'm?" Sarabeth prompted.

"—different," Brett said, crossing his ankles.

She leaned her forearms across the back of his visitor's chair and fiddled with the funky collection of bracelets on her right wrist. "I've been meaning to tell you that my kids want me to stay in Royal permanently."

He couldn't argue with the idea—the thought of her returning to LA, or going anywhere else, made him break out in a cold sweat.

Instead of firing questions at her—Sarabeth wouldn't appreciate an interrogation—he simply raised his eyebrows in a silent gesture for her to continue.

"I honestly don't know if I want to make Royal my permanent home, but I feel like I'd like to have a base here, something I can lock up and leave when I travel."

She'd mentioned wanting to travel, to see the world. He didn't have a problem with her doing that, as long as she returned to Royal on a very regular basis.

"Well, you've been all but living with me, but if you want to split hairs, you can lock up the cottage and go," he quietly told her.

"That's not a long-term solution." Sarabeth shook her head. "I think I need to find my own place in Royal. It makes no sense to rent when I have the money to buy."

His business brain couldn't argue with that but his body, and possibly his heart, didn't want her going anywhere. But that wasn't the deal, Brett reminded himself. This was just supposed to be a fun, temporary fling.

Yet what if he wanted more? What if she was *all* he wanted?

Brett stared down at his riding boots, at the worn cuffs of his jeans. He'd been engaged last month, about to marry someone else. He was insane if he was going to propose permanence after such a short time of being with, and loving, Sarabeth.

But the thought of her leaving, of only seeing her once or twice a week, of not making love with her or waking up beside her, made his throat close and his lungs shrivel. *Hell*. What had started as a need to have her, to explore her body had morphed into a need to have access to not only her body but to her mind and feelings, thoughts and emotions.

That hadn't been the goddamn plan.

What the hell was wrong with him? And what did he want? From her? From life in general? Brett had spent the last twenty or so years trying to prove that he was worth something, looking for a place and a community to see him for whom he was now, not the poor, pitiful kid he'd been. He'd built up this ranch, was wealthy beyond his wildest dreams but sometimes he still felt like that eighteen-year-old, lost, alone and adrift, looking for a place to belong.

But since meeting and spending time with Sarabeth, those feelings had, to a large extent, faded. He wasn't as tightly wound, as stressed, definitely not lonely and a whole lot happier.

Having her in his life made it better, brighter...fuller.

He was sorely tempted to ask her to stay, to make this place her home, but when his stomach tightened and his breath hitched, he knew he wasn't completely sure. And, until he was, he couldn't ask her to stay here, with him on Heritage Ranch. Because one thing he was 100 percent sure of—he wasn't going to do or say something impulsive, something that could lead to either of them being hurt. To them hating each other.

No, they'd keep it simple until he knew for certain whether this thing between them had the legs to last.

"Wow, that was some side trip," Sarabeth commented, pulling him out of his thoughts and back into the present.

He pushed his hand through his hand. "Yeah, sorry. I have a lot on my mind."

"I can see that." She tossed him a weak smile. "I'll let you get back to work."

"Yeah, thanks." Brett nodded, not wanting her to go but knowing he should shoo her out the door. He did need to get back to work but more than that he needed to *think*. About her place in his life and what he really, really wanted.

She took a step toward him, hesitated and then lifted her shoulders in a tiny, what-the-hell shrug. Standing on her tiptoes, she brushed her mouth against his...and *boom*!

As it always did every time they kissed, the world split in two and spun off its axis.

Ten

She'd kissed him because he looked a little frustrated and a lot broody. It was supposed to be a kiss of comfort but, as it happened so often with Brett, the kiss morphed at a rapid pace. His hands grabbed her hips, and he pulled her into him as his tongue invaded her mouth, setting her already spinning world on fire.

And then he was gone…

Sarabeth heard his muttered curses, watching him as he hurriedly stalked across the room. She gripped the chair again as he slammed his office door, locked it and strode over to the windows. No, he surely wasn't brazen enough to consider making love, here, *now*?

The blinds snapped shut, his lovely view of the small lake and the white pole fenced paddock disappeared, and Brett turned back to her, looking powerful and determined and so very, very sexy.

"Here and now?"

He nodded and waited for her answer. Sarabeth felt desire kick through her system, excitement and recklessness on its heels. He was the most impulsive, exciting lover she'd ever had, would *ever* have. Thrilled to the tips of her toes, Sarabeth didn't hesitate, shedding her jacket and lifting her tight T-shirt and pulling it over her head to reveal her pale pink bra.

Without breaking eye contact, she quickly toed off her sneakers and pushed her skirt down her hips, watching as gold flecks appeared in his deep green eyes. Brett's eyes slid up her bare legs, stopped on the patch of pink fabric below her belly button and wandered up to her breasts. Taking two purposeful steps toward her, he lifted the cup of her bra away, bending to tug her nipple into his mouth, alternatively sucking on it and rasping it with his tongue. Impatient, he found the clasp of her bra, and, with one hand, swiftly twisted it open.

Brett straightened and he cradled her face in his broad hands. When his lips met hers, his tongue delved and danced and Sarabeth arched her back, awed by the pent-up longing she could feel in the intensity of his kiss. She gripped his shirt, tugging it out of his jeans. Desperate to feel his hot skin on hers, she moaned her frustration and then resented the brief separation from Brett's body as he stepped away from her to pull his shirt over his head. She ran her lips across his chest, stopping to tongue his nipple, to rub her cheek on his chest hair. He was such a man, she thought. From the hardness of his muscles, the slightly rough texture of his skin and the smell that was uniquely Brett, he awakened every strand of DNA in her system.

She needed to have him, *right now*, in his office, with the late winter sun streaming through the cracks in the blinds.

Brett lifted her onto the edge of the desk, and in the process, files and papers slid and tumbled to the floor. She didn't care. Sarabeth watched him through heavy, half-closed eyes. Keeping one hand on her breast, he reached into his jeans and yanked his wallet out of a pocket. Scattering cards and cash, he found a condom and ripped it open with his teeth, dropping both the latex and the empty packet onto the desk.

Her fingers opened the buttons on his fly, and as he pushed his underwear and jeans down his hips, his hands went to her panties. With two hands and a minimal effort, he ripped the flimsy material from her body. Panties could be replaced; all she cared about was that his erection was hard and proud and that he rubbed himself against her most secret places, seeking permission to enter. His fingers, and his mouth, followed where his erection had been, and Sarabeth thought she'd liquefy under his touch.

She arched her back, and when she could tolerate no more, Brett lifted his head to adore her breasts with his mouth, tongue and lips. Sarabeth patted the desk, found the condom and stretched down to close her fingers around him and relished the sound of his breathing, heavy in the quiet of the office. The latex whispered over him, her fingers making the prosaic action the most erotic sexual play.

Green eyes met blue as she tugged him toward her, remained locked as her softness wrapped around his solidity and enclosed him in her warmth. Brett's one hand slid under her hip and the other cradled her head into his neck, both encouraging her to ride with him and promising to stand between her and the storm.

Brett moved within her and Sarabeth followed. Deeper, longer, higher, faster. She met him stroke for stroke, matching his passion, glorying in her power. Then she shuddered, splintered and through the swells of her climax, she felt Brett fracture with her in that slow, sweet little death.

She was going to be the death of him…and what a way to go.

A sudden burst of laughter, and the ring of the telephone startled Brett into remembering where they were. He gently placed Sarabeth on her feet and picked up a box of tissues from the floor. Handing her a bunch, he turned away to give her some privacy. Then, after sorting himself out, he rubbed the back of his neck. Furious, fast—amazing—sex in his office was a first and while it had been as hot as hell, it wasn't something they could repeat regularly. People routinely walked past his window on the way to the paddock and could've peeked through the cracks in the blind.

Brett turned to see her ruefully eyeing the scrap of fabric in her hands. Her ruined panties, wrecked with his caveman act.

"I'll replace them," he said, resisting the urge to beat his chest.

Sarabeth pulled her long skirt up her legs and picked her bra up off his spare chair. It had survived his decimate-her-underwear campaign, and she quickly snapped it into place. Her silence concerned him, and he waited until she pulled on her T-shirt before stepping toward her and sliding his arms around her waist.

"Are you still coming with me to the TCC cocktail party tonight?" Brett quietly asked, after lifting his nose from her sweet-smelling hair.

"If you want me to," Sarabeth quietly replied. This time, he definitely heard her lack of enthusiasm.

"Are you okay?" he asked her, his chin on her head.

Sarabeth linked her arms around his neck. "Sure."

There was that strange note again, something about the way she said the words didn't ring true. Brett pulled back from her and saw the sadness in her eyes, coated with what he thought might be fear. And longing. Then a curtain dropped over her eyes and he couldn't see beyond all that glorious blue. She had the ability to tuck her emotions away, and he didn't like it.

But until he worked out his emotions, what he was thinking and feeling, he had no right to demand to understand hers.

Damn, it sure seemed like their simple, temporary fling was becoming increasingly complicated.

Brett could tell Sarabeth was nervous. Oh, she looked sensational dressed in a slinky knee-length black-and-gold-patterned cocktail dress that skimmed her svelte figure and showed off her amazing legs. Legs that had, Brett was proud to admit, encircled his hips a few hours ago.

Man, the sex, as it always was, was shockingly great. Hot, intense, inventive. Consistently exciting. But she was slipping away mentally, he reluctantly admitted as he watched her smile at the waiter carrying a tray holding champagne flutes.

She obviously didn't want to be here but pride, and a healthy dose of stubbornness, had her dressing, putting on makeup and strapping on those stupidly sexy high heels. Brett understood her edginess. The last TCC function she'd attended had been as Rusty's wife nearly two decades ago. He hoped she wasn't worried about her appearance. As he'd told her earlier, she looked fantastic. He remembered her as a younger woman and she had the face and figure that had only improved with age...

Brett was about to excuse himself to go to her—he

didn't want her standing alone in a room full of strangers or one-time friends—but stopped when he saw her friend Jaynie approaching her. Sarabeth's smile hit her eyes and a little of Brett's tension eased.

This was their first official outing as a couple—whatever that meant—at a TCC function and he didn't want her feeling embarrassed or awkward or uncomfortable. If Sarabeth was going to stay in Royal on a permanent or semipermanent basis, he wanted her to feel comfortable living and interacting with the good, and not-so-good people, of Royal.

He liked—such a tame, innocuous word for the swirl of emotions she pulled to the surface—Sarabeth and he wanted her to be happy.

Brett tuned into Clint Rockwell's conversation with Jules, but most of his mental attention was still focused on *her*. Whoever would've thought that, a month after his aborted wedding, he would be having a blistering hot affair with the ex-wife of one of Royal's richest and most powerful men?

He could understand why people were fascinated by Sarabeth; she was incredibly beautiful, and her ability to hide her emotions and her reactions made people wonder who she was behind that serene facade. Because she seldom let people in, no one knew her pretty face hid a sharp mind, someone who had a better business brain than most men he knew. They'd be shocked if they knew she was, probably, as wealthy as her ex. They'd also be surprised to realize that she was a lot sweeter than her reputation, kind and funny and affectionate too.

Brett really enjoyed having her in his bed.

And in his life.

On the drive into town tonight, she'd told him she'd viewed some properties and he still wasn't a fan of the idea. To be clear, the thought of her moving out gave him a severe case of heartburn, and he'd spent most of the day considering what her leaving his life meant.

After their encounter in his office, he'd saddled up one of his younger stallions and galloped him across his ranch until they were both dripping from the exercise. The ride cleared his mind and gave him space to think.

He'd come to a few conclusions sitting on the bank of the river snaking through his property...

Brett loved waking up to find her sprawled over him, her face buried in the crook of his neck, her arm flung across his stomach. Enjoyed seeing her curled up in the corner of his sofa, her glasses on her nose, all her attention on the book in her hands. And he relished riding his lands with her, sharing his hot tub on a cold winter's night...

Yeah, he freakin' loved the sex, but he also loved having her in his life.

He didn't have to entertain her, mollycoddle her, constantly take her emotional temperature. She was strong and decisive and independent, and he appreciated being with a woman who was not only strong enough for him but who could also be, when he needed her to be, a pillar of strength for him. As he could be for her.

Despite them only being together a few weeks, theirs was a balanced relationship, and he didn't want her to leave his life.

In fact, he wanted her to embed herself more deeply in his, wanted her to be the center of his world. He wanted her to stay...

Brett's attention was pulled back to the present by Jules jabbing his elbow into his side. "Heads up. Rusty is heading in Sarabeth's direction, and he looks like he's loaded for bear."

Brett's eyes bounced across the guests and saw Rusty making his way across the room, an ugly smile on his face. Yep, that was his wanting-to-cause-trouble smile and she was in his sights.

He didn't like bullies, and he sure as hell wasn't going to let Sarabeth be Rusty Edmond's target...

Nobody messed with what was *his*.

"So, how come I have to hear from the grapevine that you are looking for a house in Royal?" Jaynie demanded, handing Sarabeth a glass of champagne.

Sarabeth winced. Since she'd all but moved in with Brett, she hadn't spent much time with Jaynie and she sent her friend an apologetic smile. "I'm sorry. I've been meaning to call you but—" She shrugged, heat touching her cheekbones.

"But you're spending all of your time in bed with a hot, younger guy." Jaynie nudged her and grinned. "Relax, Sarabeth, it's all good. But I am stupidly excited to hear you are staying in Royal. I thought you'd be heading back to LA."

She took a sip from her glass and sighed as bubbles popped on her tongue. "My kids are here, and I'm enjoying getting to know them as adults. And little Ben, well, he's stolen my heart."

"And there's Brett."

Sarabeth opened her mouth to respond, but her tongue refused to form the words. Yeah, Brett was here, but he shouldn't be a factor in her choice to stay in Royal. They were bed-buddies, that was all. Jaynie turned away to greet someone else, and Sarabeth looked across the room to where he stood with a few of his fellow Texas Cattleman's Club friends, guys his age. Their wives and girlfriends were a good two decades younger than her, some pregnant, some with children already. They were starting their lives together, but she'd walked that path and read that chapter.

Brett once mentioned, in passing, that he wasn't interested in having children, but it wasn't a subject she'd pursued...

Because they were just sleeping together, scratching an itch, having fun.

Sarabeth stared down into her champagne glass, thinking that she'd tried really hard to put some distance between them, but she'd yet to manage to corral her helter-skelter emotions.

She wanted a life with Brett. *There*, she'd admitted it, and she braced herself for the wave of terror that always accompanied the thought of putting her happiness in someone else's hands. Why was life testing her like this? Why did she have to crave this man, ten years younger, so much? Why did the thought of walking away from him tear the fabric of her being apart?

By entertaining any thoughts of love and a future together, she was walking across an emotional land mine primed to detonate in her face. If she allowed herself to hope and dream and want, he'd destroy her when he walked away. Because he would walk away; that's what men *did*.

But the truth was that she was crazy in love with a much younger man and she was scared to death. Scared that their age gap would eventually cause problems, that the wild love she felt for him was too feral and overwhelming and would eventually scare him off.

But regardless, he was what she wanted. Forever.

Sarabeth placed her hand of her sternum and tried to push away the visceral fear causing goose bumps to break out on her skin. She could almost taste her grief, feel the tears sliding down her face as he told her it was over. How could she carry on walking this path knowing that it would end? Was she a fool for carrying on when she knew what her future held?

If she were wise, she'd bail now, *tonight*. She should walk away before he could decimate her heart and scatter it to the wind. If she called it off, it would be on her terms—she'd know it was coming and she wouldn't need to live in a perpetual state of fear wondering when the ax would fall.

She'd be in control. And damn, control was important. She'd never allow another man to dictate what shape or form her life would take.

"Penny for your thoughts?"

Sarabeth turned at that still-familiar face and looked into the malicious eyes of her ex-husband. *Excellent.* "Rusty."

Rusty gave her a long up and down look that made Sarabeth grit her teeth. "You're still looking good, Bethie."

She hated that name, the one her mom used to call her in her sweet, cajoling, baby-doll voice. *Do it for Mama, Bethie.*

You're so pretty, Bethie. Why do you need an education when you have a face like yours?

Stop reading and start practicing your talent. Smart girls don't come first, Bethie.

"It's Sarabeth," she told him and added a silent "moron" to the end of her sentence.

"Since you're still using my last name, I can call you any damn thing I want, *Bethie.*"

Sarabeth cocked her head to the side and held his hard stare. "Can you get to the point, Rusty?" she asked. "Because we are attracting a great deal of attention."

Rusty looked around the room, and it was a testament to his power that many conversations instantly resumed and few people had the balls to meet his eyes. Brett, she noticed, was one of the few who kept his eyes on her ex-husband's face, who refused to look away. Sarabeth saw his raised eyebrow, the question in his eyes—*do you need me to come on over?*—and answered his silent question with an infinitesimal shake of her head. If she was going to stay in Royal, she and Rusty would run into each other often, and she needed to be able to deal with him and not have to rely on her big, brawny, younger lover for backup.

Besides, she was going to break it off with him, and she'd be on her own.

Rusty gripped her elbow and steered her toward the French doors that led out onto the balcony. She tried to jerk her arm from his grasp, but he maintained his grip and soon they were standing in the frigid air. Sarabeth, never a fan of the cold, shivered in her short, sleeveless cocktail dress.

"Cold?" Rusty asked.

Of course I am, you jackass.

"Do you want my jacket?"

"I'd rather be bitten by a rattler," she tersely replied. "Say what you want to say, Rusty, and make it quick."

"I want you to go back to California."

Of course he did. Her leaving town would allow him to play the part of the much-maligned husband with the gold digger ex-wife. But having her here in Royal, living life on her terms and without any help from him, blew that perception out of the water. She was not prepared to make life easier for Rusty, in any way, shape or form.

"Well, let me think about that..." Sarabeth pretended to mull it over before widening her eyes and blinking. She sent him a taunting smile. "Mmm, no."

"I'll give you a million dollars." Rusty ground the words out. "And I'll increase your monthly alimony."

"I don't need your money, Rusty."

"Of course you do. You're the type who always needs a man in her life. Harston might be paying your bills now, but he'll tire of you soon and where will you be then?" her ex said, his voice snake-oil-salesman smooth. "You're the type who needs a man to save you."

That comment cut a little too close to the bone, and Sarabeth quickly reminded herself that she'd been that person once but wasn't anymore.

"I owned and ran my own business in LA, Rusty. I've recently sold it," Sarabeth told him, already done with this conversation.

And with him.

Rusty's eyes narrowed, and his cheeks flushed with anger. "I don't believe that. You're pretty but you aren't smart, Bethie." His expression turned nasty. "I ran rings around you in the divorce and custody battle."

"Only because you had the resources to hire lawyers who were sharks and you had a social connection with the judge," Sarabeth spat back, feeling the heat in her cheek-bones. "And while you inherited all your wealth from your father and grandfather, I made mine on my own."

When his eyes flashed with anger and he clenched his hand around the railing, his knuckles turning white, Sarabeth smiled. She still knew exactly what buttons to push, and being reminded that he wasn't a self-made man, like many of his TCC cronies, was one of Rusty's biggest pressure points.

"Brett started as a ranch hand and is now one of the wealthiest and most powerful men in the state," she added, her voice low and deliberately catty. "I find that *such* a turn on."

God, arguing with Rusty was so much fun. For the first time in her life, she felt like they were standing on a level playing field, that she could give as good as she got. She barely recognized the girl she'd been when she'd married him, that wide-eyed, naive, desperate to please child willing to do anything to please her husband.

Not anymore and never again.

Rusty released his tight grip on the railing and shoved his hands into his suit pants pocket. The wind picked up and Sarabeth shivered, desperate to get inside. But if she turned and walked away, Rusty would think that he'd won and she still had a few things to say to him. And if that meant turning into an icicle, then that was the price she'd have to pay.

She'd let him speak, and when he thought he was in control of the conversation, she'd pull the rug out from under him.

"I hear that you are looking at leasing a property in Royal. That you plan on staying in town."

Man, the Royal Reporters were on fire! "So?"

"I've instructed my leasing agents not to rent to you." Back in the day, she remembered, Rusty owned quite a few properties in town. He probably owned half the town by now.

If she couldn't find a property she liked, she'd relocate to Joplin, a lovely town close to Royal. Sarabeth shrugged. "Okay."

"That's all you have to say?" Rusty demanded, disappointment flashing in his eyes.

Oh, he didn't like his lack of control over her, his inability to rattle her. She decided to twist that knife even deeper. "I can't tell you how little I care about how you feel, Rusty. I'm sure I'll find something, somewhere. Or I'll just continue renting from Brett..." She smiled and deliberately ran her fingers down her throat in a sensuous gesture. "I'm finding I quite like the arrangement we have."

As soon as the words were out of her mouth, she regretted them. She was only baiting Rusty because her ego demanded it, because she wanted to exact revenge for their unhappy marriage and their ugly divorce. It was over, in the past and that was a place where she no longer lived.

And it was definitely time to stop baiting him; not only was it exhausting, it was counterproductive. Rusty wouldn't apologize, nothing would be changed. And they both knew he couldn't stop her from renting or buying a property in Royal. She wasn't going anywhere and he knew it. They had to come to an understanding but, this time, it would be on *her* terms.

Rusty no longer held any power over her, and she didn't care what he thought or said about her, because she had the mental strength and the financial resources to deal with him. Her only concern was the damage he could do to her children.

"You've made your demands, issued your instructions and tried to dictate your terms, now it's *my* turn," Sarabeth told him, her voice as cold as the dark night swirling around them.

"Like I would listen to a thing you have to say," Rusty scoffed.

Sarabeth stepped closer to him and drilled a finger into his chest. "I don't know the full story of what happened between you and Ross, but I have no doubt that you tried to throw your weight around and interfere in his life. I'm quite sure you had quite a bit to say about Charlotte, as well..."

She waited for him to respond, and all she got was a

tightening of his mouth and a flash of anger in his eyes.
"Our kids are adults, Rusty, but if you mess with either
of them again, I will do everything in my power to bury
you. Do you understand me?"

"Don't you threaten me," Rusty growled, wrapping his
digits around her finger and squeezing it, a little harder
than she expected.

She couldn't show her fear; if she did, she'd lose this
battle so she didn't try to tug away. "I will spend every
last cent I have to protect them, Rusty."

He pushed her finger back to the point of pain, and
Sarabeth managed to hide her wince. "I said, don't
threaten me!" Rusty growled.

"Don't underestimate me, Rusty. And let me go," Sarabeth told him, unable to stop a quick gasp of pain from
escaping.

"Take your hands off her."

Sarabeth winced at Brett's hard as hell voice. She
glanced over her shoulder to see him standing to her
right, incandescent anger blazing from his eyes.

"Stay out of this, Brett. I have it under control," Sarabeth told him, returning her gaze to Rusty's face. He
didn't release her finger, and she knew that if Brett intervened, Rusty would think he'd won and she couldn't
allow that. She'd worked too damn hard to make herself
strong, to gather the courage to face him and deal with
his contempt and anger.

"Brett, back off."

"Yeah, listen to Mama, son," Rusty said, amusement
in his voice. Out of the corner of her eye, Sarabeth saw
that many of the guests were standing close to the doors
leading to the balcony, pretending not to watch them.
Damn, their argument was attracting attention. Not what
she'd planned for tonight.

"Release her. *Now.*"

Brett was close to losing it, Sarabeth realized. There was no way he'd allow Rusty to hurt her, not even a little bit. She tried to tug her finger away, but Rusty held it in a hard, tight grip. Sarabeth knew her ex was trying to make a point and because he couldn't win the verbal argument, he was trying to intimidate her. She needed him to know that it wouldn't work.

And that she'd never, ever back down from a fight with him again.

"Brett. Leave us alone," Sarabeth ordered him.

"The hell I will," Brett replied, reaching them. He looked down at her finger in Rusty's grip and turned dangerous eyes toward him. "You have a second. Just one."

"This has nothing to do with you, son."

"I'm not your son," Brett ground out, his words dripping with venom. "And, last chance, *old man*...release her."

Rusty must've seen something in Brett's eyes that had made him hesitate because he flung her finger away and took a step back. "She's not worth my time. Never has been, never will be."

Brett raised his hand, his fist clenched, but Sarabeth jumped between them, not willing to turn this into a bigger circus than it already was. She heard and ignored Brett's furious growl, and glared at Rusty.

"No, you're getting it wrong, Rusty. You're not worth my time, you never were," Sarabeth told him, her voice dripping with disdain.

Turning her back to Rusty, her eyes collided with Brett's dark green, and dangerous, scowl. She was standing between her past and what the person she wished could be her future. But he had just shown her that, like Rusty, he didn't trust her to handle a situation herself, that he saw her as the little woman who needed his intervention, his help.

By not allowing her to deal with Rusty in her own way, by treating her like someone who couldn't fight her own battles, he'd shown her that he still thought she needed rescuing. She didn't, and it hurt like hell to realize that his attraction to her was based on him thinking she was another woman who needed his help.

She'd thought they were different but equal, but his actions tonight confirmed that some part of him considered her to be the last in his long line of damsels in distress. She refused to play that part, no matter how much she loved him. She was no longer a mirror, reflecting what people expected.

"I didn't need your help, Brett. I'm not one of your strays or one of your pet projects. I don't need you to rescue me. Not tonight and not ever." Sarabeth held his eyes. Underneath the anger, she could sense his confusion and irritation.

"We're done. In fact, I'm so done I'm reconsidering staying in Royal. Not because Rusty wants me to leave but because I refuse to stay in a town where I'm seen as being helpless, idiotic and brainless."

"He had his hands on you, he was hurting—"

Sarabeth cut off his explanation with a sharp jerk of her head. "I had it under control. I asked you to back off. The fact you didn't tells me that you have no respect for me, no belief in my ability to stand on my own two feet."

Oh, she regretted breaking up with him in such a public setting—more gossip—but she couldn't find it in her to care. She was showing Royal, showing her kids that she wasn't a pushover and she was leaving with her heart dented but not destroyed. That she was strong and independent. And *fierce*, dammit.

Brett would be pissed, maybe a little hurt, but soon she'd be replaced. That was the way of the world and she was, as she kept telling everyone, a big girl. She'd deal. If she could cope with her venomous ex-husband, she could certainly cope with a sexy ex-boyfriend.

The difference was that she'd never loved Rusty the way she loved Brett.

"Don't do this, Sarabeth," Brett stated, his voice quiet but resolute. "Let's talk this through, find a solution."

Sarabeth shook her head. "No, I'm done. We're done."

"Just like that?" Brett asked brusquely. Sarabeth caught a flash of pain in his eyes and resisted the urge to fling herself into his arms, to apologize, to talk him around into giving her another chance.

And then what? They'd have another two or three months and she'd be deeper in love with him and then he'd dump her.

No, it was better this way. It had to be.

"Bye, Brett." Sarabeth stroked his arm from shoulder to elbow before lifting her hand and bunching it into a fist. Pushing her shoulders back, she forced herself to look at Rusty, whose lips were curled into a nasty smirk. "Remember what I said, Rusty. If you ever mess with my kids again, I will disembowel you. Are we clear?"

"You've got quite ferocious in your *old* age, Sarabeth."

The old age comment was a dig but Sarabeth ignored it. Really, he was such a petty little man.

Rusty turned his head, his stormy gaze landing on Brett. He lifted a finger and waved it in front of the younger man's nose. "We're not done. And I will take you down."

"You can try," Brett responded, his voice tight. Sarabeth looked at him and sighed. His face was granite hard and, with his arms folded across his chest, he looked tough and oh-so-distant. Which was what she wanted, wasn't it?

"Leave him alone, Rusty," Sarabeth told her ex, surprised at how weary she sounded. "Our relationship has nothing to do with you."

"As of two minutes ago, we don't have a relationship," Brett corrected her before turning around and walking away from her.

Rusty's laugh contained no amusement and was full of contempt. "You really do have a talent for screwing up, don't you, Bethie?"

There was no point in responding so Sarabeth just held his eye until his smirk receded. She thought that she caught a hint of respect in his eyes and told her imagination to stand down. Rusty didn't respect her and Brett didn't see her as strong and capable. Because he couldn't see her clearly, he could never love her the way she needed him to.

Sarabeth was certain she'd done the right thing.

Hadn't she?

Eleven

Brett opened up the engines attached to his luxury powerboat and smiled at Jules's whoop of appreciation. He looked over his shoulder to see his best friend lounging on the leather seats behind him, his ball cap on backward and a blissful look on his face.

They both needed a break. Jules because he was on forced leave after being shot at during a routine traffic stop, and Brett because he'd been dumped.

Dumped. Man, he sounded like a fourteen-year-old boy.

Brett sighed, grateful to be out on the water. Last night, a week after the TCC cocktail party, and feeling out of sorts and irritated and, yeah, *lonely*, he'd found himself wanting to jump out of his skin. He'd called Jules and suggested they take his boat for a spin. Of course, taking his luxury cruiser for a spin involved a three-hour drive to the elite waterside community of Mustang Point on Trinity Bay where he berthed his Riva 63 Virtus.

It was now midday, the sun was high in the sky and it was a perfect day to be on the water. Once they'd satisfied their mutual need for speed, they'd pull out their rods and throw some hooks in the water. They might or might not talk. Brett hadn't told Jules his and Sarabeth's relationship was over—though he was pretty sure that he'd heard by now—and Jules might mention the bullets that flew past his ear, but words didn't matter.

Getting away did.

His friend stood up, stretched and ambled over to stand next to Brett, who had one hand on the wheel as they flew across the lake-like waters of the bay.

Jules squinted across the bow and dropped his dark shades onto his face. "Is that Appaloosa Island?"

"Yeah."

Jules leaned forward as if to see the island better. "I've never been there, it looks impressive. And expensive."

Brett powered up again and when they were closer to the island, they could see a couple of homes on the western side of the island. "This side of Appaloosa has a few large vacation homes, all with pristine, private beaches. Farther down the coast, around the headland, there's a small, exclusive boutique resort just south of the landing. Only people with very deep pockets, the right pedigree and a connection to the Edmond family can build here."

"Rusty Edmond owns it?" Jules asked.

Brett nodded, knowing his expression was grim. He was still, and probably always would be, pissed at Sarabeth's ex.

"It's really remote," Jules commented.

"That's the point," Brett responded. "There is a private ferry available, but the island is mostly accessed by plane and helicopter. There is a landing strip on the undeveloped side for small private planes, as well as a clearing for a helicopter to land. All the supplies, food, water and building materials are brought over from Mustang Point, although I was told, when I was still involved in the project, that the resort always has emergency supplies on hand. If you are planning to visit the resort, they'll send a driver, in a golf cart or Jeep, to pick you up from either the landing, helipad or airstrip."

"Far too rich for my blood," Jules stated. Brett smiled at his prosaic comment, once again grateful that the massive difference in their financial fluidity wasn't a big deal for the other man. Jules lived a solidly middle-class life and, apart from the days when he was being shot at, loved his job. He enjoyed accompanying Brett on jaunts like this but didn't resent his toys. Brett felt as at home in Jules's small house as he did his own. Money wasn't an issue between them.

Brett spun the wheel and they moved away from the developed side of the island, hugging the coast. "The eastern side of the island is undeveloped and will be the site of the Soiree on the Bay," Brett told Jules and went on to fill him in on all he knew about the upcoming food, wine and art festival.

Steering around a bluff, he pointed to a pile of wood and the portable toilets that hinted at a construction site. Moving forward, he noticed a crew working on a structure at right angles to the beach...what was that? A stage? It could be.

Brett cut the engines and allowed the boat to bob on the swell. Reaching for a pair of binoculars tucked below the console, he lifted the glasses to his eyes and saw a tall guy walking toward the stage with a clipboard in his hand. Brett wasn't a small guy but he wouldn't want to tangle with that tall, wide and muscled foreman. He adjusted the focus on the binoculars and realized that the foreman was Jack Bowden, who'd been given the contract to build the facilities needed for the festival.

Brett handed the binoculars to Jules for him to get a clearer picture of the activities on the island.

Jules followed his lead and after a minute, whistled. "Who's John Cena?"

Brett smiled. "Jack Bowden. He owns Bowden Construction, and was awarded the contract by the committee to build the stage and other structures needed for the festival."

"The site looks organized and efficient."

"He's not a fool, and I've heard he does good work at a reasonable price," Brett said, remembering that Jack was a newish member of the Texas Cattleman's Club. "I just hope he got his money upfront from the Edmond family."

Jules lowered the binoculars and raised his eyebrows. "Finally," he stated, drawing out the word.

"What do you mean?" Brett asked, as he pulled his ballcap onto his head. He could hear the distant sound of a saw, the thump-thump of a pneumatic hammer. And the gentle smack of waves against his hull.

Jules ignored his question, hit the button to lower the anchor and walked back toward the small fridge on the upper deck. There was a galley kitchen below and sleeping quarters, but since they were just out for the day, they'd put a couple of deli sandwiches and drinks in the smaller fridge on the deck. Jules tossed Brett a sandwich and a bottle of water before walking to the leather bench seats and sitting down.

Brett, seeing the determined look in his friend's eyes, reluctantly followed his lead, slowly cracking the lid to his water bottle. He knew that an interrogation was coming and, as a result, his appetite had fled.

"I heard about the scene at the TCC," Jules said, ripping the plastic off his BLT.

"Yeah, so?" Brett belligerently responded.

Jules's steady gaze didn't waver. "Rusty's gleefully telling everyone who will listen that Sarabeth booted your ass. How do you feel about that?"

"What's it to you?" Brett muttered.

Jules didn't take the bait, his brown eyes staying on his friend's face as he steadily ate his way through his sandwich. How did he feel? Brett sighed and rested the cool bottle against his forehead. Gutted? Sad? Pissed? Lonely?

All of the above.

God, he missed her. He missed her beautiful face, the scent of her hair, her wide smile, her raspy, sexy voice. Missed her dirty laugh, the way she called him on his shit, her relaxing presence. He could be stressed to the max, but one hug from her had the tension draining away, his desire to control everything and anything fading.

Through Sarabeth, he'd learned that he wasn't responsible for other people's actions and that he couldn't be a prisoner of things he couldn't change.

And God, yeah, he missed the sex. But more than that, he missed feeling connected. In all his previous relationships he'd spent so much time looking for land mines, in clearing the decks—making sure the woman in his bed was happy and healthy and safe and secure—that he'd never taken what he needed from the relationship.

Companionship, a soft place to fall. Belonging. Being one-half of a whole. He'd always felt like he was on the outside looking in, but with Sarabeth, he never once did.

"Because I've never seen you act this way before. You don't need me to tell you that you are head over ass in love with her—"

"I'm not!" He'd promised himself he wouldn't fall into

a relationship again, allow himself to love someone again only to have the whole concept go south on him. But had he ever really loved someone or was he confusing that with his need to rejuvenate and repair?

"Dude, stop lying to yourself and admit it," Jules told him, his voice hard. "You not only love her but you like Sarabeth. So my question is, why the hell are you spending the day with me?"

"Because we've been friends since we were ten years old?" Brett asked, his tone deliberately facetious.

Jules gave him his patented, *I'm waiting* stare. Brett sighed, drained his bottle of water and stared at Jack Bowden's construction site again. Then he told Jules how he intervened when Rusty grabbed her finger, still trying to make sense of the events leading up to their breakup.

"I told him to let her go, to take his hands off her and the next minute she's turning on me. She told me that she didn't need me to save her or protect her, that I didn't respect her or believe that she could handle Rusty. That she could, and would, take care of herself."

Jules frowned and leaned forward. "All because you told Rusty to take his hands off her?"

Brett nodded. "Pretty much. Then she called it off." He shrugged, as confused today as he was a week ago.

The other man folded his arms across his broad chest, his expression pensive.

"It still doesn't make any sense. I know Sarabeth doesn't need saving. She's a successful businesswoman in her own right. She doesn't take any crap—particularly my crap. She's solid, you know?"

And that was why her about-face was so damn confusing. But he wasn't going to beg her to take him back, to resurrect something she'd killed. As he told Jules, he still had his pride.

"Yeah, and pride is going to keep your bed warm at night, help you with your strays, have bed breaking sex with you." Jules scoffed. "Stop being a dick, dude."

The man had a point.

Jules stretched before reaching for his bottle of cola, his big fingers popping the tab. "Have you seen her, spoken to her since that cocktail party at the TCC?"

Brett shook his head. She left the clubhouse with Jaynie, and in the days since, they'd not laid eyes on each other. He left his house at the crack of dawn and came back from the land after dark, and she, he suspected, was trying to avoid him too.

"What do you want from her, Brett?"

He sighed, done with this conversation. But when he tried to stand up, Jules's warning stare pinned him to his seat. He threw his hands up in the air in frustration. "I don't know, dammit!"

"Yeah, you do. You're just too much of a pussy to admit it."

Brett scowled at him. "I can toss you overboard, you know. You could swim to the beach. My boat, my rules."

"You could try." Jules smirked before turning serious again. "Now answer the question. What do you want from her?"

This conversation would never end unless he gave the ornery jerk what he wanted. And that was honesty. And maybe by admitting what he really wanted, he could, finally, be honest with himself. "I want everything with her that I didn't want with Lexi. Marriage, companionship, friendship…love."

"You're still okay with not having kids of your own?"

It was one of the biggest differences between them— Jules desperately wanted to be a dad and raise a basketball team while he was ambivalent about the concept of fatherhood. He'd all but raised himself and didn't feel the need to repeat the process.

"I just want her, Jules. Any damn way I can get her."

Brett stared at his teak deck for a long time before lifting his eyes to Jules's serious face. He scratched his head and rubbed the back of his neck, wishing his friend would say something. Brett was about to wrap his hands around his throat and squeeze the words out of him when Jules spoke again.

"Then maybe, Einstein, you should tell Sarabeth that and not me."

That, Brett decided, would be a very good idea. Of course, he would be putting his heart on the floor, inviting her to stamp all over it again. But at least he could tell himself that he tried. That he hadn't walked away without fighting for her, fighting for them, fighting for what they could have.

But he needed her to fight too, and he wasn't sure that was something she wanted to do. But something seemed off in her response to him wanting to protect her from Rusty. She knew he wasn't the type of guy to let any woman be bullied by a man—so her reaction was way out of proportion. Something else had been happening behind those pretty blue eyes, and he'd been too pissed off—and hurt and betrayed—to make sense of it.

It was time he got to the bottom of it. And afterward, if she still didn't want him, he'd find a way to live without her.

It would be hard but he damn well would.

Jules released an evil chuckle as he placed his bare feet on the coffee table separating them. He pulled his ball cap over his eyes and rested his linked hands on his stomach. "If this works out, will I have to write a new best man's speech or can I recycle the one from the aborted wedding last month?"

Brett slapped his feet off the coffee table and turned his head away so Jules couldn't see his smile. "Poop head," he said, channeling his inner ten-year-old.

"Butt face," Jules replied without missing a beat.

Yeah, because that's how adult men, friends for most of their lives, expressed their gratitude. And their love.

That same afternoon, sitting in the Royal Diner, Sarabeth heard the ding of an incoming message on her phone and, thinking it might be a message from Brett, yanked it out of the side pocket of her Kate Spade tote bag. Jaynie and Gina were laughing about something; she'd lost track of their conversation ages ago. In fact, since walking out of the Texas Cattleman's Club last week, she hadn't been able to think about anything or anyone other than Brett and how much she missed him.

The message was from her lawyer, telling her to expect the delivery of papers she needed to sign for the trusts she was establishing for her kids. Sarabeth bit the inside of her cheek, telling herself that, at some point, she would feel better, normal. Whatever the hell normal meant...

Her attention was diverted by Gina placing a hand on her wrist and giving it a gentle squeeze. "Mom, are you okay?"

She forced a bright smile for her darling daughter. "I'm fine! Why would you think I'm not?"

Gina shook her head and arched one eyebrow. "I swear, she still thinks I'm ten," she told Jaynie.

"Yep, it's what moms do. They pretend that everything is okay when they aren't," Jaynie said, glaring at the specially ordered green smoothie in front of her. Jaynie was on another diet and wasn't particularly happy about it.

Seeing that smoothie reminded her of the one she'd made for Brett, back when they were together. He'd been in a hurry, didn't have time for breakfast and she'd whipped him up one, using spinach and celery and a couple of apples. He'd hated it, and his expression was remarkably similar to the one Jaynie had on her face. It would be a while, she thought, before the smoothie craze took root in Royal, Texas.

God, she missed him.

"Mom!"

Sarabeth gave Gina a small smile, noting the worry on her lovely daughter's face. How had she managed to make something so exquisite?

"Mom, I'm seriously worried about you. You haven't been yourself since the TCC cocktail party."

"I'm absolutely fine, sweetie."

"Yeah, and a purple pig just flew past," Jaynie muttered, scowling at her. "Your daughter is not an idiot, Sarabeth, and neither am I. You are distracted, pensive and miserable. Now, what the hell happened between you and Brett?"

Damn, she wasn't going to be able to avoid having this conversation. "I ended it," Sarabeth glumly admitted. "And I don't want to talk about it."

"Tough," Jaynie retorted.

"Too bad," Gina replied.

Wonderful, Sarabeth thought, placing her phone face-down on the table. Thinking that she needed more coffee for this conversation, she motioned a waitress over and asked her to refill her cup.

When they were alone again, Gina leaned forward and

gripped her hands with both of hers. "What happened that night, Mom? With Brett and with Rusty?"

She was not going to tell Gina that Rusty tried to bribe her into leaving Royal; her daughter didn't need to know that. Neither did she need to know the ins and outs of her affair with Brett.

"Brett and I were never serious and I called it off."

Jaynie snorted and Sarabeth caught her massive, hard to miss eye roll. "What?" she demanded, irritated.

"Not serious? Oh, honey, you might be able to lie to yourself but you can't lie to us."

Oh, why was she beating around the bush? Gina was a grown woman! "We were having a friends with benefits thing. You know that."

Jaynie pointed an accusatory finger at her. "Yes, he's a hottie but stop trying to convince us that it was all about what happened in the bedroom. Sarabeth, you're crazy about that man."

"You really are, Mom," Gina added. "So why did you dump him?"

"He didn't respect me...didn't trust me to handle your father on my own," Sarabeth muttered, sounding stubborn. Good, stubborn was better than heartbroken.

"The way I heard it, Rusty had his hands on you," Jaynie bluntly stated.

Gina looked horrified. "Daddy tried to hurt you?"

Sarabeth sent Jaynie a see-what-you've-done glare. Her friend just shrugged, unrepentant. Sarabeth turned back to Gina. "I threatened him first, drilled a finger into his chest. He grabbed my finger and Brett intervened, telling him to back off."

Gina's frown pulled her eyebrows together as she digested this information. "So Daddy didn't hurt you?"

"Not really," Sarabeth admitted. "But he was definitely trying to intimidate me."

"But it could, from a distance, look like he was hurting you?" Gina persisted.

Sarabeth shrugged. "I suppose so."

She saw the puzzled looks Gina and Jaynie exchanged. "And Brett only came over when this happened? Not before?"

Sarabeth could see that they were backing her into a corner but had no idea how to get out, so she stared out of the window of the diner to look at what was happening on Main Street. Nothing interesting, unfortunately.

"Ross or Asher or even Daddy would be across the room so fast if I were having an argument with someone. And if he looked like he was hurting me, they would've punched his lights out first and asked questions later," Gina stated.

True. Dammit.

"So, Brett did neither of those things but just approached you and told Rusty to back down?" Jaynie picked up the interrogation.

Pull out the bright spotlight and the cold-water baths, Sarabeth thought, *and let's get this torture session over with.*

"So what, exactly, did Brett do wrong?" Jaynie asked.

Nothing. It was all her. Obviously. She'd admit it if they would just end this wretched conversation.

Jaynie half turned in her seat to face Gina. "I think that your mother just used Brett's response as a way to bail out of the relationship, because she's a big scaredy-cat and she didn't want to get hurt."

"Sitting right here," Sarabeth reminded her, annoyed with Jaynie's perceptive summary of her situation.

"But she is hurt," Gina responded, ignoring her. "She's miserable and sad and she misses him dreadfully."

"Still here." What was the point? They were both enjoying their little byplay.

Gina rested her chin in the palm of her hand. "Do you think that she's scared to be loved, scared to take a chance? Scared to fail at another relationship?"

"Oh, undoubtedly," Jaynie blithely replied. "She believes everyone is going to leave her so she finds a reason to walk before they can."

Ouch. But true. That was exactly what she'd done with Brett. And, because she was tired of them talking around her, she decided to try an explanation. "What's the point of us carrying on? It wasn't going to last!"

"Why not?" Gina asked, sounding genuinely confused. "And don't you dare tell me it's because he's younger than you."

"Well, he is," Sarabeth muttered, fiddling with her phone, tears welling in her eyes.

Her daughter immediately stood up to try to hug her, but Jaynie gripped the band of her jeans to pull her down into her seat. "Sympathy is not what your mom needs right now, honey."

Sarabeth glared at her oldest friend. "And what do I need?" she demanded.

"Basically, a good kick in the butt," Jaynie bluntly responded. She pushed aside her smoothie and their glances held. "I know you, Sarabeth. I've known you for a long, long time. The problem is that for you, love has always been transactional."

Sarabeth frowned and Gina asked Jaynie to explain. Jaynie pushed her bangs to the side and ran her finger up and down her glass. "Sarabeth, your mom loved you when you did well at pageants, adored you when you married the most successful man in Royal. She never loved you for *you*. Rusty—sorry Gina—only married you because he thought it was time to have kids and he had the brains and you the beauty, so your kids would win the genetic jackpot. Not your fault the man had the attention span of a fruit fly and couldn't keep his pants zipped." Jaynie patted Gina's hand. "Sorry, honey."

"I've heard it all before," Gina told her on a wan smile.

"Those men after Rusty loved your looks, but none of them saw past your pretty packaging. You then moved to LA and devoted all your time to your business and none to your love life."

"Is there a point to this?" Sarabeth asked, squirming under Jaynie's laser-like focus.

"The point is that Brett is the first man who sees you, all of you. He likes your pretty face and your skinny body, but he appreciates your mind and he seems to enjoy spending time with you, in bed and out." Jaynie tapped her hand with her index finger. "He knows who you are but that scares the hell out of you."

"Shouldn't it?" Sarabeth cried. "It's damn scary!"

"You know what's scarier, babe?"

Sarabeth wasn't sure she wanted to hear the answer but cocked her head anyway.

"Being alone is scary. Not living is scary. Giving up control and surrendering to love is horribly scary," Jaynie said. "But it's brave and joyous and lovely and wonderful. And you're an idiot if you choose to be alone, running away instead of planting your feet and trying."

Sarabeth stared at her friend for a long, long time before releasing a heavy sigh. Jaynie had a point. In fact, she had many, many points. But she still didn't know if she'd act on her advice, change a thing.

"I'll think about what you said," Sarabeth told her.

Jaynie rolled her eyes so hard Sarabeth was convinced she'd done some damage. "Your mother is damn stubborn, kid."

"Yep." Gina nodded, handing Sarabeth a soft smile. "But I remember her telling us, when we were kids, that all choices have consequences." She tipped her head to the side, her eyes openly curious.

"You've chosen to end it with Brett, Mom. A consequence of that is never seeing him again, in a romantic, sexual way. Can you deal with that? Can you deal with seeing him in Royal, seeing him date, fall in love or marry someone else? Just because you don't want to take a risk, doesn't mean he won't."

Sarabeth felt hot. Then cold. Then shaky. Hoisted by her own rope...

And tangled up by her own words.

Twelve

Brett, after sending Sarabeth a text as he started his drive back to Royal, wasn't sure she'd meet him that evening. He'd asked her to join him for a ride through his property around dusk, and although she said she would, he'd been a bundle of nerves saddling a recovered Ty and her favorite mare, Bella.

But upon seeing her walking toward the stables, blond hair pulled back in a messy ponytail, her beautiful eyes full of shadows and her creamy skin pale, he released a sigh of relief. She was here. They were going to talk.

But, damn, he was anxious. Brett resisted the urge to wipe his clammy hands on the seat of his jeans. Ty released a loud neigh in his ear and butted the side of his head as if to tell him to get his shit together.

He sure as hell was going to try.

Reaching him, Sarabeth pulled her hands out of the pockets of her sleeveless parka and took Bella's reins.

"Hi," she said, looking nervous. Her nerves relaxed him a little and he managed a small smile.

"Hi back. Want a boost up?"

Sarabeth nodded, and instead of cupping his hands for the traditional lift, he gripped her waist and easily deposited her in the saddle. Sarabeth didn't say anything but looked down at him with an enigmatic expression on her face. What was going on behind those deep, dark blue eyes?

Brett left her and vaulted onto Ty's back, impatiently pushing his feet into the stirrups. At his clicking sound, his horse broke into a trot and Brett looked behind him to see Sarabeth following. He took a mental snapshot, thinking that he couldn't wait for the rest of his life. Provided, of course, that she was in the center of it.

Hopefully, she wanted him as much as he wanted her.

But, damn, what if she didn't? The reins slipped in his sweaty hands and he grimaced. Holding Ty back, he waited for her to come up beside him and sent her a sideways look. "You good?"

Sarabeth nodded, turning her head to stare off into the distance. After a minute, maybe more, she turned back to look at him, her eyes wide and brimming with emotion. "I need to say something to you. It's not going to be easy or pretty and you might not want to hear it…"

Man, that didn't sound good. But in for a penny and all that crap. "I have things to say, too. Do you want to go first or shall I?"

Sarabeth rubbed her forehead with the tips of her fingers, and he wondered if she had a headache. He sure as hell felt one building at the back of his skull. She looked at the long, tree-lined dirt road in front of them and her shoulders rose and fell. "Can we delay this conversation, just for a little while?"

What was the point? But he was willing to hear her reason for wanting to do so. "Why?"

The corners of her lovely mouth, the one he wanted to kiss for the rest of his life, lifted a fraction. "I'm on a fast horse, there's an open road and I just want to fly."

He shook his head. "You're not wearing a helmet. If you fell…"

"You're not wearing one either," Sarabeth pointed out.

Point taken. He looked back toward the stable block. "I can go back, get some helmets."

"We're both good, experienced riders, Brett, and we're not going to jump anything. We're just going to hurtle down this empty road as fast and as long as we can. I need to work off some excess energy, and I'm sure you do too."

He could think of another way to rid themselves of this pent-up frustration, but he didn't think she'd appreciate his suggestion of going to bed. He looked at the road again and her unprotected head. "No jumping, no messing around or taking chances. And stay on the damn horse!"

Sarabeth flashed him a quick smile, dug her heels into Bella's flanks, and she and her horse accelerated away. Brett took a moment to watch her before urging Ty to do the same. He enjoyed the rocking motion of his canter and grinned when Sarabeth urged Bella into a gallop. Standing up in his stirrups, he leaned forward, feeling like a bird skimming the ground. Brett felt Ty bunch and release his muscles, steady and sure, his hooves hitting the ground as he easily caught up to and overtook Sarabeth.

Since leaving the stables the wind had picked up, and over the sound rushing in his ears, he heard Sarabeth's joyous laughter. Feeling his eyes watering, he blinked and brushed a strand of Ty's mane off his cheek, his breath starting to shorten. He could feel his thigh and arm muscles burning and he grinned, enjoying every minute of Ty's disturbingly fast pace.

They'd need to stop soon, but he had another few minutes of pure bliss before they needed to ease off the pace and return to reality and their life-defining chat. Well, for him it was life-defining; whether it would be for Sarabeth he had no idea. But talk they must. Brett started to pull on the reins and heard, above the wind and the sound of hooves on dirt and his hard breathing, a sharp snap. His saddle whipped from side to side beneath him and Brett saw the ground rushing up to meet him.

"Not too bad" and "he was okay" were his last thoughts before his head bounced off the road and he slid into darkness.

Sarabeth paced the waiting room of the hospital, her hands in the pockets of her parka, ignoring the tears sliding down her face. She had kept it together for the last couple of hours, staying calm as she called for an ambulance, not getting in the way of the EMTs when they arrived. They'd checked Brett's vitals, placed a brace around his neck and loaded him into the ambulance, all without him regaining consciousness. She'd heard the EMTs mention something about TBI—she'd demanded an explanation of the acronym and they'd reluctantly explained that it stood for a traumatic brain injury—and felt cold when they expressed their concern that he'd yet to wake up.

Once at the hospital, he'd been rushed to God knew where, and she'd been told to stay put. Sarabeth leaned against the wall next to a water cooler and tipped her head back to look at the ceiling. She couldn't live in a world that no longer had Brett in it. That was impossible and incomprehensible.

Their age difference was inconsequential. And running away from happiness because she was scared of what might happen was simply moronic. If Brett recovered—and he *would*, dammit!—she'd take whatever he could give her. Friendship, sex, a combination of both for as long as it lasted.

There was nothing like a life-threatening accident to make you see sense.

Oh, God, he had to be okay.

Sarabeth heard footsteps approaching her and turned her head to see Jaynie, Gina, Ross and Charlotte approaching her. Her son was the first one to reach her, and he pulled her into his arms, gathering her close. Sarabeth gripped his shirt and rested her forehead against his broad chest, her shoulders heaving. "I can't lose him, I just can't."

Gina laid her hand on her back and gently rubbed. "You won't, Mom. It'll be okay. He'll be fine."

Sarabeth lifted her head and swiped away her tears. She saw Jules standing behind Jaynie, his expression grim. "Can you tell us what happened, Sarabeth?" Jules asked.

She forced herself to think. "We were galloping down the road. He was on Ty and flying. Then suddenly he went one way and his saddle went the other way."

"Sounds like his girth snapped," Ross said.

Jules frowned. "Where is the saddle now?"

Sarabeth rubbed her fingertips across her aching forehead. "Uh, not sure. I called his foreman from the ambulance, told him Brett was hurt and that the horses were loose. He told me he'd take care of it. He'd have the saddle." Sarabeth saw the long look Jules and Ross exchanged and frowned. What was she missing here?

"What? What are you guys thinking?"

Jaynie, being Jaynie, didn't dance around the subject. "Brett's recently had some threats against him. Should we be reporting this to the police?"

Ross shook his head. "Let's not get ahead of ourselves. Jules, maybe you can make some discreet enquiries."

Huh? What? Who had threatened Brett? Gina was the first to make the connection. "Oh, come on!" Her eyes blazed with annoyance. "Dad is a pompous, jealous ass but can you really see him sneaking onto Brett's property and sabotaging his girth? That's ridiculous!"

Sarabeth agreed. Rusty was many things, but he wouldn't stoop so low. Would he…?

Ross wound his arm around Charlotte. "Look, the town is already abuzz with news of Brett's accident—"

"It happened less than two hours ago!" Sarabeth cried.

"This is Royal, Mom. The town heard within a half hour. Speculation is rife because everyone knows Brett is ridiculously anal about his equipment and having a girth break is not normal." Ross sighed. "Rusty recently threatened him, so you can understand why Jules and I have concerns."

"As soon as we hear whether Brett is okay, I'll head back to the ranch, find the saddle and the girth," Jules said. "We'll soon know if it was an accident or not."

Sarabeth nodded. She couldn't think about the how and why of Brett's accident right now…she just needed to know that he was okay. So why were they taking so damn long?

She looked at Ross. "Can you go and ask the nurses if they've heard anything?"

Jules squeezed her shoulder. "I'll go and ask in my official capacity as a Texas Game Warden." He shrugged, big hands holding his overloaded belt. "It might work, it might not."

"Thanks, Jules," Ross said, and Sarabeth managed to dredge up a grateful smile.

Jules nodded and as he started to walk away, one of the double doors opened and a doctor stepped into the room, pushing his fingers through his messy hair. He glanced around the room, saw the group huddled in the corner and lifted bushy eyebrows. "Brett Harston's family?"

Sarabeth didn't hesitate. "Yes. Is he okay? What's going on?"

"I'm Dr. Mike Nicolls and I'm a neurologist."

Oh, no, they'd called in a neurologist; that meant it had to be bad. Sarabeth gripped Gina's hand and squeezed. "Just tell me, *please*."

"Because he didn't regain consciousness immediately, I ordered an MRI scan to see whether he had swelling on the brain—"

Wait…what? "So, he's regained consciousness? He's awake?"

Dr. Nicolls smiled. "He's been awake for a while, and he's been demanding to see Sarabeth… I presume that's you?"

She nodded, feeling her legs buckle. If Brett was being irascible then he had to be okay. "So, he's fine?"

Dr. Nicolls nodded. "He's got a hell of a headache but he's all right. The MRI came back clear, so I'm not sure why he was out for so long but brains can be tricky things. He's got a concussion—"

"But he's fine?" Sarabeth demanded again, needing to hear it one more time.

"Fine, annoyed and wanting to leave. I'd like him to stay overnight for observation but he's balking."

"Sounds like Brett," Jules commented, relief on his face. "Where's he now?"

"He's been transferred to a private room and he's given

me—" Dr. Nicolls looked at his watch "—fifteen minutes to find you. If I don't, he'll soon start wondering the hallways himself, dressed as he is."

Jules grinned. "In a hospital gown with a bare ass?"

Dr. Nicolls smiled. "Yep."

Jules laughed. "I'd like to see that." He grinned at her, relief lightening his dark eyes.

"Well, you're not going to!" Sarabeth tartly replied, finally able to take a deep breath because she'd lost the concrete block on her chest. She pushed her shoulders back and straightened her spine before meeting the doctor's amused eyes. "Can you take me to him?"

He nodded. "Will you at least try to persuade him to spend the night? I'm not happy for him to go home, just yet."

"I'll make that happen, I promise," Sarabeth said. Whatever was best for Brett was what was going to happen. And Brett himself could just deal.

Dr. Nicolls gestured for her to walk through the door. "Good enough. Follow me."

Fifteen minutes were up and Brett swung his legs off the bed, determined to find Sarabeth. He closed his eyes as a wave of pain swept through him and multicolored lights danced behind his eyes. God, he hoped his feet worked better than his head...

Nobody had been able to tell him about Sarabeth, whether she was okay. Hell, all the nurses had been able to tell him was that he'd been in an accident, that he'd hit his head. Since the last thing he remembered was leaving his house to meet Sarabeth, he didn't know how he came to have a massive bump on the back of his head. Had they been in a car together, had he wrecked it, was she okay?

His feet hit the floor, and he winced at the cold sensation beneath his feet. He also felt a cool breeze hit his bare butt and looked around for his clothes. Nothing, dammit. Oh, well, he'd be flashing his ass to anyone who cared to look.

Finding Sarabeth and determining that she was okay was all that mattered.

Brett pushed himself to his feet and immediately swayed. He plopped down again and shook his head to clear the fog and groaned. It felt like a hundred drunk elves were digging a ditch in his head. He needed more painkillers and he needed them badly…

But he needed to see Sarabeth first. He'd stay seated, just for a minute, and hopefully the dizziness would disappear.

"You nearly split your head in two, Brett. Why the hell are you trying to get out of bed?"

Brett slowly lifted his head and there she was, standing in the doorway. His eyes danced over her, quickly cataloging her injuries… A beautiful, blotchy face, eyes red from crying. No blood on her clothing, no tears to it either. As she walked into the room, he noticed that she seemed to be moving with ease.

She didn't look injured. "You're fine."

"Unlike you, I didn't fly off a horse and crack my head," Sarabeth said, coming to stand beside him. He inhaled her subtle, fresh perfume and the panic in his throat receded. She was fine; that was all that mattered. He looked into her beautiful eyes and her fingers came up to touch his jaw.

"Is that what happened?" Brett asked. "And is Ty okay?"

"He's fine. The last time I saw him he was munching grass on the bank, not particularly concerned that you were as white as a sheet and passed out on a dirt road."

"Bastard," he said, placing his hand on her hip. She was so warm and so very alive. Yeah, all was well with his world. "Did he rear up, buck me off?"

Sarabeth moved to stand between his legs, her eyes clinging to his face. She couldn't stop touching him, a hand drifting over his shoulder, up to his neck, down his arm. "Your girth broke," Sarabeth explained.

Brett frowned and then wished he hadn't as his pain level spiked. Yeah, he might need to lie back down soon, but first he had to know what happened. "My girth? That doesn't make sense."

Worry clouded her eyes. "Jules is going back to the ranch to find the saddle and the girth. He wants to check that it wasn't…"

"Wasn't what?" Brett asked when she hesitated.

"…tampered with," Sarabeth reluctantly admitted.

Brett tried to push away the clouds of fog, struggling to make sense of her words. It was difficult. "I don't understand. He thinks someone tried to hurt me?"

"He wants to check," Sarabeth said, hurrying to reassure him. "You've had some threats against you."

Brett stared at her, thinking back. The only person who'd threatened him was Rusty. "That's nuts, Sarabeth. Your ex is a jerk but he wouldn't do that."

Sarabeth lifted her slim shoulders in a shrug. "I don't think he would either but Jules wants to check, to make sure. Ross agrees. Rusty has a hell of a temper and he doesn't like being embarrassed, and you and I have both bested him lately." She stroked his chest with the tips of gentle fingers. "Besides, have you ever stopped Jules from doing what he wants to do?"

"Never," Brett admitted. "Okay, well, it's his time to waste."

"I think you should lie down," Sarabeth suggested softly. "Have you been given something for pain?"

"They gave me something but it did jackshit," Brett grumbled.

Sarabeth dropped a light kiss on the corner of his mouth. "I heard something about you insisting on going home—"

"I am going home and you're coming with me," Brett told her. He was done beating around the bush. "And you're damn well going to stay with me."

Sarabeth smiled. "I'll come home with you tomorrow and only after the doctors have given you the all clear. And I'll stay. And when you are feeling much, much better, we'll have that talk we were supposed to have…"

Brett started to argue but saw the determination in her eyes. He wouldn't sway her and, dammit, he didn't think he could walk out of here on his own two feet. Every inch of him ached, he felt like a six-foot bruise. His ribs hurt, and his butt. And his back. Honestly, he felt like he'd gone five rounds with a steamroller.

And now that he knew Sarabeth was okay, he could relax. Just a little.

But he still had no intention of spending the night in the hospital. "I'll rest for a little while and leave later."

"We'll see." Sarabeth's lips twitched, and he didn't trust the amusement in her eyes. He narrowed his gaze at her, suspected he was being manipulated but was simply too damn sore to care.

"Want some help getting back into bed?" she asked, stepping away from him. He wanted to haul her back into his arms but couldn't get his arms to obey his brain's command.

"No, I'm good." Brett shifted back, gritted his teeth against the pain and swung his legs onto the bed. He couldn't keep a low groan from slipping past his lips. His arms held all the strength of two-day-old noodles.

Sarabeth placed her hand on his chest and looked down at him, her lovely eyes full of worry and, dare he hope, love? "You scared me, Brett," she whispered. "Don't do that again, okay?"

He lifted his hand to stroke his thumb across her cheek. "Don't go. Stay. With me."

"I'll be here when you wake up," Sarabeth promised him.

Brett closed his eyes, needing to tell her that wasn't what he meant, that she needed to know that he didn't mean just for now but for forever.

But before he could speak again, he slipped into sleep, clutching her hand resting on his heart.

Two days later, Brett woke up in his own bed feeling, mostly, like himself. He still had a headache but the pain was now manageable. Stretching, he winced at his still sore muscles but they were also on the mend, thanks to some concoction Sarabeth whipped up in his kitchen. He remembered her saying that the cream contained arnica and lavender oil and some other natural herbs.

Whatever it was, her cream worked a lot better than the conventional medicines he'd tried.

Brett turned his head and saw his phone on the bedside table, picked it up and noticed he had a bunch of messages. He skimmed through the messages wishing him well, pausing when he came to one Jules sent late last night.

I examined the girth under a microscope but I can't tell whether it tore naturally or was cut. For a definitive answer, we'd have to send it to a forensic lab.

Well, huh.

Let me think about that, he replied to Jules.

Personally, he thought that the girth breaking was an unfortunate accident; it was known to happen. But, because he wasn't a complete fool, he'd be a little more vigilant, more aware. But he wouldn't spend his time worrying. That was counterproductive.

Besides, he had bigger things to worry about, namely Sarabeth and getting her to stay in his life.

Talking of the love of his life, where was she? Judging by the light behind the drapes, it was early and dawn was breaking. Throwing back the bedcovers, Brett headed to the bathroom, used the facilities and brushed his teeth. He had to get back to work; the ranch wouldn't run itself. But before he did, he and Sarabeth needed to talk.

They were way overdue.

Brett pulled on a pair of jeans and a Henley and walked downstairs in his bare feet. At the bottom of the stairs, he looked right across his living room toward the deck and saw Sarabeth sitting on the top step of the stairs leading to the garden, a cup of coffee on the cold tile floor next to her. Her exercise mat and roller, and her workout gear, told him that she'd finished her routine yoga, Pilates and meditation session...

It was a new day, and the perfect time for a conversation.

Brett fixed himself a cup of coffee and padded over, leaning his shoulder into the frame of the open French doors. "Morning."

Sarabeth turned and smiled, and Brett's stomach rolled over. Yeah, he needed that smile in his life. "Hi. You're looking better."

Brett nodded. "I'm a little sore, but I need to get back to work."

She nodded and glanced toward the cottage she'd been renting. He saw her swallow, and then she pushed her shoulders back and straightened her spine. "And I need to pack up my stuff."

He sipped, his eyes not moving from her face. "And where do you intend to take your stuff?"

Brett held his breath, knowing that her answer would either be the start of a long, smooth glide or an uphill battle. He hoped for easy but was prepared for hard. Because no matter what, he wanted her in his life and would fight for her.

Sarabeth met his eyes and lifted one slim shoulder. "Actually, I'd just like to move it in here, but I don't know how you feel about that."

Every ache disappeared, mostly because joy infused his body and threatened to dissolve his knees. So, maybe he'd get the long, smooth glide. Just in case he'd misheard her—he had suffered a TBI not two days ago—he threw out another question. "You want to move in with me? Permanently?"

Her smile was gentle and a little naughty. "Unless there's another sexy, eligible bachelor living here that I haven't met yet?"

He couldn't joke around, not yet. This was too important.

"Why do you want to stay?" Brett demanded, walking over to her and dropping to his haunches. "Why do you want to stay here? With me?"

"Because while I don't know if we'll last forever, we're good together and I'd like to give it a try."

Sarabeth placed her hand on his knee, pushing her

fingers into the rip of his jeans, skimming over his knee. Brett shivered. With lust. And with so much love.

"I need more, Sarabeth."

"I love you. I'm crazy, madly, stupidly in love with you," she admitted, her eyes full of emotion.

"Good to know," Brett murmured, lifting his hands to hold her face. And wasn't that the understatement of the year. "I'm in love with you, too."

Sarabeth stared at him, hope flaring in her eyes. He flinched when it faded as quickly as it appeared. "Don't say that if you don't mean it, Brett. I'd rather be hurt by the truth than comforted by a lie."

Brett hit the floor, sitting cross-legged in front of her. He looked down at her bowed head, watched her fingers playing with the torn threads coming off the rips in his jeans. "Honey, I would never say that if I didn't mean it. You and I…"

"You and I?" Sarabeth prompted him when he hesitated.

"This was never meant to be anything more than a fling, a couple of weeks of fun," Brett said, taking his time to find the words, the *right* words. "There was no way I was going to start a new relationship after what I did to Lexi, and you were only going to be in Royal for three months. It was just sex, I told myself. Attraction. It wouldn't go anywhere, it couldn't."

He placed his elbows on the inside of his thighs and stared at her. "We shouldn't work but we do. You read historical biographies and I read scientific journals on new farming techniques and horse breeding. You do yoga and I couldn't touch my toes if I tried. You like classical music and I like gangsta rap…"

"I binge true crime documentaries and you binge *Deadliest Catch*," Sarabeth added.

"But we both love horses and animals and—" Brett's lips twitched "—sex. We both can cook, do laundry and we've had numerous, deep conversations about life and religion and relationships. We click and we just…work."

"I'm not going to be able to give you kids. I'm too old, firstly, and I don't want to do that again."

"Kids aren't a deal-breaker, darling. I've never had the burning urge to be a father so that's not something you need to worry about."

Sarabeth nodded, looking relieved. Then she bit down on her bottom lip before speaking again. "I don't need a savior, Brett, I need a partner."

He released a long breath. "I know and thank God for that. I don't want, or need, to always be the strong one or the voice of reason. Sometimes I'll lead, sometimes you will, depending on our individual strengths. I am looking for a partner, too, Sarabeth, and you're all that I need."

Brett watched as the last of her doubts faded from her eyes. "Are you sure?"

"Very," he told her, leaning forward to brush his lips across hers. Before he lost control and took their kiss deeper, he had a bit more ground to cover. He pulled back and waited for her eyes to open. "Are you?"

Sarabeth encircled his neck with her arms, her fingers sliding up into his hair. "Very. How's your head?"

"Fine." Brett grinned. Yeah, he recognized the signs; she wanted him naked. And while he had no objection to ripping her clothes off and making love to her on her exercise mat, he wasn't backing down before he got all that he wanted.

So, time to make this permanent. And official.

"You once told me that you hated your name. Do you want another?"

Sarabeth blinked, then frowned. "I'm too old to be

called anything other than Sarabeth. Though I do like it when you call me baby."

Brett smiled. "I meant your last name, baby. Your first name, my last. Does that work for you?"

He grunted when he found his arms full of a beautiful, squealing bundle of excited energy. She started to drop kisses on his face like an overexuberant puppy. Gently placing his big hand on her face, he pushed her back and laughed when she slapped his hand away. "Is that a yes?"

"Yes, it's a yes," Sarabeth retorted, sitting back on her heels. "Where do you want to get married? Gatlinburg? Vegas? At the courthouse? And when? Today, tomorrow, next week?"

He loved her enthusiasm and felt his chest puff up at her elation over becoming his wife. "Nope. If we are going to do this, then we're going to do it properly. You're my *it*, the only person I'm ever going to marry so I want to see you walk down the aisle toward me. I want to say my vows to you in front of a preacher. And our friends and your family and the whole damn town."

"And Royal will never forgive you if you deprive them of free booze and food again," Sarabeth teased before grimacing. "But I think I'm a bit too old for the whole white wedding dress thing, Brett."

Brett shrugged. "So, wear black, or shocking pink or scarlet. I don't give a damn, as long as you marry me."

"Black's not a bad idea," Sarabeth mused, "and it would shock the Royal Reporters. I've got to keep them on their toes after all."

"That's my girl," Brett said, laughing. He captured her face between his hands and brushed his lips across hers. "Now, you mentioned something about bed?"

Sarabeth made that hot, sexy, take-me-now sound in the back of her throat, and Brett felt his erection straining against the buttons of his jeans. Yeah, they wouldn't make it to the bed, nor would he make it to work today, but this exercise mat would work just fine.

Pulling back, he looked into her dazed expression, needing to tell her once again, how much he loved her.

Sarabeth stroked his jaw, tears glistening in her eyes. "Kahlil Gibran once said that love is a trembling happiness and that's exactly how I feel."

"I have no idea who that is," Brett said, his throat constricting with emotion as she stretched out on the mat, pulling him down to her, "but that sounds about right to me."

"Love me, Brett."

Brett spoke against her lips. "I do, baby. Always will."

* * * * *

CRAVING A
REAL TEXAN

CHARLENE SANDS

To Don, my loving husband and lifelong best friend.
Always.

One

"I'm here now, Lily," Harper Dawn whispered into the cell phone. "I don't think anyone saw me."

At least she hoped not. She'd emptied a box of dark chestnut-brown color onto her hair, changing her look from a soft honey blond to shiny brunette in a matter of minutes. She'd cut her signature waist-length locks to fall just below her shoulders now, and the transformation surprised even her. Hopefully her disguise was enough to fool the paparazzi.

"How did you manage it?" Lily asked. Her friend sounded relieved. No more than she was. Right now, she was probably the most hated reality star on the planet for dumping her seemingly perfect guy, a chef like herself, in front of millions who'd followed their love affair on national TV. "How'd you get out of your apartment complex without being seen?"

"It was tricky. My neighbor Tony walked me out. I'm

in disguise now. You won't even know it's me." She spotted Lily's car passing her on the street. "In fact, you just drove by me."

"What? I didn't see…oh, wow. Okay, I see you now on the library steps. Hold on, I'm turning the car around."

Harper laughed for the first time in three days, ever since her big breakup on *One Last Date*, and the sound was welcome to her ears. If she could fool her onetime college roomie, then this little plan Lily had cooked up might just work.

Her friend stopped the car, and Harper quickly jumped in. It was like a movie scene where Harper was the bank robber and Lily drove the getaway car. "Wow," her friend said. "You do look different. How are you holding up?"

"Better, now that I'm with you."

Lily punched the gas pedal, and they were off. "I'm glad you got away. Do me a favor and don't look at your Twitter feed anytime soon."

"That bad?"

Lily nodded. "Worse, and I can't help but feel responsible for this. I suggested you go on the show. But honestly, Harper, I had no idea it could all go to crapola so quickly."

"It's not your fault. You didn't twist my arm. Too much." Harper gave her a crooked smile. "I don't blame you. I should've known better."

"You're looking for love. Everyone should have a chance at happiness, Harp. Including you."

"I'm beginning to think I won't ever find it. Let's face it—I'm thirty years old and have had one broken relationship after another. Either I'm a bad judge of character or I'm totally unlovable."

"BS, Harper," Lily said, taking her eyes off the road to shoot her a solemn look. "You are neither of those things. You just haven't met the right guy. When you do, it'll be like creating the perfect soufflé. You'll get all gooey inside."

Harper laughed for the second time in less than an hour. "You're using foodie examples to persuade me."

"Is it working?"

"Not at the moment, but keep trying and eventually it will."

"Good. Well, here we are. This is where I leave you." Lily parked beside a white sedan in the Good Times Diner lot and handed her the keys to the rental car.

"Whose car is this?" Harper asked.

"It's a rental. In my name, so no one will be able to find you. Hopefully. Oh, and here," she said, handing her a big duffel bag. "You'll need some clothes and things. I put a spare computer in there, too."

"Lily, this is so…sweet. You've thought of everything. I promise, I'll repay you for all of this."

"Don't worry about it. Your birthday's coming up. Consider it your gift."

"My birthday? That's not for two months."

"Well, I didn't think you'd get away with walking out of your apartment complex with any luggage."

She sighed. Lily was the best friend she'd ever had. "You drove all the way from Juliet County to come rescue me."

It was an hour drive from the Tremaine estate in Juliet County to her little town of Barrel Falls. She'd only lived here a few months before she'd gotten picked for the show. And she'd put her professional life on hold to find love. Now, Lily was giving her an opportunity to escape the media that had followed her here from Los Angeles.

"No thanks necessary. Just go up to the cabin and try to relax. There's plenty of room there. You can work on your cookbook and no one will bother you. I wrote down the address. It's up in the hills and quite beautiful. Use the GPS to find your way. You've got a good two-hour drive, so be careful on the road. And we'll talk often, I promise."

"Okay," Harper said, nodding and taking a steadying breath. "Nothing like this has ever happened to me before. I feel like I've committed a crime or something."

"Harper, you followed your heart. You didn't love Dale Murphy, and you did the right thing by breaking it off. I guarantee you in a week or two, this crazy fiasco will be over and you can come home to peace and quiet."

"This is…" Harper bit down on her lower lip as tears welled in her eyes. "You're such a good friend, Lil."

Lily was the only daughter in the Tremaine family, one of the richest families in Juliet County if not in all of Texas. She and Lily had been college roomies at Stanford and vowed to remain friends for life. Both had decided on different career paths, Lily going into interior design and Harper opting for culinary school. "You'd do the same for me, Harper. I know that for sure."

Harper climbed out of Lily's car and hopped into the rental car. She waved at her dear friend.

Then she was off, driving to a remote cabin up in the Texas hills.

Take a vacation, Cade. You're working yourself too hard.

Dr. Adams had laid down the law after a physical exam had confirmed high blood pressure—way too high for a man in his early thirties. Cade had insomnia most of the time and walked the halls at night, too keyed up to sleep. He'd been pouring himself into the family business, putting in too many hours at Tremaine Corp., and his body couldn't handle the strain much longer. So said the doc.

Cade Tremaine sat down on his bed, rubbing his forehead. He'd been an athlete in high school and college, playing baseball while earning degrees in business and communications. He'd prided himself on good health and keeping his body fit. But that was before he'd lost Bree, the love of his life and the world's most perfect woman, to a cruel disease a year and a half ago.

Now, he shuddered at the idea of being alone with his thoughts, of not working, not pushing himself to the brink to keep his mind occupied and his grief at bay. Running the Tremaine ranch, keeping their oil business and real estate interests right on track was his whole life now. But the doctor had told him quite forcefully he had to take a break. Either that or go on a slew of medications to combat his physical problems.

This was the one time that he wished he was more like his brother Gage. The outgoing country music star never seemed to get rattled. He was as cool as a cucumber and let things slide off his back, whereas Cade bottled things up inside. Cade, the oldest of two brothers and one sister, had helped pick up the pieces when his father, Brand, had passed away eight years ago. And since then, Cade had done everything he could to keep the business and the family thriving.

His mother entered his bedroom. Head held high, she had stately elegance and commanded attention whenever she walked into a room. Rose Tremaine treated everyone equally, from the housekeeper to the mayor of Juliet, setting a good example for her family. They'd often teased that she was really Helen Mirren disguised as their mother.

"Cade, I see you're all packed up."

"Yeah, Mom. I'm packed."

"I'm glad you're going up to the cabin. It'll do you good."

"Will it, Mom? I don't know."

"You need a change of pace, Cade. And work can wait. We have Albert at the helm at Tremaine in your absence, and he's capable."

"We have that possible merger I've been busting my butt on."

"Cade," his mother said, "are you forgetting who helped start this company with your father? I'm here, and Albert knows he can look to me if he needs any help. But son, this is a good thing. You haven't really come to terms with Bree's death."

"How can you say that, when it's with me all the time?"

"That's exactly my point. This is a good opportunity for you to shed some of that grief you've been holding inside. You've gone on a downward spiral lately. You don't eat well, you hardly sleep. You work yourself into the ground. None of that's healthy."

"You sound like my doctor," he grumbled. He wasn't thrilled about any of this. He squeezed his eyes closed. He hated the notion of being alone at the cabin with his mental demons.

His mother kissed his cheek and patted his face. "I'm your mother, and Mother knows best. I promise this trip will do you good. I've called ahead, and everything is ready for you."

"Thanks, Mom."

His mother sure knew how to get things done.

Then his thoughts turned to Bree. Holding on to his grief meant keeping her close in his heart. Somehow, it felt like he was betraying her by trying to move on with his life.

He wasn't sure he was ready to let go.

* * *

What a difference a day or two made. Harper couldn't believe less than a week ago, she was being hounded by the media, running away from paparazzi and being touted as the most hated woman in all of TV land. Oh no, she hadn't taken Lily's advice as she should have. Instead, curiosity had gotten the best of her and she'd ventured into the Twitter-sphere, coming out scarred and shaken. Not that she didn't have some support on social media. There were a few brave souls who'd taken her side, more rational human beings who hadn't fallen for Dale Murphy's charm and wit, finding instead that he and Harper weren't a good match.

But today was a different story. She hummed along with the radio playing Gage Tremaine's latest country hit—the story of a man falling on hard times and coming out a winner because of the love of a good woman. To this day, she could hardly believe that gorgeous Gage Tremaine, famous country music star, was Lily's brother. She'd never met either of her friend's two brothers, their paths never crossing, but Lily spoke of them often while they were roomies. In a loving way, *mostly*. And now, here Harper was, staying in the Tremaine cabin, which was more like a four-bedroom estate overlooking a lake in a glorious and remote mountain community, cooking herb-roasted chicken in their state-of-the-art kitchen. The luscious scents of sage, rosemary and garlic filled the air, almost bringing tears of joy to her eyes.

This place was amazing. Peaceful. And paparazzi-free.

She pulled the roaster out of the oven and covered it with foil. The only thing missing was a kale salad. The fridge had been stocked when she'd gotten here, except for fresh fruits and veggies. Today, she'd venture out for the first time in two days to do some shopping. If Lily was right, hopefully by now the hoopla about her breakup with Dale was yesterday's news.

She put on a ball cap and tossed on her hoodie. Though the spring air was warm, the hills this time of late afternoon could get cold. She slipped on a pair of sunglasses and ventured outside. The market in Bright Landing was a short mile and a half away. She left her rental car behind and headed out on foot, enjoying the fresh mountain air.

Before long she'd reached her destination and entered the quaint but well-stocked Bright Market. She grabbed a basket and walked down the aisles, finding ingredients she needed for her salad: kale, broccoli, green cabbage, Brussels sprouts and radicchio. Her basket was brimming to the top with fruit and veggies by the time she was through.

She turned the corner of the aisle and bumped right smack into a man. A tall man, with dark hair and a chest hard as granite. "Oh, sorry. I didn't see you," she said, catching her balance, feeling grossly inelegant as an apple spilled out of her basket.

"I didn't see you, either." His voice was rich with a Texas twang, and his words made her feel like less of a clod. "Are you okay?"

"Yes, I'm fine."

He noticed the fallen apple and bent to pick it up, dropping it into her hand. Their eyes met. She blinked, reeling from the immediate impact of his dark, soulful gaze. She saw something in his eyes, something akin to well-hidden pain. And it touched her, making her wonder what had happened in his life to elicit such a look.

She realized she was staring at him, and he was staring right back. He smiled, in stunning contrast to the pain she'd witnessed in his expression just a second ago. *Wow.* His smile made something click inside and go a little wacky.

But then, out of the corner of her eye, she spotted a tabloid newspaper sitting on a rack at the checkout counter with a photo of her as a blonde splashed across the front page. The headline read, Where Is Heartbreaker Harper? Chef Dale Murphy Wants to Know.

Oh man. It was proof positive the scandal hadn't gone away. No, it was still going strong if it had reached the outskirts of a small hillside town like this. Warning bells went off. Her heart began to pound. She wasn't safe anywhere. Luckily, her disguise was holding up, because customers in the store were walking by her, and the handsome man she'd bumped into hadn't shown any recognition.

Thank goodness. "Excuse me," she said to him as she made a beeline to the checkout stand. She kept her head down and paid for her groceries. Once she was out of the store, she sighed in relief.

But that small triumph didn't keep her from trembling down to her toes, from feeling totally exposed and vulnerable again. The things they were writing about her weren't true. She wasn't a heartbreaker, or fickle or cruel. She hadn't played games with Dale's heart. She hadn't meant to hurt anybody. All she'd wanted was to find love, the long-lasting kind, and share a life with someone she felt connected to. The entire world seemed to think Dale being a chef like her meant they were perfect for each other, and for a time, she'd believed it, too. But it seemed the only real flames they'd sparked were at the kitchen stovetop. And her only real crime was that she'd found out too late she really admired Dale, the chef, but she didn't like Dale, the person, all that much.

She rushed back to the cabin in half the time it had taken to get to the store and put her groceries away. Her hands still shaking, she donned her pink-and-white polka dot apron and began putting together a salad. Cooking always relaxed her. It was the balm she needed now after seeing that tabloid. She ripped the kale and tossed it in a bowl, then chopped fresh broccoli and slivered cabbage strips. Calmer now, she began humming, grateful to Lily for giving her this chance to hide out and clear her head. Her cell phone rang, and she nearly jumped out of her skin.

Which wasn't good when you were holding a knife. A quick glance at her cell confirmed it was her friend calling. *Thank goodness.* "Lily, hi."

"Hi, Harper. How's it going?"

"It's going. I've settled in and love the place. But I just saw a photo of myself on the front page of a tabloid at the tiny market here, so I guess the story is still going strong."

"Sorry, Harp. Give it some time. It should get better."

"I hope you're right. It's hard to see that right now. And you, my friend, didn't tell me that this *cabin* is more like a dream home. I mean it, Lily. The place is beautiful. Thank you, a thousand times thank you for letting me stay here. It's so generous of you and your family."

"Well, uh, about that. I do have one teeny, tiny favor to ask you." Lily's voice went up two octaves, almost to a squeak.

"Anything. You know I'll do anything for you."

"Okay, well. You might change your mind when you hear what it is."

"I'm listening, Lil."

"My big brother, Cade, is on his way up to the cabin, too. Sorry, but my mother and I didn't coordinate on this, and honestly, sometimes a whole year goes by before anyone uses the place. But the truth is, ever since his fiancée passed away, Cade's been working himself to death. You've never gotten the chance to meet him but he's a really good guy and he's never given himself time to get over his loss. Now his blood pressure is way up. He's not eating right, either, and his doctor has warned him to slow down and take better care of himself. He ordered him to take a vacation. Which Cade didn't want to do. At all. My mom had to use clever tactics to get him to agree to leave work."

"Oh dear. I'm sorry to hear that. I guess," she said, nibbling on her lip, feeling a crushing blow coming her way, "I'd better leave."

"Don't be silly. You have nowhere else to go. I know that and you know that. Your disguise is working, but maybe only because you're in a small town and not under intense scrutiny. You can stay. It's a big place."

"But—"

"If we tell Cade the truth, he'd insist on leaving and letting you have the cabin. He doesn't want to be there, and this would only give him an excuse to go back to work. Which he cannot do. He needs to relax."

"So, what are you saying?"

"Well." Lily's voice lowered. "I've already cleared this with my mother. She's adamant that he stay. So what if we say my mother hired you to be his personal chef?"

"What?"

"You are a chef, Harper. And he hasn't been eating right. It's not out of the norm for my mother to do something like this."

"You want me to pretend I was hired by your mother?"

"Yes, but you'd have to use a different name. Even though you haven't met him, he's heard me talk about my friend Harper. He'd never recognize you from the show. The man never turns on the TV. Other than sports, that is. He wouldn't be caught dead watching a reality show. It could work. And it's only for a week or two."

"But—"

She heard a car pull up into the driveway, fallen leaves crunching under the tires. *Oh no.* Her pulse raced. She had little time to think. "He's here."

"What are you going to do?" Lily whispered in a rush.

What could she do? Lily was a dear friend. She'd put herself out to help her, and Lily's brother's health was at stake. It didn't seem as if she had a choice. "I'll do it," she said. "I'll tell him Rose hired me to cook for him."

"Oh, wow. That's a relief. Thank you, Harper. We'll talk soon and—"

"Gotta go. I hear him at the door."

"Okay, good luck."

She ended the call just as a key was turning in the lock at the front door. She stood there, waiting, holding her breath. And the irony hit her smack upside the head. She'd gone from one crazy scenario on a reality show to another nutty scheme within a blink of the eye. Oh boy, what happened to the quiet girl who'd loved to stay home at night testing recipes, happy to have the role as head chef in her hometown restaurant? Where had that girl gone?

She stared at the front door, making no attempt to go and open it. A tan duffel bag was tossed through first, landing inside the foyer. And then the man followed, carrying a piece of black luggage.

Her heart pounded as he made his way over the threshold. "You," she said almost inaudibly. It was the man from the market.

He startled and shook his head as if seeing things. Had she scared him? Immediately, their eyes met. Oh wow, those dark eyes again. They touched her in ways she couldn't name.

"You're the girl from the market."

She nodded and wiped her hands on her apron. "I am."

"What are you doing here?" he asked, setting down his luggage. He kept a safe distance from her, an honorable act on his part. He seemed sensitive to her possible fear. Then he noticed her apron and lifted his nose in the air.

The scent of rosemary-herb chicken wafted up. "Something smells awfully good."

"Thank you." She smiled. "I'm Dawn." As in Harper Dawn. Okay, so she wasn't quick on her feet, but her last name made a good enough first name in this situation. "And I'm your personal chef."

Cade stared at the woman he'd bumped into thirty minutes ago. She was standing in the kitchen doorway looking at him warily, as if she feared he'd bite her head off. That she was his personal chef gave him pause. "Funny, I don't remember hiring a personal chef."

"You didn't. Your mother, Rose, hired me."

On a sigh, Cade rubbed the back of his neck. He didn't doubt the woman. It made damn near perfect sense. His mother was a woman of action and wasn't one to take no for an answer. If she'd asked him about it, he would've told her he didn't need a chef. But honestly, deep down, the thought of having someone else around, especially a cook, meant he didn't have to be totally alone. With his memories. With his grief. With his shattered heart. "That sounds like my mother. She knows I can't cook a lick."

"Not a lick?" she asked.

"I can boil an egg. Period."

"Well, that's a start."

Where were his manners? "I'm Cade," he said, putting out his hand. "Nice to meet you, Dawn."

She hesitated a second, then shook it and smiled. A pair of delicate dimples appeared. Bree had had dimples, too, but with that, the similarities ended. Bree had been a lush redhead, with incredible green eyes and soft porcelain skin. This woman's eyes were intense blue, her skin a creamy tan, as if she'd spent a lot of time outdoors, and her hair shone in the cabin light, a rich chestnut brown.

He shouldn't be comparing the two women, but he found himself comparing women to Bree all the time. And the other women were always coming up short. It wasn't fair of him. He was better than that. Yet he couldn't seem to help it.

"I guess I'll get settled in, then," he said. It was awkward, having a young woman living in the cabin. "Do you live nearby?"

"No. Actually, I live in Barrel Falls, about eighty miles from here."

"That's not far from Juliet County. We're practically neighbors. So then, you'll be staying here, too?"

"Yes, but I promise not to get in your way. I'm...working on a cookbook. So I'll be testing out recipes and logging my results most of the time."

His brows furrowed. "A cookbook, huh?"

"A dream of mine. But don't let me keep you from getting settled. I took one of the downstairs bedrooms, if that's okay. Unless you want it?"

"No, no. I'll be fine upstairs." All four of the bedrooms were master suites, two up and two down, and each one had all the luxuries a person could ask for. He'd never brought Bree to Bright Landing, so at least he had no memories of her here.

Dawn pointed to the kitchen. "I've got a roast chicken keeping warm, and I'm just finishing up on a salad, if you're hungry."

"If it tastes as good as it smells, I'll be right down."

"Okay then." She fidgeted with her apron. "See you in a bit."

He nodded and then climbed the stairs, picking the blue room. It was his favorite, with a killer view of the lake against the backdrop of oak trees and verdant hills. He set his suitcase down and went into the bathroom to wash up. He turned on the faucet and yelped as he splashed the icy-cold water on his face. Then he chuckled, remembering that it took forever to get hot water up to the second floor. He was ten when his folks bought the cabin, and he and his brother, Gage—and Lily, too—would fight over who'd get the downstairs rooms for that very reason. In this case, the cook—or rather, his personal chef—had the honors. But now that he was older, he didn't mind waiting for warm water if it meant waking up to the hillside panorama.

Cade was dressed in a fresh change of clothes within ten minutes. He combed his dark straight hair back, noting that the thick mop was in need of a cut. He hadn't thought he'd have to worry about his attire up at the cabin, but now that Chef Dawn was here, he'd need to take better care of his appearance. He hadn't brought much in the way of clothes, just jeans, T-shirts and a few sweaters. He wasn't planning on being here all that long. Ten days at most. With nothing to do.

"Man," he muttered, glancing at himself in the mirror and seeing a forlorn face staring back at him. "This isn't going to be fun."

He opened his luggage and pulled out a framed photo of Bree and him when they were at their happiest. He had his arm around her, and they were smiling into the camera, love shining in their eyes as they stood on stage right before one of Gage's concerts. They'd been in Austin at the time, and they'd gotten the VIP treatment. Bree had been fascinated and thrilled, but instead of going gaga over his superstar brother, as so many of his dates had, Bree focused all of her attention on Cade, giving him sweet smiles and loving kisses. It was the night he realized how much he loved her.

"This isn't moving on, is it, Bree?" He smiled sadly

and set the photo back in his suitcase, then made his way downstairs.

"Are you a kitchen eater? Or do you prefer the dining room?" Chef Dawn asked as he entered the room. She held a plate in her hand, ready to dish up the food. The kitchen was spacious, and the light oak table was big enough for ten. The dining area was used only for holidays and special occasions.

"Kitchen is fine. Unless I'll be in your way."

"Not at all."

She set his plate on the counter and dished up the food: roasted chicken and fingerling potatoes with a mixture of herbs that made his mouth water. She drizzled a bit of extra virgin olive oil over the entire meal and then pointed to his place at the head of the table and set the dish down. A salad bowl was already on the table, next to a vase of colorful wildflowers. It was a nice touch.

"What would you like to drink?" she asked.

"Let me see what we have." He opened the double-door fridge and found everything neatly in place: drinks to one side, dairy products on the other, drawers full of cold cuts and shelves filled with baking staples. Chef Dawn had some mighty good organizational skills.

He grabbed a bottle of water and took his seat at the end of the table. "Water's good for now." He might need something stronger later.

"Enjoy," she said, removing her apron, folding it and putting it away in a drawer. "I hope you like it."

He glanced at the food. "What's not to like? I can already tell I'm going to enjoy it."

"I wish all my other critics were that easy."

"I guess they wouldn't be called critics, then."

She chuckled, and the bright sound filled the kitchen. "No, I guess not." She gestured toward the back rooms.

"I'll, uh, just be in my room. If you want anything else, please let me know."

"What? You're not eating with me?" he asked, as if that was incomprehensible.

"No, I, uh…no." She bit her lower lip, and Cade's gaze automatically ventured there. She had a pretty mouth, sort of heart-shaped, and right now she was nibbling on her lower lip as if it were made of chocolate candy. He had to admit she was a looker, with a pretty face and those deep ocean-blue eyes. "I usually don't eat with my…client."

He was her *client*? He guessed that was one way of putting it. "You have things to do?"

"When I'm not cooking, I'm contemplating cooking," she said. "Working on my recipes or doing research."

"Ah, got it. But just so you know, I don't mind if we share our meals. You're welcome to join me anytime." There—he didn't think he was being overbearing, but in this day and age, one had to be extra careful.

"Thank you. I'll remember that."

She walked out of the room, leaving him alone in the kitchen. He took a bite of her food. The chicken was really delicious, with a depth of flavor he'd never tasted before. Actually, he couldn't remember ever having a better-tasting chicken dish. He had to hand it to her, she was talented. And for what it was worth, this time his mother's meddling had done some good. She'd hired a great chef.

He nibbled on the food. It was delicious, but he didn't have much of an appetite lately. He'd lost some weight in the past eighteen months. Sometimes he could hardly believe it'd been that long. His life had been all planned out. He had direction and drive and was looking forward to marriage and having a family. But fate had interfered, destroying his dream.

He rose from the table and rinsed off the dishes, putting them into the dishwasher. He wasn't going to turn Chef Dawn into a housekeeper. He could lend a hand at the cabin. Besides, what else did he have to do for the rest of the day, chop wood?

He laughed at the notion, then walked into the massive living room and took note that the woodpile on the hearth was almost depleted. Damn, now that he thought about it, what better way to kill off the restlessness that crept up inside him whenever he was alone than to do hard physical labor? Yeah, he liked the idea.

Cade changed into his hiking boots and went outside, marching around to the back of the cabin, where he found an ax, protective eyewear and a hard hat in the shed. The old chopping block was right where it had always been. "See if I remember how to do this," he muttered, placing a thick log on the block and lifting the ax. One swing later, he was grinning. He loved the strain in his arms, the pull of his muscles as he landed the second blow and split the log. He hadn't lost his touch. Five logs later, with the sun beating down on him, he removed his black T-shirt and sopped up a layer of sweat from his brow. The sun felt good on his shoulders and back, and as he lifted the ax once again, he heard a female voice.

"Oh."

He swiveled around, ax in hand, and faced Dawn. She was wearing a pair of cutoff jean shorts, a blue-plaid shirt and a pair of tan hiking boots. She looked like a modern-day version of Daisy Duke. As a teen, he'd watch reruns of *The Dukes of Hazzard*, just to catch a glimpse of Daisy in her cutoffs.

"Sorry." She gulped and stared at his bare chest.

She was a good six feet away, but he felt the intimacy of the moment down to his toes. The appreciation shining in her eyes wasn't lost on him. He was grieving, but he wasn't totally dead inside. And just for an instant, a spark passed between them. Something unnamed. Something he was better off not defining. Yet it was there, and maybe it was simply a boost to his ego, having a woman gawk at him that way.

Though she probably had no clue what her eyes were revealing.

"Going somewhere?" he asked.

She cleared her throat. "I'm going for a little hike."

It sounded like fun.

"I didn't know you were back here," she continued.

"Yeah, I'm just chopping wood. Need to do something with my time."

"I could find something for you to do," she offered softly.

His brows rose. Surely she didn't mean to sound suggestive, but it had come out that way, and all of a sudden, he was imagining all sorts of things they could do with their time together. He hadn't been with a woman since Bree, eighteen long months ago. He hadn't wanted to go there, but he was here now, and for the first time, he was thinking about sex. With a Daisy Duke lookalike. He put his head down so she couldn't read his thoughts.

"I didn't mean…it's just that there's a lot to do if you like the outdoors."

It was a nice save, and he glanced at her again. "Like taking a hike?"

"Yep, there's some interesting vegetation up there that I'd like to check out. Just wanted to let you know I'll be gone for an hour. So how about dinner at seven tonight?"

"Aren't there leftovers from lunch?"

"There are. Want to have them tomorrow?"

"Sure. It was really good."

"Thank you. I'm trying out a new recipe for tonight. How do you feel about pasta?"

"Who doesn't love pasta?"

She smiled sweetly, glanced at his chest one more time and then turned away, giving him a beautiful view of her long tan legs and perfect behind as she wandered off.

It was something he shouldn't be noticing. But man, he wouldn't be male if he didn't.

Two

Harper had been taking the same hike every day since she'd arrived, because the paths were relatively remote and she didn't run into a lot of people. It was a perfect way to clear her mind without worry of being spotted. Her disguise seemed to be working.

Cade didn't bat an eye in recognition when they'd first met, thank goodness. Lucky for her, he didn't watch much television.

Seeing him just minutes ago chopping wood bare-chested brought thoughts of a rugged lumberjack to mind rather than a big business tycoon. The sight of him holding that ax with his muscles bunching, his dark, straight hair falling onto his forehead, the stubble on his jaw, put her female instincts on high alert. Which, under her dire circumstances, jarred her. She wasn't supposed to be thinking about physical attraction or the way her tummy tightened when Cade wielded that ax. No, she was supposed to be recovering from a scandal that had rattled her entire world, not ogling Lily's sexy-as-sin brother.

The May sun beat down, warming her limbs. As she climbed a rise, she spotted a blanket of wildflowers, their colors waving in the breeze. It was like a pastel patch of heaven. She stooped down and picked the prettiest of them, making another lovely bouquet.

On her way back, as she walked through a cooler area shaded by Texas live oak trees, she found a crop of wild onions along the side of the path. Their pungent scent tickled her nostrils, and she stopped to pick several of them to use in her meal tonight.

When she was done, she gathered up the onions and the wildflowers and resumed her walk, only stopping when she reached a road crossing. It was single-lane traffic on both sides. She waited as one car after another drove by, keeping her head down. For a few minutes there, she'd almost forgotten her predicament. She'd gotten lost in her thoughts, planning her next meal for Cade, but the fear of being discovered reared its ugly head again. Once the cars passed and they were out of sight, she ran across the road quickly then resumed her walk back.

When she returned, Cade was sitting on the porch, wearing a T-shirt—thank goodness—with a book that he didn't seem to be reading in his hand. Oh well, it was a nice afternoon to just be. She would love to join him in that if things were different.

He looked her way as she climbed the steps and rose from his seat. "Hi. What've you got there?"

She stopped long enough to show him. The flowers were self-explanatory. "I found some wild onions. I'll be cooking them up tonight."

"Sounds good. How was your hike?"

"Pretty good. It's an easy path, if you'd like to try it sometime."

"Maybe I will."

"How did the log splitting go?"

"Filled up the woodpile for now."

"I'd like to try it sometime."

"What?" He seemed baffled at her request. "You mean, *chopping wood*?"

"Sure, why not? Doesn't look that hard."

He grinned. "Was that a put-down?"

"Are you being a chauvinist?"

"Are you one of those women that gets offended easily? If you are, I'm going to have to zip my darn lips a lot around you." There was a teasing gleam in his eyes.

"No, I'm not, but I like being outdoors. I like nature and doing things to challenge myself."

He nodded. "Fair enough."

"I don't expect you to stand up every time I enter the room, either," she said. "But don't get me wrong, it's a nice gesture."

"Southern manners, Dawn. That's all. I've been doing it since I was a boy."

"Okay, as long as you don't—"

But it was too late—he'd already reached the door and pulled it open.

"Uh, open the door for me."

"Sorry," he said. "Old habits and all."

She laughed. She had a feeling this was one battle she was going to lose.

"What's funny?"

"Nothing, really. It's just that the last guy I was with wouldn't know a Southern manner if it hit him upside the head." Unless the cameras were on.

"Well, then. I take it he wasn't a Texan."

"No, he was from back East, and he's history now."

Why she found the need to make that point, she wasn't entirely sure. Maybe it had something to do with the way Cade jangled her nerves whenever he was near.

"Can't say as I blame you."

"You'd be the only one who wouldn't," she muttered.

"What'd you say?" he asked.

"Oh, nothing. Nothing at all."

She didn't want to ruin the day by thinking of Dale. He *was* history. If she'd made one right move lately, it was to refuse his marriage proposal. She had no second thoughts on that one. At least she could feel good about not caving in to the pressure. She'd listened to her heart and her brain. Both told her he was a no-go.

In the kitchen, she took a good long minute to wash her hands. Cade followed her in holding a bottle of red wine. The Tremaines had an extensive wine closet just off the kitchen.

"Thought wine would be good with pasta," Case said, grabbing two wineglasses from an overhead cabinet and opening the bottle. "Would you like to join me?"

She was not a big drinker, but a little wine with her meal sounded good. "I'd love to, later with the meal."

"Mind if I do?"

Heavens, it was his cabin, his wine and his family's generosity in letting her stay here. "Go right ahead."

While he poured himself a glass, she moved around the kitchen, gathering up the ingredients she needed for her dish. "Do you like mushrooms?"

"I do. Are they wild, too?"

"I haven't found any in my hikes, so I'm not sure they grow up here."

"What are you making?"

"It's something a bit different—crunchy pasta with a

mushroom and herb sauce. Topped with cheese. I've been working on the recipe, and I'm hoping it's refined enough for my cookbook."

Cade sipped wine and took a seat facing her. "Do you have a publisher for your cookbook yet?"

"Not yet, no." She shrugged. "These days if you're not renowned in the business, you have to have a theme, or gimmick, if you want to call it that, to get any feedback at all. Half of my recipes are a little bit outside the mainstream, like crunchy pasta, for instance, so I have that going for me. And I try to keep them as healthy as possible. I haven't come up with a title yet, but it has to hit the mark exactly."

Cade lifted his glass, contemplating. "How about *Daring, Dining and Dawn*?"

"That's pretty good just off the top of your head." Only her first name wasn't Dawn, and he'd just reminded her that she was deliberately deceiving him.

Her only justification was that she was doing this for his sake. According to his sister, he needed this time to relax and be calm. And right now he'd planted himself at the kitchen table, sipping wine, keeping his eyes trained on her.

It made her jittery.

Because she had this undefined attraction to him. And as much as she tried to talk herself out of it—because it was the last thing she needed—she had no real control of those sparks shooting off inside her.

"Mind if I watch?" he asked.

Yes. She minded. She had to keep focused on her dish and jot down notes for her cookbook, not have Cade Tremaine sitting so close, reminding her how he looked stripped down to his jeans. He was Lily's brother, for heaven's sake, and a guy in need of some peace. And from what she gathered, he was still grieving his fiancée's death.

"No, I don't mind at all." She swallowed, hating that the lie flowed so easily from her lips.

"Thanks."

But she didn't dwell on it; she went right into boiling water for the pasta in a big pot. Next, she turned her attention to the mushrooms, using both portobello and shiitake. She cut them into small, even pieces, getting them ready for the sauce. Once the water boiled, she added spaghetti to the pot. She had the computer set up on the kitchen table, and she logged on, making her notes. She dared a glance at Cade, who sat quietly, sipping cabernet, his eyes trained on her.

Her nerves a bit rattled, she finished her notes and closed down the computer. "What book are you reading?" she asked to break the silence.

"The latest thriller. I'm not an avid reader, but it was on the bestseller list, so I figured it might be good. It's called *Wall of Darkness*. Heard of it?"

"No, I'm not a thriller reader. So, you don't read much?"

"No, usually can't find the time. I'm trying to focus on relaxing, and people say reading is a good way to escape. Unfortunately, relaxing doesn't come easy to me. And I can't seem to get into this book."

"Thus, the wood chopping?"

He smiled. "I'll be building a fire tonight."

"Really? It isn't that cold out, but it is peaceful to watch the flames."

"I remember as a kid, coming here in the dead of winter and sitting by the fire, drinking hot cocoa and playing games with my family. My dad was alive then."

"Was he a gamer?"

"He was. My father loved competition, and he loved to win."

"Most people do. Love to win, that is."

"Do you?"

"Of course. I'm pretty good at cards. Poker, gin rummy, Uno, Go Fish. You name it and I play it."

"Go Fish?"

"I'm a child at heart."

He chuckled and sipped his wine again.

She turned away to stir the spaghetti, and when it was done, she lifted the colander, draining the liquid and then dumping the contents onto a round platter. "There, that just has to cool a bit."

She got out a cast-iron skillet next and put in a few teaspoons of olive oil, setting the burner on low heat.

Cade was quiet. He wasn't much for small talk, and she felt the need to carry on a conversation to keep the awkwardness at bay. "I hope you don't mind me trying out this recipe on you. It's probably like nothing you've ever had before."

He took a second to answer, his expression thoughtful. "If my mother hired you, you must be very good at what you do. So, don't worry about experimenting with me. I'm sort of your captive audience."

She turned to him. "But still, if you have favorites or any kind of cravings…"

Something flashed in Cade's eyes for a split second. "I'll be sure to let you know if I have any cravings," he said, expressionless but for the tiniest crook of his lips. Or was she imagining it?

"Well, thank you. I'm open to suggestions. *Food* suggestions," she clarified.

"Ah, got it," he said casually, as if he was teasing her. But that couldn't be. From what Lily had told her in the past, Cade had been devastated when his fiancée passed and had withdrawn within himself. He held everything inside until he'd nearly made himself sick. So any notion that he was flirting wasn't really plausible.

Which was a darn good thing.

She finished the dish by sliding the cooled pasta into the skillet and cooking it through until the entire batch was browned lightly on both sides, making it crispy. Then she added the tomato sauce, onions and mushrooms, topping it off with fresh basil and dabs of ricotta cheese. "Are you ready?" she asked Cade as she lifted the skillet from the stove.

"Looks delicious," he said. "You are joining me for this, right?"

"Only if I'm not intruding."

"Food tastes better when shared," he said, his brows gathering. "I read that somewhere."

A little laugh escaped her. "I think that's my line, Cade."

She set the steaming skillet down on the table and then brought over two plates and utensils, quickly setting the table. "Oh, I almost forgot." She grabbed a vase filled with the new batch of wildflowers she'd picked today and positioned it in the center. After a quick assessment of the table setting, she sat down.

The May sun lowered on the horizon, casting a pretty golden glow in the room. It was soothing, and she always loved this time of day.

"My stomach's grumbling," Cade said. "Either I'm real hungry or your food is appetizing as hell."

"Or both. Can I serve you up a portion?" She put out her hand for his plate.

"Sure," he said, setting it in her hand.

She gave him a very generous helping. "I'm not sure if I'm that hungry," he said.

"I have faith in you."

"Do you now?"

"Yes, you look like a man who can really pack it in." She smiled and took her seat, placing a napkin on her lap. She forked into the dish and took a bite, then immediately critiqued her work. "It could use more seasoning," she said. "I'll have to add that to my notes."

Cade had a mouthful of food, and after he finished chewing, he said, "Tastes fine to me."

"It's passable, but not perfect."

"Are you a perfectionist?" he asked.

"When it comes to meal preparation, I am."

"So, you're like an artist. You are your own harshest critic."

"I suppose. I never thought of it that way. I think everyone is a perfectionist about something, don't you? I mean, if you're into fashion, you're probably not satisfied until your outfit totally rocks. If you're a golfer, you aim for that hole in one. So, what is it that you want perfection in, Cade? Your business?"

"Hardly. My business is about the bottom line, but I don't need perfection in that. Only good stats while delivering good product. There are hits and misses in ranching and oil but as long as the Tremaine name stands for honesty and integrity, I'm happy." He lingered on the question a minute. "I guess I found perfection in my fiancée. Yeah," he said, nodding his head. "Bree was perfect, and I think that's all I needed. And wanted."

"I'm sorry you lost her."

He snapped his eyes to hers. "How did you know?"

Oh no. She'd been caught. She'd let her guard down, and now she had to think fast. "Oh, uh…your mother mentioned it. It was part of the interview. She told me you weren't eating well and that I should remedy that. I asked her why and she told me."

Oh boy, what a whopper of a lie. But she'd let it slip and now she had to pay the price. She hoped Rose Tremaine would forgive her, because Harper really wasn't trying to sabotage her relationship with her son.

"My mother told you I wasn't eating well because of Bree? What else did she tell you?"

"Only that. Well, she did mention something about your…your—" She briefly squeezed her eyes shut. Why on earth did she keep on talking?

"My what?"

His gaze swooped down on her like a predator's. She felt trapped and had to answer now. "Your blood pressure," she squeaked.

A tic worked in his jaw, and he gave his head a shake. "That's unbelievable. I'm thirty-three years old and my mother still thinks I'm a kid. The only reason I came up to the cabin was to get her off my back. If I stayed home, she would've been hovering like a damn helicopter."

She shrugged. "That's what mothers do, I guess. Out of love."

"Yeah, I know." He gave her a look, his dark eyes assessing her, as if sizing her up. It was reminiscent of her latest reality show fiasco, being judged unfairly by Team Dale, his loyal fans.

"I'm really sorry," she said, meaning it from the bottom of her heart. Cade had been robbed of the kind of love she'd been looking for. The kind her mom and dad had. The kind that makes you do stupid things, makes you smile all day long, makes your heart sing, because you have a secret nobody else has.

Cade's eyes softened. "You know what? You're innocent in all this," he said. "I shouldn't take it out on you because things didn't work out for me the way they should have."

Oh man. She was so not innocent. She'd told him lie after lie, and it wasn't like her. She hated this game she was playing, but it was too late to back out now.

"Don't worry about it. So, about that wood you chopped today. Still planning on having a fire tonight?"

"I…uh, yeah. I'll build a fire."

He seemed a little baffled by her change of subject.

"While you do that, I'll just clean up in here. Are you finished? Want some more?"

"It was great, but no, thanks. I'm full."

"Too full for a cup of coffee?"

"Actually, that sounds good."

"Okay, well, you go build the fire. Coffee should be ready in a few minutes."

He looked around the kitchen. "Need some help in here first?"

"Nope, I've got this."

"Okay, thanks."

He walked out of the room, and Harper hugged herself around the middle as she shivered. The air was growing colder outside, but that wasn't it. She'd just dodged a bullet, lying through her teeth to Cade. "You have to be more careful, Harper," she muttered. "Or you're gonna blow it for him." The best thing she could do was to get out of Cade's way and let him deal with his issues himself.

The living room felt more like a rustic cabin than any other place in this house. It was a large area, with polished wood flooring and a smooth stone fireplace that reached a steep ceiling. Wood beams crisscrossed overhead, and three good-size sofas formed a horseshoe facing the fireplace. Cade was just finishing up at the hearth, and she watched from behind as he started the fire. "You're good at that."

"I was a Boy Scout," he said, using a poker to arrange the wood as a slow flame began to burn.

"And I was a Girl Scout back in the day, which means I know how to make s'mores."

"Oh yeah? Do you use fancy ingredients to step it up?"

"There's no improving on s'mores. They're just right the way they are."

He rose, dusting off his jeans, and faced her. "I agree."

"Here's your coffee," she said, handing him a mug. "Do you take cream or sugar?"

"Just black is fine. Have a seat," he said, waiting like a gentleman for her to sit down.

"Oh, um. I wasn't going to impose. I have work to do. I should probably get to it."

"You're not imposing. Have a seat and enjoy the fire, won't you? At least while you're drinking your coffee." He pointed to the hearth. "It's gonna be a beauty."

She got the feeling Cade didn't like being alone. Either that or he was just being polite. But her instincts told her he was lonely. Which pretty much sealed the deal, because he looked like he really wanted the company.

"Okay, sure. Thanks."

She took a seat facing the fireplace, and he sat down adjacent to her on another sofa. "This is a nice room. It's big, but it's sorta cozy, too."

He sipped his coffee and faced the fire. "We had some good times in this room."

"That's great. Big families are nice. I'm an only child."

"Oh yeah? Where are you from?"

"My folks are Floridians. I grew up in Clearwater."

The sun had set now, and firelight illuminated the room. The fire crackled and sparked. It was peaceful, sitting here, watching the flames begin to bounce, sipping coffee. Talking to Cade.

"My baby sis, Lily, used to sit on the hearth, fascinated by the fire. We were always telling her to back up a bit, she was too close. Until one day, a spark flew onto her sweater and singed it pretty dang bad. She cried her little eyes out."

"Oh my gosh, that's awful."

"It was scary. But Lily always did have an adventurous spirit."

She couldn't sit here and pretend not to know Lily. She wasn't that good of a liar. And she felt guilty deceiving Cade. She guzzled her coffee down in three big gulps and rose from the sofa. "Looks like I'm finished."

He stood up, too. "Already?" Cade gazed into his nearly full coffee cup. "I'm just getting started."

"I really should get to my work. There's more coffee in the kitchen, if you'd like."

"I'm fine."

"Okay, then I'll shut the coffee maker off. Good night, Cade."

"Night," he said, eyeing her with that dark, sexy gaze. "Sleep well."

"Uh-huh." She scampered out of the room, trying not to raise Cade's suspicions.

Lily had made it sound so simple, but being Cade Tremaine's personal chef was harder than she thought it would be.

And that was no lie.

It was almost nine when Harper's phone rang. She'd gotten into her pajamas and was on the bed with her laptop, inputting notes. She looked at the screen, and seeing Lily's image pop up, answered quickly. "Hello," she whispered.

"Hi. Why are you whispering? Are you with Cade?" she whispered back.

"I'm in my room, and he's in the living room, as far as I know. He's got a fire going in the fireplace."

"Okay," she said in her normal voice. "He shouldn't be able to hear you."

"I know that, but just in case. I'm a little spooked by all of this, Lil. I mean I've told more lies in one day than I've ever told in my entire life."

"Like what?"

"Like what? You have to ask? I'm pretending I don't know you. And that's hard, because he's been talking about you. How you'd all come up to the cabin and play games. He even told me about you singeing your sweater by the fire when you were a kid and how you cried your eyes out."

"He told you that? I'll never forget it. I was scared to go anywhere near that fireplace after that."

"My point is, I made up a lie about your mother hiring me, and it's just gotten worse from there. I hate myself for lying to him."

"It's for his own good. Does he seem relaxed though? Is he eating better?"

"Yes, he's eating my food. But I'm not so sure he's relaxing. He chopped wood around back today, and by the way, you didn't tell me how—" She bit her tongue. She couldn't confess to Lily that she thought he was sexy, especially bare-chested, swinging the ax, with that thick dark hair falling onto his forehead.

"How what?"

"How, uh, he seems to like having company. Every time I make an excuse to leave the room, he seems disappointed. Like he needs me there as a distraction or something."

"Yeah, I know. I think he's afraid to be alone with his

thoughts. That's why he works himself so damn hard. And it's also important that you stay there. For you and for him."

"Why for me? What have you heard?" It'd been almost a week since that fateful episode of *One Last Date* had aired featuring her rejection of Dale.

"Are you sure you want to know?"

No. Yes. She needed to know where she stood in the world. "Lay it on me. I can take it."

"Well, the tabloids are saying you went into hiding, and they're calling on fans to keep an eye out for you. I'm afraid they're calling it 'the Harper Hunt' on social media."

She took a deep breath and sighed. Why couldn't this be over? Didn't people have better things to do with their lives than to go on a manhunt—or rather a womanhunt? "So, they haven't let it go yet."

"No, sorry. But they will in time. I'm sure of it."

"I just want my old life back, Lil. You know?" She heard defeat in her voice.

"Hey, you'll get it back, Harper. I know it's just going to take a bit more time. At least you're at peace at the cabin."

"I don't know about that. I'm lying to your brother, seems like every minute of the day. He took me by surprise this morning, and I blurted out my name was Dawn. I know, I'm a fast thinker, but that's the first thing that came to mind."

"Dawn? Well, at least that wasn't a total lie."

"I thought this would be easier, Lily. Honestly, I hate lying."

"It's for a good cause, and to save your own hide. So think of it as a necessary evil."

"I'll try. By the way, I have something to confess." She paused, nibbling on her lip for a second. "I let it slip that I knew about the death of Cade's fiancée and his blood pressure troubles. Let me just say, Cade's furious with your mother. I had to tell him it came up in my interview with her. You may want to warn her and tell her I'm really sorry."

"Will do. Mom will be fine with it. She appreciates you staying there, cooking for Cade. And don't beat yourself up about it, either. He won't stay mad at her for long."

"I hope not."

"Just do your job and try to stay away from Cade. It shouldn't be that hard. It's a big house. Oh, and *Dawn*... thanks." Lily giggled.

"You brat."

"Good night. Sleep well."

She hung up the phone and went back to work on her computer.

She had developed a new recipe for breakfast she wanted to try out. She didn't even know if Cade was a breakfast eater, or what time he got up in the morning. She would soon find out.

Harper had been sleeping unusually well considering she was in a strange bed in a very strange situation. Hiding out from the world took its toll. Maybe it was mental exhaustion, but for the past three nights, she'd fallen asleep and stayed asleep all night long. Feeling safe. Feeling free.

Now she popped her eyes open and stretched her arms above her head. A long sigh escaped her mouth as she enjoyed the first moments of wakefulness. It always took her a second to find her bearings and remember where she was and why she was here.

She slid a glance at the digital clock on the bedside table. "Oh no." She sat up immediately. Eight o'clock! "Oh no, no, no."

The scent of coffee brewing hit all of her alarms. Cade was up already, apparently making his own coffee.

She ran to the bathroom, scrubbed her face clean, tossed

on her bathrobe, then dashed out of the bedroom. "I'm sorry, I'm sorry," she said as she entered the kitchen. "I overslept."

Cade stood by the coffee maker, sipping coffee casually, like he didn't have a care in the world. His facial scruff was darker today, and his hair unkempt, yet no one would call it bedhead. He must've won Best Hair in high school, because even unruly, it looked fashionable…and sexy. Oh boy, she had to stop thinking of her dear friend's brother in those terms. It was a big no-no in the unwritten Book of Best Friends.

"Nothing to be sorry about, Dawn. I like to get up early." He flashed her a good long look that made her stomach ripple. "You didn't have to rush out of bed."

She could feel the heat rising up her throat. She'd forgotten her appearance. While he looked hot in a clean white T-shirt hugging his biceps, she was in a ratty robe and frumpy pajamas she'd purchased in town on her first day here.

"I know I must look a mess. I usually don't oversleep like this. Hang on and I'll fix your breakfast."

"First off, you don't look a mess."

She rolled her eyes dramatically, which put a smile on his face. "Okay, but you're not a hot mess," he amended.

No, he was the hot one. "I see the distinction."

He chuckled. "Actually, I'm not hungry right now. Coffee's fine. Well, at least I tried."

She poured herself a cup and sipped. "Not bad," she said. It really wasn't awful. So, he could make coffee and boil an egg.

He returned her nod, his dark lashes framing his eyes beautifully. "Coming from you, I'll take that as a compliment."

A bit of sunshine poured into the window, warming up

the room. "I apologize for oversleeping, I should've asked you yesterday what time you like to eat breakfast." Her personal chef skills were sorely lacking.

"I can eat, or I don't have to eat," he said, taking another sip of coffee.

She warmed her hands around her cup. "If you don't mind waiting, I'll go get dressed and make you something to eat. It's a quick recipe. Shouldn't take too long. Is there anything you don't like?"

He didn't hesitate. "Liver, pig's feet, octopus."

She smiled. "I can assure you breakfast doesn't include any of those things."

"Good to know."

"Enjoy your coffee, Cade. I'll have something edible for you in half an hour."

"Sounds good."

She turned to the oven, adjusting the digital dials. "I'll just preheat the oven and be back in a jiff."

She walked out of the room, feeling like an idiot. She'd never been anyone's personal chef before. After culinary school she'd catered for a time, and then she got the head chef job at Perfect and Pure in Barrel Falls.

Ten minutes later, after she'd showered and dressed, she walked back into the kitchen feeling almost regal in jeans and a cocoa-brown tank top, her hair combed and almost dry.

"That was quick," Cade said, looking up from the kitchen table and giving her a once-over. He'd been reading something on his phone, and the minute she walked in, he shut it down. "You look real nice."

"Thanks."

"What's for breakfast?"

"It's a surprise. A healthy take on a very delicious dish. Are you game?"

"Do I have a choice?"

"Of course you do."

"I'm kidding," he said, though he wasn't smiling. He rarely did.

"This recipe is going into my cookbook. So I want your honest take on it."

"I can do that. Don't let me interrupt what you were doing."

"I won't." Yet he didn't turn his phone back on. Instead, he watched her move around the kitchen, giving her his full attention. She tried not to let it bother her, tried to go about her business.

She sprayed and buttered a casserole dish. Then she measured out bread crumbs and flattened them into the bottom of the dish. She set it in the oven and let that cook while she diced up onions, broccoli and spinach and added in a half cup of bacon pieces. While that was sautéing, she separated two eggs, putting the whites into a bowl. Next, she added two more eggs and beat them until they were blended.

She looked up and met Cade's eyes. They were filled with questions, and she felt like she had to break the silence.

"Do you have any plans today?" she asked as she pulled the casserole dish out of the oven.

"I thought I'd take a hike."

"Good idea. I enjoy hiking. You can get adventurous out there." She dumped the mixture into the casserole dish and then added the eggs and topped it off with cheese. "I'll be taking a hike later this morning, too," she said, putting the casserole back in the oven on high heat. Then she turned and went to get something from the fridge.

"Oh yeah? Want some company?"

Her eyes went wide. It was a good thing her back was

to him. She'd just stepped in it. She was supposed to steer clear of him, but she unintentionally sounded like she was hinting that they should go together. "Don't you want to explore alone?"

She saw him shrug out of the corner of her eyes. "Do you?"

He'd tossed it right back into her lap, and she couldn't very well refuse him now. She couldn't use work as an excuse. She'd already admitted she was going on a hike. She reminded herself she was actually here by his family's good graces and it was saving her hide. She'd have to be careful around him and keep her mouth shut. "I suppose we can go together," she said, heading back to the stove.

"I'll try to keep up," he said, his eyes twinkling.

She held back a smile. He was teasing her and she liked it—a very bad sign.

She put the bowls in the sink and began cleaning the kitchen. When the oven timer dinged, she put on her oven mitts and pulled the casserole out.

"Breakfast is ready." She laid the dish on a trivet in the center of the table.

"Wow, that looks impressive," he said. "Is that a quiche?"

"Sort of. It's my interpretation of a healthy quiche, with lots of veggies. But the key is, the bread-crumb layer at the bottom replaces a ton of carbs we would've had with a butter crust. There's some bacon and low-fat cheese in there, so it's not a total loss."

"Well, it looks amazing."

She cut into the dish, placing a large piece on Cade's plate. "Here you go." She sliced herself a smaller piece and was about to exit the room.

"Where are you going?" Cade asked.

She pointed to the door. "I was just going to, uh—"

"Dawn, sit down. Please. I thought we established that food tastes better when shared."

"I'm working for you, Cade. And, well, I bet you don't share your meals with your housekeeper at the Tremaine house."

"Irene has been making our meals since I was a kid. She practically raised all of us, and she always took a seat at our table. True story."

"Really?"

"She's like part of our family."

"But surely, I'm not—"

"My mother hired you, not me. So technically you don't work for me."

"Oh, is that how it works?" She put her hands on her hips. Cade was trying so darn hard to keep her near. She thought she understood why: he hated to be alone with his grief.

"Yeah, that's how it works. If we're going to be here together, we might as well agree to a casual friendship."

"A casual friendship?"

"Why not?"

Well, he'd stumped her there. "But we don't really know each other very well."

"And we can keep it that way if you want. Lord knows I don't like talking about myself, but I don't want you to feel you have to leave the room every time I enter it."

"I don't do that," she said without much conviction.

"Don't you?"

Her shoulders slumped. "Okay, maybe I do. I just want to give you space." What could she say? She'd never been a personal chef before, and she didn't know the rules. But one thing she did know—she didn't want to blow this.

"How about, if either of us need space, we tell each other."

"I can do that."

"Good, then it's settled," he said.

"Okay, Cade." She sat down at the table with her food. "Let's eat while it's hot. Remember, I want your honest opinion."

"That's all I know how to give."

She knew that about him already. But her? She'd been lying to him pretty much since the moment they met.

Three

"You gave me a ten out of ten, Cade. You didn't have one thing negative to say about the casserole," Harper said as she walked beside him along the path leading away from the cabin.

"I ate two helpings. That should tell you something."

"So, you think it deserves to be in my book?"

"Your unnamed cookbook? Yeah, you should put it in there. What's it called anyway? Quiche Dawn?"

She smiled. "I wouldn't name it after myself. My ego isn't that big, Cade," she said, walking past him to master an incline.

He wasn't far behind. And every so often, when she turned unexpectedly, she'd catch him checking out her legs. He'd avert his gaze immediately, but she knew. Now, *that* was good for her ego, and it proved that maybe he was coming out of his grief a little bit.

When Cade had suggested they have lunch on the hike,

she'd loaded his backpack with a few items, and now he looked like a bona fide hiker with the pack on his back. Both wore sunglasses and hats, which served her well, adding to her disguise.

As she reached a plateau at the top of the incline overlooking a field, she waited for Cade. "You have to see this," she said.

Cade was beside her instantly, their shoulders nearly touching as they gazed out upon an array of brilliant pastel wildflowers. It stretched on for acres, it seemed, and it was Harper's favorite part of her hike.

"Isn't it beautiful?" she asked Cade.

"It is. It's called *Manta de Flores Silvestres*, blanket of wildflowers."

She turned to face him. "You know about it?"

He nodded. "I've been here once, a long time ago when I was a boy. I guess I'd forgotten about it. But it's something you don't see every day."

"It's breathtaking. Aside from the bluebonnets, which are in abundance, there's so many other varieties out there. I wish I had my camera. And I keep forgetting my phone."

"Well, hold on. I've got mine." He took his backpack off and grabbed his phone. "Smile."

"Oh no. I don't want to be in the picture. I'll ruin it." She backed up, getting out of camera range quickly, and stumbled on a rock behind her. She lost her footing and began falling backward.

He grabbed her immediately, pulling her up, and the momentum from his strength landed her right smack up against his chest. His arms wrapped around her, securing her body.

"Whoa, there," Cade whispered. "Are you okay?"

His lips brushed her forehead, and her heart raced much faster than when she was falling. He was hard all over, his chest a piece of granite, and being held in his strong arms made her feel amazingly safe. She hadn't felt this safe since, well, before she became a star of *One Last Date*. "I—I think so."

Yet she clung to him, closing her eyes, relishing the security of being in his arms. He held on to her without moving, without trying to back away. They were locked in place and time, and neither of them seemed to want to move.

"Dawn," he whispered, his voice tight.

She was well aware that she was plastered up against his body, chest to chest, hips to hips, thighs to thighs. "Hold me just a little longer, Cade."

He tightened his grip on her, and she relaxed against him. She didn't want to think about the ramifications of this little slipup. She didn't want to have to explain what she was doing. She only wanted to feel sheltered and secure, and Cade was providing that.

It was beautiful up here, the air fresh, the peaceful solitude of the moment calming her. But then, things began to change. She felt the pounding of Cade's heart, the tightening of his body. The calm that she felt disappeared, and suddenly her body reacted in kind, heat swarming her, sensations of desire gripping her. She didn't mean to do this to Cade, to herself, but now that it was happening, she couldn't find the means to stop it.

And so, when Cade put a finger under her chin and she lifted her eyes to his, she found hunger and want reflected back at her. "Cade," she whispered.

"I'm gonna kiss you, Dawn. Fair warning."

And when she didn't protest, didn't back away, he tenderly cupped the sides of her face and brought his mouth down on hers. It was a beautiful, soul-searching kiss, his lips firm yet gentle. A deep moan rose from her throat.

Her body tingled, and everything female about her stood at attention. Cade kissed her and kissed her, and in the kiss she felt him casting aside those months of grief and solitude while she was forgetting about her own demons, at least for the moment.

"This is crazy," she said softly between kisses. "We barely know each other."

Cade didn't disagree or try to explain their actions. "I know," he whispered.

And then they heard voices; a group of hikers were coming up the path. Both of them backed off at the same time, and they stared at each other. There was regret in Cade's eyes, in his expression, but silly her, she couldn't figure out if it was because he was sorry the kiss had happened or he was regretting the interruption.

Either way, Harper wouldn't want to change a thing. She'd needed the comfort Cade had given her, and she'd needed his kisses, too.

"Hey, folks," one of the male hikers said, coming up the incline. "Is this the right place? Is this *Manta de Flores Silvestres*?"

"This is the place," Cade answered.

"Thanks," the man said, waving on his group. "It's up here, guys."

Cade picked up his backpack and took Harper's hand. "Let's go."

"Hey, don't let us chase you away," the hiker said.

"It's okay, we're done here," Cade answered.

He led her away from the wildflowers and then stopped when they reached a tall Ashe juniper tree, the thick grass underneath lush and green. "Let's sit."

She didn't argue. She had no idea what was going on in his head.

"Okay."

Both of them sat down on the grass. He removed his backpack and took out a small, thin cloth to serve as a tablecloth. She helped by taking out the sandwiches she'd prepared: turkey and bacon on Italian bread with an aioli dressing, accompanied by homemade potato chips. There was bottled water in the pack, and she handed him one. "Are you hungry?" she asked.

He shook his head and unscrewed the cap, looking away from her. Then he finally asked, "What was that about back there?" Then as if he realized it was a bit presumptive to put all the blame on her, he added, "I didn't see any of that coming, did you?"

"No." Although she was extremely attracted to him. "I didn't see it coming, either. But just know, I've had a rough few months lately. I don't like talking about it, but my last breakup was bad and I was deeply hurt." She shrugged. "I guess I needed some comfort, and having you hold me made me feel safe for the first time in a long time. But I didn't mean to start—"

"You're not to blame, Dawn. I didn't mean to imply that. It just came out of left field. I haven't so much as touched a woman, much less kissed one, since Bree died. I guess I needed the comfort, too."

But there'd been desire, too. She'd felt it. It was hard not to notice his body tightening, hardening, reacting to hers. If those hikers hadn't interrupted, who knew where it might have led. Yet if they both refused to acknowledge it, then maybe they could go on as intended. Pretending that they didn't have a physical attraction to each other.

Only now, Harper knew for certain that Cade wasn't going to be an easy man to ignore. He was terribly appealing and boy, did he know how to kiss.

* * *

If a way to a man's heart was through his stomach, then Cade was in trouble, because Dawn's meals were delicious, and his waning appetite was gradually coming back. Maybe his mother had been onto something when she'd hired Dawn to cook for him. But that was all Dawn was to him, his chef. Period.

He finished his sandwich, both of them eating quietly, deep in their own thoughts. It was now weird between them after that prolonged embrace and the kisses that shocked his system and stirred his body. Once he'd started kissing her, he couldn't seem to stop. What had started out as innocent had changed into something more serious, a hunger that he didn't know existed within him. A light had turned on, and as long as he could shut it off, all would work out. But could he do that? Could he forget about the way her body felt pressed to his, the soft, exciting crush of her breasts to his chest, the sweet smell of her hair, the delicious taste of her lips? Those few minutes had been heaven, an awakening that went beyond his Daisy Duke fantasy.

Both of them had been hurt, injured in a way that made them wary and cautious, and it wouldn't be fair of him to pursue her. It wouldn't lead anywhere, and he didn't want to add to her obvious pain. He surely didn't want to add to his.

He balled up the foil his sandwich had been in and looked at Dawn. She had barely touched her sandwich. "Do you want to finish the hike?" he asked. "Or go back?"

Her eyes downcast, she gathered up the remnants of lunch and quietly said, "Whatever you want to do is fine with me."

He held back the urge to sigh at her indifference. "I'm up for finishing our hike. Are you?"

Finally, she looked at him. "Yes, I'd like that."

"Okay, then." He helped her repack his backpack, and they moved on. But there was no more small talk, no more easy teasing between them. For Cade, it was life as he knew it. He should be glad of it, going back to his sullen ways. Only, he wasn't. For a few minutes back there, he'd felt more alive than he had in eighteen long months.

An hour later, they were back at the cabin. "Thanks, that was a good hike," he told Dawn. "We must've gone at least four miles."

"Yeah, it really was," she said as he opened the door for her. This time she didn't berate him or give him an eye roll. No, she simply walked through the opened door and headed for her room.

"Dawn? Are you okay?"

She turned to him. "I'm fine. Just have some work to catch up on."

"All right. I guess I'll see you at dinner later."

"Yes, you will. How do you feel about fish?"

"I love all kinds."

She nodded. "Good to know." She turned and disappeared into her room.

Cade ran a hand down his face. He wasn't looking forward to being alone the rest of the afternoon. What he really wanted was company, preferably Dawn's company. He felt lighter when she was around, less burdened. And he hoped he didn't blow it with her. He'd offered her casual friendship and wondered if they could still attain that.

He climbed the stairs slowly and went into his bedroom. Taking out his cell, he called his mother, but it went straight to voice mail. "Hi, Mom. Just checking in on you. Wondering about the progress of the Able Brothers merger. Call me when you have a minute."

Next, he called his sister, Lily. Funny, but that call also went to voice mail. He left a short message on her phone, too. Gage was impossible to get a hold of, and his best friend, Rory, was out of the country right now.

After showering and getting dressed, he walked over to the window to take in the view, and his eyes drifted downward to the yard below. "Holy crap!"

What was that woman doing? He raced out of his room, taking the stairs quickly, and dashed out the back double doors, reaching Dawn before she took her first swing of the ax. "Hang on a second," he called to her.

The ax firmly in her grip, she lowered her shoulders.

"What are you doing?"

"Isn't it obvious? I'm chopping wood."

"Not like that you're not."

"Why not? Don't you think I can do it?"

"I thought you had work to do."

"I do. I did. I couldn't concentrate."

He cursed under his breath. "It's because of what happened before, between us, right?"

She averted her pretty blue eyes, gazing out on the lake. "I don't know. Maybe."

"Do you want me to apologize?"

"No. That's not necessary." She looked him straight in the eyes. "I'm just as much to blame." Judging from her expression, she really believed that.

"You were antsy so you came out here to chop wood?"

"I wasn't antsy, for heaven's sake."

"Restless? Bothered?"

She did her adorable eye roll, and he tried his hardest to keep a straight face. Otherwise she'd be swinging that ax at him. "Cade, don't you have something to do *inside the house*?"

"I do have something to do, right here. To keep you from injuring yourself."

"I'm perfectly capable of—"

"Dawn, you're not wearing eye protection. That's your first mistake. A splinter can fly up and take your eye out just as easily as I'm standing here."

He walked over to the shed and grabbed a pair of safety glasses. "Here, put these on."

She took them grudgingly. "Okay, I would've remembered that on my own."

"Before or after you took your first swing?"

"Am I getting a lecture?"

"Do you want to keep all your limbs? Because you're standing all wrong. One miss and there goes your leg." He touched his hand to her leg, just above her knee to make his point, but the contact had him momentarily speechless. Soft skin, firm thighs. From that single touch, his body tensed up, and he was reminded of how good her kisses were, how good she'd felt pressed up against him.

He cleared his throat and backed up a step. "Are you sure you want to do this?"

"I am the one holding the ax, remember?"

Cade shook his head. "Okay, fine." He took hold of her shoulders and positioned her, making sure all body parts were out of harm's way when she brought the ax down. "Okay, now, stay focused. Keep your eye on the center of the log—that's where you want to hit. And you have to keep the head of the ax straight to make the cut worthwhile. Ready?"

She nodded. He stood directly behind her, holding the handle along with her. "I'll help you raise it. All you have to do is come down straight."

She nodded. "Okay."

He had one hand on her shoulder, holding her taut, while his other hand helped guide the ax up. "Ready, now."

The ax came down in the center of the wood, only splitting the log partway.

She turned to him, her face inches from his, and their eyes met. He breathed in her scent, something akin to sweet vanilla. He swallowed, feeling the full force of her gaze. "How was that?" she asked. "It didn't go all the way through."

Something bubbled up inside him. Her raw determination mingled with her nearness rattled his nerves. She wasn't a wilting violet, that was for sure. She was a woman who enjoyed the outdoors, someone who liked a good challenge. She was also extremely appealing in this setting. And he was beginning to like her a bit too much. Which wasn't a good thing.

"That was a good try," he told her, helping her yank the ax from the wood. "You needed a little more power to finish the job. Now, just do it again. You don't have far to go and you'll finish the log off."

"By myself?" she asked.

"Unless you want my help?" He pretty much knew the answer to that.

"No, no. I can do this."

This time, Cade stood back and let her take the swing on her own.

She followed all of his earlier suggestions and aced it, the two halves of the log falling to the ground. She turned to him, took off her safety glasses and grinned. "I did it."

Her joy was contagious, and he smiled along with her. "Yes, you did. Though I wouldn't call you a lumberjack just yet."

She didn't take offense; instead her expression softened. "Thanks for your help. I guess I needed the instruction."

He didn't gloat. Well, not outwardly. "Any time, Dawn. Just promise me that you won't come out here to chop wood without telling me."

"You don't trust me?"

"It's for my sanity, okay?" He realized he was beginning to care about her, more than he'd cared for a woman since Bree. "You're still a novice."

"All right. But since you're out here now, how about I do another?"

"Another?" He rubbed his chin, feeling the rough stubble there. "I thought we'd go in and have dinner. I'm getting hungry." It was a ruthless lie, but one he knew would work. If Dawn was anything, she was dedicated to her profession.

"Oh, right. Sure." She put the ax down. "I'll get right on it."

"You go on in, and I'll clean up here."

"You sure?" she asked.

He patted his stomach. "I'm absolutely sure."

Dawn was happy with the way her whitefish tacos turned out. She'd used cod, eight cloves of garlic and half a dozen herbs to give the fish added flavor. She'd shredded cabbage and made a light salsa for the dish. Rice pilaf and fresh cherry tomatoes complemented the dish. Cade had eaten three tacos, raving about the meal, and when they were through eating, he'd lent a hand in the cleanup.

After he left the kitchen, she put on a pot of coffee and waited while it brewed. She'd wanted to bake some sort of dessert, but between the hike, the wood chopping and being totally distracted by Cade and the way he'd kissed her today, she'd run out of time.

So she dug into the pantry, coming up with a box of shortbread cookies. They were perfect to dunk into coffee. She arranged a little tray of them, setting them on the table. Once the coffee was ready, she went in search of Cade. She found him in the main room, sitting on the sofa, a fire blazing in the fireplace. He was shuffling cards and barely noticed her walking in.

The sun was just setting, and there was a briskness in the air. The fire sure looked inviting. "Cade, coffee's ready. Want me to bring it in here?"

He looked up and shook his head. "No, thanks, I'll get it myself."

Stubborn man. He didn't want her to serve him. But it was no trouble. And honestly, doing something for him made her lies to him seem a little more palatable. "Okay."

She turned to walk out of the room, and he followed her into the kitchen. "I found some shortbread cookies and thought they might go well with coffee."

He grabbed one from the dish and tossed it into his mouth. "Good idea," he said, his mouth full.

She chuckled and turned away to grab two mugs from the cabinet. "What are you playing out there?"

He came to stand beside her. "Solitaire. It's no fun, though."

She gave him a look. "Why not?"

"There's no one to play against."

She gave her head a tilt. "Is that a hint?"

"You play cards, don't you?"

"I do."

"It's real nice by the fire. We could play while we drink coffee."

"And dunk cookies?"

"Yep, that, too."

It did sound like fun, and as long as they were pretending nothing happened between them today, it could work. "Sure, maybe for a little while."

Cade picked up the dish of cookies and his coffee and walked to the sofa. She followed him, sitting on the opposite sofa, a clear glass coffee table separating them. She was wearing shorts and a short-sleeved blouse, so right about now, the heat drifting up from the crackling fire warmed her bones.

"What do you want to play?" he asked, grabbing the deck of cards. He was a master shuffler. He had these long fingers that seemed to easily control the deck.

"Rummy."

"Sounds good to me."

He dealt the cards, and as she picked up hers, she groaned.

He glanced at her. "That's not a good poker face."

"Good thing we're not playing poker."

"Remind me to play poker with you sometime."

"I can bluff with the best of them, Cade. Don't you worry."

She sipped coffee and dipped a couple of cookies as they played. Both had a second cup, and before she knew it, Cade was ramping up the fire again. He was a fierce competitor, and she didn't like to back down, either.

Cade dropped a seven on the stack, the exact card she needed. She grabbed it and then laid down her hand. "Read 'em and weep," she said. "What is it, ten games to nine now? Guess I just broke the tie."

"I'll get you next round." He pushed the cards her way. "Your deal."

He got up and went to the bar just off the dining room, coming back with a bottle of merlot and two wineglasses. As she shuffled, he poured the wine. "Fortification."

She had to agree, the wine did look tempting. "You need all the help you can get to beat me."

"Don't get cocky. You're only up by one game." He handed her the glass.

"You wanna bet?"

"Sure, why don't we make this interesting?" he said.

Gosh, she didn't mean it literally. But now that the bug

was planted, it sort of hung on. It wasn't a bad idea. "What do you have in mind?"

"Best of twenty-five games."

"To be fair, we should start from scratch."

"No, no." He eyed her over the rim of his wineglass and then took a sip. "We'll go from here. I have no doubt I can beat you."

"And I'm certain I'll win. To prove it, if I do, you have to make me dinner one night."

He shuddered at the thought. "That's more like losing. You know I can't cook worth a damn."

She smiled as she sipped her wine. "You'd have to learn."

His mouth twisted in a grimace. Clearly he didn't like the idea. "And *when* I win, you have to, to…" He stalled, eyeing her body, giving her a once-over that brought thrilling tingles down to her toes. Whatever Cade had in mind she might just enjoy. She sat up straighter, and his gaze focused on her chest. Little did he know her nipples were standing erect from his scrutiny. That one enticing look from him was enough to suddenly turn her on.

Then he gave his head a hard shake, as if clearing it out. "If I win," he began quietly, "you have to clean out the fireplace every night."

She chuckled and then downed another mouthful of wine. "Like Cinderella?"

"If the shoe fits," he said, and she giggled at his dumb joke.

"Clever, Cade. *Not*."

Then they both laughed as she dealt the cards. She had no clue what time it was. She was lost in the game, talking trash with a fine competitor and enjoying herself far too much. The fire was cozy and warm, and along with the buzz of the wine, she was in a happy place.

She finished off her wine and poured herself another glass. She took a generous gulp, downing half of what she'd poured. Cade's brow rose as he watched her. It wasn't a big deal. He was already on his second glass. Or was it his third?

"I'm fine, Cade," she told him before he even asked. "I'm a big girl."

"I've noticed," he said, dealing out another hand.

She smiled, stealthily admiring him when he was focused on the cards. He was too good-looking for his own good. And with that beard, those incredible probing eyes, he looked absolutely delicious.

She sat there, staring at her cards, feeling giddy.

"Dawn, are you okay?"

"Who's Dawn?" she whispered, then giggled.

"What'd you say?"

"Nothing." Her eyes bugged out at what she'd just spoken aloud. *Shush.* She had to keep quiet about her secret. She took a deep breath to clear her head, but things remained a little woozy. She downed the rest of her wine and set the glass on the table very, very carefully. "I'm g-getting a little fuzzy, that's all."

"On two glasses of wine?"

"Didn't I tell you, I'm not m-much of a d-drinker."

"I'm beginning to see that," he said.

She had trouble keeping her eyes open. She kept blinking and blinking and then felt the room sway. Cade was sitting lopsided on the sofa opposite her.

"Your turn," he said.

As she glanced at her cards, two of them dropped from her hand. "Whoops." She grabbed for them but came up empty as they fell to the floor.

"Okay, game's over," she heard Cade say.

"No, way. I...h-have to w-win."

He rose from his seat, and the next thing she knew he was in front of her and she was being lifted from the couch. "Can you walk?"

"S-since I was a baby." She giggled and swayed, the room beginning to spin.

She heard Cade sigh. "Just hang on to me." His arms came under her, and she was lifted up and cradled, her body brushing the side of his chest. She hung on to him tight, wrapping her arms around his neck, and caught a whiff of him, the scent of wine and musk and man. As they began to move, she stared at his strong jaw, or tried to, because it was really beautiful. "I like your beard."

"Thank you," he said, not too nicely.

"Where are w-we g-going?"

"To bed."

"Okay," she said. "G-good idea, C-cade."

He gave her a stern look.

He walked into her bedroom, and she was gently lowered onto the bed. The mattress dipped a bit as he came partway down with her, her arms neatly wrapped around his neck still. She gazed into his eyes, seeing the dark rims, but seeing something more. "Cade?"

"Shh," he said.

"Are you m-mad at me?"

"No," he said harshly. Then his voice lowered to a whisper. "I'm not mad at you."

"That's g-good. I'm really s-sleepy."

"I know."

He was close still, because her arms remained tucked around his neck.

"I should go now."

She glanced at his mouth. "Yeah."

"Good night." He bent to place a kiss on her forehead, but a cagey devil inside her curved her hands behind his head and pulled him lower, so their lips brushed. Oh boy, he tasted good, his mouth warm and firm against hers. The kiss was sheer heaven. Not a flimsy little kiss like what Dale used to give her on camera, but a deep-down, curl-your-toes kind of kiss that heightened her senses, sobering her up some.

A tiny moan rose up from her throat. "Cade."

He wove his hands through her hair oh so gently, his eyes never leaving her face. "Shh," he said, as if he was in pain.

Then he lowered down on the bed next to her, brushing his lips to hers again and again. It was delicious, the way his mouth moved over hers, how he coaxed her to part her lips and mate their tongues. Her eyes squeezed shut as she enjoyed every single moment of his masterful kisses, the way he swept through her mouth with such expertise.

From there, the kisses grew more urgent and desire swept through her body. She ached for more of him, to feel his body crushed to hers. He made her want…and she was ready to give in, to give up her doubts, to give him whatever he desired.

Her brain cleared long enough to wonder if it was the alcohol making her lose her inhibitions. Or was it Cade? She'd been attracted to him from the moment they'd bumped into each other at the market. All her thoughts rushed together, confusing her as her body stirred restlessly.

And then suddenly the kissing stopped and she opened her eyes to find Cade looking at her with regret.

"I can't do this," he whispered, an apology in his voice. His forehead touched hers, and he inhaled sharply and then rose from the bed as if he was dragged by some invisible force. Looking down at her, he skimmed his gaze over her body quickly, and gave his head a shake. "Sleep as long as you want, Dawn. You'll need the rest."

He walked out of the room and shut the door.

Harper closed her eyes. Her head spun, and she whispered softly, "My name's not Dawn."

Then she got under the covers and rolled over to fall asleep.

Things had to look better in the morning.

Four

The next day, Cade wrote Dawn a note just in case she woke early and found him gone. But he doubted she'd rise early. They'd gone to bed late, and at best, she'd have a headache this morning that would probably slow her down. He'd never seen a woman get so drunk so fast.

He exited the cabin, closing the door quietly. He'd taken a cold shower last night, and this morning he hoped an early morning jog might be just what he needed to purge thoughts of Dawn. Of her pretty blue eyes, her killer body and the way they'd kissed last night. Like there was no tomorrow, like she'd been just as starved for affection as he was. And he hadn't really understood that until their lips met, until she'd kissed him back with such unbridled passion. But he hadn't wanted to take advantage of her last night. Not in her giddy, sexy-as-hell, tipsy state. She'd had too much to drink, and he'd done the noble thing. Whatever might happen between them would have to happen when she was stone-cold sober and fully coherent, if it happened at all.

He picked up the pace, jogging a little faster now, trying to come to terms with his reaction to Dawn. She was the first woman he'd kissed and touched since Bree. And through his grief and guilt came the realization that he might just be ready to move on. Physically.

But a mental battle was going on inside his head. Dawn was a Tremaine hire, even if he wasn't really her boss. And she certainly hadn't come here for romance. Hell, no. She'd been in a bad relationship recently, and hooking up with him would probably be the last thing she wanted. He was pretty sure he could keep his distance. But a little bug in his head wondered if that was even plausible. They were together 24/7 at the cabin. And he was, heaven help him, attracted to her.

He jogged past a few cabins and came across some other runners heading his way. "Morning," he said, giving them a nod as they jogged past. He slowed as he approached Bright Market and then stopped at the threshold to wipe his brow. He entered and was greeted by a cashier wearing a bright green apron. "Good morning," she said. "Welcome."

"Morning. Can you tell me where you keep your aspirin and tomato juice?"

"Sounds like someone's in need of quick therapy," the woman said with a little smile.

"Something like that."

"You'll find what you need in aisles seven and ten."

"Thanks."

He found the items easily enough and also picked up some packaged chocolate doughnuts and two boxes of crackers. He got in line behind a young boy buying candy.

The kid dumped all of his change onto the counter, counting out quarters, dimes and nickels.

Cade stood patiently waiting; he was in no rush to get back to the cabin. And while he waited, he scanned over the rack filled with tabloids. His famous brother, Gage, sometimes made it into those papers. The sleazy reports were never accurate, and Cade certainly had no use for them. But one headline caught his eye, only because it was about a chef. The headline read, Chef Murphy on the Lookout for His One Last Date. Harper Hunt Is Still On. Whatever that meant. The guy in the photo looked dismayed. Cade couldn't believe people went on a TV show to find love. In, what, ten weeks or something? He wasn't sure because the only TV he watched had to do with sports, period.

The cashier rang up his items and he was off again, sort of dreading facing Dawn this morning. He wondered how much she remembered about last night. And he also wondered if he would ever be able to forget it.

It was quiet in the house when he entered and stood in the foyer to remove his shoes. If Dawn was sleeping, he didn't want to rouse her. He tiptoed into the kitchen and set about making coffee as quietly as possible. Then while it brewed, he walked into the living room and cleaned up the wineglasses and cards that were left on the table. It was a big reminder of how things had gotten out of hand so quickly. Dawn had been fine one minute, but after the second glass, she'd gotten smashed in the blink of an eye. What happened afterward was his fault. He shouldn't have kissed her. It was a dumb move and one he wished he could take back.

He set the glasses and mugs in the dishwasher and then stared out the kitchen window to the rustic landscape, where juniper trees were in abundance and the bright sun reflected on the lake water. He had yet to go down there, to check out the lake.

Once the coffee was finished brewing, he poured a cup and sipped. It was hot and burned his tongue. "Crap." That's when he decided he needed a lift. He dipped into his grocery bag and came up with a chocolate doughnut. He demolished it in three big bites, enjoying every second of it.

It was after ten and Dawn hadn't come out of her bedroom yet. Was she okay? Did he dare peek in on her? He had told her to sleep as long as she needed to, but now he worried that she'd gotten sick. The last thing he wanted to do was go into her bedroom and disturb her sleep and privacy. Instead, he poured more coffee into his cup, put his shoes back on and walked out the door. He'd give her another hour to rest before checking in on her.

The lake was only thirty yards away, so he headed down there and walked out onto a small dock they shared with a few other families. It was a beautiful day for a boat ride. Too bad their boat was in storage several miles from here. Cade sipped his coffee, gazing out, watching the blue jays flit from branch to branch, tree to tree, listening to the leaves rustle as they moved. He found a moment of peace here.

The sound of footsteps on the dock surprised him and he turned to find Dawn just a few feet away, her shoulders slumped, her hair barely combed and those pretty blue eyes downcast. She stopped and met his gaze.

"I'll resign if you think it's best."

Harper didn't mean to sneak up on Cade. She'd deliberately made noise as she walked toward him on the dock. He must've been deep in thought, not to hear her until she got pretty close.

"Dawn, how're you feeling this morning?"

"I'll survive," she said. Though she had a killer headache and her tummy ached. She mustered the courage to look him in the eyes. "I'm sorry about last night. About missing this morning's meal. About everything. I meant what I said," she offered softly, only because it hurt her head too much to speak any louder. "I'll give you my resignation, if that's what you want."

He smiled kindly. "No one is resigning, Dawn. So put that out of your mind."

"I would, but it's pretty crowded in there right now."

He chuckled quietly. "Listen, you didn't do anything wrong, and—"

"I'm so embarrassed, Cade. The wine hit me harder than usual."

"It's okay, we've all been there. I got you some aspirin and some tomato juice. Hopefully that will help."

"What would really help would be if last night never happened."

She braved a look at his mouth, remembering his heated kisses. The way their lips seemed to mesh so perfectly.

"We can do that. We can pretend nothing happened. And just for the record, this isn't all on you. In fact, none of it is. I wasn't drunk. I should've known better."

"You're not over your fiancée, I get that."

He winced at the mention of Bree.

"That's not entirely it. I wouldn't take advantage of you, Dawn. Not ever. You have to know that."

"I do," she said, amazed that they could have such a civil conversation about what had almost happened between them. Last night, she'd known the full pull of his magnetism, and she'd let down her guard. They'd had fun playing cards, teasing and challenging each other, and then somehow, the alcohol had sneaked up on her and she'd let her inhibitions go. Goodness, she didn't recall her exact words, but she remembered the way she felt in his arms, his kisses making her crave his touch, her breasts tingling, everything below her waist heating up. And no, he hadn't taken advantage of the situation. "I guess I should be glad you're an honorable man."

"I'm trying," he said, his face pulling taut, and she appreciated his honesty. "Listen, why don't you stay down here, enjoy the lake and fresh air. I'll get you those aspirins and tomato juice and be back in a few."

"You're not making me a Bloody Mary, are you? 'Cause I don't think I could handle any more alcohol right now."

"Nope, just tomato juice. I promise."

He moved past her and headed toward the house. "Cade," she called to him. He stopped and turned to her. "Thanks," she said, giving him a brief smile.

He nodded, blinking his eyes several times, then took off toward the house.

Well, she'd sure made a mess of things. So much for being a professional personal chef. So much for keeping her distance. From what she could remember, she'd practically jumped his bones last night. What had started out as a make-out session could've easily turned into more if Cade hadn't been the adult in the room.

She stared out at the lake, the water looking like smooth glass. It was peaceful here, and she slipped off her shoes, sat down on the edge of the dock and put her feet into the cool water. Lifting her face to the sun, she closed her eyes. In a sense, both she and Cade were seeking refuge in this place. Both were running from something, and both had their own troubles to purge while they were here.

Cade was back in minutes and immediately handed her the juice along with two aspirins. She took them gratefully and sipped the juice as he rolled up his jeans and sat down beside her. He had a bag in his hand. "What's that?" she asked.

"Lunch." He pulled out a box of crackers and some doughnuts.

"Oh man." She put her head down. "I'm awful at my job."

"Don't worry about it," he said digging into the cracker box. "I love these. And they're good for you, to settle your stomach."

"When did you get this stuff?" she asked, taking a cracker from the box.

"This morning. I went for a jog."

"You got me aspirin and juice and crackers?" She choked up, hardly getting the words out. "That's...thank you."

"Welcome. Hey, I have an idea. Why don't we say this is your day off? I can't expect you to work every single day without a break."

"You're being nice again, but you don't cook and I already feel like I've shirked my duties today."

Cade splashed his feet in the water. "You can take the day to work on your cookbook. Or nap. Or do whatever you want."

All those things sounded good to her, but was he trying to get away from her? Was that what this was all about? "And what about dinner?"

"Corky's Bar and Grill in town is pretty good. We can have dinner out for once."

"We?"

"Yeah, we. We both need to eat."

"Right now, eating anything but crackers sounds awful."

"Trust me, you'll be hungry by tonight. And the worst thing for you to do is skip that meal."

She didn't want to argue with him, but she worried about going out in public. Would her disguise hold up?

"I really don't feel like being out in a crowd. The noise and all. Maybe another time?"

"Corky's shouldn't be busy on a weeknight. And if it gets too much for you, we'll leave."

He was pretty adamant. She couldn't argue further without rousing suspicion. He was giving her the day off. She could use the time for herself, to rest, to regroup. She was still feeling out of sorts, and a nap and some privacy sounded really good. "What time?"

"How about seven?"

She nodded and grabbed another cracker, forcing herself to chew slowly and swallow it down. Cade might be right: the crackers just might ease the pain in her tummy, and the aspirin would help with her headache.

"Seven it is."

He gave her a nod. "It's a…" Then he stopped himself.

"It's a plan," she offered.

"Right, it's a plan."

Because it so wasn't a date.

Corky's Bar and Grill was crowded, and as Dawn stood at the entrance with Cade, she didn't know if that was a good thing or a bad thing. Here in the smoky honky-tonk, she'd either fade into the crowd or risk someone in the place recognizing her. Either way, Corky's was not what she was expecting. She'd envisioned a small, rustic café with few patrons and menu choices, instead of what seemed to be the hub for Hill Country partygoers.

Tonight was live-band night and luckily all eyes in the place were on the front stage, where a singing duo were belting out a Gage Tremaine song called "Rough Night."

They harmonized perfectly, and many of the patrons were on the dance floor rocking out to the music.

"Sorry," Cade whispered. "It's usually not this noisy. Didn't know about the band. How's your head?"

She'd rested today, taken a long nap and done some research for her cookbook. "Actually, my headache is gone, and I'd rather it not come back. Maybe we should go? The music's pretty loud."

And she really wished she'd refused him earlier today. Her best form of disguise, after cutting her hair and dying it dark brown, was not to wear any make-up. When she was on the show, she was made up professionally every day. She hoped it was enough.

"I'll take care of that."

Cade handed the hostess a twenty, whispering something in her ear. She nodded and then led them to a table in the far corner of the room, away from most of the people and away from the loud music. "Is this good, Mr. Tremaine?"

"What do you think?" he asked Harper.

She kept her head down, away from the young girl. "It's great."

Cade nodded at the hostess and smiled. "This is fine, Becky. How're your folks?"

"Still going strong."

"Good to hear. Tell them hello from the family."

"I sure will."

They scooted into their seats, with Harper sitting facing the wall and not the band. She wore a jean jacket over a dark blue sundress with tiny flowers, the only dress Lily had packed for her. She didn't know why she'd bothered to dress up, but after she'd seen Cade dressed in a snap-down black Western shirt and crisp jeans, she was glad she'd made the effort. He looked nice. No, nice wasn't the right word. He looked gorgeous, the stubble on his face groomed, his clothes sharp and his thick hair combed back.

"Here's your menus." Becky handed them out. "Let me know if there's anything I can do for you."

"Will do."

After she walked away, Harper asked, "She knows you?"

"She does. Becky's a local. She's been working here for about ten years or so. Her parents manage the cabin for us. They're the ones who stock the place and fix it up when friends or family use it. Becky is putting herself through online college."

Oh, so that explained the big tip.

She glanced at the menu, using it as a shield to keep her face hidden. She had to admit it was nice being out, listening to music and being served for a change. The menu was ginormous. She couldn't decide if she wanted steak, fish, tacos, pasta or chili. "What's good here?"

Cade put his fingertips on her menu and pulled it down, so he could see her face. "Steak fajitas are my favorite. If they still make them as good as they used to."

"How long has it been since you've been here?"

"Oh man. Let me think…must be at least five years or so. Came up here to celebrate my sister Lily's birthday."

Harper pulled up the menu to cover her face again. "That's nice. You know what, I think I'll have the fajitas, too, only with chicken." She couldn't change the subject fast enough.

"Want a drink?"

She glanced at him over the menu, furrowing her brows.

"A *soft* drink," he said. "I couldn't handle anything more."

She put the menu down. "What does that mean, Cade?"

He glanced at her, his eyes roaming over her face and then shifting to the sundress she wore. "Nothing, forget I said that. But you do look very pretty tonight."

His compliment went straight to her head, and warmth traveled through her body. They were tiptoeing around each other tonight. It was safer that way, but she wasn't immune to the charm he probably didn't realize he had.

"Lemonade sounds good."

"A safe choice."

"Funny."

"You know what I was thinking? We never finished our rummy challenge."

"I suppose you think you were winning?"

"Actually, I think we were all tied up."

"Really? I don't remember."

"Trust me. I do. You trash-talk with the best of them," he said.

"I'm competitive." She frowned, hating that he'd seen her less-than-awesome side. "Sometimes, that's not such a good thing."

"On the contrary, I think it's a great trait for people who want to get ahead in their lives, their careers."

"And you would know this because you're a big business tycoon and being competitive is part of the game."

"I'm just trying to stay one step ahead of the next guy, otherwise the company may not survive."

"That's a little drastic, isn't it?"

"Not when you employ thousands of people throughout the country. It's my obligation to make sure they all have jobs. Don't you want to be one of the best chefs in the country?"

"Yeah, but that's only because... I take pride in my work. I set high standards for myself."

"You also don't give yourself enough credit, Dawn.

You're very good at what you do. You're very passionate about your work."

"So are you, at least from what I can tell."

"Guilty as charged. I had two passions in my life, and now Bree is gone."

Just the way he spoke his late fiancée's name said so much about his great love for her. Harper had the urge to reach out and touch his arm. To comfort him for his loss. One day, she wanted to have that same kind of unconditional love in her life. "I'm sorry about that, Cade."

"I had to compete for her, too, you know. She was dating some guy," he said, "who was all wrong for her, and there was, well, a bit of competition between the two of us. She was worth the effort. There was no way I was giving up. And I finally broke her down and made her see I was the only one for her. We'd been so happy, looking forward to the future, until she got sick."

"It must've been hard for you."

"It's…getting better. I think coming here has helped. I might have to eat crow and thank my mom for pushing me into this."

"Well, if you're glad, then I'm glad."

Cade gave her an honest look, one that seared right through her and made her feel more for him than sexual attraction. He was one of the good guys. "Don't take this the wrong way, but I'm glad you're here. With me. It helps."

She took a deep swallow and nodded, unable to conjure up any words.

The waitress came by, breaking the tension of the moment, and took their orders. Harper was grateful for the intrusion because she'd taken his words to heart and didn't know if she could conceal the growing feelings she was having for him. Concealing her identity was one thing—concealing her heart was quite another.

They made small talk during the meal. It was just as delicious as Cade had mentioned. She was happy to see him gobbling up his food. Maybe he was slowly coming out of his grief.

When they were almost through, the band leader announced this was their last song before they took a break. "And folks, it's come to my attention that we have Gage Tremaine's big brother in the house."

Surprised, Harper swiveled her head slightly and caught the lead singer pointing toward them. She immediately spun back around and froze in place. Heads must be turning their way, dozens of eyeballs trying to get a look at Cade. She heard a small round of applause. Oh man, she didn't expect this. Lucky for her, her back was to them. Cade didn't seem to enjoy the attention, either, unlike his famous brother, who always seemed to eat it up. "Sorry," he mumbled to her. "It happens occasionally."

She nodded.

The lead singer went on. "Mr. Cade Tremaine, why don't you bring your little lady up to the dance floor and join everyone else in one last dance?"

Cade was too much of a gentleman to shoot the man down. "Do you want to dance?" Cade asked her.

She shook her head adamantly. "No."

Cade told the guy no with a shake of his head.

"Aw, c'mon," the guy said good-naturedly. "One turn around the dance floor. We'll sing a real pretty song for all of you."

"I'm afraid if we don't, there'll be more of a fuss," Cade said. Then he rose and put out his hand, giving her no choice. "We'll make an escape as soon as we can," he told her.

She took his hand, keeping her head down, her hair in her face. The band didn't start up until they reached the dance floor. "I'm a terrible dancer," she whispered.

"Then stick close and we'll melt into the crowd."

Which was exactly what she wanted. She couldn't afford to be singled out on the dance floor. There had to be at least two dozen couples dancing, and hopefully, they'd blend in. She walked into Cade's arms, and they began moving to the soulful ballad. She caught a few people watching them, and she immediately put her head on his shoulder to hide her face. Cade tightened his hold on her, keeping her within the circle of his strong arms. She'd lied to him once again. She knew how to dance; she'd taken dance lessons all through her childhood and early teens. Her folks had wanted to expose her to all sorts of things to help her find her real passion.

"You're not bad at this," Cade said, his husky voice vibrating through her body. Her cheek brushed his neck, and his delicious male scent wafted to her nostrils.

"I'm trying," she whispered.

Cade moved his hand up to her lower back and tangled his fingers through her hair. The singer's soulful voice transported her. It was magical, a beautiful moment in time. She swayed when Cade swayed, and they moved as one.

She rode her hands up his chest and around his neck and smiled when he looked down, his dark eyes gleaming and his expression open for a change, showing her a side of him she hadn't seen before. "You're beautiful, Dawn."

She batted her eyelashes, not to be melodramatic but because he'd spoken genuinely and she didn't know what to say to him in return. He was beautiful, too. He was a real gentleman, a man who'd been hurt, scarred probably, and who was just, at least in this moment, opening up a little. Knowing that did things to her she couldn't name, but it was a good feeling.

She hated the lies, the cloud of deception she was under. She hated to do that to Cade. He didn't deserve it. Every time he called her Dawn, she squirmed. Whatever was happening between them—and make no mistake, there was definitely something happening between them now—she remembered the falsity of their relationship. But she'd promised Lily to stay on here and keep her brother from sinking into a deep hole. Now that she'd gotten to know Cade a little bit, she wanted to continue. She wanted to pull him out of his grief and help him recover. Not necessarily because he was Lily's brother, and not because he was deadly handsome, but because she cared about him from the bottom of her heart. Which was crazy. She'd known him less than a week. But then again, she'd gone on a reality show and had been expected to marry a guy after less than ten weeks. So, she supposed on that premise, it wasn't altogether that crazy.

"Cade, I...like you." That was lame. Was she still in grade school? But it was honest, and being honest with him now was just what she needed to do.

He brushed his lips to her hair, just above her ear, in that place that brings tingles. "I like you, too."

He pulled her closer, and she immediately understood just how much he did like her. Heaven help her, she was as turned on as he was. No lie.

"Can we pretend we just met tonight?" he asked.

She whispered in his ear. "And then what?"

"Then, I bring you to the cabin and we..."

"Play cards?"

He blew out a breath, as if in pain. "After, we can play cards, Dawn. Is that what you want?"

She did. She really did. They'd been denying their attraction to each other for days now. She brought her mouth to his and kissed him soundly, so there would be no doubt. He was delicious all over, his mouth just one of the places she wanted to taste. She pulled away to see hunger in his eyes and feel the heat emanating from his chest.

"Let's get out of here," he said, taking her hand and leading her to their table. He dropped a hundred-dollar bill down, picked up her purse and handed it to her, and together they made a quick dash out of the place.

He stopped once they were outside to kiss her again, his mouth devouring hers. She was so swept away that she remained silent in the car on the way home.

In the house, Cade led her up the stairs, her hand clasped in his. She'd only been up here once before, when she'd first gotten here, which seemed like an eon ago now. He stopped at the threshold to his bedroom and took her face lovingly into his hands, searching her eyes for any sign of refusal, before bringing his mouth down on hers again. The kiss was wrought with desire, filled with hunger. She had to steady herself from the impact of his kiss. Thrills ran through her body, her heart fully involved already.

"I… I didn't expect this." He brushed hair away from her face with the tenderest touch.

"I didn't, either, Cade," she whispered.

Her heart pounded like crazy; everything she'd ever wanted in a man was standing right in front of her. It was inconvenient he was Lily's brother, and that Harper had lied to him, but none of that mattered now. From the moment she'd first met him in the market, she'd felt an immediate connection to him. A spark that only continued to burn bright with every minute she spent with him.

"Come with me. I want to show you something." He led her into the bedroom and over to a trio of large windows facing the lake. He stood behind her, his hands on her shoulders. The moon was full tonight, and the lake waters glistened with a fine sheen under the stars.

"It's so peaceful."

He rubbed her arms up and down slowly, his touch a low-burning flame on her skin. Then he moved her hair to one side and nuzzled her neck, kissing her with tiny little nips. Tilting her head, she gave him more access, closing her eyes. "Are you sure, Dawn?"

She turned in his arms and slipped her fingers under the spaghetti straps of her sundress, lowering them one at a time down her arms. Then she slid the dress off her shoulders and past her hips. It draped down to the floor, exposing her nudity but for the bikini undies she wore. She gazed deep into his eyes. "I'm sure. Are you?"

Cade's lips twitched. "Oh yeah."

He pulled her into his arms, crushing her into his chest. The contact was immediate, fiery and wild. He brought his mouth to hers again as he roamed her body with his palms, caressing her shoulders, her back and then lower. He palmed her cheeks through the skimpy material of her undies, applying sweet pressure to pull her tight against him, handling her like something precious, yet something he desperately needed.

In the back of her mind, she hoped this wasn't just about sex. About relieving an itch. From what she gathered, he hadn't been with a woman since his fiancée died. She didn't know that for a fact, but she assumed. And now, here she was, living under his roof, about to make love to him. Was this only because she was convenient?

His next kiss wiped that thought from her mind. Whatever this was, she was all in. She'd never experienced anything like this before, this need, this craving, to be with him. It was almost unexplainable. But for her, it was real.

The snaps of his shirt were easy to pull apart. It came off quickly and then her lips were on his chest, her hands roaming his upper torso, his amazing rock-hard muscles.

He made her breathless. And bold. And she wanted more of him.

"Dawn," he whispered. And she mentally flinched. She didn't want him to call her that. She didn't want the deception to go on, though she knew it had to.

And then his hands were on her breasts, his fingertips teasing, caressing, until all the nerve endings below her waist quivered. And when he was through tormenting her in the best possible way, he took her hand. "Come to bed with me."

He led her to his massive bed and lay down, taking her with him. She ended up atop his body, her breasts pressed to his chest. He sucked air into his lungs. "You have no idea how much…"

She swallowed hard, afraid of what he was going to say.

How much he needed a woman. How much he'd wanted to do this since he laid eyes on her. How much she'd tempted him.

"H-how much what?" she asked quietly.

"How much better I feel when I'm with you."

Oh God. It was the perfect thing to say, and she couldn't deny that she felt the same way about him.

"Really?"

He blew out a big breath. "Yeah, really."

She wanted to cry from the beauty of that statement. Cade was a special man, and she wanted him in a very special way. "Me too."

He kissed her then, and there was more meaning in

his kiss this time. It was different and good. Better than good. It was Cade.

They tangled in his sheets for half the night, Cade caressing every part of her body with equal attention. His tongue in her mouth made her crazy, his mouth on her breasts made her wild, but his mouth below her waist made her cry out joyously. And when he was deep, deep inside her, every pleasure she'd ever known was magnified by a thousand. When he was through with her, she was totally complete, totally sated. She could languish in his bed forever and never get up.

But morning came too early, sunshine spilling into the vast bedroom windows. She woke beside Cade, his arm around her shoulder, her head on his chest. She watched him sleep soundly. He was solid as granite, handsome and virile, but he was also a considerate lover, not satisfied until she'd had multiple orgasms. And just maybe she'd worn him out a little bit last night, too. She smiled, remembering how delicious it'd been to make love to him, to generously give to him what he'd given to her.

She carefully kissed his chest, wanting nothing more than to stay with him, but she had work to do, and she wasn't going to shirk her duties again. She tiptoed out of bed and went downstairs to shower and change.

As she moved, her body ached just enough to remind her of the sensual night she'd spent with Cade. She was sore in all the right places. It'd been a long time since she'd been with a man. Before Dale, she'd been in a few relationships that were all wrong for her. But today, after being with Cade, nothing felt more right. She embraced the aches as a badge of honor. She only hoped Cade had no regrets, because she sure as hell didn't.

After showering, she dressed in her usual uniform of jeans and a cold-shoulder top and walked into the kitchen, her domain. She was comfortable in her surroundings now and turned on the radio, keeping the sound low so as to not to wake Cade. She danced around the kitchen, pulling out bowls and pans, setting the coffee to brew, feeling happier than she had in a long time. She refused to let reality intrude, to make her feel guilty about anything.

But deep down she feared Cade would wake up and think this was all a big mistake. Despite the sweet things he'd said to her last night, despite how he'd held her tight in his arms, refusing to let her go back to her own bed.

"You belong here," he'd said, right before he'd drifted off to sleep.

She whipped up eggs in a bowl and added fresh bacon bits, diced ham, chopped olives, artichokes and onions, and then grated in a cup of Gruyère cheese. She dumped the mixture into a cast-iron skillet, added a few spices and heated it on the stovetop. Then she set about making honey-glazed corn bread from scratch. She took the bowl in her arms, using a spatula to combine all the ingredients as she continued dancing around the kitchen, humming along with the melody pouring out of the radio.

On her third spin around, she stopped up short, coming face-to-face with Cade. He was leaning against the kitchen wall, arms folded, his drowsy eyes on her. She swallowed, her gaze flowing over his bare chest and his jeans sitting low on his hips. His hair was an unruly, thick mop, the locks falling into his eyes, and the scruff along his jawline was one day darker.

"Beautiful," he said, pushing away from the wall and approaching her. He took the bowl from her, setting it on the counter, then laced his right hand with hers and spun her around to the music once, twice, and then pulled her up into his arms on the third spin, his hands locking behind her waist as he kissed her hungrily on the lips. "I missed you when I woke up."

Again, the man knew just the right thing to say. "It was getting late, and I made us a frittata for breakfast." She poured him a cup of coffee. "Here, enjoy."

"I did. Did you?"

"Is there any doubt?" Didn't he know what a fantastic lover he was? "I mean, I usually don't dance around the kitchen when I cook in the morning."

"It's a nice look on you. You should do it more often. I'll be glad to help with that anytime."

She smiled before she sipped her coffee and liked that they weren't getting all serious about what happened last night. Sometimes you could overthink things, and right now, all she wanted was to feel the way she was feeling. "I'll remember that."

She poured the corn bread mixture into a greased pan and set it into the oven.

"Should be done in thirty minutes," she said, mostly to herself.

Then she took a seat adjacent to Cade at the table and both of them gazed out the window. "It's a beautiful day."

"It is," he said. "You, uh, you want to do something today?" He cleared his throat. "Together?"

She wanted nothing more than that. She could take a day off from her recipe research. "What did you have in mind?"

She trusted that he wouldn't say some cliché jerk thing; she already knew Cade wasn't made that way. He wasn't going to assume anything or force the situation, and she was grateful for that. "A ride? There's some really pretty landscapes around here I'd like to show you."

Her smile stretched wide across her face. "I think I'd love that."

He paused with the coffee cup at his mouth, his eyes gleaming. "So would I. It's a date."

Dating Cade? She liked the sound of that, and it no longer seemed like the end of the world that she was extremely attracted to him.

Five

Harper sat on the cushioned white seat of a ten-guest party boat and looked out at the lake. Warm breezes blew by, ruffling her hair as the boat caressed the lake waters. When Cade asked about going for a ride this morning, she'd assumed it was a car ride, but he'd surprised her by taking her to the main dock, where he'd arranged to have the boat ready.

Now, out on the lake, she felt freer than she ever had. She removed her sunglasses and let down her hair—which was already curling at the ends from the boat spray— just letting herself be without fear of anyone recognizing her. It was glorious and liberating. Here, on the lake, with only a few other boats in sight, she wasn't in any danger of being recognized.

"Over there is where my brother and I would anchor and try to fish when we were kids." Cade pointed to an inlet that was lush with trees and undergrowth. "But the only thing we attracted was a parade of baby ducklings led by their mama. Didn't help that Lily would toss them bread crumbs. She was afraid they were starving."

"Sounds like Lily," Harper said, then realized her blunder. Her heart sped up, and she held her breath.

"What'd you say?"

"I mean, sounds like Lily is…good-hearted."

"She is, but sometimes that gets her into trouble."

The only thing Harper thought to do was change the subject. "I would've packed a lunch if I knew we were going out on the water."

"No need. I got it covered."

"You do, do you? Did you actually put together a meal?"

"Hell, no." He laughed. "I wouldn't subject you to that. There's a little restaurant just around the bend. We can have lunch there, or we can get it to go."

"To go," she said immediately.

Cade gave her a glance from behind the steering wheel and nodded. "To go it is. We'll find a good place to anchor and have lunch on the water."

"Thank you, Cade. This is…nice."

"You're nice," he said, giving her a charming smile. He reached for her hand and gave it a little tug. She went willingly and landed on his lap. "You want to captain the boat?" he asked, his mouth just inches from hers. Her bottom was snugly set on his thighs, and her body quickly reacted.

"Maybe I just want the captain," she whispered.

"Dawn," he said almost helplessly. "I've been wanting you all morning."

His lips came down on hers in a crushing, bruising way, and she couldn't hold back the tiny little moans rising up her throat. He kissed her long and hard, his tongue mastering her mouth, his hands mastering her body. They were in the middle of the lake, alone for the most part, but still out in public.

"Do you want to—"

"Yes," she answered.

He groaned and kissed her again, and she was ready for whatever was to come.

He dropped anchor in the remote inlet, then lifted her off his lap and brought her under the shade of the canopy at the front of the boat. There was a long horseshoe-shaped seating area there, for the most part hidden from view. They kissed again, and then both dropped down onto the cushions, relentlessly touching each other through the confines of their clothes. She ached for more, to be one with him.

When he touched her breasts, she lay back and whimpered. "Hold on," he whispered, kissing her again and again. Then he came over her, unzipping her jeans and pulling them partway down. "Let me do this for you," he said.

And then his fingers were on her, stroking her, and every touch, every caress brought her to the brink. She'd never made love almost fully clothed before, but Cade knew what he was doing. Between his kisses and his caresses, it didn't take long for her little moans of ecstasy to grow louder, fiercer. Her hips arched, the muscles in her legs tightened and then...she shattered. Pleasure flitted around her like butterflies, bringing their beauty and grace. She was devastatingly done.

Cade zipped her jeans and brought her into the circle of his arms, his eyes on hers. There was so much spoken in that moment without words. Perhaps for the first time in her life, she was really in tune with a man. With Cade.

"You still want lunch?" he asked.

She shook her head, unable to speak just yet.

"We'll head back home and finish what we started here."

Yes, she wanted that. Very much.

She wanted Cade, and he wanted her.

It was as simple as two plus two.

Cade steered the boat to the slip by the house and locked hands with Dawn helping her onto the dock. He had to touch her, to stay connected with her and keep reminding himself she was real. She was the balm to his darkness, a woman who had captivated him from the very start. She wasn't a one-night stand or a fluke. She wasn't a woman who wanted to sleep with Gage Tremaine's brother. Just remembering how his touch completely made her come undone on the boat had him becoming a greedy soul, wanting more of that, wanting to keep Dawn close.

Hand in hand they strolled to the front door of the house. He stopped at the threshold and kissed her again and again, loving those tiny whimpers rising from her throat. Reluctantly, he broke off the kiss to open the door. Taking her face in his hands, he searched her eyes. "How are you?"

"Good. I'm good," she whispered in a sultry voice.

"Me too. Now that we're home."

She gave him a pretty smile, and he brought her inside the cabin. He wasn't going to ask her again, or make sure this was all right with her. He'd had his answer back there on the boat, and from her urgent kisses. He led her to her bedroom and closed the door. Her room was smaller than his, her bed a queen, but he didn't mind being in close quarters with her. In fact, he couldn't think of anything better.

He brushed his lips over hers, ran his hand through her hair. "Take off your clothes, sweetheart."

"You take off yours," she answered back.

"Planning to." He unbuttoned his shirt, then unfastened his belt and drew it off with one long pull. He kicked off his shoes, all the while keeping his eyes trained on Dawn as she stripped down to her panties.

"All done, slow poke."

He grinned. "You trash-talkin' me, angel?"

"Have to. You're taking your sweet time."

"You'll thank me later for that."

And then they were on each other, lips meshing, bodies colliding. He caressed every single inch of her skin, absorbing her softness, the supple, sweet body that gave to him so generously. His palms grew hot from rubbing her perfect breasts, loving the firm feel of them, the rosy tips that pebbled up and invited him to do more. He brought his mouth down to lavish one pink tip with love and then the other. She squirmed under his grip and he grew even harder. Gently, he moved her to the bed and lowered her down, her head on the pillow, her incredibly long legs lying across the bed, her eyes on him, glistening like the lake waters.

He sheathed himself with protection and moved over her, lowering down into her awaiting arms. She ran her hands through his hair, rumpling it, then caressed his face, kissed his mouth. They just seemed to fit perfectly everywhere, and when kissing wasn't bringing them close enough together, Cade thrust inside her, his hands on the bed giving him momentum to take her fully, to reach as deep inside as he could go.

Her whimpers met with his groans, pleasure and heat and lust all mingled. "Oh, damn, Dawn," he uttered in a plea. Raw sensations whipped through him as he continued to move, to gaze into her passion-filled eyes. Her reaction to him was his biggest turn-on, the way she seemed to enjoy everything he did to her.

She was not just a one-night stand. Definitely not.

She was scary good with him, beautiful under him, drawing every ounce of passion from him, meeting him thrust for thrust.

"Cade," she whispered, reaching up to his neck and pulling him down for a fiery kiss. She destroyed him in the best of ways, taking all of his breath away.

And then her mouth clamped down, her body stiffened, as she pleaded with him not to stop. And he knew the exact moment of her climax, the earth-shattering second of her release.

Man, he was amazed, stricken to the core. And watching her like that fueled his desire.

He moved harder and faster, and then he combusted, his release an earthquake of pleasure and satisfaction. He rolled off her, taking her with him, to hold her tight. To keep her close. "That was the…best," he uttered.

She nodded, and snuggled his chest.

Where had this beautiful woman come from?

She seemed too good to be true.

After their incredible day together—and even more incredible night—Harper found Cade in the kitchen the next morning. The coffee was brewing, and he was over the stove, burning bacon in a cast-iron skillet. She giggled a little, and he turned, obviously surprised to see her there. "Mornin'," he said. He leaned over to kiss her cheek. "Damn, you look good in my shirt."

"Thanks. What on earth are you doing?"

"Well," he said, sighing in defeat. "I was trying to cook you breakfast."

"Really? That's sweet."

"Actually, it was a very bad idea." He set the spatula down to give her his full attention. Putting out his arms, she walked straight into them. It felt safe there, and right, being cocooned by him, feeling his lips on her hair giving her morning kisses. When she woke up a few minutes ago, she feared he'd left her to sleep in his own room, but instead, she found him here, trying his hand at cooking.

"It's never wrong to cook. If you want, I'll show you how."

"You're willing to teach me?"

"Sure. I'd love to."

"You think you could take me being underfoot all day?" He touched his finger to her mouth, outlining the shape of her lips, parting them with his fingertip.

She drew his finger into her mouth and suckled. "I think I can handle it."

Danger flickered in his eyes. "You are something, angel." His voice turned husky and deep, like a growl.

Uh-oh. She backed away from him and the stove, putting a good distance between them. "I can be a devil sometimes. Especially in the…kitchen. So watch out, bud."

He tossed his head back and laughed, a good, hearty sound that made her grin, too.

Then he pulled her into his arms and gave her a good long, punishing kiss that curled her toes and made her beg for breath. When he was through, her heart was pumping hard.

They broke the embrace simultaneously, staring into each other's eyes. Something amazing was happening between them. For her, anyway. And she didn't think she was wrong in assuming for him, too. But no words were spoken between them yet, nothing more than casual conversation and sexy talk.

Harper didn't want to be the first to make a big deal of it. To put words to their actions. It was better to ride out this thing between them and see where it went.

"So, do you want a lesson in the kitchen or not?"

"I can't believe I'm saying this, but yeah. I want a lesson. Are you gonna tease and tempt me all through the day?"

She grinned mischievously. "Probably. But only if provoked."

"I'll remember that."

Harper showed him how to make the perfect omelet, giving him tips all along with way. She taught him how to chop and dice and julienne. And they danced around each other, trying to concentrate, trying not to touch each other, at least until the lesson was through.

They ate his omelet and drank coffee at the kitchen table as Cade shared some more of his life with her, little anecdotes about growing up a Tremaine. But each time he asked about her life, she had to give him a condensed, measured version, so as not to include the part that included Lily. Or her *One Last Date* fiasco. She so wanted to be truthful with him and hated the lies. But now was not the right time to come clean. Not when their involvement was just budding. She couldn't even call it a relationship, it was too soon for that, but her feelings for Cade were growing stronger every day. She couldn't stop it even if she wanted to.

"The kitchen's a mess," she said after her second cup of coffee. "I'll clean it up." She rose to get started, but his arm snaked around her and tugged, and she fell right into his lap. It was like magic how that always seemed to happen.

"I'll help," he said, giving her a dusky, dark-eyed look.

His cell phone rang, and he grabbed it off the table. "It's from my sis," he told her.

She nodded and bounded up from his lap, her stomach clenching. Thankfully, he didn't seem to notice her panic. She made noise while cleaning up the dishes, and he rose and walked into the other room to have a conversation with Lily.

She was so bad with deceit, she didn't want to know what they were talking about. She didn't want to over-hear anything that could cause her to slip up with him. She scrubbed and rescrubbed the pans and bowls, taking out her frustration on them. It was almost as good as chopping wood.

"Hey, you trying to rub the paint right off them?" Cade asked good-naturedly as he strode back into the kitchen.

"What? Oh no. I like to make sure everything gets really clean."

He was behind her and she didn't turn around, didn't face him, but continued washing with the same vigor.

He picked up a kitchen towel and began drying the pots and pans. "You don't have to do that," she said, putting on her personal chef hat. "It's my job."

"I made this mess, I'm damn sure gonna help you clean it up."

There was no point arguing. Cade had a stubborn streak, and a keen sense of duty, she was learning.

"Okay."

"That was my sister. She was just checking in. Making sure I'm being a good boy, eating my peas and carrots. I told her you were a fantastic cook, and I've never been more relaxed. I've hardly thought about work lately."

She nodded, keeping her head down. "Is that true?" she asked softly.

Cade wrapped the kitchen towel around her waist and grasped the ends in one hand to bring her to face him. "Yes, it's true. And it's because of you."

"Me?" She started shaking her head. "Because of..."

"That part's great, Dawn. Don't get me wrong. I mean it, I love being with you that way. But it's also because you made me see how empty my life was before. How I let my grief take hold of me."

"I'm no expert, but I think grieving is actually healthy for the soul. But at some point you need to get over it."

He began nodding, looking at her like she'd accomplished some great feat. "Because of you, I've been hiking, foraging, taking the boat out, learning how to cook. It's like I can breathe again."

She didn't want the praise. She didn't want any credit. She didn't deserve it. "You would've done all those things without me."

"No, I wouldn't, *Dawn*. I know I wouldn't." He spoke her name softly, with reverence, as if she was a good woman instead of a fraud.

She was trapped by the dish towel, searching the depths of his dark, beautiful eyes. Trapped by his charm, his honesty, his strength. And in that moment, she knew. She was in love with him. Deeply, crazily, stupidly in love with him.

He was the perfect guy. And she was a grossly imperfect girl.

But it didn't seem to matter. Because what she was feeling wasn't going away. She loved him. She loved Cade Tremaine. He was her one last date, whether she wanted it that way or not.

"Dawn? Are you okay? You're blinking like crazy. Got something in your eyes?"

He stared at her, concern on his face.

"No, I'm…f-fine."

He was thoughtful for a while. "If it makes you uncomfortable, I won't speak of it again. I don't want to do anything to upset you."

"You couldn't," she said truthfully.

"I like that you have that much faith in me." He pulled on the dish towel and brought her up close, so no space divided them. The feel of his rock-solid chest made her lose her train of thought. Goodness, they'd made love twice last night, and it'd been amazing both times, but this morning, just a touch, a kiss, had her wanting more. She couldn't tell him she loved him, but she could show him.

"In you, yes. But not in your rummy skills."

He laughed. "Is that a challenge?"

"For later maybe," she said.

"Do you have work to do?" He appeared disappointed.

"No, yes. But honestly, Cade." She rose up on tiptoes, licked at his delicious lips, giving him a mind-blowing kiss. Then she whispered, "The only thing I want to do right now is you."

Cade looked shocked for a second, then he grinned. "Aw shucks, angel. I really wanted to play cards." Then he took her hand and led her up the stairs and into his bedroom.

Cade lay on the bed alone, looking out the window at the flourishing spring scenery. He was in a happy place, the happiest he'd been in a long while. And it was strange that when he was with Dawn, he didn't feel guilty—he didn't feel that same powerful grief that ate away at him.

After they'd made love this morning, they'd dozed off in each other's arms, and now it was approaching the afternoon. Whiling away the time had never been his style, but doing nothing with Dawn was better than doing something with anyone else. His work, the office and all the problems he fixed on a daily basis were what had driven him lately and kept him sane. But not here, not with Dawn. He didn't need those things right now.

With his arms behind his head, he sighed, realizing he'd come to a conclusion. All he needed was her.

The door to the shower clicked open, and he imagined his dark-haired beauty stepping inside and soaping up. Immediately, his body reacted, everything going tight and hard below the waist. He couldn't seem to get enough of

Dawn, and lucky him, she seemed to feel the same way about him.

He rose from the bed and strode across the room, entering the bathroom. The glass shower door was too fogged up for him to see anything more than her outline, so he opened the door a tad and peeked in.

"Cade," she said. "You scared me."

"Sorry." But he wasn't, not really. She was covered in tiny soap bubbles, her body glistening under the spray. "But I was thinking I need a shower, too. Want some company?"

He'd never tire of seeing her naked. She had two perfectly round butt cheeks, just enough for him to hold in his palms, a waist he could practically wrap both hands around, breasts that were full and just slightly elongated. Perfect.

"What took you so long, sleepyhead? I didn't think you'd ever wake up."

She had a sassy mouth on her, too, that kept him on his toes. "In about a minute, you'll think it was worth the wait."

He pulled open the door and stepped inside. Hot, steaming water rained down on him, and it felt like heaven on earth. He grabbed the soap out of her hands and turned her away from him, making soap bubbles of his own on her shoulders, her back and then lower, to foam up her beautiful rear end, cupping her cheeks and soaping them, making her sigh restlessly. He came up behind her and reached around to cleanse her breasts, his hands lifting those firm globes and washing them with infinite care.

"Cade," she moaned and turned in his arms.

"Under a minute," he whispered.

"I know. You're kinda hard to resist," she said, wrapping her arms around his neck.

He smiled. If she only knew how much he wanted her.

How hard she was to resist. In a matter of just a few days, he'd come to think this woman was his angel. His savior.

She took the soap from him and lathered him up, kissing the places she touched. And then she was soaping him below the waist, her hands working magic on him, stroking him until he was about ready to combust. She was relentless in her quest, and when she replaced her hands with her mouth, Cade couldn't hold on any longer. He couldn't deal with the pleasure she was delivering with her mouth, her tongue.

He stopped her just in time and then lifted her up and carried her out of the shower, quickly drying them off and taking her back to bed. There, he sheathed himself with protection and brought her to the brink, again and again, until both were breathless, sated and spent.

Six

Harper spent the next few days teaching Cade to cook, hiking and boating with him. She was in total sync with the universe, enjoying every second with Cade, every minute they spent in bed and out. In their ongoing rummy game, she was up forty games to his thirty-eight, and she loved teasing him about losing to her. He had a competitive nature and it irked him every time she won. And if she got on a winning streak, the devil in him would distract her with his kisses. One time he actually stopped the game entirely to carry her into the bedroom and make love to her, she believed to end her winning streak. But neither of them minded the interruption. They were hungry for each other morning, noon and night. And when they'd pick up the cards again, each one would go right back into killer mode.

Right now, Harper had a winning hand. She laid her cards on the kitchen table. "Read 'em and weep," she said. "I win again."

"Damn." Cade tossed his cards down. "I was so close."

"Sorry," she said, grinning. She could hardly believe she'd been with Cade one full week. The time seemed to slip by so quickly, and she had no idea how long he planned to stay. How long they'd go on like this, in their own private, sheltered world. Technically, she was here to cook for him for as long as he needed. Lily had mentioned ten days to two weeks, but Cade made no mention of when he planned to return to Juliet County. He also made no mention of his feelings for her. Oh, he was full of compliments, and that made her ego soar. He told her she was beautiful, a talented chef and a kick-ass competitor. But he never spoke of the future. He never mentioned them having a real relationship.

She was in limbo. And part of her was wary of where she'd end up. But another part of her was too darn happy to worry about what would happen next. She was enjoying the here and now way too much.

"My deal," she said, scooping up the cards on the table.

"Hey, uh, Dawn?"

"Hmm, what?" She shuffled the deck.

"I think I'm ready."

She stopped shuffling and gazed into his dark eyes. "Ready?"

"To cook for you. I want to make you dinner tonight."

"Really?" She smiled, noting confidence in his expression as he waited for her reaction. "I'd love that."

He touched her face, stroking his thumb along the line of her jaw. "Thanks for not telling me I'm not ready." He leaned over and gave her a kiss. She loved how when he ended a kiss, he gently tugged on her lower lip with his own lips, as if he wanted to taste every last morsel of her.

"This isn't your way of distracting me, is it?"

"No. Maybe. No," he said finally. "I've been thinking about it a lot."

"What, may I ask, are you making for me tonight?"

"Braised short ribs, with riced potatoes and creamed asparagus tips."

"Wow. I'm impressed. You're shooting for the fences, aren't you?"

"Go big or go home," he said, grinning. "How about we end the game for now? I've got some shopping to do. Wanna come?" He rose from the table.

"Shopping for food is my second-favorite thing to do." Then as he loomed above her, she took in his long, sturdy, muscular body, a body she'd become familiar with in the most primal of ways. A body that stole her breath and made her heart race. "Uh, make that my third-favorite thing to do." She lifted off her seat. "Sure, I'll go with you. And don't you dare ask me what those three things are. You already know."

"I wouldn't dream of it," he said, gripping her rear end with both hands and squeezing gently. A reminder of his sexual prowess, she supposed. But it was working. Every time he touched her, it worked. "I would love to know what position I'm in, though, first, second or third?"

She smiled and backed away from him, giving him a look that said, *drop it, bud.* "We have shopping to do. Ready?"

He nodded, getting the hint. "It's a nice day. Wanna walk to the market?"

"I'm always up for a walk."

The weather was warming up lately, getting up in the mideighties. They hadn't had a fire in the fireplace for the past two nights, and as she stepped outside wearing her usual disguise of a ball cap and sunglasses, the sun's warmth cascaded down on her.

Cade took her hand, and they navigated the two-lane road leading to the store. Harper noticed more cars along the road, more people out walking. It was May and, she supposed, vacation time for students who'd already finished their spring semester. Maybe some folks were taking early vacations to beat the summer rush.

They entered a busier-than-usual Bright Market and scanned the shelves, grabbing what Cade needed for dinner. She helped pick out the best cut of meat and suggested some fresh herbs for the dish. As she was rounding an aisle, a girl who was on her cell phone bumped into her, knocking into her shoulders extremely hard. Harper's sunglasses flew off, and she came face-to-face with the girl and her two friends. All three appeared to be college-aged. "Oh my gosh, I'm so sorry," the girl who bumped her said.

"It's okay. Just maybe next time don't look at your phone when you're shopping." It came out harsher than she intended. But one of her good friends in culinary school had lost her mother due to a distracted driver, so it was a sensitive subject.

The girl's mouth twisted. "And next time maybe take your shades off when you're in the store."

The other two girls were staring at her. Rather than make a big deal out of it, she reached down to pick up her glasses and scrambled to put them back on. Which must've looked weird, since she really didn't need them on in the store and the girl had called her out on it. "I've had eye surgery recently," she fibbed. "Can't be exposed to light."

The girl who'd bumped her gave her an odd look and then the three took off, whispering and looking back at her. It was probably nothing, but a queasy feeling gnawed in the pit of her stomach, and she was suddenly chilled to the bone.

"Everything all right?" Cade came over and put a hand on her shoulder.

"Everything's fine. Just some snarky girls. No big deal."

"You sure? You seemed rattled."

"I'm...fine, Cade." She plastered on a smile and gazed down at his shopping cart. "Have everything you need?"

"You tell me," he said, smiling. "Do I? Oh, you were talking about the food."

She chuckled. He was definitely loosening up, and she needed to do the same. "Looks like you do, both ways."

"Okay, then let's get out of here so I can wow you in the kitchen. Among other places," he whispered in her ear. He had turned out to be such a tease. And she loved every second of it.

"Let's try the kitchen first and see how you do."

"You mean if I get an A grade, I get to wow you in the—"

She put two fingers to his mouth. "Shh, Cade." She looked around. Those three girls were in the checkout line now, and one of them was staring again.

"On second thought, I think we need a good bottle of wine for tonight."

"We have wine back at the cabin, quite a bit of it."

"I know, but you need to pick up cabernet sauvignon. It works best with your dish."

"Okay, you're the chef." He spun their cart around and headed to the liquor aisle. Harper gave one discreet look back at the checkout, noting the girls had left the market.

"You know what, I forgot something," she said. "You go get the wine, and I'll meet you at checkout."

"What'd you forget?"

She smiled coyly. "Body lotion."

His brows arched, and he smiled. "See ya."

She left him, grabbed some lavender body lotion down

aisle nine, then rushed up to the check stand, scouring over the tabloids. Luckily, there was only a mention of *One Last Date*, but no photos of her. Apparently, she'd been relocated to page four. All good news.

She breathed a sigh of relief.

Now she could look forward to dinner with Cade tonight back in the safety of the cabin.

"The thing is, once I start preparing the meal, you can't come in the kitchen until it's ready," Cade said to her when they finally got back to the cabin.

"Really?"

"I'm doing this all on my own." He began putting the groceries away. "And later you can tell me where I went wrong."

"Okay, but I have faith in you. You're going to do great."

"You do? You have faith in me?" He set his handpicked potatoes out on the counter.

"Of course I do."

He rubbed his hand over his chest, looking a bit perplexed. "I don't want to let you down."

"You won't." She reached up to kiss his lips. "Just do your best. I'll leave you to it."

"Enjoy your afternoon off. What're going to do?"

"I'll be in my room, doing some research, but if you get in a bi—"

This time, he gave her a quick shut-up kiss. "Go." He pointed to the door. "I'm good."

"I'm going, and yes, *you are good*."

She went into her bedroom and caught her reflection in the mirror. The expression on her face could only be described as bliss. Pure joy, happiness like no other. What was in her heart was plastered all over her face. She couldn't believe how much she cared for Cade, how happy he made her.

She sat on the bed and picked up her phone. She'd gotten three text messages from Lily asking for a good time to talk. Since she'd been with Cade almost nonstop lately, she hadn't had time to call. She punched in Lily's speed dial, and Lily answered on the first ring.

"Hi, it's me."

"Harper? It's good to hear your voice. It's been a while."

"I know. It's been…well, I've been spending a lot of time with your brother."

There was a pause on the other end of the phone. "Is this something we need to talk about?"

"Maybe, but first tell me what's going on. I feel so isolated here. In a good way, but what can you tell me about my situation?"

"Well, the search for Harper continues. But it's simmering down. I think. I mean, you're still on the news, but not as much as when you first dumped Dale."

She blew out a breath. "Oh, that's positive."

"It's been close to two weeks now. But that's nothing in tabloid land. They can milk a story for months. Especially a high-profile one like yours."

"We went to Bright Market today. I was fully disguised and I didn't see my picture on any of the front pages. I thought that was something."

"We?"

She ignored Lily's question. "How's your mother doing? And the rest of the family?"

"Well, Mom is doing fine. But now she's worried that she isn't hearing enough from Cade. She thought he'd be checking in every day, bugging her about the business. Giving him grief for making him stay away so long. But he hasn't been calling at all. So, what's up with that?"

"Lily, I, uh. I think you should know, Cade and I are getting along really well now."

"You mean he's not busting your chops, not hating your healthy meals?"

"No. He's been…great. We've been spending time together. Hiking, boating, playing cards. Uh, keeping busy."

"Harper, what aren't you telling me?"

Harper squeezed her eyes shut. She scrunched up her face. "Oh, Lily. I want you to know, I came here with all good intentions. I take my profession seriously, and I was trying to do just that. Trying to be Cade's personal chef and no more. But we're pretty much alone here, and I've been isolated, trying to keep out of the public eye. It started out with us taking hikes together. Then, one day he surprised me with a boat ride, and now we go out on the boat a lot. We have this ongoing rummy game, too, and it's been…"

"What are you telling me? That my brother is having fun? That he's not stressed out anymore?"

"He asked me to teach him how to cook."

"Cade is cooking?" Lily's voice rose to a higher pitch.

"Making me dinner as we speak. It's all his doing. He wanted to learn."

"Wow, Cade is cooking. Having a good time. I think I hate you."

"Oh no, Lily. Please—"

"Kidding, Harp. I couldn't hate you. I love you for getting Cade out of his rut. Sounds like he's coming out his grief. And the two of you are…"

"We're close, Lily. I'm falling for him and I think he feels the same way. I didn't mean to take advantage of the situation. You have to know. It's not a fling, Lil. It goes much deeper than that. I'm in love with Cade. I love him very much."

"Oh, Harper," Lily said softly. "Are you sure? I mean, you just came off that roller coaster with Dale."

"I didn't love Dale. Not like the way I love your brother. He's…amazing."

"How does he feel about you?"

"Honestly, I don't know. We don't talk about feelings. At least not now. But he's happy, and I'm happy. And I don't know where this is heading. But I thought you should know."

"Honey, I'm ecstatic for you and Cade. But there are so many variables. Like, you've been lying to him since the day you met him."

"I know," Harper whispered. Saying it aloud made it seem that much worse. "I've been thinking about that a lot. My conscience has been bothering me. I want to tell him the truth so badly, but I don't want to betray your trust and screw things up. You've been such a loyal friend."

"I don't know what to tell you, Harper. Honestly, if Cade is happy now and you two have gotten close, maybe you should tell him the truth. I think he can handle it."

"You do?"

"I mean, I hope so. But it's up to you. Whatever you decide to do is fine with me."

"And your mom?"

"I'll talk to her. Make her understand. Hey, love is messy sometimes. Mom will be glad that someone new is in his life. That he's come out of his grief. That's big."

"This is happening so fast, and it scares me. But I think I have to tell him."

"Whatever you decide, I have your back."

"Thanks." She nibbled on her lips, contemplating the task ahead. "I'll figure out a good time to tell him, Lil. When the time is right."

The table by the fireplace was all set with the best dishes in the cabin. The wineglasses sparkled, and candles flickered from every corner of the room. Cade had laid out pillows to sit on, and a low-simmering fire burned in the fireplace. The meal was ready. So was he. He wanted to please Dawn; it mattered to him that he would. He'd done this for her, to be a part of her world and show her that he cared.

He didn't know when or why it happened, but he was in deep with her. He couldn't imagine being here at the cabin without her. She'd pulled him out of his slumber and made him see light again. She was pretty and funny and sweet. It'd been his lucky day when she came into his life. She'd torn down his defenses, leaving him open and vulnerable, and he was falling hard for her. Nothing felt more right.

He strode to her bedroom door and knocked.

"Cade?"

"It's me," he said, walking into the room. He grabbed her hand and lifted her up from her seat at the secretary desk. "Close your eyes."

"Why?"

"Just close them and come with me."

He covered her eyes with his hands, just to be sure. They penguin walked out of the room with him behind her until they reached the table by the fireplace set for two. "Okay, open them."

He stepped to her side to gauge her reaction. She opened her eyes and peered at the table, the fireplace, the candles, and her loving expression told him all he needed to know. "Oh, Cade. This is beautiful."

"Like you," he said, kissing her cheek.

"I love it."

"Well, I hope you like the food as much as this."

"It smells wonderful."

"Have a seat," he said. "I'll plate up the meal."

She smiled. "You're using all the right lingo."

"I should. I've been through three digital cookbooks today."

She laughed and then took her seat on the pillow.

He strode into the kitchen, his chest puffed out a little. He'd made a good impression with the table setting—now he only hoped the meal was edible.

The riced potatoes looked good. They were a breeze. All it took to rice them was a strong arm and some herbs and butter. It was amazing how much different they tasted than regular old mashed potatoes. He laid those down on the plate first, then arranged two of the braised short ribs on top. He crisscrossed the asparagus on a slant, so that the stalks towered above the meat on an angle. For an amateur, it wasn't half-bad.

He brought the dishes to the table, serving Dawn first. She was staring at the fire, watching the embers burn. "Here you go."

She turned a discerning eye on the food, and her expression changed. "Cade. Wow."

"You haven't tasted it yet."

"I don't have to. I can see you did this perfectly. The presentation is half the battle. I know it's gonna be delish."

He rubbed the back of his neck. "Hope so."

Feeling accomplished, he took a seat. He hadn't been this content since before Bree. He sighed and waited for Dawn to take the first bite.

She managed to get a little portion of each dish onto her fork and then brought it to her mouth. She closed her eyes as she chewed, as if she could discern the different flavors that way. "Oh, yum."

"Really?"

"It's good, Cade. Really, really good."

He grinned. "Thanks."

She gazed at him, pride beaming from her eyes. "You did a great job on the meal."

"You didn't taste the biscuits yet. They didn't rise like I hoped."

She looked over at the basket on the table. The biscuits were flat and crunchy. "Making perfect biscuits is an art. I'll still eat them."

"You don't have to."

She grabbed one from the basket and chomped on it. She chewed and chewed. "Not bad for a first time."

"You're just trying to make me feel better."

"No, I'm not." She gave him an adorable wink. "I'm saving that for later, in the bedroom."

"Well in that case, I'll make you dinner every night."

She smiled as he poured wine, and then she raised her glass. "To you," she said, giving his glass a clink. "And your new cooking skills."

He went along with that, but secretly he toasted Dawn coming into his life, saving him from sinking into the quicksand of grief.

Cade sat on the bed, glancing down at Dawn. He didn't think he'd ever seen a more beautiful sight than the brunette lying there, her hair tousled, her expression so serene. She opened her eyes and immediately reached for him, wrapping her arms around his neck. "Mornin'," he said, bending to give her a kiss.

"Hmm." She sighed. "Why are you getting up so early?"

"Babe, it's not early. It's ten o'clock already."

They'd had quite a workout in bed last night. Just thinking about it made his body tighten and his pulse race.

"Ten o'clock?" Dawn popped up, the sheets covering her delicious body falling off her. "Why didn't you wake me?"

"Because you looked like Sleeping Beauty. Snored a bit, too."

"Cade, you know I don't snore."

"If you say so."

She tossed a pillow at him, and he went down laughing.

She laughed, too, as she scrambled off the bed. He reached for her, but she was too fast; she wiggled right out of his arms. "Oh no, you don't. We're late. I still have to put together lunch and we haven't even had coffee yet."

He gestured with his arms. "Look around and show me who cares?"

"I care. I'm being paid to feed you. And we've planned that trip around the lake. We were supposed to get an early start, remember?"

"Yes, but that was before we tripped all around the bed last night, remember?"

"So, you don't want to go?"

The disappointment in her voice tortured him. That, and the fact that she was buck naked in front of him, her lips in a pout. He'd rather spend the day in bed with her, but he wouldn't go back on his word. "Of course I want to go. We're not on any time schedule. Why don't you get ready and I'll meet you in the kitchen? I'll make coffee."

She smiled, a big, wide grin that warmed his heart. "Okay. I'll only be a few minutes."

"Oh, and wear those denim shorts—you know, the ones that are all torn up."

"You mean my Daisy Dukes?"

He swallowed hard. "Yeah, those."

She blew him a kiss. "I sure will."

He laughed and walked into the kitchen, shaking his head. He was in deep with Dawn, and it was the best place to be. She lightened his mood and made everything fun.

Somehow, after all this was over, he'd find a way for them to be together.

He set coffee brewing. As he reached into the cabinet, bringing down two mugs, he heard a car pull up on the drive, and he frowned slightly in confusion. Who could that be? He walked over to the window and found three more cars pulling up behind the first one. Then a Channel 10 news van pulled up. "Oh, crap."

He knew what this was about. He wasn't gonna let these guys intrude on his vacation.

He opened the front door and walked out onto the porch. Cameras snapped his picture, and questions were immediately slung at him. He held up a hand, gesturing to stop, and leveled them all a hard look. "Not a step farther," he said, standing his ground at the foot of the porch. If he allowed them, they'd be shoving their microphones in his face.

What on earth did his brother, Gage, do now to warrant the paparazzi seeking him out for a comment? Hell, he'd been down this road before, too many times.

"Where's Harper?" one reporter asked.

"Are you hiding out together?" another one shouted.

"Do you know the entire country is looking for Harper?" The questions were hurled at him, one right after the other.

"Who the hell is Harper?" he replied. "I think you've got the wrong guy here."

"Harper Dawn," a reporter shouted. "The woman you're living with."

"What?"

Just then, the door creaked open, and Dawn exited. "Go back inside," he told her. "This isn't about you."

Dawn didn't heed his warning, but instead stepped up next to him. Color drained from her face, her expression dire. She put a hand on his arm. "It is about me, I'm afraid. Cade, I'm so sorry."

"Sorry?" He blinked and blinked again. What was she talking about?

But at her appearance on the porch, the entire crowd started shouting questions at Dawn. His mind muddied up. What was happening? The reporters kept calling her Harper. Harper Dawn.

"When did you dye your hair?"

"Is it for your disguise?"

"Does this mean you don't love Dale Murphy anymore?"

"Yes, I'd like the answer to that myself." A man walked up, slender with blond hair and deceptively cool blue eyes. As if he were a god, the sea of paparazzi separated to let the guy through.

It was like a freak show gone bad, and Cade was right in the middle of it.

Harper silently prayed for guidance. The reporters were relentless. And Dale? Now, that was a surprise. Where had he come from? Why was he here looking forlorn? Her heart pounded hard against her chest.

She turned to Cade. He was...oh dear God, he stared at her with a mixture of confusion and panic. As if he was hoping for all of this to be some giant mistake that she could explain away. "Dawn?"

She squeezed her eyes shut briefly, shaking her head. "I'm so sorry, Cade. My name's not Dawn. Well, it is, but I'm Harper Dawn. And I was going to tell you—"

"It's true, then? You're not who you say you are? You're in some sort of disguise?"

She swallowed hard, tears forming in her eyes, but she refused to let the cameras catch her crying.

"She's Harper Dawn," the blond man said, "and I'm here to win her back. To remind her of our dream. We had beautiful plans to open a restaurant together. To be married, partners in love and life. I want you to be my one last date."

All the cameras turned toward Chef Dale, catching his plea. He stood there, bold but sympathetic in the eyes of the world. He was good, she'd give him that. He always knew how to capture the spotlight. She didn't love him. She never really had, but his charm and wit had had her fooled for a time. That's where she'd gone wrong.

The man she loved was standing beside her, and with each passing second his expression grew more and more grim. Cade was looking at her now like she was a monster. An ugly, lying, two-faced creature that disgusted him.

"One Last Date?" Cade's mouth twisted. "That reality show?" He looked out at the reporters, the news vans, now three in number, and she could see it in his expression as the full impact of her deceit hit him hard.

"That's right," Dale said. "We met on the show, and we fell in love."

"I didn't," she said to Cade, shaking her head adamantly. "I didn't love him."

Cade dismissed her denial. "You're a damn reality star?"

She shook her head. "No, no. It's not like that."

"She got cold feet is all," Dale said, "and ran off. But I'm not giving up on you, Harper. I'm here to ask for another chance."

Cade flinched and then gave her a look filled with pain and anger. Then his eyes narrowed, zeroing in on her. "Harper? My sister has a friend named Harper...do you know Lily?"

Oh crap. "I think we should go inside and talk, Cade."

"And deprive these vultures of a story?"

"Cade, please." She pleaded with him with everything

she had inside. Her eyes burned from holding back tears. "Please."

He looked her up and down, battling with his decision, then jerked his head toward the door. "Get inside, *Harper*."

She flinched. Oh man, this was a mess. "Are you c-coming?"

"It's my cabin."

She walked inside first, Cade directly behind her. He slammed the door shut and locked it. She was trembling, her legs weak. She had trouble breathing, her heart was racing so fast. Cade hated her. She could see it in his eyes. At least he hadn't left her out there—he hadn't tossed her to the wolves. They were still outside, shouting questions.

Cade walked straight to the liquor cabinet and poured himself a scotch. He downed it in one gulp, then poured himself another.

"Cade, please. Let me explain."

He glared at her from across the room, desolation in his eyes. She'd hurt him. She'd destroyed his trust and anything that they may have had. *Oh God.*

"Sit down," he ordered.

She took a seat on the sofa adjacent to the fireplace. The same one where they'd played rummy so many times, the same place where Cade had served her his first home-cooked meal.

He stood for a while, pacing. Not saying anything. Just gulping scotch and, apparently, trying to calm himself down.

When he finished the glass, he poured another, then took a seat. "Explain."

She began at the beginning, telling him how she and Lily had become friends. And how she'd been dating, wanting so badly to fall in love and be married. She wanted a family before she was thirty. She had a life plan that included opening a restaurant, and so when Chef Dale Murphy had been picked for *One Last Date*, Lily convinced her that she should join the show. Harper had deep reservations about it, but the producers loved the idea of putting another chef on, so before she knew it, she was chosen to be one of twelve women vying for love.

All the while she was explaining, Cade stared at the fireplace, refusing to look at her. His face was hard, and nothing she had to say seemed to change that.

"So, after I refused Dale's marriage proposal, I became public enemy number one. The press was horrid to me, hounding me everywhere I went. They knew where I lived, where my parents lived. I had nowhere else to go. So Lily offered to let me stay here at the cabin."

"Nice of my sister," he muttered sarcastically.

"It turned out you were coming here, too. They knew if you were told I was coming up here, you'd have an excuse to stay home and work. I didn't want to do it, Cade. But I was in a bind. And so Lily came up with the idea of me being your personal chef. It seemed harmless enough at the time. That way, both of us could stay here."

Cade rose from the sofa, looking down at her. "You got paid to sleep with me."

"No! I wasn't paid a thing." She lifted from the sofa to face him, hating that he'd jumped to such a conclusion. Hating that he thought that little of her. "I'm sorry, Cade. Really, really sorry. But I think you know, us being together intimately wasn't in the plan. It just happened." And it had been earth-shattering.

"For all I know, you were in on this from the beginning. Did the creators of the show get to you? Is that what this was all about? You did it for the ratings? Because honestly, I can't figure out what kind of woman has to go on a damn reality show to find love. Certainly, not one for me."

That stung, and she bit her lower lip, holding back tears. "Cade, that's not true."

"You lied to me over and over. About *everything*."

"I was going to tell you the truth. Honest, I was."

"I don't believe that," he said, his voice a deep growl. "I'll *never* believe that. You made a fool out of me, Harper. I feel like such an idiot. But you did show me a good time. You sure know your way around the bedroom."

She jerked back and gasped. She wanted to slap his face. He was being intentionally cruel. Maybe she deserved his wrath for bringing all this down on him, but she'd never thought Cade could be so hurtful. He tossed his tumbler into the fireplace. The sound of shattering glass echoed in the silence of the room, seeming to seal their fate. "I'm leaving," he said. "Stay or go, it's up to you."

As in, he didn't give a crap about what happened to her. "I'm…leaving, too."

From now on, she'd have to battle the paparazzi, but it would be a whole lot easier than trying to convince Cade she'd never meant to hurt him.

Seven

"I'm not leaving here until you speak to me." Lily stood in front of Cade's office desk at Tremaine Corp., tilting her chin at him stubbornly. His sister was the last person he wanted to see today. Well, make that the second-to-last person he wanted to see. His day had gone from bad to worse, and Lily was just the topping on the cake.

He rubbed the back of his neck and leaned back in his chair, staring up at her. "What is it this time?"

"You're working yourself to death, Cade. You're never home, and Mom's worried about you."

"I'm fine. Just busy doing what I love to do."

"You're not supposed to be working these long hours. You're under too much stress."

"Not as much stress as my last vacation," he shot back. "Remember, when you and Mom set me up?"

"We didn't set you up, brother. And if you'd stop feeling sorry for yourself long enough, you'll realize it. How many times do I have to apologize?"

"The best thing you can do for me is let it go."

"Cade, please."

He rose from his desk, his temper flaring. "No, Lily. Not this time. Have you seen the newspapers lately? My picture is splashed across the front page, with Chef Dale and Harper, or whatever her name is. I just love seeing my picture in the tabloids in a love-triangle-gone-bad headline. Geesh, Gage must be laughing his head off. He's usually the one on the front page." He looked out his office window and sighed. "How do you suppose that affects my blood pressure?"

"It's only been a few weeks. It'll die down soon."

He turned to face her. "A few weeks too many."

Every time he thought about *Harper*—he still thought of her as Dawn—his stomach knotted up. He didn't want to remember the good times. He certainly tried not thinking about how pretty she was, how sweet her body felt crushed up against his, how she moaned his name when he made love to her. He fought those thoughts on a daily basis, having only the reminder of her grand deceit to sway him back to reality. To the truth of her betrayal.

"Cade, Harper is terribly sorry. She's living with her folks now, barely holding on. She's not working. She's trying to keep a low profile. These past few weeks haven't been easy on her. The media won't leave her alone. She doesn't have security guards to keep them away, the way you do."

Cade hated hearing it. He hated that her folks were being hassled, too. It wasn't fair. They were innocent in all this. "I'll send some security to help out. For her parents' sake."

"Just for her parents?"

"Yeah, Lil. Don't read anything else into it."

"I've already offered, but Harper won't hear of it. She refused help."

"Then that's that." So why was his gut twisting? Why was he feeling like crap all of a sudden?

"Is there anything else?" he asked Lily. He wanted her to leave so he could put these feelings aside and dive back into his work.

"Yes, now that you asked." Lily plopped down on the leather seat facing his desk. "Sit down. We need to talk about Mom's seventieth birthday."

"What about it?"

"It's happening in less than a month. We have to make arrangements. I need your input."

He took a seat and shook his head. "You don't need me. You can do this."

"You expect me to plan a party for 150 people on my own? No way, bro. That's a big undertaking. Gage is flying in special the day before her birthday, so that leaves you and me."

"Hire a company or party planner or whatever to do it."

"Not gonna happen. Mom wouldn't appreciate it as much, and you know it. We need to make this special for her."

"Okay, fine. I'll help. But today's a killer."

"How about on Saturday morning?"

"Fine, we'll talk on Saturday."

"Great." Lily gave him a big smile. "I'll see you Saturday. And Cade, just so you know, Harper is doing about as well as you are right now."

"Go," he commanded, pointing to the door. Lily bounced out of the office with pep in her step. What on earth was she so happy about all the time?

He went back to work, looking blankly at his computer screen, Lily's last words echoing in his ears. *Harper is doing about as well as you are right now.*

He'd fallen for her, and she'd made a fool out of him. He shouldn't feel anything but contempt for her. Yet knowing that she was hurting, too, didn't make him feel any better.

It just made his day even more horrible.

"That's a sweet girl," Harper said as she stroked Queenie's pure white fur. The cat sat on her lap purring, her little motor running full speed. "It's been a long time since you've gotten this much love from me, hasn't it?" she asked softly, running her hands over the cat's back, sinking her fingers into her fur and then rubbing her behind the ears. Every so often she'd stop petting her and the cat would turn to look her in the eye, as if to say, *do more.*

Why not? She didn't have anything else to do. She hadn't left her parents' house since she'd gotten here two weeks ago, and now only an occasional news van would show up in front of the house. Lucky for her, her father was a survivalist. They had enough food and supplies for months, and her parents had hunkered down with her, lying low. They claimed they were glad to stay at home and not give the press what they wanted. She loved them for trying to protect her, but it was a great inconvenience to them.

Her mom made sure to give her extra hugs every day, and her dad would give her a good-night kiss before turning in. Just like when she was a little girl. They were the best, and she hated putting them in this position. That's why she'd gone up to the cabin—to avoid causing them this grief. Not to mention the embarrassment of the scandal she'd created. A love triangle, the tabloids had said, with her right smack in the middle of it.

She didn't know if she'd ever get back to doing what she loved, to being a chef. Right now, she was known as a heartbreaker. Period.

"Honey, I brought you some hot tea."

Her mom's cure for whatever ails you was always herbal tea. She didn't have the heart to tell her mom she preferred coffee.

"It's raspberry hibiscus."

"Sounds yummy. Thanks, Mom."

Her mother set two teacups down on the cocktail table and took a seat on the sofa next to her. Queenie hadn't moved a muscle, and her mother gave the cat a loving scratch under the chin. "She really is a queen," Harper said.

"We've spoiled her."

"The same way you've spoiled me."

"Oh, honey, we're not spoiling you, we're supporting you and letting you know we have your back. Dad and I hate to see you so sad."

"I'm not *that* sad, Mom. Just at loose ends."

Her mom reached for her hand. "I know it seems hopeless right now. But this will pass. You just have to be patient."

"I've worked so hard to make a name for myself. I have a publisher interested in my cookbook, but I haven't had the heart to work on it for weeks now. I gave up my job to go on *One Last Date* and now, just because I couldn't go through with a marriage proposal, no one will hire me because suddenly I'm this big villain."

"Not to everyone."

"I appreciate your support, Mom."

"That's not what I mean. Have you looked on social media?"

"Social media? Mom, what do you know about that?"

"Hey, your mom wasn't born in the stone ages. I know about those sites. I've been reading some of those posts, and there's more than a few people who are on your side. They say you stuck up for your principles and decided to follow what your brain and your heart were telling you to do."

"Really?"

"Yes, really. So not everyone's against you. And for those trolls who are bashing you, I say, so what? They don't define you. *You* define you."

Harper sipped her tea. Her mother was amazing, giving her this pep talk and making her see things from an entirely different perspective. It gave her a mental boost. "Thanks, Mom. That means a lot to me."

Her mother gave her hand a squeeze. "That's my girl. You need to get back out there. You need to show them that you're not going to let them hold you back."

Her cell phone rang, and she looked at the screen. "It's Lily," she told her mom.

"I'll let you girls talk," her mom said, rising from the sofa.

"Mom, I can call her back. We haven't finished our tea."

"No, no. It's fine, sweetheart. You can talk to me anytime. You talk to Lily and tell her I said hello."

"Okay, Mom. Thanks." She sat up straighter and answered the phone. "Hi, Lily."

"Hi, you."

It was great to hear Lily's voice. They spoke every other day, keeping in touch with each other without mentioning the sore subject of Cade. "How's your day going?"

"Okay, I guess. I'm knee-deep in preparations for my mother's birthday. It's a big challenge. I don't know how party planners do it."

"Some might say the same about interior decorators. All those choices, but you manage to put together amazing looks. I guess it's all about your passion."

"I guess so."

"Speaking of passion, any luck on getting a position?"

"No one's beating down my door for my culinary talents, I can tell you that. I miss working."

"Are the sleaze buckets still out there?"

"Actually, it's been much better. They're not camped out in front of the house anymore. I've yet to go outside, though, afraid someone will be lurking around a corner."

"That's no way to live."

"Tell me about it."

"Well, I have a solution to your problem, but I want you to hear me out before you say anything. Promise?"

"The last time I promised you something, I wound up on a reality show."

"I know, but this is different. It'll be good for your career."

Harper took a steadying breath. After her mother's pep talk, she had a newfound desire to get back to her old life. Where she was respected as a chef, and as a person. Where she could walk down the street holding her head high.

"I'm listening, Lil."

"Remember to let me speak. As you know, I've been working on my mother's birthday bash and I've been going full steam ahead, but I ran into a roadblock, and it's something you can possibly help me with."

"Me? What can I do to help?"

"Well, you see, Mom's very fussy about certain things, and dining is very important to her. Her favorite caterer needed emergency surgery yesterday and she had to cancel on us. It's not her fault or anything, but now, with such short notice, we're sort of stuck. I was thinking, hoping, that you could take her place as our chef. Of course, we'd pay you, and you'd have a team to help you. So, um, I know it's a lot to ask, but you've been wanting to get back to work, and this is a really good gig. Would you consider doing it?"

"I assume Cade will be there?"

"Of course. It's our mother's seventieth birthday."

"Then no. I can't help you. Sorry, Lil."

"Wait a minute, you haven't even thought about it."

"I don't need to think about it. Look, I appreciate you thinking of me, but there's no way I'm going to impose myself on your family and cause any more trouble. You and I both know Cade doesn't want me there."

She heard Lily sigh on the other end of the phone. "And I also know you're in love with him."

"So?"

"So, are you giving up so easily? You must not love him enough to fight for him. But if it was as amazing being with him as you said, then I'd say he was worth one more try. He's a good guy and you brought him out of his heartache, Harper. You ended his grieving, and that's really something."

"He hates me, Lily."

"You know what they say. There's a fine line between love and hate."

"That's a cliché and doesn't pertain to me."

"Still, clichés exist for a reason. And I say it does pertain to you. It's a chance to take on a challenge, both in the kitchen and out. We have two weeks to prep. One hundred fifty guests to feed and you'll have to be here to set up the menu with my mother, to train your team. We've got a cozy guesthouse on the property you can stay at while you prep. And you'll be making a name for yourself as an accomplished chef. Doesn't that sound perfect?"

"It would be if…"

"If what?"

"I'll do it only if Cade agrees. I'm not going to spring this on him. Everything has to be cleared by Cade or I won't come."

"I'll talk to him," Lily said.

"No, Lily, I'll speak with him. That's if he'll get on the

phone with me. After all, I'm the one who got in this mess, so it's up to me to make things right. Or as right as they can be, under the circumstances."

"Okay, I think that's fair. You've got the job, if Cade agrees."

"Thanks, Lily." She hung up the phone and closed her eyes. If she was going to do this, it had to be now. Otherwise, she might just chicken out.

She immediately texted Cade. Hi Cade, it's Harper. I'd like to speak with you on the phone. Is it okay for me to call you? Please.

Now the ball was in his court. All she had to do was wait for him to reply.

Or not.

Cade sat in the game room in his favorite suede chair, fully focused on the television screen as he sipped bourbon straight up. *One Last Date* was an idiot concept, and he'd often wondered about the people who actually went on that show. Granted, he'd never once tuned in before, and he was surprised at the occupations of the contestants. There were attorneys, nurses, stockbrokers and *chefs*.

He sat mesmerized watching the women—well, one woman—in her quest for love. Pretty curly-blond-haired Harper Dawn seemed to be the fan favorite, and he could hardly believe she was the same woman he'd spent time with at Bright Landing. The transformation blew his mind, and it had taken him a few episodes to actually believe that Dawn didn't exist—never existed. Harper was a completely different woman. She had paired up nicely with Chef Dale Murphy. Both shared a love of food, cooking and entertaining. They looked good together.

Cade fast-forwarded their kissing scenes, barely able to watch further. But he persisted as Harper looked straight into the camera, giving her testimonial about what she wanted in a man. About her feelings for Dale. But there was something missing in her speech. And as Cade continued watching episode after episode, he began to notice little things about Dale Murphy, culinary chef. He spoke to Harper constantly about opening a restaurant together, about how they made a good team, but on their cooking dates, Dale would question Harper's judgment and give her backhanded compliments. It was apparent he was trying to make himself look the more competent chef by his subtle innuendo.

The more Cade saw, the more he thought the guy an egotistical jerk.

"Cade, are you in here?" His mother, Rose, walked into the room, and he immediately paused the show.

"Yep, I'm in here."

He sipped his drink and looked up at her, caught in the act.

"Bingeing on something?" she asked, taking the seat next to him.

It was obvious he was. "Just trying to keep up on the times."

"By watching *One Last Date*?"

"It's must-see television."

"You're watching Harper, trying to make sense of all this."

"Mom, what kind of woman goes on a reality dating show to find love?"

"Someone who's ready for love, I suppose."

He shook his head. "I don't get it. Dawn—I mean, Harper—was a different person than I'm seeing here. I'm not sure which one she is. I don't know her at all. And the lies she told, the whole deception, I'm sorry, but I can't help but compare her to Bree. Bree never would've done anything like that to me. Heck, not even Madeline would've done something like this." Madeline was an old girlfriend, someone he'd dated for an entire year before he met Bree.

His mother took his hand. "Cade, in your mind Bree was perfect. She was a saint compared to other women, but she was rare. Not everyone can be that perfect. You shouldn't measure all women against Bree's memory. People make mistakes, especially when they're backed into a corner. And I hate to see you give up on someone you obviously care about because of her mistakes. And mine. And Lily's. Try to remember that as you finish watching these episodes. Keep an open mind, son. You don't want to shoot yourself in the foot."

"Dad would say that." He smiled.

"And where do you think he got it from?" His mom squeezed his hand and rose from the seat. "Love you, Cade."

He nodded, his heart warming. "Love you, too, Mom."

And an hour later, he was still watching the show, having reached episode seven, when his cell phone buzzed. He glanced at the screen. It was Harper. His eye began to twitch. He never thought she'd contact him. He had mixed feelings about reading the text, but his curiosity got the better of him. He opened the text, scanning it quickly. She asked if she could speak with him, if she could call him. He wrote back. It's late. Maybe tomorrow. His finger was on the send button, and he stared at his curt reply. No sense being a jerk about it. He erased it and wrote instead, We can talk tomorrow, okay?

She returned the message immediately. Okay, thanks!

Cade's gut clenched. He had no idea what she wanted, and that put him on edge. Maybe he shouldn't have been so quick to agree. Did he really want to speak with Harper?

He wasn't sure. She was all he would think about when he let down his guard.

Folding his arms across his chest, he hunkered down into the cushions of the chair, determined to watch *One Last Date* to the bitter end. He didn't think he'd get much sleep tonight, anyway. Not with thoughts of Harper Dawn invading his head.

"Honey, it's good to see you cooking again. Are you experimenting with a new dish for your cookbook?"

"I am, Mom." Harper was at the stove, putting together an egg-white scramble, a healthy alternative for breakfast. "I've decided to take hold of my life again. What do you think of *Healthy and Hearty with Harper* for the title of my cookbook?"

"I think it's wonderful."

"It's pretty catchy, right? I'm going to dedicate it to you and Dad if the publisher offers me a contract." So far, she'd only gotten offers to do a tell-all book about her time on *One Last Date*. That was so not happening.

"That's sweet, honey. Your dad and I will be honored. And it's not *if*, but when it gets published."

"You have such faith in me. I wish I felt that confident."

"Give yourself some time. This whole ordeal has you rattled. But I think it'll work out in the long run. You're talented, Harper."

"Thanks, Mom. Love you."

"Love you right back."

An hour later, Harper paced back and forth in her bedroom. Her mother had kept her room pretty much intact from when she lived here. She loved the warmth and coziness that still remained, the thick lavender comforter, the pillows in the shape of hearts, the posters of a younger Tim McGraw and Rascal Flatts on the walls. Whenever she came to visit, it was always a comfort to sleep in her old room.

She glanced out the window. The time for stalling was over. She needed to call Cade, and her future could very well be in the balance. She dialed his phone number and waited. It rang, two, three, four times, and just when she thought it was going to voice mail, he picked up. "Hello."

"Hi, it's me," she said.

"Which me is it?" he asked.

Oh boy, he wasn't going to make this easy.

"It's Harper. The same person you know, except by a different name."

"I doubt that, but go on."

She counted to three before answering. At least he hadn't hung up on her. That was encouraging. What wasn't encouraging was the way her heart pounded and her stomach churned just hearing his deep, masculine voice. It did things to her. Reminded her of happier times.

"How are you, Cade?"

"Fine. Perfect."

He didn't ask how she was, and that should tell her something. "I, uh, that's good to hear. Are you busy? Because I can call you later if you are."

"Harper." He always seemed to say her name with contempt, or was she reading too much into it? "Say what you have to say."

"Okay, well, you know how sorry I am about the way things turned out. And I don't suppose you want to see me and I'm not asking for that. But what I am asking for is a chance to help out your family and try to get my reputation back as a chef. Right now, because of the scandal, I haven't been working. I, uh, quit my job to go on the show, and I'm not sure restaurants are going to hire a chef that comes with so much controversy. And, well, since Lily is in a bind to find someone to prepare your mom's birthday meal, she asked me to do it. But," she rushed out, "I will only take the job if it's okay with you. I mean, you wouldn't have to see me. I promise to steer clear of you. I'll be working hard prepping the meals and training the crew. I told Lily it all depends on what you say."

"So, let me get this right. You're asking my permission to come here as a chef and work my mother's birthday bash."

"Yes, that's right."

She heard him sigh into the phone. There was a long pause. "I'm not sure it's a good idea."

Tears welled in her eyes, not from losing the job, but because Cade hated her so much he really wanted nothing more to do with her. "I...understand. Well, then there's not much else to—"

"I'm not sure it's a good idea, but yeah. I won't stand in your way if you want the job."

"So, I have your blessing?"

"Hardly that. But Mom needs a chef and you need the work."

"I'll take that." Her spirits lifted. "Thank you, Cade."

He remained quiet, and she decided to end the call before he changed his mind.

"Bye, Cade." Gently, she hung up the phone and fist-pumped the air several times before flopping on her bed with a big grin.

She was going to make the Tremaine party the best they'd ever had.

Even if she'd have to tiptoe around Cade the whole time she was there.

Eight

"I'm so glad you're here," Lily said, giving Harper a big, squeezy kind of hug. Her friend's arms felt good around her. Harper needed to know one person was happy she was here. But she couldn't think about Cade right now. She had one week to pull this all together.

"Lily, you're such a great friend. I needed that kind of welcome."

"You're an equally good friend, and you look good."

Harper rolled her eyes. "I don't, but thanks for saying that." She looked out at the view of the estate from the steps of the guesthouse. "Wow, your home is amazing. I've seen pictures of it, but they don't do it justice."

"I can't believe you've never been here before. Seems weird."

"I know. I guess the timing was never right for me to visit."

"Yeah, I remember how busy we both were back then. But you're here now, and I can't wait to show you around.

But first things first. Here's the key to the house." Lily handed it to her.

She glanced down at the key. "What's also weird is you're always handing me keys to your family's homes."

"Nothing weird about that."

Lily was always upbeat. It was hard not to be happy around her. Hard, but not impossible. Right now she was somewhere between nervous and excited.

"Come on, let's go inside."

As they stepped into the house, the vibe Harper got was nothing short of perfect. It was a spacious guesthouse with a Southwestern flair, lots of windows, tall ceilings and a rock fireplace. She walked into the kitchen and smiled. It was well stocked, with long granite countertops and all the appliances, big and small, a chef would ever need. "Nice kitchen."

"If you think this is nice, wait until you see the kitchen in the main house. It's state-of-the-art."

"Now you've got me really excited."

"Let's take your luggage to your room." She grabbed one bag as Harper grabbed the other and they moved down the hallway. "Take a peek and pick whichever room you like."

Both were pretty. One was in a neutral tone, with furnishings that would suit either a male or female guest, and the other was done in warm melon and cream tones. It was an easy choice. "I like this one."

"Yep, that's my favorite, too," Lily said.

She was suddenly overwhelmed with gratitude. "Thanks for all this, Lil. And for picking me up today at my apartment. You didn't have to go so far out of your way."

"I wanted to. Just in case any stray photographers dogged you."

"Luckily, I think they've moved on. At least I hope they have ever since Dale said he's given up on the two of us.

I think he just wanted the sympathetic press to help him launch his new restaurant."

"That sleaze."

"I don't blame him. I think he was convinced we would be perfect together. But unfortunately, I realized the only sparks we generated was when we were cooking in the kitchen. That was it. There was nothing real between us romantically."

"You made the right decision, hon."

"At least I did one thing right." She smiled. She was not going to be Debbie Downer this week and ruin Lily's mood.

"Well, enough talk about the past. Why don't you settle in, and I'll come get you, say, in two hours. We'll have a meeting with Mom and nail down the menu. She's anxious to see you."

"Gosh, it'll be good to see her, too."

"Sounds good."

Lily gave her a kiss on the cheek. "Welcome to our home, Harper."

"Thanks, Lil."

After Lily left, Harper unpacked her bags and put her toiletries in the bathroom. She thought she was too keyed up to rest, but suddenly a bout of fatigue hit her. She took off her clothes, put on an oversize T-shirt and set her phone alarm to wake her in forty-five minutes. That should give her plenty of time to dress before meeting Rose. She lay down on the comfy queen bed and closed her eyes, managing to shove aside all of her doubts and fears about this job and this place and simply let her mind clear.

A few raps on the front door woke her from her nap. She glanced at the time on her phone—Lily was really early. "Coming," she called out. "I'll be right there."

She padded to the front door and opened it. "Sorry, I thought you said two hours—"

But she didn't finish her thought, because it wasn't Lily who stood on her doorstep.

It was Cade.

"Oh, uh…" For a few seconds they just stared into each other's eyes. Then Cade's gaze lifted to her honey-blond hair—now back to its natural color—and the waves that swept over her shoulders. Next, he moved down to her chest, reading the words on her T-shirt: Chefs Like It Hot. His brow lifted at that and then his gaze traveled farther down to her exposed thighs. He took all of her in, his expression unreadable but for a certain gleam in his eyes.

"You look…"

Her heart pounding, her hand automatically touched the tips of her hair. "Different, I know."

But he looked different, too. He was wearing a white dress shirt tucked into a pair of slacks—business clothes. So different from the guy who wore jeans and T-shirts all day long back at the cabin. Although, with the sleeves rolled up and his collar open, he was just as drop-dead gorgeous and sexy.

He nodded, his lips tight as if he was remembering her disguise, her lies.

"What are you doing here? I mean, you have every right to be here, since this is your house, but I never expected you to—"

"I thought it would be less weird if we saw each other in person privately first, rather than giving the family a show if we bumped into each other in front of them."

She nibbled on her lower lip. For a second there, she'd had hope. "I see… It's weird now, too."

"At least we don't have an audience."

Because he would hate that. She was grateful that he didn't mention *One Last Date* and that audience.

"I'm sorry, Cade."

"I didn't come here for an apology. I know you're sorry."

Well, that was to the point. "Would you like to come in?"

He swept his gaze over her body once again, quickly this time, and he shook his head. "No."

But his eyes said something different. His eyes gave him away. He didn't trust her. She knew that. But he seemed to be struggling, trying to remain distant.

"Is there anything else?"

"Not really, no. Just wanted to break the ice."

"Consider it broken," she said softly. "And thanks again for agreeing to let me do this. It means a lot."

He gave her another nod. "Anything for Mom's birthday."

The meaning wasn't lost on her. He'd do anything for his mom, including enduring Harper's presence at the estate for an entire week.

"Goodbye, Cade." She shut the door, but his arm came out immediately to stop her.

"Wait." He sighed and shook his head. "That came out wrong."

"Did it?"

"It honestly did. I'm not here to hurt you."

"It's okay, Cade. I've got to get dressed. I've got a meeting with your mom in a few minutes. So, if you're through, I'd better be going."

He let go of the door. "Yeah, sure."

She closed it slowly and heard Cade curse under his breath as he walked away. "That went well," she muttered before slumping against the door, trying to hold back tears.

The Tremaine kitchen was almost the size of a small house. There were three large workstations, long counters and two double ovens, not to mention the Sub-Zero refrigerators. Two sliding glass French doors led out to a wraparound patio shaded from the afternoon sun by an awning and a yard that would easily hold 150 people. A large stone fireplace sat in the corner of the patio, and the lawn furniture would be perfect for the guests to sit and have drinks and appetizers. She envisioned the scene in her head. It would be lovely when all was said and done.

"Hello, Harper."

The sound of Rose's gentle voice made her turn from the French doors. They'd met a few times and had had lunch once when she'd come to visit Lily at school and later at graduation. "Hi, Mrs. Tremaine."

"It's Rose, please. Thank you for coming on such short notice." She walked over to Harper and gave her a brief hug.

The gesture meant a lot. She'd take all the hugs she could get lately. "Of course, it's my pleasure."

"It's good to see you, Harper. You're looking well."

"Thank you." But Rose Tremaine looked like the epitome of Southern grace and style. Her silver-pearl hair flipped at the shoulders and shone brilliantly in the daylight. Her eyes were clear sky blue, and so pretty. "It's great to see you, too."

"Mom, Harper is all settled in at the guesthouse," Lily said.

"I hope you find it comfortable."

"It's very comfortable. And this house, especially this kitchen, is like a dream come true."

"Can I get you two anything?" Lily asked. "Some iced tea or lemonade? Or something stronger?"

"I'm fine," Harper said.

"Lily, why don't you bring a pitcher of iced tea over with some glasses? And Irene made some fresh blueberry muffins this morning. Bring those, too."

"Sure, Mom."

"Irene is the family cook," Rose said. "She's been with us twenty years. She'll be around all week to help with the party."

"Great."

"But before we talk about the menu, I need to apologize to you about the mix-up at the cabin."

Heat rushed up Harper's throat, and her cheeks burned. She didn't want to talk about this. She was trying to put it all behind her. "There's no apology necessary, really."

"Lily and I put you in a bad spot. We realize that now."

"But you really helped me, too, since I had nowhere else to go. It was just an impossible situation. And, well, I never meant to hurt anyone."

"Cade's a big boy. He'll come around."

"He's not happy I'm here."

"I wouldn't be too sure of that, Harper. But my meddling days are over. Now, shall we talk about the menu? I was thinking surf and turf. But I'm open to all of your ideas, too."

"Sure, I'm thrilled to talk about my ideas." She opened the file folder she'd brought along. She had been writing down her notes ever since she accepted this job. "I have a list of five options for the meal plan. Or we can combine, as you fit."

"You're organized—I like that."

"I love what I do. It helps."

She and Lily and Rose stayed at the table until every detail of the menu, including appetizers, drinks and desserts, was nailed down. Rose handed her a list of caterers in the area, many of whom would be willing to work alongside her as sous chefs. She would be calling them later today. And though Harper could do desserts, she opted to bring in a pastry chef. Once all their business was conducted and

Harper was satisfied, she rose from the table. "Thanks for your input," she said to Rose and Lily. She grabbed her folder filled with notes and tucked it under her arm. "I'm excited to get started on this. I'll be at the guesthouse, in case either of you think of something we missed."

"Oh, I think we've covered everything," Lily said.

"Dinner is at seven," Rose said.

"Oh, but I can't, uh… I'll be working into the night."

"Nonsense, Harper. You have to eat. And while you're here, you're our guest. We wouldn't dream of not having you for dinner."

"Yes, ma'am. But then there's the matter of…"

Lily took her hand. "Mom's right, Harp. There's no reason why you can't have dinner with us."

"That's right," came the masculine voice from behind her. She turned and faced Cade, who was standing in the kitchen doorway, looking handsome as always. "You should have dinner with the family. I won't be joining you."

The implication was clear. Cade was avoiding her, but he didn't have to be the one doing the avoiding. She'd promised she would steer clear of him. "I don't want to drive you off," she said quietly. "It's not what we agreed on."

"Harper, I have dinner plans of my own tonight."

"Oh, uh, I see." Was it the truth? Was he having dinner with a woman?

"Well, I've gotta get to the office. See you all later," he said.

Everyone said their farewells, and after he was gone, Harper exchanged glances with Rose and Lily. Both had sympathy in their eyes.

"Brothers," Lily mumbled.

Rose remained silent.

"I guess I'll see you in a few hours at dinner."

Lily and Rose both nodded.

Harper walked out of the kitchen, an ache in the pit of her stomach. At the very least, Cade was missing time with his family to avoid her. At the very worst, he had a dinner date with another woman.

"Irene, this meal was delicious," Harper told the Tremaine cook. She was a woman in her early fifties, a little bulky around the middle, with a pleasant smile and pale green eyes. "I ate up everything, and I usually don't do that."

"Coming from you, I'll take that as a compliment. Thank you, Chef Harper."

"It's just Harper, unless the sous chefs are around." She and Irene exchanged smiles. "Which, I'm happy to say, are all lined up. We'll have a staff of seven."

"That's wonderful," Rose said. "And yes, the salmon was delicious, Irene."

"It really was perfectly cooked. It's hard to get just right," Harper added.

Irene beamed. "Thank you. I'll bring coffee and dessert out now."

"Oh, none for me, thank you," Harper said. "I'm so full, I couldn't eat another bite."

"Are you sure?" Lily asked. "Irene makes a to-die-for caramel apple pie."

She patted her tummy. "I'm sure. Maybe I'll grab a bite tomorrow. Thanks for dinner, everyone. I think I'll turn in early tonight."

Lily walked her out, lacing their arms together like the true friend she was. "So, tell me. How was your first day here?"

"Actually, it went pretty smoothly. Better than I expected."

"That's good. You didn't seem to react to seeing Cade again."

"That's because he paid me a visit earlier today to break the ice. He didn't want to have an audience when we first saw each other again."

"Is that right? You didn't tell me."

"I'm telling you now."

"Hmm, he wasn't as shocked as I thought he'd be."

Lily drew her closer and whispered in her ear. "I think I know why."

"Why?"

"He's been watching *One Last Date*. Mom let it slip one day, but she wouldn't elaborate."

"Are you sure? I can't see Cade watching the show. That's not something he would do. He thinks the whole idea is ridiculous."

"I'm only telling you what I know."

They'd reached the front door. "Whatever. I've got too much on my mind to think about it." She kissed Lily's cheek. "Thanks for being the best friend ever."

Lily took a bow. "That's me. Best friend extraordinaire."

They both giggled at her silliness, and then Harper walked out.

The night was cool, and she decided to take a walk around the premises, partly because she'd eaten too much and needed to exercise, and partly to clear her head about Cade. Of all the millions who'd watched *One Last Date*, he was the one person she'd hoped never would. Goodness, she'd revealed so much about herself on that show, exposing her feelings, which she usually held inside. Those producers had a knack for drawing out her deepest emotions. And when she'd rejected Dale when he was down on one knee, all hell had broken loose.

She closed her eyes, wondering when that memory would fade. The sound of horses snorting drew her gaze over to the stables, and she began heading in that direction. It wasn't far from the main house, but the moon had vanished behind the clouds, so she made her way under the guidance of ground lights, crossing the road.

A car came to a careening halt from behind, and she jumped back and turned. Headlights beamed in her face, and she squinted at the blinding light. Her heart pounded.

Someone jumped out of the car, slamming the door. "Geesh, Harper. Are you okay?"

She put her hand to her forehead to block the headlights' glare. "C-cade?"

"Yeah, it's me." He walked over to within a foot of her and looked her over from head to toe. "You sure you're okay?"

She nodded. "I'm fine."

"I didn't see you. Damn it, I could've hit you." He ran a hand down his face. "What were you doing on the road all the way down here?"

"I, uh, was taking a walk and heard the horses."

The gravity of what almost happened finally dawned on her. She swayed back, and Cade caught her arms. He stared at her and his jaw tightened, his eyes in shadow as he gave her arms a gentle up-and-down rub before letting her go. His gentle caress, though brief, touched every part of her body.

"You wanted to see the horses?"

"Yes, I just needed a little more time before turning in."

"Hang on a second." He walked back to his car, a silver Beamer, and turned off the engine. Immediately the bright lights disappeared. "There, that's better," he said, coming to stand beside her. "Come on. Let's go."

"Go?" She shook her head, confused.

"I was heading to the stables. I like to check on my horses whenever I can."

She pointed in the opposite direction. "Maybe I should

walk back to the guesthouse, let you go see the horses on your own."

Cade sighed heavily. "You want to see the horses. I want to see the horses. I think we can manage that."

"If you're sure. I'd love to see them."

"Follow me," he said, taking off and not giving her another chance to decline.

She caught up to him on the third stride, and together they headed toward the stables. "How many horses do you have?"

"The ranch has over twenty. We're breeding them. It's a small operation that our wrangler, Nathan Haines, heads up. I have three horses, Pepper, Cinnamon and Sage."

"I see a trend here. I like it."

"Bree named them," he said. "She didn't like power names. Said they were cliché."

"How so?"

"Well, Storm is big around here. So is Bolt or Thunder."

"I see what she meant. Is it hard talking about her?"

Cade's mouth twitched, but then he shook his head. "Not so much anymore." He gave her a look, one she couldn't quite grasp. "You helped me with that."

She swallowed a big lump in her throat. So, she was his rebound girl, who came before the one who would hold his heart for good.

They entered the stables, and they were magnificent. The facilities were clean, and it was obvious the horses were well taken care of in the large stalls. Somehow, she figured if Cade had anything to do with it, it wouldn't be any other way. She followed him to where his three horses were kept, and as soon as they spotted him, their ears perked up and they rushed to greet him, hanging their heads over the gate. He grabbed a bunch of carrots and handed Harper a couple. "Here, feed Sage. She's real gentle. Don't be afraid to show her some love. She eats it up."

"As long as she doesn't eat my hand."

He laughed, and the sound was beautiful to hear.

"I'll get the other two."

She watched him feed and love up his mares, stroking them and speaking sweet words in their ears. It almost made her jealous, if one could be jealous of such regal animals. But she had no right to be jealous. She'd blown it with Cade, and though he was civil to her, that ship had sailed.

"You know, if you ever want to ride her, I'll let Nathan know. He could take you out one day."

"Oh, thanks. But that isn't happening. I have too much work to do for the party."

"Yeah, I heard you have a great menu planned."

"Thanks. It'll be a challenge."

"You'll do fine. Better than fine."

"That's nice of you to say."

"I wouldn't say it if I didn't mean it."

She smiled, and he blinked a few times. Tension mounted between them. She could feel it in the way he looked at her, the softness in his eyes, the way he'd touched her earlier. It was murder standing here, with him being nice to her like this.

She couldn't hope.

She wouldn't hope.

"I'd better get some sleep," she told him. "It's getting late."

"I'll drive you back."

"No, I feel like walking."

"I'll walk you back, then."

"Cade, why?" she implored him.

"Why what? Why do I want to see you safely back

home? Maybe it's because I almost ran you down tonight. It sorta freaked me out. I can't lose anoth—"

"Cade, I can walk back by myself. Thanks, but I think it's best for us to keep our distance. This…this is hard for me, too."

She gave Sage one more pat on the head, turned and walked out of the stable. Hoping Cade wouldn't follow her.

His mother and Lily were sipping coffee in the kitchen when Cade came downstairs the next morning. They were the last people he wanted to see right now. They'd caused all this trouble, and now he was feeling the brunt of seeing Harper and wanting her when he should be keeping his distance. The irony was, he'd set the terms that they were to steer clear of each other, and he was the one wanting to break the rules.

For no other reason than he missed her.

She was all wrong for him, he knew that, but she was like a magnet, pulling him toward her, and he couldn't seem to break free.

He turned to leave before his mom and sis spotted him. "Hey, Cade. Where're you going?" Lily asked. "Come have coffee with us."

"Yes," his mother said. "Irene made your breakfast. Don't let it get cold."

"I'm not hungry," he said, turning and walking over to the table. He slumped into the chair, put his elbows on the table and ran his hands through his hair.

"You look awful," Lily said. She was a master at saying the obvious. "Bedhead and bloodshot eyes."

"I didn't sleep much," he said.

Lily poured him a cup of coffee and placed it in front of him.

"Hope you're not coming down with something, Cade."

His mother's face crinkled for a second, the way it would when he was a kid and had a fever.

"I think he is. I think it's called Harper syndrome."

He slanted his sister a look. "Very funny."

"I thought things with you two were running smoothly," his mother said. "I mean, my goodness, you've barely seen each other."

"Maybe he's seen her more than we know." Lily was prodding him, trying to pry information out of him.

"Lily, give it a rest. I almost ran her down last night with my car."

"What?" Mom and Lily both chorused in disbelief.

"How?" Lily asked.

"What happened, son?"

"I was coming home from my dinner with Madeline and her dad when—"

"You went out with *Madeline*?" Lily jumped in.

"Yes, and her dad, Martin O'Shea. It was business— my business and none of yours."

"If Madeline was there, it wasn't all business," Lily pronounced.

His sister could be a real pain in the ass sometimes. "Okay, whatever you say." He wasn't about to explain his relationship with his ex-girlfriend right now. Her dad and the Tremaines had been doing business together for over a decade now. Martin O'Shea owned a chain of hay and feed stores throughout the Southwest. Cade hadn't dated Madeline in over four years, though he was surprised to learn she wasn't seriously involved with anyone right now.

"Hush, Lily. Go on, Cade. Tell us about last night." His mom had had a way of breaking up would-be fights ever since he and his siblings could talk.

"Well, I was driving down our road, and it was black as pitch last night. I didn't expect anyone to step foot on the road without looking, and I slammed on my brakes just short of hitting Harper. God, talk about a deer-in-the-headlights look. On both our faces."

"Poor Harper. Is she okay?"

"I think so. She wouldn't let me drive her or walk her home."

"That's your doing, Cade." Lily rubbed salt into the wound.

Cade stared down at his coffee cup. "The thing is… I might still…" He sighed then and shook his head. "I don't know."

Cade glanced at his mother. Sympathy filled her eyes. "I think it's best if you sort out your feelings. Before either of you gets hurt again."

"Harper's only obeying the rules you set down," Lily said. "Well, speak of the devil." His sister's eyes went to the kitchen doorway, and in walked Harper.

"Good morning," she said. "I hope it's okay—Irene let me in."

"Of course it's okay," his mother said, getting up. "Come have a seat. We have more than enough breakfast to go around."

"Oh no, thanks. I've already—"

Cade turned around in his seat to face her, and their eyes met. She stopped midsentence, searching for words.

"I've already had…m-my breakfast." She stared into his eyes, and he couldn't quite break the connection. She was so pretty in the morning, her face a ray of sunshine, her blond hair curling down her shoulders. She wore a red-plaid shirt and jeans and looked like she fit in around here. Too much.

"Excuse me," she said. "I'll come back a…a little later. It's nothing important." She turned, and before Lily or his mom could stop her, she was out the door.

"Crap." Cade pushed away from the table and went after her. He hated seeing the indecision on her face. He didn't want her to feel unwelcome in their home. His mom and Lily adored her, and that should be enough. But obviously it wasn't.

"Harper, wait," he called out.

She kept walking, out the front door and down the path. When she finally got far enough away from the house, her shoulders slumped and she turned around. "Why are you following me?"

"Why did you run off just then? We were all having coffee. You could've joined us."

"I don't want to break the terms of our agreement." Her chin went up.

"I think you're taking that a little bit too literally. We're bound to see each other around the house, the grounds. In the morning at breakfast, in the evening at dinner."

"You mean you'll actually have dinner with me, and not make other dates."

"I had that date on the books before you got here."

"Who was she?"

"*She* is a friend and her father is a business associate. She's nothing like you."

Harper squeezed her eyes closed and turned to walk away.

He stood his ground. "I meant that as a compliment to you."

She turned. "Your compliments are sorely lacking, Cade."

He grinned. He hadn't done that in a long while. "You're just as sassy as ever."

She lifted a shoulder and smiled back. "Can't help it."

"I know." He'd always liked that about her. "Want to go for a ride later? After work and before dinner?"

"Ride?"

"On Sage?"

Her face lit up at the mention of his mare. "I'm going to be busy all day."

"Can't you plan to be unbusy for an hour?"

"I, uh…"

"Come on. I want you to feel comfortable around here. There's no reason you have to leave a room every time I come into it."

"So, how does riding help?"

"You'll just have to wait and see."

"I have a lot of ordering for the party to do today. And I might have to go into town to do some shopping of my own."

"I'll tell you what. I'm going to be at the stables at five o'clock. If you can make it, fine. If not, just text me."

"Okay. That sounds fair."

"I'm going up to get ready for work," he said. "It's safe for you to go have breakfast with Mom and Lily now."

She rolled her eyes. "Cade, sometimes you make me crazy."

"Yeah, well. Welcome to my world."

Harper sat in the car, Lily in the driver seat, as they headed home from their trip into town. "I feel like we really accomplished a lot this afternoon," her friend said.

"We did. Thanks for your help. I feel we're making good headway. And the chairs and table settings you picked out are beautiful. I can picture how it will all look in the backyard, Lil. It's going to be a grand party."

"I hope so. Gage is in charge of the music. His band promised to play some sentimental tunes as well as their usual country rock. I can't wait for you to meet him in person."

"Just think, I get to meet a superstar."

"To me, he's just one of my brothers."

"Last time I checked, most brothers don't have a bunch of Grammys and pack stadiums with swooning fans from all around the world."

"Would you believe when Gage started out, all he really wanted was to play music in local clubs. He loves what he does, and he once said, as long as the good Lord lets him continue to make music, that's all he would ask for."

"I get that. I'm pretty much the same. I just want to earn a decent living doing what I love to do. He sounds like a pretty levelheaded guy."

"Gage?" She laughed. "Hardly. He's cocky as all get-out, and won't hold back at busting anyone's chops. But fame didn't do that to him—he was born that way."

"Still, I can't wait to meet him."

Lily pulled up in front of the guesthouse, and Harper grabbed the bag of spices she'd picked up at a specialty store. Some were exotic flavors, others were staples, but all were necessary for the dishes she was going to prepare. "Thanks for the ride. And the company."

"Yeah, we done good. Only five days to go before the big party."

"I'll be ready."

"So, what are you going to do the rest of the afternoon?"

It was three o'clock. "Me, uh, maybe I'll go over my recipes. Maybe take a rest."

"I have a better idea. Why don't you go on that ride with Cade?"

"You know about that?" she squeaked.

"Not because you told me. I overhead Cade telling Nathan to have the horses ready later."

"I haven't agreed to go. I probably shouldn't. I won't."

"Who are you trying to convince of that, me or you?"

"You. Me." Her shoulders slumped. "I can't put myself through that, Lil."

"You claim you love my brother. Is that still true?"

She nibbled on her lip. She hated admitting it, even to her dear friend, because saying it aloud only made the hurt go deeper.

"Harper?"

"What?"

"Do you love Cade?"

She thought about how he'd been at the cabin, the sweet guy who couldn't cook a thing when she first met him. The guy who chopped wood bare-chested like nobody's business, who also fought and won his battle with grief there, too. The guy who'd shown her what real love was truly like. "Yes, oh God. Yes. I can't deny it."

"So why not fight for him? Why not forget about staying away from him? Give yourself a chance with him. If he didn't want it, he wouldn't have asked you to go riding with him."

"I think I bruise his ego when I run off whenever he shows up. He doesn't want me to feel unwelcome here at your home. That's all it is."

"That's a load of horse poop, Harp. Cade still cares about you. He may not be over what happened yet, but won't you be sorry if you leave here never knowing? If you let him go without a fight?"

"Lily, why do you have to make so much sense all the time?"

"Go, Harper. If nothing else, enjoy a peaceful ride with a handsome hunk."

"*Hunk?* He's your brother."

"Ew, that did sound weird, but you know what I mean."

"I do. Cade *is* a hunk. I'll give it some thought, Lil. See you at dinner."

* * *

As soon as Cade sauntered over to her by the corral, Harper's mouth opened, and she hoped to high heaven there was no drool dripping out the sides. He was holding the reins of Sage and Cinnamon, wearing boots, jeans, a black snap-down shirt and a Stetson. He was her cowboy fantasy come to life, and it wasn't fair that Cade could have such an effect on her. She wasn't made of stone. How could the man completely unravel her with just one look?

"Hello," she said, a bit tongue-tied.

"Hi. I'm glad you came."

She nodded. "I had a productive day. So, I'm here, but I have to warn you, I haven't ridden a horse since I was ten years old. And then it was one of those rides where you go round and round in a big circle."

"Sage is a real sweetheart. She won't give you any trouble. And I'll be right beside you."

She snapped her eyes to his, and his mouth twitched in that beautiful way she remembered. A stream of warmth coursed through her belly, making her giddy. "G-good to know."

"When you're ready, put your left boot into the stirrup, grab the saddle horn and then swing your leg around."

She attempted that easy feat three times before turning to Cade. "Epic fail."

"Nope. You just need a little boost. Try it again."

This time, when she tried to grab the saddle horn, Cade was behind her, giving her butt a steady boost up, so that she could swing her leg around and mount the horse.

"There you go," he said.

"Thanks." Her rear end tingled from his touch, and her mind went to places it shouldn't go.

He adjusted her stirrups and handed her the reins. He mounted Cinnamon, all the while giving Harper instructions on how to hold the reins and make the horse turn left or right or halt. "Got it," she said, though she didn't feel as confident as she sounded.

Cade made a clicking sound, and both horses took off at a slow gait.

The sun was warm on her shoulders, the sky a splash of colorful blues. "There's nothing like seeing the ranch on horseback," Cade said, seeming to think aloud.

Sage kept up with Cinnamon, so they rode side by side. "It's pretty this time of day."

Cade nodded. "It is."

She'd promised herself she wouldn't ask Cade why he'd asked her on this ride, so she held her tongue and let him steer the conversation. Only, he didn't say much. Instead, he simply rode quietly until they were in a silent rhythm with each other. The house was no longer in view, and they came upon a little stream running over a rocky creek bed. Trees shaded the entire area. It was a lovely spot.

"We'll stop here and water the horses."

He dismounted, then came over to her, his arms up, waiting to catch her if she fell. She managed to climb down off the horse without incident, and Cade put his arms down. "Good job," he said. They walked to the creek bed, and the horses followed, finding their way to water.

"This is my favorite spot on the entire ranch."

"I can see why. It's lovely here."

"You really think so?"

"I do," she said quietly.

"I once thought I'd build a house here. Something smaller than the main house. Just big enough for a family."

"You were gonna build a house here for you and Bree." She sighed and turned away from him, so he wouldn't see what was in her eyes. He wouldn't see the hurt in her expression. They say, fake it until you make it. But she couldn't fake her feelings anymore. She couldn't pretend it didn't hurt being out here with Cade. She couldn't compete with angelic Bree.

He grabbed her hand, and she whipped her head around to meet his eyes. They were dark, brooding, filled with regret. "No. Actually, I wasn't. The idea came to me later, while at the cabin."

"While at the cabin?" Her voice squeaked. "You mean when you were a boy?"

"Not when I was a boy, Harper."

"Oh."

"I shouldn't have told you that," he rushed out, looking away. Looking like he wished he'd never spoken those words.

"There was no reason to," she whispered back. It only proved what she already knew: she'd blown it with him.

"No," he said, pulling her closer, giving the hand he held a gentle squeeze. "No reason at all," he said quietly.

Their chests collided, and Cade focused on her lips. He ran his other hand along her jawline, and the simple caress turned her insides upside down.

"Cade?"

"Shh."

Then he brought his mouth down on hers, and the touch of his lips to hers was like a bright spark on a dark, gloomy night. It connected them, made them whole again. It was scary good, delicious and amazing all at once.

Cade cupped her face in both hands and positioned her mouth to his. He devoured her, parting her lips, his tongue sweeping through her mouth until all she could do was whimper and moan.

Cade kissed her while walking her backward until she came up against a tree. He pressed his hard body to hers, and the friction was heaven on earth. He caressed her breasts through the material of her blouse until she wanted to scream. Then he moved his hand lower, teasing her below the waist, and she arched into his touch, trying to absorb the full impact of the pleasure he created through the soft denim. She heard her jeans zipper slowly being unfastened, the teeth spreading open, inviting Cade in. His hand flat against her, he pushed aside her panties and caressed her folds, the skin sensitive, pulsing. She was on the brink, unable to hold back. "Cade."

She gritted her teeth, and her body splintered in a release that shook her to the core. It was earth-shattering, and a few moments ticked by as she came down from this high.

Cade seemed pleased. He kissed her again and again and whispered, "Dawn."

Dawn? In the heat of passion, he called her Dawn. She backed away to gauge his eyes, but he was distracted by his phone. It rang and rang.

He stared at her for a long moment, blinking.

"You better get that," she said, suddenly confused and sinking fast.

He finally answered the call. "Lily, what the hell?"

She overheard Lily's panicked voice. "It's Mom, Cade. She took a fall down the stairs."

"Damn it. How is she?"

"She's pretty banged up and refusing to go to the hospital. She won't let me call an ambulance."

"Okay, I'll be right there." He hung up the phone and shook his head. "We've gotta go. My mama's hurt," he said, walking away to retrieve the horses.

"Oh no," she gasped. She ran over to Sage and tried to mount her, but Cade was there, hoisting her up none too gently.

Cade grabbed both of their reins. "Hold on to the saddle horn tight."

Then they took off at quick gait. Cade kept checking to make sure she was holding on, not losing her balance. He probably didn't want to have another fall on his hands. When the Tremaine home came into view from a distance, she called to him. "Cade, I'm slowing you down. I can get back from here. Hand me the reins."

"You sure?"

She nodded. "I'll walk Sage back. You go."

"Okay. Thanks."

She took hold of the reins and watched as Cade put his head down low to the mare's mane and flew like the wind. There was nothing that man couldn't do perfectly—except maybe get her name right. That bothered her more than it should. It was as if he wanted Dawn, not Harper, and couldn't seem to see them both as the same person.

Her feelings were all jumbled up. She didn't know where she stood with Cade, but that didn't matter now. All that mattered was that Rose Tremaine would be okay.

Nine

Cade had taken his life in his hands when he threatened to cancel his mother's big birthday bash if she wouldn't let their family doctor take a look at her. Nobody threatened his mother and lived to tell about it. She was a force to be reckoned with. As it was, three days later, his mom was still barely talking to him. Luckily, she'd only fallen down three steps, not the entire flight of stairs. She'd bruised her legs pretty badly, and her knee had swelled up. Her cheek had been scraped where she'd hit the banister, and an eggplant-colored bruise popped up there. Nothing a bit of makeup wouldn't cover, or so she claimed. Nothing was going to stop her birthday party from happening. She was looking forward to having her entire family home. And that was that.

Lily, the sneak, had laid their mother's recovery all on Cade, claiming she had too much to do for the party. According to Dr. Adams, a few days of rest was all Rose needed and then she could dance at her own party. The doctor was an invited guest, so he'd be in attendance if anything else happened.

Irene made his mother's meals, and Cade brought them up to her in the morning before work and in the evening after he got home. It wasn't an ideal situation, but Rose wouldn't trust anyone but Cade with her recovery. He got her out of bed every morning and helped her walk around her room. Her knee still bothered her, but the meds the doctor had given her helped with the swelling.

Cade glanced out the window of his mother's room. The stables were in view, and he spotted a pretty blonde walking alongside the road...with Gage? When did his brother arrive home? Cade hadn't seen him yet, but he was sure talking up a storm with Harper. The two had their heads together, looking too close for comfort. Damn. Cade hadn't spoken to Harper since the night of the accident. He'd only texted her about his mother's condition. She'd said all the right things in her reply about how glad she was it wasn't more serious, and how she hoped Rose would be better in time for her party. But that's where it had ended.

"Mom, when did Gage get here?"

His mother looked surprised. "I didn't know he was."

"Well, he is. He'll probably be up soon to see you." That's if he'd tear himself away from Harper long enough to visit his mother before she went to bed.

"Good. At least he won't fault me for wanting to have fun at my party."

"Mom, are you still mad at me?"

He continued to gaze out the window. Gage had enough charm to sweep any woman off her feet, and Harper seemed to be enjoying his attention. What girl wouldn't want to meet Gage Tremaine, superstar?

"I wasn't really mad, Cade. I was angry at myself for

being clumsy and for everyone insisting I go to the hospital when I knew I didn't need to. But just so you know, if you ever speak to me that way again, I'll disown you," she added for good measure.

"That's nice, Mom," he replied, distracted. Gage and Harper had stopped by the corral fence from what he could see, having a fun ole time. What in hell did they have to talk about?

"Nice?" his mother asked. "Cade, you're not listening to a word I'm saying. Who's out there with Gage? Must be Harper. She's the only one who seems to hold your attention lately."

"Wh-what, Mom?"

"Cade, look at me."

He turned, shaking his head. "What is it, Mom?"

His mother smiled as if she knew a secret no one else did. And she was going to share it with him. "If your brain and your heart are in a battle, always go with your heart."

"It's not that simple. I still have issues with her."

"You're thinking too much. Harper is a talented, sweet and smart girl. If you care for her, let her know. And if you don't, let her go."

Cade took one last glance out the window. It looked as if Gage and Harper were finally saying their goodbyes. Gage headed toward the main house and Harper toward the guesthouse. The relief Cade felt seeing them go their separate ways rattled him.

"Mom, I don't want to make another mistake."

"I get that you were injured when Bree died."

"This isn't about Bree anymore, Mom. It's about trust. I'm struggling with trusting again, and I don't know if I can trust Harper."

"Have you noticed the way she looks at you? Now, that's a woman who knows what she wants."

Cade sighed. If only he could have faith in that, in her.

"Son, I'm getting a little tired. Will you round up your brother and bring him in to see me before I turn in?"

"Sure, Mom."

"And, Cade. Think about what I said."

"Will do."

Harper was all he had been thinking about lately. He didn't need his mother to tell him that. He felt guilty leaving Harper in the lurch when his mother had been injured and not calling her afterward. The truth was, he'd been shaken to the core by their encounter at the creek, unable to halt his desire for her. Was it only about sex? Was he missing her, Harper, or was he simply fantasizing about Dawn, the girl he'd met and fallen for at the cabin?

Cade opened the front door just as Gage was walking in. "Hey, dude, good to see you." Gage smiled and opened his arms and the two bear-hugged. "It's been, what? Three months?"

"Something like that." They resembled each other, with their strong jawlines and thick shocks of dark hair. Both were over six feet tall, too. But Gage had blue eyes that all his fans seemed to think were dreamy. "It's good to see you, too. Mom's upstairs, getting ready to turn in."

"How is she?"

"Doing well. It's been murder getting her to take it easy, but I think she's gonna dance at her own party tomorrow night."

"Ah, I'm so glad. Would've been here sooner, but I had to do an interview in Houston. Man, I'm glad my tour's almost done."

"Well, it's good to have you home."

"Thanks, bro. Hey, I met your girl outside. Harper? She's real nice."

Cade folded his arms across his chest. "She's not my girl, Gage."

"She's not? Man, maybe she should be. She's got a lot going for her."

"What does that mean?"

"Hey, I follow the headlines. Hell, half the time, I'm the one in them. But Harper, she got a raw deal."

"She told you that? But you just met her."

"Don't get your panties in a knot," Gage said, grinning. "I watched the show. Whenever I could. And Harper and that Chef Dale guy weren't right for each other. The fans turned on her just because she recognized that fact before she made a big mistake in marrying him."

Cade's mouth tightened. Now he was getting romance advice from Gage, the guy who'd broken more than a few hearts in his day.

"If you're not interested in her, then maybe I—"

"Forget it, Gage." His brother was trying to bust his chops. That's all it was. They'd grown up competing with each other, but never over a woman. "Just so we're clear— Harper is off-limits."

"Yeah, I figured," he said, his mouth twitching in the start of a smile.

"You haven't changed."

"Why should I? I like who I am. Do you?"

No, Cade didn't like who he was right now. He liked the man he was at the cabin, a trusting soul who'd fallen in love with a wonderful woman. "Mom's waiting for you. Let's have a drink together later?"

"Sure, I'm always up for that."

Harper couldn't believe she'd just met Gage Tremaine. He was larger than life, and when he'd introduced himself to her over by the stables, she had to admit she'd had a fangirl moment. But it had only taken a few minutes talking to him to learn two things about Gage. First, underneath the heartbreaker superstar facade was a decent man who cared a good deal about his family. Second, Gage wasn't Cade. Not by a long shot. And thinking of Gage's brother only made her hurt even more. Because in two days, she'd be leaving, and her time with Cade Tremaine would be over.

She made herself a cup of tea and plunked down on the sofa, staring at the television, not really paying attention to what was happening on the screen. Tomorrow was the big day, and she needed to get a good night's sleep. She'd exhausted herself, but in a good way, training her sous chefs and going through a dry run with the staff to make sure everything would work like clockwork for the party. She put all else out of her mind, focusing solely on her job. The menu was set and all deliveries had been made. Now, it was just a matter of creating a delectable meal with all the trimmings.

The knock on her door startled her. She wasn't up to visitors. She was exhausted and totally unpresentable, wearing gray sweatpants with her greasy hair piled atop her head. She thought about not answering the door, but the knocking was persistent and she had a pretty good idea who it was.

"Just a minute," she called out. She ran into the bathroom, washed her face and brushed her teeth, then groaned at her reflection in the mirror.

"Harper, are you okay in there?" Cade called out.

"Fine," she said, and walked over to the door. Cade was the very last person on earth she wanted to see right now. She whipped open the door. "What?"

He looked her over from top to bottom, and his expression didn't change. "Hi."

"Hello," she said, folding her arms.

"Sorry to bother you so late."

"It is late."

"Will you invite me in?"

She shook her head. "No."

"I get why you're mad, Harper. I shouldn't have…"

"Why are you here, Cade? For a man who sets down rules, you certainly don't abide by them."

"I know. I've been—"

"Confused? Hurt? Unsure? Well, so am I. But I'm one other thing. I'm exhausted and not up for this, Cade. I have a big day tomorrow. So, I'm going to say good night now."

"Harper?"

"Glad you got my name right this time." She closed the door, pretty much in his face.

Which only made her feel worse, instead of better.

Ten

Saturday morning, Harper, dressed in chef's whites, was sitting in the dining room with Rose, Lily and Gage. "I'm glad you joined us for breakfast," Rose said. "You've been working very hard this week."

"Thank you. It's great to see you up and around."

"I'm up and ready for my party," she said, taking a sip of coffee. "I'm only sad my dear friend Tonette won't be coming. She's very ill and her daughter, Gianna, is taking care of her. I'm afraid my friend isn't…" Tears came to Rose's eyes. She couldn't say any more.

"Oh, Rose, I'm so sorry to hear that," Harper said.

Rose was such a strong woman, but Lily had said Tonette's illness had taken a toll on her. The two were like sisters.

"Mom, Gianna is with her. Tonette understands. We'll visit her next week," Lily said. "Just like we always do. I promise."

"Okay. Thanks, honey. I enjoy our visits." She patted

Lily's hand. "Do you know where Cade is? I thought he would've come down by now."

Irene served them bacon and eggs, and, according to the Tremaine cook, Gage's favorite: yeast rolls. Apparently, she wasn't wrong. Gage grabbed three rolls and buttered them like a pro.

"I wouldn't be expecting him for breakfast," Gage said. "He sorta drank me under the table last night."

"Geesh," Lily said. "You guys with your drinking games."

"Not games, sis. We're not eighteen anymore. He did some serious damage, then went up to bed."

All eyes turned to Harper, and she put her head down, trying to keep heat from burning her cheeks. She hadn't been hungry before she sat down, being too excited to start the day with her sous chefs and prepping the meal. But now, her stomach churned and she surely couldn't bear to take a bite of anything. She slugged her coffee down in a big gulp.

"Harper, why don't you tell Gage about the menu you planned for tonight."

"Oh, sure," she said, grateful for the change of subject. "Keeping with the surf and turf theme, we'll start out with bourbon-and-pineapple steak-and-shrimp kabobs, among half a dozen other appetizers."

"You could stop right there," Gage said, "and I'd be happy."

"Oh, hush," Rose told Gage. "Let the girl finish."

Gage winked at her. "Sorry, Harper. Please go on."

She gave him a smile. "We'll be baking fresh, rustic sourdough bread for the table. And then serving a cranberry-pecan salad with raspberry vinaigrette. And the main dish is prime rib roast, served with a side of linguine with scallops and artichoke hearts in a white wine cream sauce."

"My stomach's grumbling already. I'm impressed," Gage said.

"Me too," Lily said. "Harper's a great chef. Her food always tastes so delicious. She even taught Cade to cook, if you can believe that."

"Cade cooking? Now, I'm really impressed. Maybe you can teach me, too, Harper. I can hardly toast bread."

Harper looked at Lily and she shrugged. "What can I say? My brothers are hopeless in the kitchen."

"Or maybe just hopeless," Cade interjected, and all eyes turned to the doorway.

"Well, speak of the devil," Gage said.

Cade sauntered into the room, looking like he'd had a rough night. His hair was rumpled, his eyes bloodshot, and his clothes a wrinkled mess. Always at first sight of him, love surged inside Harper, softening her heart. And then she remembered all that had transpired between them. Last night, she'd spoken harshly to him and sent him packing. She had every right to do that. He couldn't come in and out of her life as he pleased. She was glad she'd spoken her mind, yet she did feel a bit guilty, looking at the wreck he was this morning.

"Cade, come sit and have some coffee with us," Rose said. "Looks like you need it."

Cade gave everyone a glance, then stopped on Harper, noting her chef's uniform. "Morning," he said to her.

"Good morning," she replied.

"Big day?"

She nodded. "For everyone. Actually, I should get started in the kitchen. The crew will be here in half an hour." She rose from the table. "Thanks for breakfast."

Cade's mouth twisted in a frown. This time she wasn't trying to avoid him. "I really have to start work," she told everyone, making her point to Cade, as well.

"Of course you do," Rose said. "But be sure to take a break every once in a while. You didn't eat a thing for breakfast."

"I'll eat later, I promise."

"I'll join you in the kitchen in a few minutes," Lily said.

"I'm counting on it," she told Lily.

She was just outside the door when she overheard Cade say to his brother, "And no, she's not gonna teach you how to cook."

Harper rolled her eyes, but then the more she thought about it, the more it made her smile.

Harper spent the morning working hard with her staff to prep the meal. She chopped vegetables, sampled the meat and scallops for taste and texture, and made sauces and marinades. She worked on a fruit tower, using some secrets she'd learned in culinary school to make it stand over two feet tall.

Outside, in the backyard, tables were being set up. She heard Gage and his band members constructing a stage and doing sound checks.

A flower delivery arrived, including bouquets of pastel roses to decorate the first floor of the house, while a dozen arrangements for the tables were placed in the dining room to keep cool until just before the party started at six o'clock.

Lily was in and out of the kitchen all day, helping as much as she could until she was called away to check on something else. By one in the afternoon, Harper felt like it was all coming together. She watched her team work and was proud of the job they were doing.

To her surprise, Cade walked into the kitchen, dressed in sharp clothes, his eyes keenly alert. The transformation from morning to afternoon was truly stunning. Again, her traitorous heart did an Olympic-quality somersault.

"I've never seen you in your chef's whites," Cade said. "I like it."

"Thanks." She continued chopping bell peppers.

"How's it going?" he asked, glancing at the half dozen sous chefs working in the kitchen.

"Well, we're right on target, so you can report back to Lily all is going smoothly."

"That's not why I'm here."

She kept her head down, finding more veggies to chop. "Oh no?"

"I came to ask you to give me some time after the party. I'd like to speak with you privately."

"Cade."

"I mean it, Harper. We really need to talk. Just give me twenty minutes of your time."

"I don't know." She gestured to the room with all its organized chaos. "I can't think clearly right now."

"That's why I want to see you after this is all over."

"Okay. Fine. I'll see you after the party."

A smile crossed his face, one that melted her silly, stupid heart. "Great. I'll see you soon."

By late afternoon, the kitchen was abuzz. Guests would begin arriving in minutes, and Harper and her team were ready. She couldn't be prouder of the way they'd worked together these past few days. With the clinking of a glass, she summoned their attention, and they gathered around. "I just want to thank you all for your hard work this week. I couldn't have asked for a better team to work with. We've accomplished quite a bit, and everything is looking great. So again, thank you from the bottom of my heart. It's the witching hour now, the party's about to begin and we've got more to do. So, let's all get busy."

Lily walked in with Rose, both looking glamorous in long shimmering gowns. Rose was walking without a limp, a regal picture in soft pink. She beamed from ear to ear. "This all looks marvelous," she said, glancing at the food.

"Thanks, but you're the one who looks marvelous. Both of you do."

"Mom's about ready to greet her guests. But she insisted on seeing you first."

"Harper," Rose said. "I'm so happy you're here. You've taken over the kitchen and done a professional job. I can tell already it's going to be truly wonderful. I only wish you could attend the party instead of working in here all night."

"Rose, that means the world to me. Thank you."

"Mom, I'll make sure Harper gets some time at the party."

"You do that, Lily."

After they walked out, Harper looked down at her chef's uniform and grimaced. She was a total mess, with grease stains and raspberry smudges covering her entire coat. She excused herself and walked out the door, heading for the guesthouse, where a fresh white coat was ready to go.

A valet was opening car doors in front of the house, and she came face-to-face with a red-haired woman just exiting her car. She was striking, supermodel-sleek, wearing an emerald green gown with a plunging neckline.

"Oh, hello," the woman said to her. "You're Harper Dawn, aren't you?"

"Uh, yes, I am." Harper had trouble not staring at the woman's impeccable features.

"Cade did say you were catering the party tonight. I'm

Madeline O'Shea." She put out her hand. "A very good friend of Cade's—and the family, of course."

Madeline? She remembered Lily telling her something about Cade's ex-girlfriend. She was pre-Bree and, if she recalled correctly, someone Lily wasn't too fond of.

Harper slid her hands down her coat to wipe them clean before taking the woman's hand. "Nice to meet you."

"I recognized you from the reality show," she said. "I'm a loyal fan of *One Last Date*. But Cade never would watch it. He thought it was insane and thought any woman who had to go on a reality show to find love was well… *I'm too nice to say*. He hated being dragged into that whole mess with you. He as much as told me so over dinner the other night."

Harper hadn't spent weeks on *One Last Date* not to recognize a woman with her claws out. Madeline was staking a claim on Cade. But it was news to her that Cade had taken Madeline out to dinner while she was waiting for a call from him. Oh boy, she was such a fool. She'd always vowed not to let women like Madeline get the best of her, but wow, she was good. And from the wicked smile on her face, Madeline knew it.

"If you'll excuse me, I have to go." Harper brushed past her, holding in her anger, her rage, but she couldn't quite shelve her pain. It spread through her body like wildfire.

Once she arrived back to the kitchen in a pristine white coat and wearing a toque on her head, she had calmed down somewhat. The party had started, and she focused on overseeing the serving of the appetizers.

Lily wandered into the kitchen twenty minutes later. "Hi, just checking in. Everything's going smoothly out there. I'm hearing good things from the guests."

Harper gave her a solemn nod as she sliced freshly baked bread with a vengeance. "Thanks."

"Harper, what's wrong? I can tell you're not happy. What's going on?"

"It's nothing."

"It is something. I know that look. Remember, you can't fool me. I'm your bestie since college, and we know each other inside out."

She shrugged and set down her knife. "Nothing I want to talk about."

Lily grabbed her arm and tugged her out of the kitchen and into the downstairs study, where Lily gave her a stern speak-to-me look. "Something's wrong. What is it?"

She sighed. "What do you know about Madeline O'Shea?"

Lily blinked a few times. "You want to know about Madeline?"

"Yes, I met her a bit ago and…"

"She gave you grief," Lily finished for her. "The truth is, Madeline's never gotten over losing my brother to Bree. She's been after Cade ever since Bree passed away."

"You mean, Cade dumped her for Bree?"

"*Dumped* isn't the right word. They weren't getting along and Cade realized she wasn't the woman for him. She did not take the breakup well. Shortly after, Cade started seeing Bree."

"Madeline told me she went out to dinner with Cade this week. Did you know about that?"

"I wouldn't worry. Cade does business with her father, and so he sees her occasionally. But it always seems to be about business."

"But you're not sure?"

"I'm sure of Cade. He's crazy about you, Harper. I wouldn't give up on him."

"Does he know he's crazy about me?"

Lily grinned. "Probably not, but Gage and Mom seem to think so, too."

Harper rolled her eyes. What good was it that they all thought so, if Cade was too blind or gun shy to know it? "Lil, I've gotta get back to work. Thanks for the talk."

"Sure, any time." Lily kissed her cheek. "You're kicking butt out there, girl. I'm so proud of you."

Harper returned to the kitchen, feeling slightly better. Her sous chefs were all giddy listening to Gage Tremaine sing as they prepared the meals. He had a dynamic voice that streamed into the house. His tone was unique, and it was no wonder he'd become such a superstar. But he'd had his share of scandals lately. Though the Gage she'd met hardly seemed to be such a bad boy. And Lily claimed he was innocent of most things written about him in the tabloids.

Harper could relate.

She kept busy throughout the evening, making sure the dishes were going out on time, hearing the rumble of conversations mingling with music and laughter. It put her in a good mood. She liked Rose, who was definitely a powerful woman with a soft spot for her children. She deserved to celebrate her birthday in the best of ways, surrounded by family and good friends. All 150 of them.

After all the meals were served and dinner was over, Harper breathed a sigh of relief. All they had to do now was sing "Happy Birthday" to Rose and have cake and the other desserts the pastry chef had cooked up, and her work would be done.

It was a bittersweet moment, having accomplished so much while she also felt so unsettled. She walked over to the double French doors, opening one to hear the full power of Gage's sultry, deep voice. When the song ended,

Gage looked out onto the crowd, finding his mother sitting at a table with her friends. He spoke into the microphone, "Mom, it's your turn on stage now. Come on up. Cade, Lily and I have something special for you."

Harper had to see this. She'd promised Lily she'd come outside the second her work was done. She unbuttoned her white coat and took off her hat, fussing with her hair a bit and straightening out the dress that had been crushed under her uniform. Then she walked out onto the patio. The stage was set back and illuminated with several strategically placed spotlights. Overhead, twinkle lights sparkled.

Lily took her mom's arm, while Cade took the other and they escorted her up on stage. The cake was brought over on a cart and placed in front of the stage so everyone could view it. It was a true work of art, thanks to the pastry chef Harper had hired.

"So, what do you get a mom who has everything?" Gage asked the crowd while taking his mother's hand. Rose gazed into Gage's eyes in a tender moment. "You have all three of your kids sing you a birthday song. One that was written just for you."

The crowd let out a collective sigh. Tears formed in Harper's eyes at the love all three had for their mother.

Gage played the guitar and did most of the singing with Cade and Lily as backup. The ballad was touching and emotional, creating an unforgettable moment. And when it was over, they were all given a standing ovation. "Happy birthday, Mom," they said over the applause, each one giving Rose a kiss on the cheek.

Harper clapped so hard her hands hurt and then made her way over to Rose and Lily by the stage. "Happy birthday, Rose." She kissed her cheek, too.

"Oh, Harper, thank you. The meal was delicious. I can't

tell you how many people complimented the food. Everything was superb."

"I'm happy to hear that."

The band played on, and Gage approached the three of
them. "Mom, can I have this dance?"

"Of course, son. Excuse me," Rose said, smiling. "My
son wants to dance with me."

"You go, Mom."

"Have fun," Harper said.

A few seconds later, Nathan came over to say hello,
his focus on Lily. He seemed to hang on her every word,
and then he quite tactfully asked, "Would one of you ladies care to dance?"

Harper took a step back. "You go on, Lil. I'm so tired
I can barely stand, much less dance."

"You're sure?"

"Of course. Go on, Nathan, take Lily around the dance
floor."

Harper found a wall to lean against to watch the festivi-
ties. Even though she was tired of being on her feet, she
tapped her foot in tune with the country sounds, finally
able to enjoy the party. Several of the Tremaines' friends
made a special effort to come over to compliment her meal,
explaining Rose had pointed her out to them. And not a
one of them mentioned seeing her on *One Last Date*, thank
goodness. It was a triumphant moment, boosting her spirits and inspiring her to finish her cookbook.

She looked around, searching for Cade. He seemed to
have disappeared after the birthday song. Unfortunately,
her search ended when he suddenly appeared on the dance
floor with Madeline's arms draped around his neck, her
body crushed to his. Even though the music was upbeat,
they moved slowly, as if they'd shut out the entire world.
And then Cade kissed her, right there on the dance floor,

in front of everyone. Harper didn't know how long the kiss lasted; she wasn't about to wait around to find out.

All she knew was that her heart had finally shattered, and there was no hope left. This whole mess was finally over. She walked into the kitchen to give it one final inspection. Luckily her staff had taken care of everything. She didn't have one more obligation to the Tremaine family, so she grabbed her things and walked straight out the front door.

Cade searched the crowd for Harper. He wanted to spend at least a few minutes with her during the party, but he couldn't find her. He approached Gage and his mom. "Have you seen Harper anywhere? She's not in the kitchen and her staff hasn't seen her, either."

"Nope. I haven't seen her," Gage said, shaking his head. "But you better hope she didn't see you with Madeline. That was not cool, bro. What in hell is going on with you?"

"*Madeline?* You think she saw me with Madeline?"

"Everyone near the dance floor saw you locking lips with her," his mother said, condemnation in her voice.

"It's not what you think. Hell, that woman causes nothing but trouble. She's a damn drama queen."

"I hope you're not talking about Harper," his mother said.

Lily approached, her expression grim and aimed directly at him. "What did you do now?"

"Why, where's Harper?"

"She's at the guesthouse. She wants to leave, ASAP. But she doesn't have a car and she won't ask me to leave Mom's party early. I'm supposed to take her home first thing in the morning, A-hole." Lily looked toward her mother. "Sorry, Mom."

"It's okay, honey. I agree."

All eyes turned to Cade.

"Are you going to let that girl go?" his mother asked.

"Man, she's a keeper, Cade," Gage said, shaking his head, giving him a don't-be-a-dumbass look. "Even I recognize that."

"I know. I know." Cade's gut clenched. He might have blown it with Harper for good, and that would be the worst thing that ever happened to him. Well, except for losing Bree. But losing Harper was right up there on the same level. "I need to talk to her."

"She doesn't want to talk to you. She texted me specifically to keep you away from her."

"I have to see her. Tonight. Give me your phone, Lily."

"No way."

"Cade, what are you up to?" his mother asked suspiciously.

"I just need to explain. And straighten all this out. But I can't do it without Lily's phone and her car keys."

"Now you want my keys?"

"If you want your best friend becoming a part of this family, you'll give them up."

"Really?" Lily grinned, and her entire demeanor changed.

"Man, you have it bad," Gage said. "Take pity on the guy and give him what he wants, sis. Or we'll never hear the end of it."

"Okay, but if you do anything to hurt her, I'll never forgive you," Lily warned.

"And I'll disown you," his mom said, halfway serious.

"Then I'll kick you to the curb like yesterday's garbage," Gage said, making his point.

"Got it. Now hand them over," Cade said, finally seeing some light.

He only hoped it wasn't too late.

* * *

Harper let the warm water of the shower rain down, cleaning her body of a full day in the kitchen. The grease, the oil, the scents of herbs and garlic all needed washing away. But so did her aching heart. She wished there was a shower for that. Something that could wipe away her uncontrollable sobs. Something that could free her body of fierce and unyielding pain. She could call Cade Tremaine a jerk, a fool, an idiot, but none of that seemed to make her feel any better. Because she still loved him. Desperately and helplessly. So didn't that make her the bigger fool? The grander idiot?

She let the warmth spread over her body until her tears no longer mingled with the water spraying down. Until the warmth gave her courage enough to face the cold reality that Cade was out of her life now.

For good.

She stepped out of the shower and dried off with a towel. Her phone buzzed on the countertop, and she picked it up to read a text from Lily. The party broke up early. I can take you home now, if you're set on leaving tonight.

It's late, Lil. I can't impose on you that way.

I'll spend the night at your place and drive home in the morning. No problem.

Harper glanced at the clock. It was ten thirty. She could be off Tremaine land and in her own bed before midnight. Nothing would make her happier. And Lily would be there in the morning to keep her company. Maybe to help nurse her wounds.

That's a good plan, she texted back. Thanks, my friend.

I'll be there in thirty minutes.

Harper made fast work of packing up her stuff. She didn't have all that much here, so it was easy to gather up her clothes and dump them into her suitcases. Any regrets she had in leaving this place were stifled when the sight of Cade and Madeline kissing entered her mind. Something squeezed tight in her belly every time she thought about Cade. He'd probably wanted to tell her he was getting back with Madeline when they were supposed to talk tonight. So, she was saving him the trouble.

Damn him.

The doorbell rang precisely thirty minutes later, and she was more than ready. She grabbed her bags and glanced out the window to see Lily's car in the driveway. She opened the door. "I can't thank—" She gasped, stunned to find Cade at her threshold, not Lily. "What are you doing here?" She looked over his shoulder for Lily. "I'm waiting for your sister."

Cade took a deep breath, and his lips turned down. "Lily's not coming."

The look on his face frightened her. "Did something happen to her?"

"No, nothing like that. Lily is fine. Trust me."

She laughed in his face. What a joke, asking her to trust him. "I don't."

"I know. I'm sorry about that. That's why I'm here, to explain and make things right. I knew if I asked to speak with you, you'd slam the door in my face again."

"And you'd be right. I saw you tonight with Madeline. You kissed her on the dance floor. So, there's nothing more to explain. She made it clear how things are between you."

Cade's eyes darkened to coal, and his face twisted up at the mention of Madeline's name. "She had too much to drink. The next thing I know, she's dragging me on the dance floor and kissing me. I didn't want to make a scene in front of all the guests. But if you saw the whole thing, you would've seen me give her a stern talking-to afterward. I made it clear that I wasn't interested in her that way and handed her over to her father. Regardless of what happens between you and me, I still wouldn't go back to Madeline."

He seemed sincere, and she took a moment to digest what he claimed had happened with Madeline. She wasn't going to deny that his explanation made sense. And maybe she'd jumped to conclusions a teeny, tiny bit too soon. Still, she had doubts. "You lied to me. You pretended to be Lily in the texts."

"And you lied to me for days, pretending to be someone you weren't."

"That's not entirely true, Cade. I am the same person I always was. And I've apologized for that many times."

"And I've forgiven you." He put out his hand. "Will you take a drive with me?"

That caught her off guard. "Why?"

"So we can talk. Really talk. I have something I want to show you. I'll take your suitcases and drive you back to Barrel Falls myself if you still want that after you hear me out."

Harper gave his proposition a moment of thought. It seemed like a win-win. If she didn't like his explanation, she'd be assured of going home tonight. It was the best she was going to get.

"Fine."

He grabbed her suitcases as she closed up the guest-house and followed him to Lily's SUV. He hoisted both bags into the back end, then opened the car door for her. He was still such a gentleman. She was beginning to appreciate all that Southern charm.

Once she was seated and buckled up, Cade climbed in and started the engine. To her surprise, he whipped the car around, leading away from the main road and heading deeper onto Tremaine land.

She sat quietly, not asking any questions as they passed the stables and then took off down a bumpy path. One she recognized, perhaps. But it was dark out, the stars above giving only slight illumination. "You know, my family threatened to toss me out on my ass if I didn't go after you."

"Smart family. I like them all."

"They like you. Better than they like me, I think."

"So, is that what you're doing? Going after me?"

He turned to her and nodded. "It took me a while to figure some things out. I admit, I'm slow on the draw at times. Especially after I met a gorgeous brunette who wrapped me around her little finger. It was new to me, being with someone else. Giving of myself. One day, you were this sweet tomboy hiker and herb-loving chef, and the next day I find out you're one of the biggest reality stars in the country. It threw me off and made me really think about what I was doing with my own life."

He stopped the car a short distance from his favorite place by the stream and got out. She didn't wait for him to open the door for her, but when she exited the car, he took her hand. He faced her as they both leaned one shoulder against the car.

"Harper, I condemned you for going on that show. I shouldn't have. It was wrong. I shouldn't have judged you."

He touched a wisp of her hair and then gazed deep into her eyes. She was mesmerized, caught up in him, in this beautiful place. A few stars shined above, but it was enough to see the sincerity on his face. Her heart was racing; it hadn't stopped since the moment he showed up at the guesthouse.

"Why should you be any different than anyone else?"

"I should be different because I care deeply about you. I watched all ten episodes of *One Last Date*."

She gasped, her hand going to her mouth. She knew from Lily that he'd watched some of it, but he'd seen every second, every moment of what she'd gone through. "You saw it all? I wish you hadn't."

"I'm glad I did. I saw how you struggled with finding the right man, how much you wanted to find love. You weren't in it for the fame, to make a name for yourself, like some of the others. I could tell you were authentic. You put yourself out there, and it wasn't easy. But I was proud of you for sticking up for yourself when you realized you didn't love Dale, that though you had a lot in common, and he was perfect on paper, you couldn't see spending the rest of your life with him."

"Thank you. That means a lot to me."

"Sweetheart, how could I blame you for trying to find love over the course of a ten-week television program when I fell in love with you in less than a week over bad rummy games, hot, sweaty hikes and cooking lessons? Harper Dawn, I'm crazy in love with you."

"Oh, Cade," she breathed out softly. "I love you, too. So much." Tears misted in her eyes. And she touched his face to make sure this was real. "But are you sure you didn't just fall in love with Dawn by the lake?"

He grinned. "I fell in love with Dawn and with Harper. Even if I hadn't seen you on *One Last Date*, the woman you are today, standing right here in front of me, is the woman I love with my whole heart. I discovered that love can happen in the craziest ways, under unique circumstances. And I wouldn't change a minute of my time getting to know you."

"Are you sure?"

"I'll prove how sure I am, but first…"

He took her face in his hands and crushed his mouth to hers, kissing her like there was no tomorrow, kissing her like he could devour her. She'd never felt so loved, so incredibly joyous.

Cade ended the kiss and smiled, a big, wide over-the-moon kind of boyish smile. "C'mon," he said, taking her hand. He led her down a slope and there, hidden under the arching branches of two trees overlooking the stream, was a table set for two with white linens, flowers and a bottle of champagne in a silver bucket. Cade lit half a dozen small candles, and the table flickered to life. "I wanted to have our own private celebration tonight."

"Is this why you insisted we have a talk tonight?"

"I couldn't interrupt your work, Harper. I knew how much it meant to you. But I'm selfish enough to want you all to myself. Here in my favorite spot."

He pulled out a chair for her, and she sat down. He sat across from her and took her hand in his. Before he could speak, she had to ask, "The last time we were here was when your mom got hurt. Why didn't you call me after that?"

"I should have. But it was here that I realized how much I loved you. To be honest, it scared me a little. It wasn't about Bree anymore. It was about opening myself up again to that strong of an emotion. And Mom was hurt and needed my help, and there was the party. But Harper, sweetheart, I never meant to hurt you. I'm no expert in love, but I know now, you're the only woman for me."

Harper's eyes went wide, and she held her breath as Cade got down on one knee. "Harper Dawn, I love you more than I can put into words. But know I'll do everything in my power to make you happy. Will you marry me?"

It was her deepest wish to marry a man who loved her unconditionally. And Cade had proved that he did. He loved her through lies and deception and was man enough to see the woman she really was. "Cade, I couldn't be happier than I am right now. Yes, I'll marry you. I'll be your wife."

He placed his class ring on her finger. "I'll get you the ring of your dreams," Cade said, "but for now please accept this ring as my pledge of love."

Cade took both of her hands, and they rose together. "I don't need a new ring," she said softly, "when I have the *man* of my dreams right here."

Cade kissed her softly this time, sweetly. There was no longer any rush. They were bonded together through true love.

"What do you say about us building a house together? Right here, and you can design your own kitchen and finish that cookbook you're working on."

"It'll be a place for us to raise a family, Cade."

"I like the sound of that."

He kissed her again and then opened the champagne bottle, the cork popping and bubbles spilling out. They toasted to their future, and to Cade being her very own *one last date*.

* * * * *

COMING SOON!

We really hope you enjoyed reading this book.
If you're looking for more romance, be sure to
head to the shops when new books are
available on

Thursday 4th
March

LET'S TALK

For exclusive extracts, competitions
and special offers, find us online:

- facebook.com/millsandboon
- @MillsandBoon
- @MillsandBoonUK

Get in touch on 01413 063232

MILLS & BOON

THE HEART OF ROMANCE

A ROMANCE FOR EVERY KIND OF READER

MODERN

Prepare to be swept off your feet by sophisticated, sexy and seductive heroes, in some of the world's most glamourous and romantic locations, where power and passion collide.
8 stories per month.

HISTORICAL

Escape with historical heroes from time gone by. Whether your passion is for wicked Regency Rakes, muscled Vikings or rugged Highlanders, awaken the romance of the past.
6 stories per month.

MEDICAL

Set your pulse racing with dedicated, delectable doctors in the high-pressure world of medicine, where emotions run high and passion, comfort and love are the best medicine.
6 stories per month.

Celebrate true love with tender stories of heartfelt romance, from the rush of falling in love to the joy a new baby can bring, and a focus on the emotional heart of a relationship
8 stories per month.

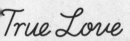

Indulge in secrets and scandal, intense drama and plenty of sizzling hot action with powerful and passionate heroes who have it all: wealth, status, good looks…everything but the right woman.
6 stories per month.

Experience all the excitement of a gripping thriller, with an intense romance at its heart. Resourceful, true-to-life women and strong, fearless men face danger and desire - a killer combination!
8 stories per month.

Sensual love stories featuring smart, sassy heroines you'd want as a best friend, and compelling intense heroes who are worthy of them.
4 stories per month.

To see which titles are coming soon, please visit
millsandboon.co.uk/nextmonth

MILLS & BOON
MODERN
Power and Passion

Prepare to be swept off your feet by sophisticated, sexy and seductive heroes, in some of the world's most glamourous and romantic locations, where power and passion collide.

Julia James
Heiress's
PREGNANCY
SCANDAL
MILLS & BOON
MODERN

Jennie Lucas
Chosen as the
SHEIKH'S ROYAL
BRIDE
MILLS & BOON

Kim Lawrence
A WEDDING
of the
ITALIAN'S DEMAND

Sharon Kendrick
The
SHEIKH'S
SECRET BABY
MILLS & BOON
MODERN

MILLS & BOON

HEROES

At Your Service

Experience all the excitement of a gripping thriller, with an intense romance at its heart. Resourceful, true-to-life women and strong, fearless men face danger and desire - a killer combination!

MILLS & BOON
True Love
Romance from the Heart

Celebrate true love with tender stories of
heartfelt romance, from the rush of falling
in love to the joy a new baby can bring,
and a focus on the emotional
heart of a relationship.